EROTIC CITY

D1165824

EROTIC CITY

&

PYNK

GRAND CENTRAL
PUBLISHING

NEW YORK   BOSTON

This book is a work of fiction. Names, characters, places, and incidents are the product of the author's imagination or are used fictitiously. Any resemblance to actual events, locales, or persons, living or dead, is coincidental.

Copyright © 2008 by Pynk

All rights reserved. Except as permitted under the U.S. Copyright Act of 1976, no part of this publication may be reproduced, distributed, or transmitted in any form or by any means, or stored in a database or retrieval system, without the prior written permission of the publisher.

The quote on the front cover of this book ran in the February 25, 2002, issue of *Publishers Weekly*, for *May December Souls*, which was published under Pynk's real name.

Grand Central Publishing
Hachette Book Group
237 Park Avenue
New York, NY 10017

Visit our Web site at www.HachetteBookGroup.com.

Printed in the United States of America

First Edition: November 2008

10 9 8 7 6 5 4 3 2 1

Grand Central Publishing is a division of Hachette Book Group, Inc.
The Grand Central Publishing name and logo is a trademark of Hachette Book Group, Inc.

Library of Congress Cataloging-in-Publication Data

Pynk.
    Erotic City / Pynk.—1st ed.
      p. cm.
    Summary: "A fast-paced, sexy ride through the very liberated and very free life of Atlanta club owner Milan Kennedy"—Provided by publisher.
    ISBN: 978-0-446-17957-7
    1. African American women—Fiction. 2. Nightclubs—Fiction. 3. Atlanta (Ga.)—Fiction. I. Title
    PS3613.O548E76 2008
    813'.6—dc22

                        2008012628

Book design and text composition by L&G McRee

This Pynk book is dedicated to past, current, and future swingers everywhere. Swing on!

ACKNOWLEDGMENTS

Thanks for experiencing my virgin erotica ride. It's been a steamy journey as I've traveled into the amazing world of swingers, not to mention the juicy world of erotica. I wanted to create a piece that was about more than just sex. I wanted *Erotic City* to be about the lives of swingers.

First and foremost, I offer deep love to my cherished family and friends, those of you who support me and understand that I write so that I can breathe, and for accepting the oh-so very erotic side of me.

I want to express my sincere appreciation to my grand editor, Karen Thomas, to Jamie Raab, Latoya Smith, Linda Duggins, Sam Kelly, and everyone at Grand Central Publishing who has contributed to the debut of *Pynk*.

To you, the readers, thanks for picking up this book. Milan Lee Kennedy is more than happy to host you at her dirty south, sexual playground.

To Brent for the "life" e-mails, Mz. Poison (the flogging mistress) for agreeing to be interviewed, to Anthony for your hot, invaluable information, to HB for hanging tough, and to Adrienne, my test reader—thanks, thanks, and more thanks.

And, I am very grateful to Maureen Walters at Curtis Brown, Ltd., for negotiating this deal.

In October 2009, I'll give birth to my sophomore erotica novel, *Sexaholics*, also from Grand Central Publishing. My characters, Miki, Valencia, Brandi, and Teela are in sexual rehab, and, if you let them, they will turn you out! Who will break their addiction to sex, and who will fall off the no-fuckin wagon? A wild preview chapter is at the end of this book.

Also, please check out the "shop" page on my Web site at www.authorpynk.com, where you'll find hot items for your own personal enjoyment, as well as my official *Pynk Hard-Candy* book thongs. Consider it a sexy piece of jewelry for the crack of your book!

Until then remember, no glove no love, and twenty-one and over. Keep it tight and keep it pynk!

Smooches,
Pynk
XOXO

authorpynk@aol.com
www.authorpynk.com
www.myspace.com/authorpynk

WARNING

If nudity or sexual acts offend you,
please do not enter.

Signed: Erotic City Management

CAST OF CHARACTERS

- **Milan Lee Kennedy:** thirty-two-year-old owner of Erotic City, where the hot and hip Atlanta swingers swing

- **DeMarcus "Lavender" Lewis:** Milan's thirty-year-old boyfriend, a former professional boxing champ

- **Ramada Hart:** Lavender's crazy-ass ex-girlfriend

- **Tamiko Rae Kennedy:** Milan's baby sister and best friend who's a virgin swinger

- **Jarod Hamilton:** Mr. Big Stuff with a fetish or two

- **Nancy Clark Kennedy:** the forty-two-year-old, vanilla ex-stepmother who prefers young chocolate studs . . .

. . . all make Erotic City cum alive!

EROTIC
CITY

1

"Erotic City"

⌘

Sunday, March 30, 2008
12:45 a.m.

I wanna be your bitch, mistress." He was muscular and hairy, wearing pink lingerie and high heels. His submissiveness reeked.

The curvy mistress replied, "Follow me, my slave." Her domination made his torpedo salute underneath the sheer lace fabric of his panties.

"Can I lick your feet?" a naked man asked a heavyset woman.

"Only if I can give you a foot job." She took his hand as he led the way into fetish mania.

"Do you want some?" the tall lady asked the short lady who was fixated on her beautiful, bountiful ass.

"Hell yeah," she replied with a look like she was about to rob the National Bank of Pussy.

She was about to get her swinger-newbie cherry busted.

That's just how the shit went down.

Fuck so pretty you and me, Erotic City come alive.

Coming alive four nights a week Erotic City did indeed. Fucking so pretty its members did like clockwork. Each and every Thursday through Sunday, hidden among the alluring, sophisticated nighttime bling of midtown Atlanta's sexy cityscape. It was the perfect place for a whole lotta dirty-south, sex-in-the-city encounters. Folks were getting down, shakin the sheets until the sun came up.

Watching.

Choosing.

Flirting.

Talking.

Touching.

Kissing.

Licking.

Eating.

Sucking.

Spreading.

Penetrating.

Fucking.

Swallowing.

Screwing.

Cumming.

Swinging.

And not always in that order.

Sometimes cumming before talking.

Three scantily clad, twenty-something women, one white, one black, one Asian, sat at the circular studded bar, bouncing their heads, singing in unison, sipping on pink champagne in the main purple room. One wore red, one wore white, and one wore blue. A red bustier and strategically ripped black denim jeans, a white bikini top and low-rise boy shorts, and a blue teddy with lace-up thigh-high stiletto boots.

The sounds of "Erotic City" by Prince, the club's theme song, bumped through the air, mixed with the moans of passion and pleasure, all illuminated by soft, mood-setting, dim lights.

The red room smelled like Butt Naked incense. The dance floor included a stage with two brass stripper poles, just in case the introverted had suddenly turned extroverted and desired to show off his or her suppressed seduction skills. The wide-screen triple-X-rated fuck flicks showed along the wall of the gold orgy room as a visual reminder of what folks had cum there for. And the blue room, the S&M dungeon, was equipped with a spanking bench, shackles, and every bondage toy one could ever beg for, and of course there was a pink pussycat room for ladies only.

Sex seeking, upscale club members walked by striding smoothly, exacting the speaker-banging beats with each step.

The sexy Asian woman turned coolly and came face-to-face with zebra-printed drawers being worn by a sculpted, tanned white man with a six-pack. He strutted behind her back, looking edible. Her look devoured him from head to toe. She licked her lips from west to east. It was clear he was at full attention. He approached a short, lean woman who was wearing fire engine red lipstick to match her red pussy hairs. He took her welcoming hand. The woman looked back and winked at her man's admirer as they headed off to the hot tub. The Asian woman blushed and nervously fingered her jet-black hair. She darted her sights away with demure hesitation, as if to excuse herself for raping the model-like man with her hungry dark eyes.

Her guilty vision then stopped at an open door. A group of three women and two men in the intimate silver room, most of whom were naked, were twisted up together in X-rated entwinement upon burgundy loungers. Two fucked missionary. A chocolate woman with a more than healthy amount of round ass was riding seven inches of tricky-dick for dear life. And then there were two Coke bottle shapely women frantically muff diving in a sixty-nine that looked more like a ninety-six. It was an asses up, heads down orgy with balls swangin and titties hangin.

"Get up" was all that could be heard as a toffee-colored man walked up to the group. He had salt and pepper hairs on his head and chest, and was wearing only an ivory towel wrapped at his thick waist as he delivered his no-nonsense demand.

One of the participants of the sixty-nine let out a girlie growl and continued her face-fuck against a stranger's fleshy inner split.

His woman, the giver, the muffin-muncher, barely twenty-nine, moved her auburn hair to the side and looked up at him with half eyes as she backed her cum-coated lips away from the smiling clay dugout. There were two looks that shone on her face. One was a look as though she was high on lust, and happy to take on the label of vagitarian, as if she were on a strict vagina-only diet. The other look was as though she'd found the sudden interruption a complete nuisance.

"Watch that group of five down on the burgundy lounger in the silver room. Brian reports a jealous man who's pissed off about his woman who's involved in girl-on-girl." Milan Kennedy pressed the release button on her Nextel two-way as she glanced through the smoke-tinted one-way mirror from her office, looking down toward the first floor.

"Upset? Why? For woman-on-woman head?" her lead security person joked, sounding confused.

"Just check on it, Lavender."

"Gotcha."

Milan disconnected the unit and took a seat at her massive mahogany desk. She was preparing to go over profit reports for her city of sex . . . her pride and joy, Erotic City.

Curly-headed Lavender sprinted down the stairway with a wireless earpiece that flashed a tiny blue light, looking every bit the professional boxer he was some years back. Lavender was the name he'd been given during his boxing days, which seemed to stick with him. DeMarcus George Lewis was the name he was given at birth, though very few called him by any name except the one he'd earned in the ring. He spoke with his heavy voice. "Hey, Jarod. Come on over to the silver room right away."

"I'm on my way." Bald and yellow Jarod took long hurried steps, quickly passing what he knew to be the usual . . . parted legs spread-eagle, deep-throating females swallowing long tools while getting fucked by nameless studs who came to play, deep, sweaty pussies drenched with desire for penetration from a willing penis hard enough to break glass, and masturbating singles in fe-verish strokes, attempting to reach their peaks . . . all in the name of getting off.

Without even stopping to notice the surroundings, Jarod, who was Milan's sister's boyfriend, and Lavender arrived in the silver room simultaneously. Lavender spoke first. "Sir, is there a problem here?"

The angry man, branded with frown lines on his forehead, who was older than his woman by maybe twenty years, secured the grip on his waist towel and replied without looking up. His eyes were fixed upon his lady's shapely back as she began to stand. No was all the man said.

Lavender spoke to the young woman's back as well. "Ma'am, are you having trouble with something?"

She ignored him, taking a deep breath and a lengthy exhale. Her dainty shoulders dropped bit by bit like sticky molasses being poured from a mason jar.

Her hot and bothered man spoke instead. "I just caught my lady with her face between that woman's legs." He pointed at the other woman's frame.

The other woman's face turned toward him with a combination of satisfaction and worry. Satisfaction for the fact that he'd walked up just after she came in his woman's mouth, and worry for the fact that perhaps she would not be able to enjoy his young lady's tongue-screw skills again.

Jarod took over as club spokesperson. He kept one hand on his leather holster and unsnapped it. "Sir, our rules clearly state that couples have to work things out calmly or leave."

Lavender kept his eyes on the woman, trying his damndest not to stare at her perfect cinnamon butt cheeks. Scripted in purple ink on the small of her back was a fancy tribal design tramp-stamp. The sight of the tattooed artwork rang a loud and vivid bell. The sweet scent of Poême made its way to his nostrils.

She began a slow-motioned turnaround.

The man continued, "I paid nearly two hundred dollars, supposedly for my lady to eat some woman's pussy? We're not leaving."

Jarod gave the man a cautious once-over and took one step closer toward the man's face. "Sir, have you been drinking?"

Irritation persisted to envelop the man's sentences. "Hell no. I barely got my dick out. I brought my own strong-ass liquor in here and haven't even had one sip."

"Hello," Lavender said with a cautious head nod as the woman completed her about-face.

The statuesque, pecan woman replied, "Hi, De-Marcus. I mean Lavender." Her voice sang a sultry tone. Her searing eyes, which looked like they belonged only in the bedroom, were big and brown. She did not blink.

Jarod spoke to the man with firm delivery. "You and your lady get dressed. It's time to go."

The man locked his attention upon his lady's face, which was still locked upon Lavender's face. "I'm not going anywhere. And did you say Lavender?"

The woman licked her lips before she spoke. "Yes. Baby, this is Lavender Lewis."

"How's it going, Ramada?" Lavender asked, trying to cut the cord of their eye string. A sustained, forced blink seemed to do the trick.

"Fine and you?" Facing the gentleman, big-breasted Ramada stood in suede pumps, with rock-hard nipples and a hairy vagina.

Lavender now glanced at the carpet, on the floor, that is. "Fine."

Jarod took two steps back in confusion.

"What the hell is all of this?" the man asked. "All of the niceties and shit."

Ramada ran her fingers through her flat-ironed hair while she spoke. "DeMarcus, this is Ray. Ray, this is De-Marcus, or Lavender as he's called."

Lavender extended his hand. "Pleasure to meet you."

The man paused, put out his hand and gave a firm shake. "Lavender? You work here?"

"Yes. I'm the head of security."

"And you knew this?" the man asked Ramada.

Ramada wore a sticky smirk. "Honey, this is the scene of the crime. I told you about that, didn't I?"

"Crime?"

Lavender rubbed the hairs on the back of his neck and gave Jarod the eye. "Jarod, they're cool. They can stay. Anyway, Ramada, it's good seeing you." He focused on her man. "Sir, is there anything we can do for you?"

Ramada replied for her boyfriend while giving Lavender a naughty wink. "No, I've got him." She turned her naked body away from Lavender and grabbed her man by the hand, kissing him softly on the lips. He barely reciprocated. She moved her body closer and grinded up against his crotch, maneuvering the towel as it dropped to the floor.

The hard-on that her boyfriend now wore did not match the dismay on his face. Ramada looked over at Lavender. The look on her face was playful and serious. She dropped to her knees, securing herself to take her man's stiff penis into her mouth as though dick sucking was her own personal creation. She shellacked his shaft with her maple brown lips, stroking his length with her left hand, rubbing his swollen balls with her right. She bobbed up and down as her hair bounced about. She closed her eyes while Lavender coolly turned to walk away.

Jarod gave it another second but eventually moved his feet, following close behind.

Ramada's man's eyes remained wide. His fists were tight. But the lines seemed to fall from his forehead the deeper his shaft traveled down her talented throat.

Lavender shook his head and forced himself not to look back.

"Lavender, I need to see you upstairs. Now." Milan's voice rang in his ear, firm and anxious.

"I'm headed that way," he said. He commented to Jarod as they took the flight of stairs. "She always did have a thing for the ladies. He'd better get used to that shit."

"Girl's got mad skills," Jarod commented, looking as serious as a heart attack.

Lavender checked to make sure his microphone was off. "She always did."

"Damn, talk about SuperHead," Jarod replied as he walked back toward the second floor bar area. "Uh, uh, uh."

Lavender headed up another flight to Milan's office . . . the office of the woman who was the love of his life. The woman he knew was now pissed the hell off.

2

"Juicy Fruit"

❦

Sunday, March 30, 2008
1:15 a.m.

Milan greeted Lavender with quick words as he stepped inside her office and closed the door. She stood before him. Her high, curved cheekbones showed a slight flush and her slanted, dark brown eyes were intense. "Is that who I think it is?" Her breath paused.

"Yes." Lavender gave her a peck on the lips before making the red leather guest chair his seat.

She exhaled and crossed her arms, leaning against the desk, exposing her model-thin, bare legs. She had on a pink top and a short skirt with black Mary Jane pumps. "What the hell is that about?"

He shrugged his broad shoulders. "I have no idea."

"And what was up with that man?"

"That's her boyfriend."

She chuckled. "Boyfriend? Since when does crazy-ass Ramada have a man?"

"Like I said, I have no idea and I could care less." Lavender looked at his radio and lowered the volume.

Milan stepped closer to him. "Lavender, I want them out of here." She was firm.

He looked up. "Why?"

Milan pointed her pink index fingernail his way. "You know she brought her tired ass up in here to fuck with you. The girl is one slice short of a full damn loaf." Tightness formed around her mouth. "I'm not having that type of game playing in my place of business." She stepped back, turning away.

Lavender rose to his feet and spoke from behind her. "Milan, considering that I came here with her last year and ended up leaving with you, you have nothing to worry about. Besides, your motto has never been to fight fire with fire."

She turned back toward him. "Then why now has she decided to come in here and flaunt herself at the very place where you and I met? This is our place of business. Have you even told her that you own a part of Erotic City as well?"

"Not yet."

"See, Lavender. I see the game. I don't have time for this shit."

"Then don't make time for it." He smiled but kept track of her right hand, knowing she wasn't the type to slap, but also knowing women.

Milan's face was blank. "I've been patient with all of Ramada's crap. But I'll tell you now, I will not put up with her if she's gonna pop up out of the blue and come up here playing her silly ass games. No telling what she's got up her sleeve. I'm serious. I don't trust her."

"Baby, I know you've been cool about Ramada. And, yes she's been trying to make my life a living hell.

And I know you've stuck by me over the past year. But I'm telling you there's nothing to worry about. Now, I'm gonna go back out there. All you need to do is keep your head up."

He noticed her eyes were red. He tipped her chin his way, demanding a full-on stare. She gave him only half a glance. He placed his hands on her upper arms and pulled her close. She rested her head on his chest.

He took a peek beyond the one-way mirror and accidentally caught an eyeful of Ramada bending over to allow for her man's entry. Lavender blinked twice and kissed his own woman on the cheek. He loved every inch of her china-doll face. To him it was perfection. Her porcelain, pale skin was oval and flawless. Her long, coal black hair was pulled back and twisted into a tight bun. She wore large silver hoop earrings that hung from her dainty ears, and a silver cuff that shone along her upper arm. She looked just like her mother. Her bushy eyelashes framed her Asian eyes that he knew so well. Stubborn eyes that still offered a look of dissatisfaction, as if yearning for more than he'd communicated. He knew a question was brewing.

"You're not gonna ask them to leave?"

"No, I'm not and you're not either. And I really don't think they're worried about us." With a focused look he said, "I love you."

She glanced at the white gold crucifix that hung from his wide neck. Avoiding his eyes, she then focused on his beautiful upper arm. His black shirtsleeve ended at the very top of the LL initials etched on his bicep. And just below that was a boxing glove tattoo.

Lavender placed his hand on her slender upper thigh.

The feeling of her smooth skin made him smile. He raised her knit skirt, finding that as usual, she was panti-less. He spoke as he used his fingers to trace a path to her vagina. He slipped his middle finger to her clit, gently flicking it. It was stiff and moist.

"Lavender." She said his name as if unsure.

He pressed his fingertips toward the opening of her pussy and inserted his middle finger, probing her familiar walls. Her moistness made his dick pulsate into full grown. He pushed his long finger as deep as it would go, swirling inside of her tightness. She gave a soft moan. Her eyes half closed. He exited the sweet vagina he'd claimed as his and his alone, bringing his finger to his mouth. He sucked her shiny glazed wetness from his skin.

Milan grabbed his finger and took it into her own mouth. She licked the sides and sucked the tip and gradually pulled his finger out and rubbed his own finger along his neck.

"There. A little pussy perfume." She lowered his hand to his own crotch. "You and junior calm down now. And I love you, too." She flashed a glimmer of content.

He reached inside his pants to adjust himself. "Damn, girl. You know you don't have a thing to worry about."

"Well, thank God for that. Anyway, there's more where that came from. But for now, it's business before pleasure." Her face had indeed softened.

"I'm on it. Besides, we've got Big Mack and his boys upstairs in VIP."

Milan pulled down her skirt and shook her hips back into the perfect fit. "Baby, you know tonight is couples and single females only. I don't like to break the rules."

"He came in as part of a couple, like most men do

anyway, come with a woman just to get in. Nothing we can do about that."

"Yeah, well, he needs to be in here with his wife." She shook her head.

"I've got this. I'll check on you later. I'm out." He blew a kiss and she caught it in her hand.

She glanced at the wall clock. "Hey."

He turned as he held on to the doorknob. "Yeah."

"Happy one-year anniversary."

"Happy one-year to you, too." He gave her a mischievous look before closing her door.

Milan sat at her desk and logged on to her flamingo pink laptop, preparing to get some work done. However, her eyes insisted on a glimpse of the silver room again. She stood. Ramada's man was still fucking her royally from behind, and this time it was his face that was situated between the thick thighs of the Hispanic woman. He sucked her wide-open red-velvet pussy as the woman stood over his face.

Milan tried to look away, but curiosity took her by the hand and insisted. She imagined Lavender, long and strong, screwing Ramada in the same vulnerable position. Ramada was handling the dick well, and her ripe 38DD breasts flopped around. Lavender always was a breast man, always checking out the biggest tits in the place, no matter where they'd go.

Just as Ramada began to bust a jerking, sputtering nut, a woman stuck her long tongue inside of Ramada's wide-open mouth. Ramada's man, now obviously willing to play the game, backed away from the oral vagina, closed his eyes, and continued grinding. And another man was sitting back with his white, veiny dick in hand, stroking himself within an inch of Ramada's round ass. His liquid expelled onto his cupped hand and melted. He simply stared at the other fuck buddies as though he must have died and gone to swinger heaven.

Milan looked away and spoke aloud. "Her psycho ass will be on the no-entry list from now on." She sat down in her chair and resumed looking over her computer files. "That kinda mess doesn't work on Milan Kennedy. She's gotta come up with some better shit than that," she told herself.

About thirty minutes later, just as Milan again checked out the view, she caught a glimpse of the upstairs VIP. room. She saw a group of people moving about in the midst of an obvious commotion.

Lavender's voice belted from her two-way. "Milan."

Milan snatched it from her desk. "What's wrong, Lavender?"

"We've got a problem. We have someone in VIP. claiming that after saying no, she was forced to suck Big Mack's dick at knifepoint. She's called the police. It's Ramada."

"What?"

"It's Ramada." He said it again with an extended exhale.

She paused. "I'll be right down." She disconnected the radio and ran to the door. "Damn, that fuckin baby-mama bitch."

3

"She's Always in My Hair"

ᑼ

Sunday, March 30, 2008
8:07 a.m.

As was the morning ritual, because Milan always burned the midnight oil, the rich aroma of a hazelnut breakfast blend permeated her home, reminiscent of the local Starbucks coffeehouse. The pot was now half full.

Milan Lee Kennedy, tall and slender, butterscotch and sophisticated, stood in the spacious, lavish living room of her blond-stone estate in Alpharetta. Most of her furnishings were cream colors with bold-colored accents like hot pink, purple, or red. That's how she liked it. Colorful and bold.

Most of the fabrics were woven jacquard and the window treatments were formal. Her style was contemporary classy.

She used her gold letter opener to loosen the seal of the envelope from the music publishing company. It was the first of what was to be quarterly checks from her deceased famous dad's music royalties.

The dollar amount would have made some eyes pop

in amazement, though Milan had expected the five fig-
ures. Over the next three quarters, those checks would
add up to almost eighty thousand dollars. Her other two-
acre home in the Palmetto Bay area of South Miami her
well-known father had left her in his estate. It was a
gray-stone, five-bedroom English manor, with a black-
bottom pool, located in a cul-de-sac. He had also left
her a large amount of money, which she had already in-
vested and saved. And she had enough income from the
success of her house of fucking, Erotic City, to take care
of her other financial needs.

Fame and wealth had greeted Milan and her younger
sister, Tamiko Rae Kennedy, since the day they were
born. They were heiresses. Their father, Charlie "Scatman" Kennedy, a legendary singer and pianist, had always been on the road, but he had never failed to take
care of home, financially that is.

Wearing a red silk robe, Milan sat upon her orange
pillow–top sectional and leaned back, extending her
long legs along the cushions. She glanced at the glass
cabinet that contained her dad's six Grammy Awards.
She remembered and smiled. That side of her dad was
remarkable.

She pressed the button on her BlackBerry Pearl. Her
ring tone was Sisqó's "Thong Song." "Hello." Milan was
in first gear.

"Hey, sis. What's happening with you?" Tamiko, who
was younger by two years, had an energy level that was
fifth-gear hyper.

"Not much. Just going through some mail."

"I got my royalty check. Did you get yours yet?"

"I did." Milan cautiously sipped her caffeinated black

brew from a pink Diva mug and glanced out at the lush backyard past the beveled glass of the double French doors.

"It's funny how this money's nothing more than a reminder of Daddy's death."

"I know what you mean."

The sound of clanging dishes sounded in the background. "Have you decided what to do about the Miami house yet?"

Milan replied, "No. I'll just leave it as is for now. What about you, living all alone in Peachtree City? Daddy barely even started furnishing that house after Nancy left and took nearly everything. That's a big place."

"It is. I'm slowly getting things set up. His energy is all around. I even found a box with his old vinyl records. He hadn't even unpacked them."

"Good. We can pass them down when we start our families."

"True. So how are things with you?"

Milan held the mug with both hands and curled her legs beneath her. "Tamiko, I know you heard about what happened last night."

"What?"

"The police were called out to the club at like one-thirty in the morning. Lavender's ex came in there starting some mess."

"Not his crazy baby's mama again?"

"I could add some choice words to go along with the word *crazy.*"

"It just doesn't make sense that she would even come in there considering that's where you met Lavender."

"Yeah, but she had the nerve to show up last night

trying to get under his skin, screwing everybody all up in his face. And when that didn't work, she snuck into VIP and went down on Big Mack, and then had the nerve to claim she was forced."

Tamiko's sigh could be heard. "Big Mack, the rapper?"

"Yeah."

"First of all, what was he doing in there?"

"What do you mean?"

"I'm just saying. It seems somebody like Big Mack could get all the erotic pleasure he needs."

"You mean sex, Tamiko?"

"Yes. You know what I mean."

"I'm sure he can. But we get a lot of famous people in there. We've got this strict policy that whatever happens in the club, stays in the club. We call it the Vegas rule. Also known as the Swing 101, never kiss and tell rule. Most of our members know that."

"I guess that didn't happen this time."

"Not after Ramada took it upon herself to call the police when she went out to her car."

"Oh, what a drama queen."

"She claims he was drunk and pulled a damn switchblade after he was deep down her throat and then she says she backed off, changing her mind. She said he told her he'd slit her throat if she didn't finish the job."

"What? Don't you guys have cameras in there?"

"Not in the rooms like that. I mean it would be legal, but our patrons are so worried about privacy, we couldn't violate that. I try to keep an eye on things from my office, but our bouncer checked them before they even came in the club and he found nothing."

"Oh Lord. So what now?"

"It's pretty much her word against his. You know the old girl has a history of making things up." Milan took another slow sip.

"Yeah, I know that's right. Where is Lavender, anyway?"

"He's sleeping. We got home at like six this morning and he fell out. But hell, sleeping is the last thing on my mind."

"Wow, Milan. I'm really sorry. But I'm sure everything will be okay."

"One thing I know is it's sure to be all over the news today. I refuse to even turn on the TV."

"I hope it isn't. And you guys need to try and keep your heads up. You'll be fine."

"Let's hope so." Milan rubbed the back of her neck and asked, "Have you heard from Nancy? I still need to talk to Attorney Wyatt about what she might do to try and get her hands on Dad's money."

"She hasn't called lately. Last time she called my number it was to deny Dad's claims that she was screwing her trainer."

"Man, thank God their divorce was final one month before he passed away. He worked way too hard for his money. She lost her rights to his estate when she accepted the divorce settlement. I know she seems to run to you when she has something to say. But I'm sorry, I just can't accept the fact that now that he's gone, she decides to get her hands on even more than he gave her. It's never gonna happen." Milan placed her coffee cup on the glass side table.

"You know I agree. I'm on your side. Maybe because I was in the house with her a little longer than you, she and I bonded a little more. But she knows where I stand."

"She should have thought about that when she was lucky enough to steal him away from Mom. She played his chick on the side for too long before he married her. And have Daddy tell it, it seems like she snuck around on him most of those years. Call me what you want, but I can't stand her ass."

"You know I don't blame you. Anyway, what're you doing the rest of the day?"

"I'm headed out to late service before I lose my damn mind."

"Okay, but make sure you get some sleep when you get back since you've gotta go back to work again tonight."

"At least we'll have a few days off until Thursday. Thank God we're only open four nights a week. What're you guys doing today?"

"Jarod and I might catch an early movie before he goes to the club."

"Tell him I'll see him later." Milan adjusted her legs and sat up straight.

"I will. I'll talk to you tomorrow. And I hope Lavender's okay. I can imagine he's feeling pretty bad."

"Yeah, considering he always tells me he has her under control. Anyway, let me stop."

"Yeah, you stop. Bye, big sis."

"Bye, baby sis."

4

"Whip Appeal"

Where're you going?" Lavender asked with squinted eyes, carefully exiting his brief slumber. He rubbed the back of his curly head to soothe his daze.

He'd spent the night at Milan's house for the fourth night in a row. His three-bedroom home in Fairburn was now rarely occupied. They'd seemed to make Milan's home their convenient sanctuary, mainly because she lived a bit closer to the club than he did.

Only wearing his boxers, he laid his muscular, long body upon the woven purple sheets of her platform canopy bed, buried underneath a layer of soft covers. The dungeon bed was fully equipped with a sex swing and overhead bars. The oversize playpen provided plenty of room for a kinky royal rumble.

As usual, Milan was a mere stitch away from naked while she stood in her well-organized walk-in closet deciding what to wear. "I'm going to church."

He could see her from glorious head to toe. "Without me?"

"You were sleeping."

"You could have tried to wake me up."

She spoke without aiming her sights his way. "Well, I didn't." A click of her tongue followed her words.

He lay on his side, adjusting the down pillow under his head. "You need to be right here in bed with me. With your fine ass." He adored every inch of her. Even her shadow.

"I need to get ready to leave." She snatched a wine-colored skirt from its hanger.

"Milan, come here. Cut out that tough girl act." He patted the bed and stared as though begging for her happy side.

"Why?" Her one-word question was resistant.

"Just come here."

She still ignored the sight of him. "I'm getting dressed."

"Don't make me come and get you." His tone was playful but the look on his face was stern.

She laid the skirt on the oak dressing table, smoothed the fabric with her hand, and tried to fight off a half grin. Her one dimple flashed. "Please. Your ass is not getting out of that bed and you know it."

"What I know is that you need to walk yourself right on over here so I can talk to you."

Milan exited the closet and stood in place, bringing her hand to her hip. "What?" She slowly brought him her eyes.

"Cut out the attitude."

She took another step. "Lavender, I am not in the mood right now, okay?"

"Neither am I. So say that while you're walking." He pointed toward the side of the bed.

Milan stood still. She shook her head and looked down, and then took the few steps to her man. She stood before him, wearing her tiny purple panties and a very tiny smile, and dropped her eyes down at his face. She folded her arms along her flat belly.

He shifted his body and scooted back, leaning against their leather headboard. "Good girl. Now, I'm sorry. I'm sorry for the fact that Ramada came up in the club and started all this crap. I don't blame you for being mad. I won't try to excuse myself from this shit. I asked you to trust me and I was wrong." His eyes agreed with his words. "We'll get through this."

She shifted her weight. "Lavender, it's tough to think about anything else right now. I've worked hard to make the club what it is, and I can't afford anyone trying to bring it down. It's been rough. You know that."

"I do. And I'm in this with you, for many reasons."

She gave a grand sigh. "Well, I appreciate your apology."

"Thank you."

Milan's heart gave a soft twist in her chest. She took small, slow steps forward, leaned onto the bed, and crawled toward him as she planted a kiss on Lavender's lips. The pucker was loud. Their stares were focused and deep.

He said with a commanding smile, "Can you spare a few minutes for your man?"

Her eyes were baby doll big. "I might be able to work that out."

"Please allow me to bury the hatchet." Lavender's stare traveled from her face to her full breasts. He pulled the covers away from his body and removed his boxers. His good-morning penis had already extended its full length, and she noticed immediately. Her tawny nipples began to harden at the sight of him.

Milan took off her panties and gave them a toss. She positioned herself to straddle him like she was mounting a motorcycle. His dick met the exact point of her vagina. She rubbed her juiciness along his shaft, and he moaned.

He said, "You always do it to me. You always make my dick hard at the sight of you."

She spoke not a word, though her eyes answered him, and she eased herself upon his dick, guiding him into her body with a slow lowering of her dark pinkness. He swelled inside of her and she contracted with every inch of entry until his dick was completely gone from sight, deep inside of Milan, exploring her from the inside.

Milan began to bounce her slender body. Her long, shiny black hair hung past her shoulders and swayed in response to her sultry movements.

Her pussy sucked his dick and sucked it well.

He buried himself inside, stretching her. "Take that dick," Lavender said while grinding himself to the exact rhythm of her hungry fucking skills. He looked up at her face, examining the obvious expression of dick-riding pleasure that coated her skin. It was a look of utter ecstasy. Milan's eyes were shut tight, and her bottom lip met her upper teeth. Her breathing was fast paced and so was her bounce.

Her voice was suddenly sex symbol seductive. She always talked shit. It was the bad girl in her. She was always a vixen in the sheets. "I love to fuck my dick. My dick is right where it belongs. Deep inside of this pussy, hiding out like it fucking ran away from home. I should just keep it and walk around with my dick all day so I can cum on it whenever I want."

"Hell, I wish you could."

"Now I know why Ramada is pulling that crazy shit. This hard-ass dick is so damn good. But this is mine now and ain't nobody gettin any of this. Nobody."

"If you say so."

"I say so."

Lavender closed his eyes. He ground faster and re-opened them. "You wouldn't let Dee ride this dick?"

"Dakota? Hell no. Dakota can only wonder what this black dick would be like."

"So I can't go into the silver room and get some head then?"

"You try it and see what the fuck happens." Her hard-working pussy escorted her firm reply.

"I guess I'll just keep watching everybody else while they fuck strangers. But I can't have any, right?"

"Fucking me right here is all you need."

"You are greedy, aren't you?"

She spoke with a deep but soft roar. "Damn right and so are you. That swinging shit is over for your ass. We'll leave the fuck parties to the rest of 'em."

"You say so."

"I fuckin say so." Milan leaned forward and her tits grazed his chest. She pressed her fists into the mattress and bounced her backside against him. She raised and lowered herself from his pee hole to his sac, over and over again, taking time to look back to catch the view of her grinding skills in the oval dresser mirror. Her ass wasn't the biggest, but she definitely knew how to show him what she was working with.

"Fuck, that shit feels good."

"This is my dick." Her sentence was serious.

"Ride it like you could break it off."

Milan twisted her grind, rolling it slightly, almost like a clockwise stir, pressing her weight onto her left knee and then her right. She made a motion as if she was walking straight up on the dick like a StairMaster.

"Damn."

She said, "Give me that circle fuck. Fuck me in a damn circle. Harder."

He did just that and grunted.

"I can't believe you're still talkin like you wanna fuck a stranger. You've got a damn stranger right here. Who do you want me to be? I can be Conchita and say, 'Ay, Papi,' and talk about cabalgue este pussy. I can be Inga and speak German to your ass. Nimm diese Muschi. Hell, I can be Gina and speak Italian. Prendie questo pussy. Who the hell do you want me to be, damnit?" Her accents were precise and erotic and angry.

"I want my woman to fuck me like she won't be satisfied until I come all through her ass. I want you to take this big dick deep down into the back of your pussy, right there, where I feel that sweet spot I love to hit. I want you right there, pumping yourself along my dick so I can explode."

"Like this." She worked it like she was getting paid.

"Hell yeah."

"Then cum for Mommy. Give Mommy her stuff, baby." She bucked and shook and pumped and choked his dick with the force of her gyrating vagina, bouncing her tig-ol-biddies like rubber balls to the sounds of raw skin hitting raw skin. The scent matched the erotic audible.

"Fuck." Lavender squinted his eyes as though trying to find himself in the back of his own head.

Her voice was now a provocative whisper. She aimed her words toward his ear. "Gimmie my stuff. And I want all of it. Make it squirt so hard I can taste it in the back of my damn throat. Shoot that shit, Lavender. Christen your woman right, like you know you can."

He froze in place and raised his ass from the sheet like his dick was a missile. His legs flexed straight out in front of him. He fully extended his dick and shot his warm ejaculate into his woman at a hundred miles per hour. "Uhggghhhhgh. Fuck." His eyes shot open lightning fast upon the very last squirt.

"That's it, baby. Yes. Damnit." She still rode him like a cowgirl, leaning back and placing her hands on her own pointy nipples, rubbing the tips with a fast motion while she squinted her pussy in preparation for her own approaching orgasm. She squeezed her pubis muscles, or her sex muscles, as hard as she could just before the spasm of the orgasm hit. And then it exploded. "Yeah, yeah, awwww, uuggh." Milan threw her head back in direct measure of the strength of her burst. She then draped her upper body upon him.

His discharge and her juices blended together along the trail of his testicles. They truly did fuck so pretty.

Lavender lay beneath her. The weight of her smooth, satisfied body was his pleasure to support. He was, as usual, in awe of his woman's freaky ability to please him, and please herself. His not-so-willing-to-deflate dick still filled her up. To him, she was simply a-fucking-mazing. Way more amazing than his ten-year relationship with Ramada, the mama of drama.

"I'm going with you," he said as he kissed her along her ear.

She leaned upward. "Okay, with your bringing-other-women-into-the-bed self. I'm leaving those words right where they are. You definitely need to go to church. We both do."

Milan rolled off, came to a naked stance, and headed to the bathroom.

He watched her walk away. "Good Lord. Simply amazing." He turned his head away, shaking it in awe, and picked up the television remote. "Any more coffee?"

"Yeah."

He turned on the forty-inch plasma. The sound of a Geico commercial could be heard.

Milan yelled from the bathroom as she turned on the shower. "Please don't turn on the news, honey. Not this morning. Not just yet."

He spoke like he was still trying to snap out of his post-lust state. "Why?" He remembered. "Oh. No problem, baby." Lavender clicked the TV back off. "No problem at all."

Milan closed the shower door.

The ring of his titanium iPhone sounded while he came to a stance. He reached over to the nightstand to pick it up and touched the screen.

His face shifted to a smile. "Hey, Great Mama."

"Hi, DeMarcus. How's it going out there in Atlanta?"

He spoke while standing in the buff. "Oh, pretty well. We're about to head out to church. The late service."

"You and Milan?"

"Yes."

"Good. She's a nice girl."

He looked around for his boxers and asked, "How are you?"

"I'm good. I've been thinking about you a lot though. I had a dream about you early this morning and wanted to check on you."

"You did?"

"Yes. And it kept me up."

"I'm sorry. What was it about?"

"Oh, about you being down. You know, just you having problems with Taj's mom. I had a dream she got you in some trouble and we were all worried. Something about blaming you for something you didn't do. I don't really remember but I do know we were worried about my sweet little great-grandson, Taj."

"Nothing like that's going on here. Everything's cool." He picked up his boxers from the foot of the bed and stepped into them.

"That's good. I'm glad. But after that, I couldn't wait to get back from church myself so I could call you. That dream had my heart heavy, you know?"

"You just relax and don't worry about anything. Taj is fine. I'm fine."

"So what's been going on with Ramada anyway? Has she moved on yet?"

"I have no idea."

"I hope she has. She used to call a lot when you two first broke up. You know she tried to talk bad about you so I had to cut her off. I'm not having that."

"I know that's right."

"When are you coming out here to see me? I miss you."

"We're gonna try to get to Miami soon to check on Milan's house out there." He reached over to make up the bed with one hand.

"Oh, that would be nice. Real nice. Well, tell Milan hello. I'll let you two go ahead on and get to church. I said a prayer with your name on it at service this morning."

"Thanks. We'll do the same. I'll call you soon, okay?"

"Okay, DeMarcus. You know I love you."

He fluffed up the pillow as he spoke. "Yes, and I do you."

"Bye." As usual, she was the first to hang up.

He wondered if his God-fearing grandmother really did feel something in her spirit about what had happened. She was usually very in tune to his emotions. It had always been that way, even when he was going through tough times back in the ring. He and his grandmother just had a connection that was unbreakable.

Milan stepped out of the bathroom smelling like tea rose.

He told her, "That was Great Mama. She says hello."

"Oh, okay, good. She always does know just when to call."

"That's true."

"Let's just hope the news doesn't make it down there. You might need to tell her first just in case."

"Maybe so. But then again, maybe not. Lord knows she's been through enough."

He stepped past Milan, popping her rear while he headed to the shower next.

Milan turned to keep an eye on Lavender's muscular physique as he passed. She smiled from ear to ear at the man she called hers. "You know best," she said. And she really hoped that he did.

5

"Mama Said Knock You Out"

∞

Saturday, September 13, 2003
10:42 p.m.

It was evening in Las Vegas, the city of sin, gambling, and sex, and don't-ask don't-tell. Las Vegas Boulevard was on fire. The lights that set ablaze the city of perpetual motion reflected along every square inch of the never-ending strip. It was a dry, desert heat. It was fight night.

It was fall of 2003 and Lavender Lewis was a strong specimen of a twenty-five-year-old with a bright future ahead of him.

He stood in the ring at the glorious Mandalay Bay Hotel among the busy chatter and piercing cheers of the postfight commotion. The huge, multipurpose arena was packed. Celebrities who had filled the first few rows of seats of the sold-out house were on their feet, along with nearly everyone else. The standing ovation was electric.

Lavender was surrounded by his Team Lavender manager, and his trainer slash grandfather, Cedric Lewis, as

well as his bodyguard. The referee and announcers stood
before him. And by his side was his girlfriend of five
years, Ramada Hart. His cherished grandmother, who he
nicknamed Great Mama, stood in the front row, holding
Lavender's four-year-old, curly-headed son, Taj George
Lewis.

The slightly balding, middle-aged Fox Sports jour-
nalist held the rounded microphone just under his own
chin and spoke extra loud with his finger to his ear,
fighting to hear himself above the bustling, boisterous
crowd.

"Lavender Lewis, here you are, the second youngest
heavyweight champion in professional boxing history,
and all after only two years. Your amateur record is
twenty-four and six, and last year you won twelve out
of fifteen bouts, all knockouts. Now here, in only round
five, you knock out Lorenzo Gomez to win the WBC
Heavyweight title. What's going through your mind
right about now?"

Lavender stood proudly with his new gold champion-
ship belt in his hand. He was drenched in a slick coating
of his own sweat, wearing his trademark lavender satin
trunks. At the moment Lavender began to speak, his
manager proudly threw his lavender satin robe over his
shoulders. The back of it read LL. The crowd cheered
even louder. His face looked unscathed, other than a
small red nick on his chin. He smiled out loud. "First
off, I want to give thanks to God for my blessings and for
my gift. I knew I wanted to fight ever since I was thirteen years old. I trained in the gym at the boxing club
in Miami where I grew up, the same gym where my father trained before he died. My grandfather retired from

boxing but trained fighters there and I'd go with him. He and my grandmother basically raised me. But today, here I am having been trained by the best, and I stand in this ring with the heavyweight belt in my hand. The same belt I used to dream about. I'd lose sleep thinking about this day, man. I love this. I'm honored and I want to thank everyone who's been a part of this so far." The applause grew louder and then dissipated.

"Would you say Lorenzo Gomez underestimated you?"

"I'd say Lorenzo is a fighter. And he's definitely powerful. He came at me like an ox. He stood strong, and one time when I threw a right hook that connected to his head, he didn't even flinch. He barely blinked. I was like, look at this." Lavender rubbed the sweat from the bridge of his nose. "He's tough, man. I just think I was able to dodge most of his punches, and maybe it's because he had his guard down a few times, I don't know. But I have a lot of respect for him as a man. He's a true fighter."

"Looks like he got a couple of good shots in before you knocked him out though. Tell us about those."

"Well, one was a right cross to my chin. On that one, I felt like I was about to pass out. I'm telling you, he's a strong dude."

"Will you give the Macho Man Gomez another shot?"

"That's tomorrow's news. I want to celebrate tonight. I'll talk about that when the sun comes up. I do plan on a long career though, I'll say that much. I'll look back ten years from now and will have won all three titles."

"Anything else you want to say?"

He added a rhythm to his speech. "Just that I am, the smooth as silk, Lavender man, brilliant and vivid, a mixture of purple and white. My dad, George Lewis, wore purple trunks and my grandfather wore white. I come from a long line of Lewises. And I will continue the legend of the Lewis fighters in this sport. We thank you." He flashed his trademark smile and held his wide, flashy WBC belt high in the air. The crowd again erupted in cheers.

"Well, congratulations, Lavender Lewis. Back to you, Jim."

Lavender turned to hug his woman, Ramada, and their embrace was firm. Her hair was in a ponytail and she had on a tight, pale yellow halter dress with jeweled high heel sandals. Her back was strong and her face was flawless. She dabbed a small, slow moving tear that traveled down her right cheek. The photographers' bulbs bounced off Lavender's and Ramada's faces as they kissed on the lips, trying to keep it clean. Lavender turned to follow his manager's lead and stepped down from the ring to the beat of "Mama Said Knock You Out," making the trek back to his dressing room. He took a moment to blow a kiss to his dear Great Mama and loving son, then disappeared beyond the dark curtain. The crowd still cheered, "LL! LL! LL!"

Within two hours, Lavender, his manager, and his bodyguard were in the penthouse suite of the hotel. The three men were having sex with three different groupie women in the same room, and then they swapped. And the women were happy to oblige, as long as they had their chance to fuck the amazing and talented Lavender Lewis.

Three days later, early one morning once back home in Miami, a conservative-looking Italian doctor in a white coat stood over Lavender and his grandmother as they sat in a small examining room at South Miami Hospital.

The doctor's face was blank. He spoke slowly. "The magnetic resonance imaging scan shows two subdural hematomas."

Lavender asked with question marks in his eyes. "What the hell is that?"

"You have bleeding on the brain," the doctor said. His face was apologetic.

Lavender's grandmother spoke up immediately. Her words were rushed. "What? What do you mean bleeding on the brain? He's been feeling fine, just a little groggy, that's all. He can't possibly have any damage. Our boy barely got hit."

The doctor seemed to choose his words wisely. He talked while giving both Lavender and Mrs. Lewis equal focus. "One of those blows caused a traumatic brain injury and blood has collected between the outer covering of the brain and the middle layer. Basically, there were small perforations in the vein caused by a punch. Symptoms have a slower onset in that area. That's why you described some confusion or disorientation. The MRI we took before the fight was totally normal."

"Oh Lord Jesus." The elder Mrs. Lewis put her age-worn hands over her mouth.

Lavender asked quickly, "So what's next?"

"We'll monitor you for a while. Sometimes a craniotomy is required, which requires opening the skull and removing the clot."

Lavender's grandmother's eyes told on her level of alarm. She shook her head. "Oh no. Please no."

Lavender put his hand on his grandmother's knee.

The doctor spoke to her and then to Lavender. "We just don't know. There's a chance that the hematomas can heal, though we'll just have to wait and see. But, Lavender, you won't be traveling anywhere right now. We want you to stay put and relax and come back to chart the injury."

"Doctor, my grandson will be okay. In Jesus' name, I'll see to that," Lavender's grandmother said, placing her hand over her grandson's hand while a weighted tear rolled down her seventy-year-old cheek. "I'll see to it."

Monday, October 4, 2004
3:31 p.m.

Lavender sat still in his sprawling home office in Miami. His boxing memorabilia and cherished Plexiglas-framed gloves and trademark lavender shorts graced the maple-paneled walls.

The custom-made walnut plantation shutters were barely open. The afternoon sun seemed to beg to enter through the narrow slats. As was the case recently, Lavender had planned it that way. Even one year after his last fight, the light of day battled with his moods. His gloom and doom thoughts had won over long ago. And so the darkness remained a welcome resident. It was his comfort zone.

He had been sitting at his desk for hours, wearing royal blue sweats and sports socks. His longer than normal hair was unkempt, and his five o'clock shadow was at ten o'clock.

Lavender squeezed and released a hand exerciser over and over with his right hand and held on to a glass of Hennessy in the other. It was Crown Royal yesterday and Rémy the day before. His manager entered the dark room and Lavender stopped his grip but started hittin the Henn. He gulped, admitting the liquid into his system as though it could cure his ills. He drained the last of it.

His eyes were stuck upon one wall in particular, seemingly without blinking. It was the wall where a photo of his last fight hung. It stared back at him in an annoying way.

Lavender's speech was monotone and angry and his words dragged. "I've tried to get a license over and over again. The Nevada State Athletic Commission won't do it because of the damn hematomas. How many hour-long hearings have we had and they still won't lift the medical suspension?"

His manager spoke angrily as he sat in the brown chair on the other side of the rectangular desk. "This still makes no sense to me. I've talked to a team of doctors and neurosurgeons from all over the country who say you're in no more danger than any other boxer. They agreed that there are football players with even more serious head injuries than this, and they still continue their careers. Yet the commission refuses. They still voted five-zero anyway."

"This isn't football. This is what it is." Lavender still stared.

"Well, we'll keep challenging the commission. We'll file papers in federal court."

"My career is over."

"Maybe so. Maybe not."

Suddenly, Lavender's office door opened at a snail's pace. The creaking seemed to go on forever. Lavender's grandfather had been staying with him. He peered in and said, "Excuse me, DeMarcus. Your career might be over. But not your life. Your destiny is better than your history. Remember that." He stood and stared until Lavender's eyes joined his. Lavender smiled. His grandfather smiled. And then he closed the door just as slowly and disappeared.

Two weeks later, his grandfather died.

6

"Hate on Me"

✆

Sunday, March 30, 2008
10:58 a.m.

New and upscale Open Word church in Cumming, Georgia, was as big and popular as big megachurches get. And Pastor Michael Bellaire was as charismatic and renowned as big megachurch pastors get. He was tall, he was charming, and he was very, very rich.

Rolls Royce and private jet rich.

Eight-figure bank account rich.

Twenty-thousand-square-foot mansion rich.

The brotha was rich.

Milan and her sister, Tamiko, grew up in the church, mainly attending with their mother in Miami. Even after their mother passed away when they were teens, some Sundays they would go to church with their father and his new young wife, Nancy.

As the late morning orange sun and pale blue, cloudless skies hovered overhead, Milan and Lavender stepped away from Milan's pearl white CLK 320 coupe. The license plate read "EROTICA."

They were dressed impeccably. He was in his silver gray single-breasted suit with a black shirt, black tie, and vintage Prada black leather shoes. And she wore her pencil skirt and tailored jacket with silver-and-burgundy herringbone slingbacks. Her extralong natural pearls were tied in a knot just under her wide breasts. Milan and Lavender proceeded step for step.

The regular churchgoers always greeted the well-known couple. Lavender had only moved to Atlanta three years earlier, but was often recognized. He was muscular with a neck like a running back. He stood six one, weighed two ten, and was the epitome of tall, dark, and handsome. And before meeting Milan, he had been a heavyweight ladies' man.

"That's a doggone shame," one church hat–wearing woman said outside as she and her friend walked just behind the couple. She failed to keep her slow-moving words under her breath. She looked back at Milan's license plate and then examined the couple.

"What did that mean?" Milan asked Lavender.

"What?" he asked as he adjusted his collar and placed his navy blue Bible case under his arm.

"Hypocrite," the woman mumbled behind their backs.

Milan turned her head to check out the ladies as Lavender placed his arm around her waist. She turned back around after the women offered zero eye contact.

Lavender stepped up and held the glass door open for Milan to proceed first. As he walked in right behind her, he held the door open for the ladies as well. They proceeded inside offering him a nod. "Thanks," one of them said to him, proceeding to the right, mumbling to her friend.

"Hi, Ms. Kennedy, Mr. Lewis," a woman said to the couple. "God bless you." She handed them each a daily program and an envelope.

They accepted the handoff and both replied in unison, "Hello."

"Nice to see you both. Praise the Lord," she said with vigor. Her name was Beverly Sepulveda, a woman in her late forties who had known Milan from church years earlier.

"You, too," Milan said, beaming her way.

Beverly was always warm, always smiling, and always praising the Lord.

Once inside and down the main aisle, Milan and Lavender found their regular seats. They stood in place as Milan placed her purse and Bible under her seat. A forty-something couple in front of them turned back, giving careful examination just as the choir winded down their final praise and worship song, "The Spirit of the Lord."

Upon taking in their glances, Lavender smiled and bowed his head, closing his eyes in silent prayer, as did Milan.

The couple turned back around and bowed their heads, too.

Moments later, Pastor Bellaire stepped up to the podium, clean and dapper in his light-brown-and-white-pinstripe suit, a white silk tie, and winter white leather ostrich-skin shoes. He stood tall with his clean-shaven head. He was a graham cracker–colored Mr. Clean. He had Afro European skin and wore a tightly trimmed goatee. Everyone in his place of worship arose to his or her feet as a symbol of respect, and they all applauded, loudly. His short and perky wife, Tatiana, smiled proudly as she stood, clapping the loudest.

"Hallelujah. Praise the Lord. I'm so happy to be here today to talk to you about your life. You may be seated.

"I want to ask you this morning if you've ever noticed that sometimes, for some people, everything they touch turns to gold? We think they've got the Midas touch, right? In Greek mythology, King Midas had the ability to turn everything to gold. He was known for his garden of roses.

"The difference between those people and people who seem to struggle is they never rest. They tend to their gardens with time and focus. They never become complacent. They never give up. They eliminate excuses because an excuse gives you permission to stay where you are. They seize the moment. They stay ready so they don't have to get ready, if you know what I'm saying. They are passionate about what they do. Passion is like fuel. It gives you energy to get where you need to go. They have found what they love and they surround themselves with people who are passionate, too. Passion is contagious, you know. And, they have visualized themselves being where they want to go.

"Now, I know some of you are thinking that some of the successful people you know seem to be some of the biggest sinners you've ever seen in your life. It's like they're shouting in church on Sunday and shacking up on Monday."

"Hallelujah. I know that's right," one man could be heard shouting behind Milan and Lavender.

"But don't worry about Joe and Jeffrey and Jenny. Life is abundant and it's yours for the taking. See it as an all-you-can-eat buffet. Be a victor. Hold your hope. Don't worry about why your friend's marriage is working and yours is broken. Bless them and focus on your own marriage. After all, a marriage is two sinners saved by grace who live together. Tend to your own crop, your own house. And know that if along the way you find a path without obstacles, it probably doesn't lead anywhere. Be thankful for your challenges because there is a hidden opportunity in every crisis. Don't let the devil throw a pity party and invite you as the guest of honor. Life is not about what happened to you, it's about what happens through you. Look to your neighbor and ask, 'Can I get an amen?'"

"Amen," Lavender and Milan said to each other.

Milan heard one word from the woman sitting to her right. And it wasn't amen.

"Jezebel."

Milan immediately turned toward the young woman, who stared straight ahead. Milan looked around and then at Lavender, who kept his focus on Pastor Michael.

Milan sat still, crossing her arms and legs, pulling her distracted mind away from the thoughts of the sometimes cold and distant vibes she'd get in the Lord's house.

This is obviously something I'll just have to get used to, she told herself, twisting the oversize pearl ring on her baby finger.

Pastor Michael said, "It's not what they call you that matters, it's what you answer to."

The woman next to Milan folded her arms and leaned

away just as Lavender put his hand over Milan's knee and gave a firm squeeze. She turned toward him and squeezed him back with a smile.

More than an hour later, Milan and Lavender were in the slow-moving line of cars waiting to exit the parking lot of the church. Lavender wore his Marc Jacobs stunna shades as he looked down to fiddle with the radio.

Station 102.5 announced out loud, *"As we reported earlier, Gwinnett County resident, popular rapper Big Mack was charged with assault early this morning after attending a sex club in midtown Atlanta called Erotic City. An unidentified victim has allegedly accused him of assault with a deadly weapon after claiming that force was used in an effort to engage the victim in the act of oral sex. The owner of Erotic City was charged with one count of negligence. Our records indicate that Erotic City opened its doors in 2006. The owner, Milan Lee Kennedy, is the daughter of legendary singer Charlie Kennedy who passed away last November. Both Big Mack, aka Mac McCoy, and the club's owner are due in court for an arraignment soon to discuss the charges."*

Milan did not flinch. She did not blink. She simply stared forward and swallowed. Without looking, she reached into her purse and pulled out her tinted sunglasses, securing them along her youthful face. She leaned her head back and rested her elbow along the door, bringing her hand to her chin in thought.

Lavender pressed the button to switch from the radio to the Jill Scott track that was Milan's favorite, "Hate on Me."

He took her hand and squeezed. "Everything's gonna

be all right. We'll be fine." He pulled out onto the street and headed to Milan's home.

Milan had no reply.

Silence sat in the car with them the entire way home.

7

"When I'm with You"

❧

Sunday, March 30, 2008
4:00 p.m.

Later that afternoon, Tamiko Kennedy and her man, Jarod Hamilton, rode back home from a matinee at the Fayetteville Pavilion theater. They rode in his freshly detailed, coal black Audi A8 with deep gray privacy windows and black leather seats. They always made a point to attend movies on a regular basis. It was just one of the things they liked to do together.

She asked, "Still can't believe what happened last night at the club. Was it a crazy scene or what?"

"Not really. Most people left once the police got there."

"Do you think Big Mack did that?"

"I have no idea. I was downstairs. With the only witness being Ramada, who knows?"

"True." Tamiko smoothed her black bangs along her forehead and brought her long hair from behind her back to over her shoulder. She was a couple of shades browner than her older sister, a little bit shorter and about twenty pounds heavier. She looked more like her black father than her Asian mother. "I thought that movie was pretty good. Did you?"

Jarod drove with his sunroof open, allowing the cool afternoon air to circulate above his freshly shaven head. He sat with a bit of a gangster lean, with his elbow resting on the middle console. "Uh-huh. The bad guys came around in the end. But the ladies were pretty hard on the brotha who cheated on his wife. She fooled around too, now."

"Yeah, but not until he did."

"Hey, two wrongs don't make a right."

"I agree."

He rubbed the top of his head. "Would you do that?"

"What?"

"Run right off and get with someone if you were fooled around on."

Tamiko focused on the neighborhood view that passed by. "I have been. And I didn't. And I won't. But I don't need to worry about that, right?" She gave her sights to Jarod.

"Oh no. Not from the kid."

"Good."

"Good." He turned up the jazz radio station a notch.

Tamiko looked his way and spoke to his profile. "Would you fool around if I did?"

"To be honest with you, I probably would."

"Really?" Tamiko turned the volume back down. "I thought you said two wrongs don't make a right. That's a double standard."

"That's just keepin it real. That's just a man trying to get his mind off of stuff."

"Not sure if I like your honesty."

They came to a red light. "The thing is, foolin around would mean it's over anyway, right? But, we don't have to worry about that so, we're straight." He reached for her with his eyes.

She smiled and leaned over to kiss him on his cheek. She said, "We are," and glanced out of the passenger side window.

They met about a year ago, around the same time as Milan and Lavender. Jarod had applied to be a body-guard for Tamiko's dad just before he got sick. Tamiko was working as her father's assistant. Her dad didn't hire Jarod. First of all, her dad thought he was too young, even though he was twenty-seven at the time. But also because at the last minute, her dad's best friend asked him to hire his son. But by then, Jarod had already shown up for the scheduled interview at a hotel in Vegas where Tamiko's dad was about to make what would be his last performance onstage. And Tamiko was bitten. Hard.

Jarod bought his new luxury car to chauffeur people around the vastness of the greater Atlanta area. He was born in Decatur and knew the city like the back of his hand. He'd started his own car service company last year and it was paying off well enough. He had his regular clients who made his business a success. By night, he worked for Milan as Lavender's right hand. The man never slept.

During the day from eight until five, he dropped off and picked up clients. And from nine at night until four in the morning, he worked at Erotic City. When he did have a night off, the second thing that was most on his mind was sex. And even though Tamiko spent her time putting all she had into trying to turn her love of fashion into her own clothing line called Cheekz, she worked some serious overtime of her own trying to please him. But, she felt it was worth it. She considered Jarod to be her best friend and her soul mate. Unlike with the other men she'd bonded to who left her broken hearted, she wanted this one to be different.

A while after arriving home, they lay in bed in the master bedroom suite of Tamiko's place. It was the home her father had bought when he'd married Nancy seven years ago. The outside was red brick with a clay roof. The inside of the five-bedroom McMansion had rich, cherry hardwood flooring and mahogany paneling. The walls were dark tan with buff crown molding. Most of the rooms were sparsely furnished being that Nancy took just about everything as part of the divorce settlement, but the main bedroom and sitting area were complete. The large area even had a full wet bar and a two-sided fireplace.

Atop the fitted leopard-print comforter, both buck naked, they watched a *Baby Got Back* porno. As usual, Jarod's favorite X-rated star, Cherokee, was doing what she did best. Bouncing her world-class ass. And what an ass it was.

"How'd you get to be such a butt fiend?" Tamiko asked, keeping both eyes on the gingerbread-colored, talented, booty shakin porn star.

Jarod's left hand gripped only half of his rock-hard penis. "I couldn't tell you."

"It's like it's a fetish or something?"

"I wouldn't call it that."

"Well, what would you call it then?" Tamiko rested

her head upon his buffed shoulder and looped her leg in between his legs.

"Me liking big butts isn't out of the ordinary, is it? I mean, a fetish is something you like that's out of the ordinary that you fantasize about and spend all day thinking about. Something kinky like getting hit in the back of the head. Now, that donkey punch shit is crazy. Shoot, man, mine is mild. I just love the female body."

Tamiko's eyes bugged toward the flat screen. "Well, whatever you want to call your preference or fixation, I'd call that booty way, way out of the ordinary." She examined every inch of it. "She is one of a kind. What does it do for you though? Supernatural butts I mean?"

"You know. Just something to pad the pushin. Something to hold on to. Something to watch." And watch he did. Jarod began stroking himself, rubbing the enormous head of his dick with his long thumb. "Look at that shit." The movement of his stroke was like erotic clockwork. "That is a thing of beauty."

Tamiko turned onto her stomach, still adjusting her sights to watch the movie. "That is way too much junk in the trunk, if you ask me."

"Look who's talkin. You got all the backside in the Kennedy family anyway. Thank God." Jarod popped her butt and it shook in response. His glimpse lingered.

"Oh, so you're trying to talk about my sister, huh?"

"No, but you've definitely got a whole lot more. I'm just saying."

"Shoot. Milan's got enough breasts to make up for it. I wish I did. I got my hips from the big girl side of my dad's family."

"I ain't mad at 'em." He returned his eyes to the movie.

Tamiko shifted her stare to Jarod's handsome face. His teeth were Colgate perfect and his eyebrows spanned perfectly over his wide brown eyes. "Good thing you don't have a brother. The ladies of the world couldn't handle that."

"As long as you can handle it, I'm cool."

"I try."

He made a moaning sound and gave even longer strokes to himself. "Damn. Uh, uh, uh."

"Speaking of fetishes, let's hope there's no big booty white girl coming on next. You will lose your mind then." She shied away from viewing the gifted porno stars again. Instead, her eyes dropped from her man's face to his extreme endowment. His forever dick was medium brown, slightly lighter toward the top third, and it curved to the left, toward Tamiko. The rounded head of his circumcised cock was like an extralarge mushroom. It morphed down into a wide shaft, seeming to be the size of a damn forearm. He and Tamiko had measured it as twelve inches, with a girth of almost seven inches at its thickest point. It looked like a hammer and banged like one, too. It was a sight for sore eyes.

8

"Mr. Big Stuff"

❧

Sunday, March 30, 2008
5:17 p.m.

In the beginning, Tamiko was afraid to suck Jarod's
dick. She didn't have much practice, having only been
with two average-size men before him. Both who pro-
posed and both who she'd caught cheating.

But giving her horny ex-boyfriends oral sex, and giving
Jarod oral sex was the difference between a Volkswagen
and a damn Hummer. He put the *E* in *endowed*, and it
took her a few months to master his mighty hungness.
Though after a while, she quickly found that one thing
she was actually good at was swallowing a huge dick like
it was a Tootsie Roll. And those dick-sucking skills kept
Jarod hanging around.

Tamiko had a wide mouth, with thick dick-sucking
lips and a long tongue. And the trip was that she
seemed to have no gagging reflex whatsoever. She
knew how and when to use her hands to assist her once
she'd gotten his man-muscle as far down her throat as
it would go. It was an art to her. But when it came to

taking her man inside of her pussy, now that was a dick of a different color.

She loved to make a downright slippery mess when she sucked him off. When she was done, the sheet under his ass would be soaking wet. Tonight, she'd decided to keep a bottle of beer beside the bed, just so she could wet his dick-whistle the way he really liked her to.

"Keep watching your girl. I've got this," she said. She moved his right hand away from the firm grip he had on his man-size tool.

Just as she shifted her body from lying beside him, he spread his legs almost automatically, making way for her driver-seat position. She moved downward and rested her tummy along the covers, tossing her hair behind her, and propped her elbows so that her hands could reach his wonder dick. Her legs hung off the bed and her maple ass was sprawled out. He caught a downward glimpse and took a deep breath. His face said he knew what he was in for.

Jarod put his right arm behind his head and leaned back, keeping his eyes on the sight of caramel Cherokee, with her d'ass tattoo on her right cheek, riding a dick doggy style, with the camera all up in the crack of her mammoth booty. Her ass jiggled like Jell-O. There was a loud slapping sound each time her cheeks would clap together.

Meanwhile, Tamiko's tongue tickled Jarod's broad tip, and then his dorsal area. She traveled down to his substantial balls and kissed them.

He lay back like a puppy getting his belly scratched.

He shifted his eyes to view Tamiko, though he only saw the top of her head. She placed her hand under his thigh, signaling for him to raise his legs and she slipped her tongue up and down along the wrinkled skin of his tight asshole, poking inside, tossing his salad. He moaned and his eyes opened wide. He caught another glimpse of his girl Cherokee at work and tensed up. His asshole clamped around her stiff tongue. His dick surged and he let out a long, slow "Unghhhh."

Tamiko smiled at his manly anatomy and moved up to his hard-on. He lowered his legs, watching her as she took his dick deep into her mouth.

She opened her mouth extra wide and slid him in, again and again, stretching her lips around his size, inching herself along, making sure to keep her teeth away as best she could. She backed away and spit, stroking his shaft with her palm, giving expert wrist rotation with every long stroke, similar to the stroke she'd learned by watching him jack off so often. She moved over to the nightstand and grabbed the bottle of Corona.

"You are bad." His statement was accentuated by raised eyebrows.

"My mouth is dry." She took a long swig and replaced the bottle.

She kept the chilled brew in her mouth, and brought her lips back to his penis, slowly inserting him deep inside with the beer meeting his hardness.

"Damn, that shit feels good."

She sucked, and moved her head like a bobble-head doll, making sloshing sounds and allowing small dribbles of the liquid to drip down and saturate his testicles. Again she took him all the way back, as far as it would go, and swallowed him to her tonsils. She held a handful of dick at the base and her mouth was full. He could feel the back of her throat. She growled.

He said, "That's my baby. Get all that shit in there."

Tamiko came up for air and again grabbed the bottle, this time drinking a few swallows for herself.

"You know I'm ready for that pussy, don't you?" This time it was his eyes that said he was serious. "Turn over."

Tamiko propped herself up on her knees while Jarod sat up and positioned himself behind her. He still had a view of the movie. Cherokee was still going at it.

He stuck himself inside of his woman. She jerked. He pulled out and slipped back in, this time slower.

"That's my big man, there," she said, almost purring.

"You know it."

Tamiko eyed the movie and grinded. There was a white woman, built like a sista, now joining in on the action. Tamiko was not surprised.

Jarod said from behind Tamiko, "Damn, she's got a body."

She shook her head in her mind only and concentrated on trying to make her man cum. She slid her ass up and down, taking most of what he had to offer, and stopped. She squirmed. "Let me get on my back."

He agreed and she turned over, opening her legs wide, exposing the view of her Brazilian-waxed pussy. He entered her again. She pulled away and took a long breath. He entered again and dug deep.

"Baby, wait." She shifted her body and worked the angle to accommodate all that he had.

Tamiko managed to screw him that way long enough to get a good rhythm going. Jarod made those sounds. Those sounds he'd make when he was about to cum. But usually he'd make them after a couple of hours of serious buck-wild fucking. With Jarod, she had to pack a serious lunch.

He pressed straight back inside and braced himself when Tamiko jerked. She froze.

"No, don't stop. Keep it up, just like that." He panted hard while long drips of his salty sweat began to fall upon her titties.

Tamiko moved back toward the headboard and took another deep breath.

"You're scooting again," he said with a mix of frustration and compassion.

"Not so hard," she told him.

Even when she faked it, it never helped him get his rocks off. He needed constant, exact stimulation.

He paused and pulled out slowly. "Here, on your side." He crawled off and she lay to her left. He came up from behind and entered her again. She kept her hand alongside his thigh to control him, and grinded in tiny circles. His voice sounded pleased. "That's it."

What seemed like a two-hour marathon ended up being barely one. Tamiko watched the clock to make sure. She reached back and did a wetness check, but found that it was indeed a dry fuck.

"Wait. Let me lick your balls." She always knew that if all else failed, his own masturbating would do the trick.

"Okay," Jarod said sounding on edge.

He rolled onto his back and Tamiko moved between his legs. She took his hand and placed it on his dick. She spit four long dribbles of saliva on the head. He shellacked his dick with her fluid and stroked in a circular motion.

Her face met his crown jewels. She licked them with her flat tongue, up and down like an ice cream cone, over and over, again moving up to wet his dick with spit.

The movie had been long over. Jarod closed his eyes and lost himself in his own visual production. He again sounded like his moans were about to turn into grunts.

She kept her focus upon his balls. They were drenched with her repeated saliva that ran down from his dick. Just as her jaw began to cramp, he slowed down, squeezed his base, and said, "Here, baby. Take this."

She quickly met his tip with her wide-open mouth, and he released his hand, shooting his hot, cloudy cum into her mouth. She took every drop and swallowed while looking up at him with big, receiving eyes.

She wiped her mouth and stood. Through the mirror, Tamiko watched him watch her backside with a satisfied look on his face.

She stepped into the bathroom and closed the door. Her feet pressed upon the Spanish limestone. In the dark, she sat upon the toilet and peed, rubbing the sweat from her forehead. Even when she was done, she sat still. She heard him speak to her.

"You handled me like a champ."

She remembered him telling her the first time they had sex that most women complained that he took too long. Most women would only get theirs and then go to sleep. He said one woman referred to sex with him as one long boregasm.

"You just don't give up," he said.

She sat still, without a reply. Unsatisfied and exhausted.

She stood and flushed the toilet and then turned on

the light and the shower. She climbed inside, slid the chocolate shower curtain closed, and squeezed the almond body wash onto her hands. Tamiko rubbed between her legs and all over her skin and to her breasts. She removed the elongated showerhead and lowered it toward her pussy. The pulsating aim of the spraying water shot upward at the point of her fleshy vulva and her heated shaft. It teased her tender meaty point. She relaxed her muscles and brought the tip of her finger up to the spot of her clit, rubbing her finger back and forth. And Tamiko brought herself to a slow, quiet climax, gently squeezing her ass and thigh muscles as she busted a good, self-servicing nut of her own.

She sighed and rinsed her body and returned the showerhead to its place. She turned off the water, hearing her no-girl-head-giving boyfriend in the throes of a deep, I got mine, loud-ass snore. As usual.

He would need to get up and head to work in an hour.

She went into the den and sat, in thought, wondering, "Is that all there is?"

9

"Controversy"

ᎧᏇ

The bright neon lights read E.C. The initials shone loudly outside of the erotic club of swing in the heart of Hotlanta. It was considered fairly early as far as the club was concerned, yet the parking lot was nearly full.

The tuxedo-clad valet had been busy since the doors had opened at nine o'clock. Parked down the street were two news vans, both with satellites perched high up into the black sky. The photographers and reporters kept their distance but also kept a close eye on the front door as though waiting for something else to happen, for someone well known to show up and get their freak-nasty on, or perhaps waiting to catch the club's owner for an impromptu interview. Only, Milan had made sure to arrive early in the afternoon, way before the madness she'd so correctly predicted.

Inside, Milan sat in her office, eyeing the goings-on from the top floor as always. She sat back with her legs crossed, swiveling in her high-back chair with her mind racing. She spoke toward the speakerphone.

"Don't they know we have no liability in this thing? And they'd better not photograph the cars in my parking lot. That's a gross invasion of privacy. Am I the only one who sees this?" She tapped her long fingernails along her desktop. "I mean, some famous guy patronizes us and all of a sudden we're responsible for his actions. Not that I believe the accusations in the least." She stood up, wearing her grape pants suit, and walked across the Persian rug to the front window.

Family friend and lawyer Hunter Wyatt replied, "Milan, as you know, because it happened on your premises, and because of the celebrity status of the accused, this is big news. It's not like it happened at a local restaurant or at a park. The world of swingers is mysterious enough so people are curious. You know you can't blame them for that."

Milan spoke just short of loud while she gave a peek through the vertical blinds. "Well, I guess next thing, we'll see *Entertainment Tonight* or *TMZ* out there. People who come here deserve some privacy."

"I understand that."

"But, Hunter, I'll tell you who I can blame, aside from Ramada herself." She made her way to her desk and sat along the corner while she grabbed her hair and fluffed out her length. "What I can do is blame the prosecutors. They know that each and every person who steps through that door signs a waiver, stating that we are not responsible for the decisions our patrons make while they're in here. We have very strict rules and you know as well as I do that there was no knife."

Milan grabbed an ink pen and scribbled circles upon a Post-It.

"Do we really know that?"

"No one found a knife. We have metal detectors at the door. We don't even allow cell phones."

"Maybe so, but because one of Big Mack's bodyguards left before anyone knew what was going on, he could have snuck a knife out of there. And it didn't have to be metal."

She paused her cryptic artwork. "Oh I see what you're doing, Hunter. You're playing devil's advocate. Very good. But that's my point. He still never would have gotten in here."

"Anything is possible, Milan."

"Maybe. But it would be highly unlikely."

"Look, I know you don't want any unnecessary attention to your club. This should blow over. It's just the news of the day because of the curiosity about Big Mack's lifestyle. Especially because he's married."

"Yeah well, married or not, that's on him and his wife."

"Seems she's left him already. I guess she had no idea he was into swinging and she told a radio station they're through. She also knows he had some stripper come in with him so he could get in as part of a couple."

"Now, that is true."

"Anyway, from what Ramada Hart says, she wasn't willing to finish her act upon him, wife or no wife. She tried to stop performing, and as you know, she says she was forced to finish."

"I know I've told you about her past relationship with Lavender. They have a child together and she's been dealing Lavender hell cards from the day their son was conceived. Plus, she came in here with her so-called man and then went to another room to give a blow job without him so much as knowing she was anywhere other than in the ladies' room. She puts the *D* in *drama*. I think she wanted to start some mess since Lavender's still with me, and she did it one year to the day that she lost him. But, this is really a case between her and Big Mack. I'm all for standing up for victims who're forced to do anything they choose not to participate in, but other than not allowing either back in here, there's nothing much I can do. Shoot, if you came in here to get your freak on it would be none of my business. But, that would never happen, I'm sure." She gave a mini laugh.

"Very funny. And you are correct. It never would. Not with my wife. Not without my wife. It's simply not my cup of tea."

"Like I said, that's on you."

"Point made. I understand. We'll deal with this next week. Let me do what I do best, okay? Defending, not swinging. And I was able to get the date pushed back since the prosecution's trying to find some more witnesses. Nothing's happening right away. Just let me do this."

Milan reached for a stack of mail, shuffling through the envelopes. "Okay. Go ahead. And I'm sorry about that little jab. You know me."

"Yeah. What I do know is you got your determination from your dad. That'll get you far, Milan."

"I just want to get past this. Sorry to call you at home so late."

"No problem. Anytime."

"Good night." Milan hung up, though she was not impressed by the fact that Attorney Wyatt used the word *anytime*. Anytime should have been her dad's former attorney's response, as he was being paid by the hour. And paid well. The last envelope in the stack was a bill for his retainer fee at three hundred per hour for an estimated thirty hours of work. And that was supposed to be a reduced rate. But, as usual, his high price was well earned, and Milan knew it.

Lavender appeared at the door to Milan's office looking like he was in full work mode. His adulation was evident. "Baby, do you know we're at full capacity and we've only been open two hours? It's amazing. We've never had a Sunday night like this since I've been here."

Milan glanced over at one of the front door monitors. "We've never had a night like this period. Bad publicity is still publicity. I'm sure they're just a bunch of lookie-loos. Curious folks window-shopping for some T&A. But it is impressive considering Channel 3 is camped outside."

He pointed to the monitor as the bouncer screened a group of new members. "Baby, those people are doing more than looking. Eight out of ten beds in the group room are taken."

"So, I guess we should thank your nutty ex-girlfriend then, huh?"

"Now, I didn't say that."

"Well, just know that I'd rather have an empty club and no drama than a packed house and court dates up my ass."

"I'm with you." Lavender headed back toward the office door. "I'm not gonna let anything happen to you or this club. That is a promise."

"I'm gonna hold you to that," Milan told him as he exited her office with a wink.

She talked out loud to herself, standing at the over-size one-way mirror, watching the crowded goings-on below. "I just have a bad-ass feeling about this. A real bad-ass feeling."

10
"Sex Shooter"

ॐ

Monday, March 31, 2008
1:15 a.m.

Her name was Trudy.

She was a regular.

They called her Big Booty Trudy.

And she was a squirter.

A gusher.

A shooter.

A female ejaculator.

Trudy was called the eighth wonder of the world of sex kittens. A bombshell. Not only for her gi-normous, second-to-none backside, that was actually a twenty-pound moon, looking like two midgets were fighting to stay in or get the hell out. It would cause quite a commotion wherever she'd go.

But she was mainly known for her unique ability to cum in liquid form, shooting her fluid up to two feet ahead. Her waterworks talents were spellbinding.

Some men in the club would joke that it was raining whenever they'd see the twenty-seven-year-old's stream a-flowin. Envious female haters would swear she was really peeing on herself, but either way, Big Booty Trudy had a way of erupting that was a sight for sore eyes. And those who were on the other side of her eruption usually shot their shit within two-point-two seconds just from the sheer amazement of it all.

Trudy laid it on the lucky stud of the evening with an expert wobble-wobble, shake-it shake-it move.

Her satiny chocolate flesh was needy.

She converged upon him, squatting in a reverse cowgirl. His dick peeled her lips apart. She pressed her pussy to its base.

Her back was branded with a cursive BBT. Her cheeks were flushed. Major spillage hung over each side of him.

Her roundness and girth pressed along his thighs. She did a solid bounce move, riding him like a pogo stick. It sounded like someone was getting their ass smacked with a wooden paddle. She gave new meaning to the term *more bounce to the ounce*.

He didn't get fucked.

He got bucked.

Her long weave was Shirley Temple curly and it swayed in direct response to her strong grind.

She always smacked on a wad of Bubbilicious watermelon bubble gum. She'd chomp down on it every time she got her fuck on.

Her wet pussy and massive ass ate his dick like she was downright hungry. She could toss a man around inside of her and slide up and down like his dick was a stripper pole. She was legendary.

She bounced upward, making sure to secure his tip

entry and abruptly lowered herself to the base of his scrotum, plopping down hard.

She squeezed her inside muscles tight to grip his length, securing it all the way back, almost inserting it into the entrance of her cervix. His dick slid into place.

She bore down, screaming inaudible sounds, and shot four steady streams of colorless fluid outward, gushing straight forward onto the carpet in front of her and onto his legs. Her tight pussy throbbed.

"Uuungh," he yelled like his tongue was tied up, catching a back-end view of her squirting eruption just as he shot four streams of cum deep inside of his glove, deep inside of her connoisseur vagina. His eyes leaped and his mouth flew open while she still swam in the downshift of her mighty orgasm. It smelled of sweet clover.

Nameless, he gave one more grunt and went rigid. "Damn, woman. What the hell?"

She spoke through her moans. "That's just me, baby. That's how I do it. You didn't know?" She blew a large bubble that popped and then scooped it back in her mouth with her wide tongue. The light green wad was being converged upon just as his dick had been.

His eyes were still large. "That shit is crazy."

"You struck gold," she told the stranger. Her thick, soup-cooler lips smacked together.

She then kissed him like he meant something, scooped up her clothes, and stepped out of the private room.

With a still-hard dick, he just sat back in wonder of the sex-shooter extraordinaire, Big Booty Trudy, who was truly the shape of freaky things to cum.

11

"Ex-Girlfriend"

⨯

Monday, March 31, 2008
11:39 a.m.

The next morning after a long night of making sure the Erotic City patrons were on their best behavior, Lavender had already been up and out of his own house and to the gym. He was headed to Milan's house.

Milan lay in bed. As usual she'd slept in her light brown birthday suit. She was half awake, thinking about how she needed to wash her hair and stop by the cleaners and buy some groceries for when Taj spent the night on Wednesday and pay the car insurance and talk to her attorney again about her greedy stepmother Nancy and the case involving loony Ramada. Milan's brain was in overdrive.

She rolled onto her back and opened her eyes, looking at the tray ceiling. She began her daily PC muscle exercises, or Kegels, and tried to stop her mind from racing. Her home phone rang. The cordless was on the dresser and not on the charger on the nightstand. She jumped up and took long steps, reaching over to grab it before the third ring, noticing that the call was blocked. "Hello."

"Let me talk to Lavender." The all-too-familiar voice was stern and rushed.

Milan's eyebrows dipped. "You know what, Ramada? You need to learn to say hello when you call."

"I'll call back. Let it go to voice mail."

"You can just go ahead and call him on his cell, that's what you can do. Don't you ever call here again after you had the nerve to—"

Click.

Pissed off, upset, and disgusted, Milan's middle finger wanted to press redial and her mouth wanted to take over from there, using the words *bitch, ho, freak, psycho, and fucking piece of stank ass shit.* But Milan's better judgment took over. Her man's baby's mama, who had just filed bogus charges, already knew not to call. Especially Milan's home. And so, Milan put the cordless on the cradle where it belonged and headed to the bathroom. She snatched on the light and closed the door. The phone rang again, four times, and then stopped. It was all she could do not to tackle the phone and beat Ramada to a pulp with her words.

Minutes later she crawled back into bed and brought the purple covers to her chin. But she couldn't help but grab the cordless, dial her own number, and enter her password. She held the phone with a firm grip.

"Lavender, this is your one and only son's mom giving you a heads-up to let you know that I have filed a petition to increase the child support amount since you're rollin hard enough to co-own a club and didn't tell me. Hell, you said

you lost all of your boxing money in bad investments. Liar. Anyway, don't say I didn't tell you." Click.

Milan pressed the end button and pushed the phone back onto the charger just as Lavender walked into the room looking sweaty and tired.

"Hey," he said. He spoke while tossing his gym bag and walking straight to the dresser, rummaging through the one bottom drawer that contained his underwear, pajama bottoms, and some white tees. He grabbed a shirt and threw it onto the bed and approached Milan as she lay back with her head propped up upon two boudoir pillows against the headboard. He leaned down and pressed a kiss to her lips. "Good morning."

She gave a quick frown. "Morning. Lavender, you need to tell Ramada to stop calling my house again. It makes no sense to me that she would call repeatedly other than to piss me off. I know you didn't give her the number, but she got it anyway. Maybe from when Taj called from here but the bottom line is she uses it. And for her to have the nerve to call after what happened the other night is just insane. I'm gonna have to change my number now."

Lavender gave a concerned frown. "What happened?"

Milan tucked the sheet under her arms and then used her hands to accentuate her frustrations. "She just called and I told her to call you on your cell. But she had the nerve to tell me to hang up so she could leave a message. I'm telling you, Lavender. I'm about fed up with her. You need to check her." Milan grabbed the phone, dialed voice mail, entered the code, and held it out toward him. "Listen to this damn message she left. Press one."

Lavender took the cordless, pressed one, and sat on

the edge of the bed, bending down to take off his gym shoes. He sat still and listened, and then disconnected the phone, placing it on the bed. He took his cell from the leather holder along his waist and dialed Ramada's number. He pressed the speaker icon, inhaling loudly, exhaling even louder, talking right over Ramada's live greeting.

"Ramada, why are you calling Milan's house?"

"Because you damn near live there. I always know where I can find you."

"You can find me on my cell. You're calling here to fuck with Milan. I'm telling you for the third time, do not call this number again."

"Or else what?"

Milan sat back and stared at the back of Lavender's head.

"Ramada, we shouldn't even be talking on the phone after the other night."

"Did she give you the message I left?"

"Yes."

"And?"

Lavender leaned forward and rubbed his eyes. "Let me talk to Taj."

"No."

He got louder. "Ramada, put him on the phone."

"No. He's sleeping."

"Wake him up."

"I'm not waking him up. He barely slept last night after having trouble breathing. And I, for one, am relieved to see that he's getting some sleep."

"Oh, so he's snoring again?"

"Yes."

"Funny. He doesn't snore when he's with me."

"You just don't notice it. You're probably too busy banging your swinging woman."

Milan buttoned her lip and tossed away the sheets. She arose from the bed, entered the bathroom.

"Like I said, he doesn't snore when he's with me."

"How can you even hear him? You snore, too."

"Maybe that's why it bothers you so much." He cut his eyes toward the bathroom door and noticed that Milan still had a glimpse of him.

"Oh please. So, you're saying his snoring reminds me of you? You're so egotistical."

"You couldn't stand it when I snored. You complained all the time."

"This has nothing to do with that."

"Maybe you can't get your sleep, so you're making a big deal out of it."

"Why does everything revolve around you? Your son could have serious problems when he gets older if he doesn't have this surgery."

"I've checked with doctors who say he'll outgrow it."

"He won't. He'll end up sleeping with a C-Pak machine. Do you want your son to grow up like that?"

"Ramada, make sure you have Taj call when he wakes up. And I'll get him Wednesday after school." He stood up and grabbed the cordless.

"Did you get my message?" Her annoyance was thick.

"I said yes."

"But you didn't tell me what you thought."

"What about it?" Lavender stood next to Milan's nightstand and set the home phone down.

"You must have an audience. You're acting so foul."

Milan exited the bathroom with her toothbrush in her mouth and walked out of the room and down the hall.

"Good-bye." He disconnected his cell and took the same path out of the bedroom and down the hall as Milan, who was still naked, standing in the kitchen upon the blond Pergo floor.

Milan opened the stainless steel refrigerator and stared inside. Her eyes switched between the orange juice and the bottled water. "You know none of this has anything to do with a last name, or seeing my house, or little Taj's adenoids, for that matter. That woman is still in love with you." She grabbed a carton of juice and shut the fridge.

"She's not in love. She's just a damn pain in the ass." Lavender leaned back against the counter as his cell rang. Ramada's name appeared. He pressed ignore.

Milan opened the cupboard and took a glass from the shelf. She set it down and poured half. "Yes, she is that. A royal pain in the ass for both of us."

"And I'm sorry about that."

"You two need to talk about what's really going on." She downed half of the juice in one long gulp.

"Nothing."

"Then why is Ramada having such a hard time moving on? It's really so obvious." She drank the rest and placed the glass in the sink.

"She's just a drama queen."

Milan crossed her arms under her breasts. "Ten years with a drama queen, huh? Well, it would be really nice if I didn't have your drama queen's mess in my life. You're in my life. What you go through, I go through. And I know that without your baby's mama, there'd be no Taj. But I'd like you to protect me from all this crazy drama. If I had a baby's daddy, I'd shield you."

"I plan to. But as far as the surgery and child support amount, I'm standing up for both and I hope you do, too."

"I want what's best for Taj. It bothers me that he's got a mother as wacky as her. But I'm not so sure he shouldn't go ahead and have that procedure done." She picked up her toothbrush from the countertop.

"Why?"

"If it's gonna help him in the long run, why not get it done while he's young?"

"Because he might outgrow it."

She pointed the toothbrush in every direction as she spoke. "The doctors would know best. It's a shame that you two can't iron that out without going to court. Next thing you know, she'll file a petition for that, too. You guys are in and out of court more than anyone I know. It's like a substitute for screwing or something. All that damn misplaced passion."

"She's just trying to make me miserable."

"Yeah well, she's making us miserable. Not to mention the crap at the club." Milan headed out of the kitchen and back down the hall.

Lavender spoke while following her. "So, what's up with the charges against the club anyway?"

"I'll know later today."

"We need to know at the same time. I know you and Attorney Wyatt go way back, but if there's any more communication with the lawyers, I need to be in on it."

She did not look back. "Cool."

"Make that happen."

"I will." She entered the bedroom and opened the panty drawer next to her bed, rummaging through her G-strings and V-strings and XYZ-strings.

His tone seemed milder. "Milan, if we can get away tomorrow, just for one night, let's do it. Let's go to our spot in Panama City and celebrate our first anniversary."

She spoke while selecting a strawberry lace pair of undies with a pink-jeweled butterfly that perched at the crack of her ass. "That sounds good."

"And thanks for putting up with all of this mess." Lavender was right up against her cheeks from behind and he hugged her around her waist. His hands were clasped along her pierced belly button where her sunburst tat resided.

She closed her eyes and leaned her head back along his chest. "Lord knows you deal with enough baggage that comes along with being with me. It's a give and take. And so, I'm in this with you."

"And so am I. You're my girl?"

She turned toward him. She pressed her breasts to the fabric of his gray T-shirt. His freshly pumped muscles rippled beneath. He had a chest that would give any man pec envy. Her hand rested on his boxing glove tattoo. She looked up and into his eyes. "I'm your girl."

He peered down at her tits and gave a devilish grin. Down below, Lavender junior was slowly receiving the message that something was up.

The beep tone sounded on his phone. He looked down by his side. He had

1 new voice mail.

Milan shifted away from him and proceeded to her closet saying, "Damn, that was a long-ass message. And just how freaky were you guys cause she is still straight-up dick whipped?"

Lavender shut down the power to his phone. He lost his grin and lost the thrill of his frustrated hard-on.

Ramada's timing always had a way of fucking things up.

12

"After the Love Is Gone"

❧

Friday, March 30, 2007
9:11 p.m.

Less than one year earlier, Ramada Hart awoke from a long nap with Lavender in his Fairburn home. The afternoon had quickly wound into a dark sky that fell over them as they slept. She glanced at the digital clock and couldn't believe her eyes. Time had flown in slumber land. As usual, their time spooning together knocked her out like a left hook.

She turned toward Lavender and planted a loud kiss on his forehead. He opened his brown eyes and gave a woozy smile. He shut his eyelids in slow motion.

Ramada reached under the maroon satin sheets and took his dick into her hand. It was tucked away and at rest. She found her way past the drawstring of his plaid boxers and went skin-to-skin upon his resting package.

It was as though his penis was alone with her and it was willing to play suck-and-cum without its master, if she would only keep things between it and her. It grew gradually as though to stay low-key. Lavender's eyes reopened slowly. But his little man couldn't help but continue its sneaky expansion. Lavender turned onto his back and Ramada prepared to place herself up close and personal, when he moved her hand away. He pulled back the covers and threw his right leg to the side of his California king bed, springing to a stance, wiping his eyelids with the back of his hand. He headed straight to the bathroom. He said not a word.

She lay upon her back and placed her forearm over her eyes. She remembered that Lavender was mad about a phone call from her long lost ex earlier that day. She and Lavender had fallen asleep at odds. The few hours of slumber did nothing to erase his memory.

Ramada slipped from the bed in her midnight blue pajamas and threw on a cream-colored, ruffled robe.

After so many years, she knew better than to push the issue. She needed to give him time. It was his jealous streak that she knew so well. *He always gets like this when he starts trippin about someone else*, she said to herself.

She headed to the front of Lavender's ranch-style home toward the kitchen. On the way she walked past Taj's bedroom door. He had spent the day at his best friend's house in the subdivision. The young boy's mother had called Ramada right after Taj was dropped off to ask if he could stay until Sunday. Ramada agreed because she knew the boy and his family were moving to Dallas the next month and he'd no longer be able to see them. And also because she and Lavender had been talking about going to Erotic City anyway.

Lavender walked into the long and narrow kitchen and grabbed a small Capri Sun from the ebony refrigerator while Ramada prepared to make a cup of evening coffee. "Are you sure you want to go out?" she asked.

"I'm sure." Lavender inserted the tiny straw, keeping an eye on Ramada. "Coffee this late?"

"I wanna make sure I stay up."

"We just had a three-hour nap. You'll be up."

Ramada scooped heaping teaspoons into the filter. "Are you okay?"

"I'm fine. Are you?"

"I'm good."

"Good. I'll get dressed. You wanna leave in about an hour?"

"That's fine. Do we need to talk about any rules?" she asked.

"We've covered all of this before."

"Well, it's been a while since we went to The Playpen. And we've never been to this club before, so I just wanna make sure."

He recited the rules as though they were etched in his head. "No flirting unless I show you who I'm interested in. No making a move unless we're both attracted. No kissing. Use condoms."

"Okay. And we won't leave each other's side other than to go to the bathroom. Unlike last time."

"Last time I went to the bar." He pointed to her with his eyes. "You tripped."

She filled the pot with water. "You didn't tell me I'd be standing alone for thirty minutes."

"Let's not go there."

"Let's not." Her sigh was small.

Lavender noticed and said, "Ramada, we can go some other time. It's on you."

She poured the water, slid the pot under the filter, and walked up to Lavender. She used both hands to hold his hand. Her voice and her eyes were now seductive. "I'm down for it. Taj is gone. I think we need to spice things up anyway. Besides, you know how I love watching you please another woman." She looked him square in the eyes.

He did not blink. He turned his head to the side and took a big sip of his juice. He swallowed and then balled up the package. "Then like I said, I'm gonna go get dressed." He took a step from her, raised his hand up high, and made a three-point shot into the trash can near the side door.

Ramada turned away from him and opened the cupboard, reaching for a ceramic coffee mug. "I'll hit the shower in Taj's room," she told him.

"You do that." He still had not forgotten.

13

"Little Red Corvette"

❧

Friday, March 30, 2007
11:59 p.m.

By midnight, Ramada and Lavender paid their couple's membership fee and were buzzed inside of the adult playground, Erotic City, hand in hand. They both had looks of sexploration on their faces.

Lavender led the way, looking grown and sexy. The club was not too crowded and not too empty.

"Little Red Corvette" played as they weaved through the dance floor and headed for the bar. Ramada took a seat and Lavender stood. He'd brought a bottle of Crown Royal.

"Here you go," Lavender said close to the ear of the female bartender. It was the rule to store your bottle behind the bar. No glass was allowed because some members walked around barefoot. And it was self-pour only, because like most sex clubs they didn't have a liquor license.

The bartender was young and brunette and dressed meagerly in hot pants and a tight black peekaboo top that hosted her oversize breasts. She took the unopened fifth with one hand and pressed her eyeglasses close to the bridge of her pointy nose with the other. "And your membership number?" she asked.

"It's 30291," he replied after glancing at his card. He noticed her undeniable cleavage, boob man that he was.

Ramada noticed him noticing but was unfazed.

The lady bartender spoke to Lavender but offered her smiling eyes to Ramada's fully occupied red bra. "You want to break it open now?" She placed a big orange sticker on the front of the bottle and wrote their number in black marker.

"Yes, please."

"As long as you pour. You want two glasses?"

He nodded. "Yes. On the rocks, please."

"Coming right up."

Lavender stood close to Ramada while they both checked out the premises. Ramada nodded to the beat of the music.

The bartender returned and placed their ice-filled cups in front of them. "My name is Destiny."

Lavender nodded. "Destiny."

Ramada grinned.

The bartender grinned back and handed them back their bottle.

"Appreciate it." He opened it and began to pour. "Oh, and some Coke, too, please."

"No problem." She wiped off the counter and gave another smile to Ramada, reaching down to grab two cans of soda. "Is this your wife?"

"My lady."

"Pretty lady." She placed a can near the cups.

"Thanks." Ramada blushed.

"You're welcome," the lady said, stepping away to another couple.

Lavender shook his head and laughed as he mixed their drinks and placed a five-dollar tip on the bar. "Yeah, the ladies always have loved you. I'm not surprised." He took a big sip.

Ramada took her drink and swirled around the ice cubes with her finger. "You, too."

"You're sure you were never with a woman before we met?" Lavender asked.

"I'm sure."

"Because you know what to do, I'll say that much." He took another swallow.

Ramada took a small sip and licked her lips. "You taught me everything I know."

"That might be the other way around. I thought the lady we got with at the hotel was gonna loose her mind when you . . . well, when you were doing whatever it is you do down there."

"I do the same thing you do to me. Besides, I'm not the one who made her cum. You did." Ramada again checked out the other swingers. "That orgasm was from when she was getting some Lavender dick." Ramada locked sights on someone. "Speaking of dick. What do you think?"

Lavender tried to trace her stare. "What?"

She pointed in the exact direction. "About him?"

Lavender saw who she was speaking of. "About him what?"

"He's cute."

Lavender looked away and faced her. "Ramada. What are you doing?"

She nodded toward the dark and cute, twenty-something man. "Flirting. We said we'd ask each other." The man walked away, but turned to see that she was still looking at him, looking at her.

Lavender placed his half-empty drink on the bar, resting his foot along the bottom on Ramada's chair. "Why are you acting like we suddenly agreed to allow men in on this? This is a female-female-male threesome. That's it. That's how we do it. That's how it's always been."

Ramada found a new direction to look in. "Yeah, but he was cute. But I hear you, Mr. Double Standard."

Lavender simply stared at Ramada.

She said, "What about who I like?" Her eyes continued to scan the room like she was T&A shopping.

"As far as women. We already went over this."

"I just wanna make sure I've got it right. So, if I like that sexy bartender, or, let's say, that person over there, and you do, too, then we're cool." She nodded in the direction of someone else.

Lavender did not look where she was looking. "I'm still working on your double standard comment. No man is gonna see me, or you, do our thing. Period. Call it whatever you want."

"But a woman can see you do your thing, right?" she asked. Her eyes were still busy.

He leaned back against the bar and crossed his arms. "Ramada, we've been here three minutes and we're having problems already. I'm not gonna take one for the team because you've suddenly got the hots for some man."

"It's getting hot in here, so take off all your clothes" is

what folks on the dance floor were singing in unison, dancing like a group of strippers.

Ramada used her pinky to point toward the end of the dance floor. "I'm trying to get you to look at that lady over there. She's looking at us." Ramada set her drink down without looking. "I'll be right back."

Lavender picked up his drink and watched where she was headed. She stepped like a runway model, wearing her red bra and jean shorts with two-tone, denim and red peep-toe heels. She stepped up to a woman.

He guzzled his drink and replaced his cup on the bar. Ramada and the woman approached.

"Lavender, she's bi curious and she wants to play," Ramada said, giving flirty eyes to the woman, and to him. She asked the skinny woman with the big eyes and long blonde hair, "Do you like him?"

The woman's eyes flirted. She held her silver clutch bag close to her chest. Her black cat suit seemed painted on. She had a bronze summer tan in the spring. She looked tall, but about six of her inches were mirrored platform stripper shoes. Her undeniable marshmallow scent matched the fragrance of M by Mariah Carey. "He's cute." Her eyelashes batted.

Ramada asked Lavender. "Do you like her?"

He checked her out up and down. What was not to like? She looked like a living, breathing calendar girl. As his eyes made their journey, he noticed her subtle, shapely hips and tiny waist, flat stomach and wide mouth. "Yes."

"Then let's go," said Ramada.

She led the way and Lavender brought up the rear, watching them both from behind. Ramada headed to a private room and removed her clothes. Right away, she lay on her back upon the white sheet and exposed her crotchless red panties, opening her legs and bending her knees back, still keeping her heels on.

Lavender pulled the door to. He stood at the foot of the twin bed.

The woman pulled off her tight clothing, exposing her small chest, and kept her eyes on Ramada. She said to Lavender, "Aren't you going to show me how you do it. How you turn her on? Or should I go first?"

Ramada's anxiousness was apparent. "I don't care which one of you starts but one of y'all needs to start eating some pussy."

"Go right ahead," Lavender said, waving his hand toward Ramada while he took off his clothes. The woman knelt to her knees upon the bed and buried her face in between Ramada's neatly trimmed vagina. She immediately found Ramada's hood and exposed her oversize pearl. Curiosity was trying to kill the cat.

Ramada rolled her eyes back and reached one hand out toward Lavender. Her words were throaty. "Now you come here."

He stepped to her and she took his penis in her right hand. Before she could get going with a mouth-boning session for her man's at-attention dick, the woman shifted from Ramada's most private part, grabbed Lavender's dick from her, and stuck it as far back inside of her mouth as he would go. Lavender looked shocked and his dick agreed. It pulsated as if it could have said, "Damn."

Ramada got up, wearing only her skimpy panties, and stood behind Lavender, rubbing his sensitive back and massaging his shoulders as he looked down upon his new friend's extraspecial dick-sucking skills. The fact that she was a stranger had him extra hard.

Ramada looked back toward the doorway, and there stood the young man who had been eyeing her earlier, peeking inside. She tossed her cognac hair back in a girlie way and gave him a bad-girl stare. She brought her tittie to her own mouth and sucked her nipple while turning to eye him just below the waist. He stepped in farther.

Suddenly, the woman backed her head away and positioned her hungry vagina to meet Lavender's saliva-wet dick. She had a foil package from a gold magnum XL penis hat in her hand, which she opened with her teeth and placed on him, and then she opened her legs wide enough for him to see where she was coming from . . . where he needed to be.

Wearing only his socks and with tunnel vision, he braced himself and leaned forward to feed her, rubbing his dickhead along her light brown, long pussy hairs. He plunged inside. It was wet and hot and tight.

She jerked and pressed toward him for more. "Uhhhh," she said softly. Her right leg shook the deeper he got. And so did her moans.

His eyes involuntarily closed and he dipped inside with a fury.

The man who was standing at the door was now kneeling behind a totally naked Ramada, sticking his stiff tongue in and out of her ass, licking her butt cheeks, and fingering her honey pot from behind like he was trying to hit her G-spot.

As Lavender moaned, Ramada said, "Yeah. Get that shit," keeping her hands on Lavender's spine, his hot spot. She began breathing heavier and leaned her tits along Lavender's back, as though assisting him in getting his fuck on.

Lavender turned to his side to get a view of their X-rated, three-part entwinement and saw the fourth party, the young man, with his hands and mouth all over his preorgasmic woman. Lavender's eyes widened in alarm. He pulled out and peeled off the condom. He tossed it and said to the woman, "Excuse me."

He came to a fast stance and put his clothes back on. The man stood up and gave Lavender a look like he was ready for whatever.

Ramada hurried to Lavender, who was fighting himself mentally, working to chase away an instinct to physically beat her ass, or his. But he knew that if he did, he would literally hurt somebody. But the thought of killing at least one of them kept his dick hard. He gave a forceful exhale.

Ramada's eyes begged along with her frantic words. "Baby, wait." She tried to take his hand.

He raised both hands in the air. "Baby, no. It's cool. If that's what you want, it's fine. But find someone else who's cool with it, too. I'm not. I told you. I don't share."

"But, baby."

"No. You knew the rules. It's all right."

"You didn't want to discuss the rules."

The lady who'd just had the dick of life yanked out of her lay on her back completely still, with her abandoned vagina looking unsatisfied. The man looked at her. But she only looked at Lavender, just as Ramada did.

"You three enjoy yourselves. Good night, Ramada." Lavender headed straight for the door.

Ramada stood and took two big steps as he walked away. "Wait." She managed to touch his arm.

He yelled without looking back. "Get your hands off me."

"Lavender," she yelled louder.

He saluted the guy and said, "As you were," and stormed out of the room, heading a few doors down to the men's room. He stood before a ceramic sink and glanced at the tiny sample bottles of Scope. He broke open a bottle, swigged and then spit, and looked down at the travertine floor.

At that moment, the same man walked in and stood at the urinal. The man unzipped his pants, pulled out his dick, and started to piss. Yet he managed to talk as well. He had a slick look of brotherly love in his eyes. "Man, I'm down. Didn't mean for you to leave, dude. I thought maybe . . ."

Before the man could finish his sentence, Lavender tossed the tiny bottle and immediately headed back out, walking faster than fast. What was a lingering hardening of his penis had now shrunk down into two inches of softness.

He passed by the door of the open room and saw Ramada, giving him the evil eye, while the woman continued what she had started in the first place. Eating Ramada's pussy, woman-to-woman.

He stepped away and walked back to the bar. "Hey there, Destiny. You know that Crown Royal with 30291? It's time for more if you wouldn't mind."

"Sure. And Coke?"

"No thanks."

As the minutes turned into hours, Lavender danced a

little bit and drank a whole hell of a lot. He didn't see Ramada again. He sat at the bar and noticed the crowd begin to thin out. Just then, a tall, mixed-race woman approached and took the next seat. She wore bright orange.

She said with a smile, "You've got a lot of restraint."

"Why?" he asked, studying her undeniable cleavage.

"You didn't kick that man's ass. We were ready for you."

"Oh you saw that, huh?"

"I'm the owner of this sex in the city. I see everything." She sat next to him.

"Oh really? How's that?" Lavender asked, checking out every inch of her.

"One of my security people walked by and saw what was up."

"I see."

"That guy was probably more interested in a bromance than your woman."

"I caught that vibe."

"You'd better watch yourself." She looked around and he continued looking at her. "So, what do you do?"

"Security."

"Really. Where?"

"I head up security in Buckhead for the chain of XVIII Karats jewelry stores."

She looked impressed. "I see. That's where all the shot callers and big balers go. You wouldn't happen to be in the market for a job, would you?"

"No, I'm afraid not."

"Well, if you change your mind, let me know."

The lady bartender wiped off the portion of the bar near him. He shifted his eyes to her chest and back to his conversation. "I don't think so. I couldn't be around all this full-time."

"How do you know?"

Lavender raised his brows. "Oh, I know."

"Once you're around it long enough, you'd become immune to it, I promise you. Kinda like when people move to Vegas. After a while, you just stop gambling." She asked, "You been in the life long? Swinging I mean?"

"It's been a big part of my life for a long time."

"I see. Mine, too." Her two-way radio flashed and she pressed a button to clear it. "So, I hope the rest of your evening goes smoother. I'm Milan, by the way. It was nice meeting you." She came to stance and offered her hand.

He held her hand and asked, "Where are you going?" Her chest was eye level.

"We're about to close. It's already four in the morning."

"I see." His two words dragged. He rubbed his throbbing forehead.

She noticed his bloodshot eyes and asked, "Are you okay?"

"I'm good. You think you could call a cab for a brotha? I think my ride left me. Actually, I'm sure of it," he said slowly.

"I can do better than that. How about if I take you home?"

"You would do that?"

"I would do that."

He nodded her way. "I'd appreciate it. I don't normally drink this much."

She smiled. "I'll be right back." She began to walk away.

"I'll be right here. My name is . . ."

She replied while still walking, waving her hand over her head. "I know who you are. I'm from Miami. Give me thirty."

He said too low for her to hear, "You've got it." He turned to guzzle the last bit of his drink but the bartender had already taken it away. "Yep, I'll be right here," he said out loud as the room began to play funny little tricks on him.

This has to be the last straw for weird-ass Ramada. It just has to be.

Five weeks later, Lavender and Milan were in love and fucking like there was no tomorrow.

And they only fucked each other.

14

"Head"

⨎

Tuesday, April 1, 2008
1:30 p.m.

Here you go, Mr. Lewis. Just initial by the X to accept the nightly rate and then sign at the bottom."

"Sure." Lavender took the pen in hand and read the fine print.

An older man appeared from behind the counter of the grand Marriott Bay Point Resort and Spa in Panama City Beach. The ambience of the beachfront hotel was charming and laid-back. The man picked up a file from a nearby desk and turned to exit, but stopped. He looked up at Lavender and Milan.

The man spoke loud. "You ever gonna box again there, boy? I remember you."

Lavender nodded with certainty as he signed. "No, sir, I'm afraid not."

"We were looking for big things from you a while back."

"I'll bet you were." Lavender replaced the ink pen and handed the girl the sheet of paper. "So was I. One more fight after winning the belt and I would've gotten the big money."

Milan looked at him like she couldn't believe his honesty.

The man said to the girl behind the desk, "That was a bad boy there. That joker could fight."

"Oh really?" asked the young girl.

"Yeah, I'm telling you for sure. He was smooth. Just like his daddy."

"Thanks."

"Lavender right? Lavender Lewis?"

"Yes, sir." Lavender flashed a smile.

Milan's smile was even bigger. She placed her hand on her man's lower back.

"Well, you two kids enjoy yourselves." The man headed toward the door shaking his head and grinning. "Yep. That's a bad boy there." He stopped and positioned his feet while jabbing his fists as though he was giving a one-two punch. He laughed out loud and headed out of sight.

The woman gave a chuckle and handed the lovebirds their key cards. "Your room is upstairs and to the right. The elevators are over there. It's room 6004."

Milan said, "Oh good. That's our regular room. This is our favorite hideaway, you know?"

"Good. We're glad to have you back." Then she said, "Aren't you Charlie Kennedy's daughter?"

"Yes."

"It's nice to meet you. I saw you on a show they did on TV. One not long ago. I think it was about the history of jazz. I love jazz."

Milan grinned. "Oh, okay. What's your name?"

"I'm Sharita. You're very beautiful."

"Thanks, Sharita. It's nice to meet you."

"Sorry about your dad," the girl said as they shook hands.

"Thanks."

They headed up the elevator to the sixth floor and down the hall. Lavender slid the key card and held the door open as they stepped inside. It was a contemporary-looking one-bedroom suite. The hotel was fairly new and the room looked like it was designed for an O magazine photo shoot. The sage green and white colors in the living room were tropical, with tan and green sun-blocking drapes. The bedding was white with bright red throw pillows and a folded green spread at the foot of the bed. It had an office area and a full kitchen, and a large sliding glass door that led to a very private balcony.

Milan said as Lavender closed the door behind them, "Baby, someone left their flowers in the room." She pointed toward a dark green vase that was filled with fresh, deep-red roses.

"Oh really?"

She placed her laptop case on the square coffee table and stepped up to the flowers, sniffing the tallest bud. "They're beautiful." She looked at Lavender's expression.

"What?" He gave a clueless look.

She picked up the small note card that read, "Milan." She asked, "I know the hotel didn't have my name, did they?" Her face said she was adding things up. "Lavender. You didn't."

Lavender stood next to her emptying out his pockets and pulling off his blue cap.

She turned back toward the card and continued to read. "Here's to a day away from it all. Happy Anniversary."

He said, standing behind her, "I love you."

"Oh, baby. That is so sweet. Thank you." She turned to him.

"You're welcome."

She gazed up at him. "How'd you swing that?"

"I called the hotel and asked for the nearest florist. Made sure it was delivered to our regular room by noon."

"That is the sweetest thing you've ever done. That means a whole lot."

"You mean a whole lot." His eyes told on his playful mind. "Do you think going out to eat can wait about an hour?"

"I do." She unzipped and unbuckled his pants. He removed his kicks and stepped out of each pants leg. Milan knelt before him.

She liked to talk to his dick like they had a thing going on. She spoke low, directly at the split of his tip. "How's my baby doing? You been okay? Let mama thank you."

She pressed tiny kisses upon his dick skin. She wiped his tip all over her face, sometimes asking him to close his eyes to see if he could tell which part of her face he was at. He always got it right, from her eyes to her ears, to her chin to her nose. And especially her small, tight mouth. "Here. Let's go lie down so you can really relax."

Lavender helped her up and they entered the bedroom. He pulled back the sheet and lay upon his back, naked from the waist down.

Milan lay beside him and lifted his shirt. She sucked the tip of his dick like it was an all-day lollipop, back and forth, over and over, until she finally had it all in her mouth. She pulled it back out and pressed her lips together firmly, allowing him to find his way inside so that it was like his dick burst into her tightness. She did it repeatedly and he cooperated.

His dick slid in with exactitude.

His toes curled.

His pulse pounded.

Not even ten minutes later his dick lost control. She gulped his quickie nectar. Even the postcum.

"Thank you for the flowers," she said, resting her face along his washboard belly.

He said, "The pleasure was all mine."

15

"Do Me Baby"

✦

Later that night, after hitting their favorite seafood place along the nighttime shore for all-you-can-eat crab legs, they stopped at the local drive-through liquor store for a quart of Seagram's Extra Dry Gin and grapefruit juice.

Milan giggled as they sat at the window waiting for their order. "This is the life. Some gin and juice and cups of ice like we're ordering fast food."

"Just pickin up a little drive-through liquid panty remover."

"Oh, like you're really gonna need that."

They pulled off with their brown paper bag and two cups full of ice, holding hands and listening to Yung Joc's "It's Goin' Down."

As soon as they hit the hotel room door, Lavender stepped in behind Milan and began to pour them a double on the rocks. Milan headed to the side of the bed and disrobed. She grabbed a towel from the bathroom and went out to the balcony that overlooked the evening beach.

The sandy shore and dark waters of the Gulf of Mexico were illuminated only by the glow of the shimmering moonlight. It graced the darkness like sparkling diamonds. The illumination was breathtaking. And the stillness of the quiet view was peaceful, which was just what the doctor ordered for them both.

A few people stepped along the shore. One couple was sitting on the sand near the abandoned lifeguard station.

Milan placed the towel on the blue-and-white patio chair and sat back upon it, raising her feet along the banister. She looked through the spaces between the bars of the railing, down at the view below, taking in the welcomed coolness of the night air. "This is the life. Away from it all."

"It is." Lavender handed her a drink and closed the sliding door behind him. The only view he took in was between her wide opened legs. He swigged his drink and took a seat at the same time.

He took another sip and placed his hand along her thigh, moving it toward her middle. He ran his fingers along the shape of her vagina and slipped his middle finger toward her clit.

She downed a big swallow and said, "Watch it now, baby."

"Hell, I know my way around there."

She nodded in agreement.

"Actually, let me inspect it closer. It's so dark out here, I might need a better view." He placed his cup on the side table.

Lavender knelt down and adjusted himself so that he rested upon his hip and faced Milan's pussy. She brought herself to the edge of the chair to assist him and stretched her legs out.

Milan took a minute to look down at the passersby again. She could see each silhouette clearly and wondered if they could possibly see her about to get her pussy eaten.

Lavender began kissing her opening and moved his mouth to kiss her inner thigh. His lips and his left-hand fingers teased her.

Her body buzzed with lust. She quivered, enjoying the thrill of the licking. She balanced the cup in her hand.

He used his fingers to spread apart her labia and pointed his tongue to her rams-head clit, licking the skin around it and flicking the tip back and forth. He used short, probing strokes and applied pressure with each lick. He inserted his stiff tongue in her vagina, giving her an oral fucking. The wetness could be heard. He played slip and slide with her opening.

"Damn, baby. Damn."

She closed her eyes, though she kept thinking about the fact that they were outside, being watched by the ocean and the sky and the moon. Her eyes opened. She moaned deeply with a guttural sound.

He latched his mouth around her entire clitoris, flicking it in circles and giving it a butterfly whipping.

Milan's hips shook while he made the sound of an airplane about to take off. The vibration of his lips was like a tiny, hot vibrator against her firm point.

He guided her hips forward a bit more with his hands and hungrily positioned his face deeper, taking ownership of her hard clitoris into his mouth. He sucked it using short, luscious motions. He increased the tempo as she began to thrust her split toward his mouth.

She snuck a peek down at him and cheered him on like the soldier he was. "Uh, suck that shit, baby. Ummh, that's it." She looked out at a man and woman who walked hand in hand along the sand. They were looking up at the view of the hotel, and it seemed as though they looked up at the balcony of room 6004, seeing Lavender's back, and his head between her long, wide open legs. Milan's breathing accelerated. She still grinded, generously fucking his face.

Lavender continued to suck her, moving his head up and down in a slight motion, using his tongue while sliding her between his lips. Her legs trembled. Her clit pulsated between his lips. She froze up.

He could feel its pulse pounding in waves back at him. He moaned, "Uh-huh. Uh-huh."

"Damnit!" she yelled loudly. She dropped the plastic cup. The remaining gin and juice formed a small puddle on the balcony floor. He still continued giving head.

And then, Milan's pussy popped with a stream of juices that seeped and spilled like her drink. She bit her fist to mute her loud screams. "Shit," she said, making a point to try to keep it down. Lavender still did not retreat from the strength of her multiple orgasm.

She moved her hips and placed her hand along the top of his head to push him away. The force had created a sensitivity that she could no longer bear.

Lavender looked up at her with smiling eyes and glazed lips and went back down to taste her secretions with his absorbent tongue. He grinned and put his hand on his penis, which was hidden under his clothes. It stood tall like it was next in line, waiting patiently to get in on the action.

She spoke sexily. "Take those off. You juiced this pussy up, now you need to fuck it."

Lavender came to a stance and pulled off his shirt. Milan moved the chairs back and leaned onto the banister, placing her hands on the rail, facing the voyeuristic beach. Lavender stepped out of his pants and boxers and positioned himself behind her, bending down slightly to secure his point of entry, but not before he inserted his middle finger to locate the exact, cum-laden spot.

"Yep. You're ready," he said.

He placed one hand on her lower back, and guided his penis to the entrance of her vagina. He parked it there and put both hands alongside her hips. He first inserted just the head, and gave a few shallow thrusts.

She wiggled him inside. "Deeper, baby. Gimme all that good dick. Fuck me." She tried to bridle her X-rated volume as she shook her hips back at him.

He teased her for a bit and slowly leaned forward, sliding inside, farther and farther, diving in headfirst. Her swollen opening took him in, hugging his dick with welcoming walls.

Milan held on with all her might, again watching those who seemed to have no idea that their presence made the juices flow even stronger.

"This is some good shit here," he said loudly.

"Uh-huh." Milan was being hit hard.

He shook his wide dick in and out of her like he was about to break it off inside.

"This shit is slippery. Damn, baby." His level of turn on was obvious.

"Uh-huh." Milan was being dick-dunked.

He thrust his shaft down the throat of her deep pussy, and he, too, looked out along the ocean and the view of the people strolling along. He spotted one single female who looked as though her eyes were fixed upon them, too. She was a young curvy Latina.

His crucifix swayed as he laid the pipe. His dick grew even harder. "You know I'd like to fuck that one right there while you watch."

"You would?" Milan immediately spotted her man's object of affection.

"You'd stand behind me and rub my back while I took that from behind like this."

"I know you'd get it good, too."

"I would."

She said, "I see her looking. Go deeper, baby. Get you some."

Lavender pumped his well-defined ass muscles back and forth into Milan's willing cunt. He thrust his hips all the way forward and took full advantage. He could feel the extra wetness stirred up by the strength of his stroke.

He kept his sights on the young woman and held tighter to Milan's hips, slamming into her with every muscle in his body as Milan's pussy adopted him.

"Get it good, baby." Milan continued to buck. "Uh-huh, uh-huh. Yeah."

After one extra deep push, his meat had all it could take and it began to surrender. His violent expulsion traveled from his balls to his head. He bit his lip.

He suddenly yanked himself out, holding on to his base, and railed on her viscously as his climax rushed out of him. He let out a long, intense, unintelligible groan. His excess of pleasure slurred his speech. "Oh umh ahhh umph uummmmgg." Her backside looked like the top of Mt. Everest.

"Uh-huh," Milan said, looking back at his stream of semen. "That's my baby. You're a damn Picasso."

"Uh-huh," was all he could say.

He took one step back and held his hand under his stiff dick.

Milan still leaned over the balcony. She noticed the young woman begin to slowly walk away, still seeming to look their way. "That was a long nut there. Damn."

"Damn is right. You're my bad girl." His heavy breathing was obvious.

"Just doing what we do."

He leaned down to kiss her back. "That's what I'm saying."

Milan reasserted, "You and your damn fuck fantasies. Don't get your ass in trouble."

16

"She Get It from Her Mama"

❧

Milan and Tamiko's mother, Ming Li Kennedy, had been free spirited and extra wild in her younger days. She was born in Miami, but her Japanese mother and Chinese father divorced when she was ten. They divorced because Ming's mother had an affair. Even though Ming's father had many women before that, he left her and went back home to start a new life without them.

Ming's mother was reared in Japan with an emphasis on a woman's physical pleasure being a means to encourage women to have many children. The traditions accepted the fact that men would be away from the family, visit brothels or bordellos, and Ming's father did just that. The women did not stress their men about their absence. The traditional belief was that women didn't enjoy sex as much as men, and women's sexual needs were for purposes of procreation only. Ming's mother did not agree.

Ming and her mother rarely agreed on anything. She had raised a radical daughter. Ming left home when she was sixteen. She did what she had to do to take care of herself, living here and there until she found an older man who fit the title of sugar daddy. He wanted her all to himself. He took care of her as long as she would play the role of trophy woman.

Ming looked the part. She was breasty and five seven, both of which were unusual for the women in her family. She always wore her straight black hair in a sophisticated precision cut just above her shoulders. Her bangs were short and thick. And she was never seen without makeup, not even lipstick.

By the time she was twenty-seven, she left him and started working for the first time in her life. She spent another ten years getting to know herself and exploring life and having fun, but she never did experience love. Not with him. Not with anyone. That is until she was well into her thirties when she met the rich and famous entertainer, Charlie Kennedy.

Charlie was a playboy for years and never had any kids that he knew of. His focus was being a single man on the road, enjoying all that life had to offer the well known. That included having as much sex as he could, whether it was from a semiregular girl, or a complete stranger. He believed men just wanna have fun. And the money he made allowed him full privilege of doing just that.

He would go to underground nightclubs in every city. He was always recognized and was one of the last ones to leave. But he never left alone. For Charlie Kennedy, there wasn't much he hadn't tried.

One weekend Charlie traveled to Hawaii for a concert, and he met Ming. She was actually lounging out on a beach called Bottoms Up while on vacation from her dreaded job as an executive assistant for a marketing company. The stretch of beach in Maui was clothing optional, and both Ming and Charlie took that option.

Charlie walked up to Ming after noticing she'd lowered her oversize sunglasses past the bridge of her tiny nose to get a better view of his generous anatomy, and he made a spot for himself on the towel next to her. Within six months, the two were married.

After years of enjoying being single and without children, Ming quickly found herself pregnant at the age of thirty-eight, giving birth to Milan while they were in Milan, Italy, for one of his performances. She also gave birth to Tamiko two years later in Atlanta, where they had bought a second home.

It was a given that Charlie would be gone most of the year, and Ming would assume the role of homemaker and mother. She was somewhat familiar with that concept even though she didn't stay around her mother long enough to really get a good grasp of it. She didn't agree with anything old-fashioned. But, despite her sometimes radical nature, she respected her man as the head of the household in Miami or in Atlanta.

Ming enjoyed being a mother. She was more progressive and hip than most moms. Milan's and Tamiko's friends always saw Ming as the cool mom and envied the girls for their mother's easy spirit. Milan inherited her mother's attitudes about sex. That it was not a sin. That men would be men. And that women, too, could be women.

On the regular, Ming would walk around the house in her white cotton underwear, sometimes without a bra. And she had been a chain smoker for thirty years. It was a fact that when she was at home, she'd have a drink in one hand and a cigarette in the other.

The one-quarter Japanese and one-quarter Chinese mixture in both Milan and Tamiko were physically obvious. They had almond-shaped dark eyes, high cheekbones, and jet-black hair. Their black father's genes were more obvious in Tamiko.

Charlie was crazy about all three of them, and he'd shower them with gifts, though over time Ming's gifts became less frequent. After about fifteen years of life with Charlie, Ming received a call from a woman who said she'd been in love with Charlie for years and that it was time Ming knew. She said she had met Charlie at a law office where she worked. Ming listened and calmly hung up. She never confronted Charlie about it. She knew he'd recently been gone twice as much as before, even though everyone knew his career was starting to dwindle.

One day, the day he was to return from a flight to Chicago, he didn't come home. He'd returned to Atlanta but moved into a home with Nancy Clark. Nancy was young, she was white, and she was known as being a Hollywood groupie. She'd caught a big fish in Charlie Kennedy. Even if he never performed another day in his life, he was a multimillionaire.

When the girls were still in high school, their mother got sick and within ten months, she passed away from lung cancer. But not before she'd gotten herself hooked up with a boy toy of her own, who was twenty years her junior. She was never one to sit around and cry over spilt milk. From the moment of her death, they saw Nancy as a home wrecker who they were forced to live with, hopefully for as short a time as possible.

Milan moved out first, getting an apartment with her

dad's money, yet wasting it any way she could. She got deep into the pipe and ended up getting evicted. Not from lack of money, but from staying too high to remember to pay her bills. The first time she smoked a blunt was when she was only ten. At the age of twenty, she moved in with a man she'd met in a nightclub and he kicked her out a few months later. She lay around all day and spent money all night.

Tamiko got her own place in Stone Mountain and Milan moved in with her. Tamiko couldn't stand seeing her sister do nothing but sleep and party. She encouraged her to go to school or find a line of work or invest her money, but Milan refused.

One night, they got a call that their father had a stroke. He recovered but only performed two more times, as his voice was never the same. He lived another three years. Milan stepped up to take care of him. She bought a home in Atlanta and spent half her time with him around the time she opened Erotic City.

Tamiko became his personal assistant, handling all of his business matters.

Meanwhile, instead of taking care of her husband, Nancy was running the streets. Charlie believed Nancy was having an affair or two and wanted a divorce. Nancy refused to move out until the divorce was final. And the day it was, Milan called the moving van herself. The divorce agreement stated that she would accept a six-figure amount and waive her rights to any of his property and earnings. One month after that, Charlie died of a heart attack.

Suddenly, Nancy Clark Kennedy wanted her fair share.

Her fair share for spending so many years of her life with a rich and famous man.

Her just monies in spite of the fact that she was left out of her dead ex-husband's will.

17

"Like Father, Like Son"

⬿

Wednesday, April 2, 2008
4:44 p.m.

It was late afternoon. Milan and Lavender had just returned from their relaxing stay in Panama City. They both picked up Taj from school and headed to Lavender's house for the night.

"Milan, can I please have some cake?" Taj asked as he sat on the black velvet chair at his father's breakfast nook. His wide, hungry young eyes were stuck on the crystal cake dish on the counter. His fourth-grade homework was spread out along the glass kitchen table.

Taj was the spitting image of Lavender. He had curly hair and was very muscular for his age. Even a little stocky. He looked like a football player in the making.

Milan wore a long, rose-colored robe, searching the cabinets to see what she could throw together for dinner. She'd never made it to the grocery store to stock up on items for her home, or Lavender's. Her hair was up in a banana clip, and she was barefoot.

Milan said with a smiling face, "Taj, we're about to eat

dinner soon. How about if we have some dessert when
we're done?" She headed to the refrigerator and checked
the freezer.

Taj peeled his eyes away from the cake and looked
down at his work. "Okay. Did you make the cake?"

"No. Your dad bought it at a place on Memorial Drive.
It's really good."

"I love caramel cake. I love all kinds of cake."

"Join the club."

Lavender walked into the kitchen wearing a white
wife-beater and jeans after taking Taj's bag into his bedroom. He rubbed the top of Taj's head as he walked by.
"Hey, little man. I see you've jumped right into getting
your homework done."

Taj nodded. "Yeah."

Lavender stepped up to a stack of mail that he'd
placed on the sink when they'd walked in earlier. He
made a point of placing a kiss on Milan's cheek along
the way. "Hey, baby."

"Hey. How about some spaghetti for dinner? You've
got ground turkey and some Ragù. Do you have any
noodles?"

"I should." He pointed to the large closet. "Should be
in the pantry somewhere. Maybe on the bottom."

Milan opened the double doors and looked around.
"Oh, I see it. How about it, Taj? Is spaghetti okay with
you? I can make garlic toast, too." She placed the box of
spaghetti on the oval island.

"Yeah. I love spaghetti."

"Good."

"We usually just have pizza or corn dogs at my mom's."

"You do? I love corn dogs," Milan told him.

He scrunched up his nose. "Not me."

Lavender looked through the envelopes and stopped at one from the Fulton County Court. He peeled the letter open and read in silence.

Milan searched the oak under cabinets for a copper pot. "This'll be fun. We can have an early dinner and then, once you're done with your homework, we can watch a movie or something."

"Dad. Can we play Madden later, too?" Taj held the pencil eraser to his chin.

Lavender's ears took in half the question. "Ahh, yeah. Sure."

"Dad says he's the Madden king and I'm the Madden prince."

"Oh really?" Milan replied, looking over and noticing Lavender's focus.

He seemed to unglue his mind and his voice got happy. "Well, that's because I am." He replaced the letter back into the envelope and handed it to Milan. "Who won last time?" he asked Taj, heading toward the kitchen table.

"I did."

"That's because I let you win."

Milan checked out the return address and said, "Honey. You, let someone win? With your competitive self? Are you sure?"

"I had mercy on my son."

Taj looked surprised. "No you didn't. You lost fair and square."

"Fair and square, huh? Okay, well, I think tonight would be a good time to go ahead and have a rematch. And this time, I'll have zero mercy on you."

"Maybe I'll let you win." Taj sounded confident.

Milan said, "Oh, see. He's got you."

"No, son. If you wanna be the best, you can't let people win." Lavender pulled out a chair and sat next to Taj.

Taj asked, "Did anybody let you win when you were boxing?"

"No way. Not even once."

Milan said, "Your dad had zero losses."

"I thought somebody beat you. I thought that's why you stopped fighting."

Lavender told him, "No. It was just time to stop."

"Well, I'm gonna work hard at beating you tonight." Taj grinned.

"You do that."

Milan raised her eyebrows. "Uh-oh, I think he went to the Lavender school of trash talking."

"Yeah well, once you finish that homework, and we finish eating, let those sticks do the talking," Lavender said.

"I will. Hey, Dad. Mom said you guys are changing my last name to her last name. Why?"

Lavender asked, "She told you that?"

"Yeah."

"Well, we'll see."

"Dad, you always say we'll see."

Milan smiled, flashing her dimple. "Yes, he does, Taj."

Lavender smiled back and leaned closer. "Anyway, so what are you working on?"

"Math."

"Let's see what you've done so far."

They went over Taj's schoolwork. Milan saw Lavender's happiness. It showed on his face and in his voice.

She opened the flap on the envelope and unfolded the paper. It read *Petition to Modify Child Support Instructions—Request for Increase in Child Support—Petitioner Ramada Hart—Respondent—DeMarcus George Lewis—Minor Child—Taj George Lewis*.

Lavender told his son, "Good job with that math, Madden prince."

"I'll be the Madden king one day. Taj Lewis, the Madden king. I wanna be named after you, dad. You're *the* Lavender Lewis."

"You are named after me, son. For now let's move on to this English homework. Only one sheet to go." Lavender looked over at Milan, who placed the letter back on the sink. "And dinner's on the way, right?" he asked.

"Yes it is. Coming up, champ."

Taj watched Milan as she turned on the top burner to the stove. "I like her," he said. He looked back down at his paper. "No matter what Mom says about her."

18

"Beautiful"

☙

Wednesday, April 2, 2008
6:09 p.m.

Being that the temperature was in the seventies, the early evening was unusually warm for April. Traffic was heavy, especially traveling from 400 into Buckhead. And available parking spaces were scarce. Tamiko pulled into a space after staying on the bumper of a woman who pulled out slowly. She put her car in park and exhaled, remembering that her sister had returned from her much-needed getaway.

"What are you doing?" Tamiko asked her sister from her jeweled cell as she exited her rust Range Rover. She pressed the alarm button toward her shiny truck. "You sound cheery."

"I am, actually. I'm at Lavender's house. We just had dinner. We're hanging out here for the evening. Taj is spending the night until we take him to school in the morning."

"Oh good. So he picked him up from school?"

"*We* did."

"Oh excuse me, little family. Whatever it takes so you guys don't have to deal with what's her name."

"Exactly."

"Girlfriend actually let you guys have him during the week?"

"She had something to do. Who knows?"

"Probably go see one of her attorneys. I can't believe she filed those charges and then you guys still have to interact with her."

"I can't either."

"Anyway, at least Taj and Lavender get some bonding time."

"True."

"Okay. Well, I'll let you go. I know you can't talk. I'm out and about in Buckhead. I was just calling to see how Panama City went, but I'll call you later."

"It was wonderful as usual. But yeah, let's talk later."

"Love you, big sis."

"Love you, baby sis."

Tamiko was sexy casual in stonewashed jeans, a dark brown top, a sparkly belt, and animal print pumps. She walked inside of the Hancock Fabrics store near Sidney Marcus. She headed straight to the fabric aisle and grazed her fingertips along the varied textures of stretch material that complimented the tiny threads of dark green hues she wanted to use for her flared skirt creations.

A young man who was wearing a Georgia State cap stood near her, looking at the selection of metal zippers. He had on black jeans, a black-and-white Akademiks hoodie, and red, low-top Nikes. He kept both eyes on Tamiko. He looked down at the metal zippers and back over at Tamiko, focusing somewhere near the supreme roundness of her authentic apple bottom.

Tamiko kept him in her peripheral view and walked over toward the next aisle.

He followed.

"Excuse me," he said.

She turned around, knowing he was behind her. "Yes?" As she pivoted quickly, her long hair bounced over her shoulder.

"Oh, I just wanted to ask if you come here often." His wide sideburns and baby mustache were lined up tight. His lips were chiseled and his teeth were ultra-white.

Tamiko grinned while taking in his looks. "I do. The question is, do you?"

"Well, I saw you when you first came in and I, well, I just wanted to say hello."

"Hello."

"Hello."

She pulled the strap of her brown purse onto her shoulder. "So, you're stalking me in other words, huh? Cause you don't look like the fabric store type." Her face said she was both kidding and serious.

"Okay. I guess that's fair." He checked out her left hand. "So, are you married?"

"No."

"Good."

She waited a few seconds before she spoke again. "I'm flattered but I do have a boyfriend. So, I'm not available to get to know new people, or should I say other men." She glanced at his face and then to the shelf.

"Believe me, I can respect that. I'm just saying he's a

very lucky dude. But if I were him, you'd definitely have a ring on your finger." He sounded serious.

"A ring, huh?" She smirked and examined his brown skin. "Aren't you still in college?"

"No. I'm thirty-one."

"Thirty-one? You're kidding me. You don't look it."

"I know. People say that all the time. I guess it's a good thing."

"I guess. I know you get carded everywhere you go." She grinned.

"I do."

Tamiko's phone rang out. "Well, mister young looks, I have to get this call." She removed her phone from her purse.

"No problem. You stay beautiful, beautiful." He shook his head. "Man better hold on tight. I'm Kellen by the way."

"Take care, Kellen." Tamiko gave a quick smile as she stepped toward the next aisle. He stood in place to watch her tight jeans from behind. She pressed talk. "Hello," Tamiko said at the same time she read the caller ID. Her smile flipped.

"Hi, Tamiko."

"Yes, Nancy. What is it?"

"I just wanted to check on my stepdaughter."

She snapped her tongue. "Check on your stepdaughter? Anyway. So what's going on?"

"Nothing. Just calling to say hi."

"Oh, so you must've heard about the mess at Milan's club, right?"

"Well, I do think your sister is in a bit of trouble."

"Milan will be just fine."

"Oh, so I see she has you thinking the worst of me again."

"I can think for myself."

"Well, I'm family, and as her stepmother, I am worried."

Tamiko headed toward the notions aisle and turned to look back behind her. "Worried about what?"

"That maybe this woman will try and get some money from you guys."

"Look who's talking. Anyway, first of all it wouldn't be the club's money, and second of all why are you worried about it in the first place?"

"Because it could be a financial strain on everyone."

"Please don't act like you're trying to protect our assets. Everyone doesn't even include you." Tamiko rolled her words.

"Why are you so angry with me?"

Tamiko's eyes narrowed. "I'm talking like this ever since you didn't show up at Dad's funeral, yet you claimed to love my father so deeply. And then you send both of us that e-mail about filing a claim to get money from his estate. It's not going to happen. So like I said, I can't figure out why you're calling me. Other than to be straight-up nosy."

"I haven't filed anything yet."

"Oh, so the e-mail was like what, a threat? A warning or something?"

"You know, I just don't understand. As good as I was to you when you lived with your father and me, I can't figure out why you, of all people, would want to just erase me from your life. We have memories together and you know it. We did have some good times."

Tamiko switched the phone to her other ear. "Those memories were a long time ago. You and my dad went through some major times after that. You moved out and accepted the settlement. We have that in writing. And from what I know, you found yourself someone else and moved on."

"See, that's what your dad told you. Your dad said a lot of things about me that just weren't true."

"Oh, so my now dad's a liar?"

"I'm not calling him a liar. But some of the things he claimed were going on, weren't. He thought I was fooling around on him. I'm telling you that's not true."

"Well then why didn't you fight for more money when he was alive? Why now?"

"Because I guess I thought he'd leave me something after all these years. Something."

"If you spent the money you agreed to that's on you."

"That's not the point. But unfortunately, now that you and Milan have turned against me, there's nothing I can do but try to go through the legal system."

Tamiko continued to walk farther down the aisle. "Go ahead and try."

"Maybe you feel I've changed and that I'm being greedy, and that's your right. But Milan has always been angry with me."

"You'll have to ask her about that. But I do know that our father didn't stipulate you in his will. He didn't want you to have the money you're asking for. Milan is honoring his wishes. And so am I."

"But I was in his will until the divorce was final. And I know he didn't leave all that money to charity."

"And?" Tamiko stood in place tapping her foot.

"And, who knew he'd pass away right after that?"

Tamiko sighed. "We knew. He never fully recovered from his stroke and you know it. Where were you?"

"I was kicked out. And, Tamiko, don't forget, I'm not some groupie. I was his wife."

"Was." Tamiko looked back, and then down another aisle.

"Don't do this. Let's keep the lines of communication open."

Tamiko heard a beep tone and looked at the screen. "You made your choice. Go ahead and file the papers. We don't need to talk. Our lawyers can talk. Now I've gotta go."

"Tamiko."

"Good-bye." Tamiko clicked over as she shook her head. "Hey, baby."

"What's up?" Jarod asked. The sound of traffic backed up his voice, along with the sounds of a Boney James track.

"Oh, I'm in the store. My dad's ex-wife is trippin. She had the nerve to call me after that e-mail she sent."

"Trying to get that money, huh?"

"Jarod, you just don't know this woman. I know I don't talk about her much, but she's turning out to be more of a trip now than when I lived at home with her."

"From what you tell me, she won't get anything. She agreed to an amount and she needs to move on."

"I have a feeling she'll do what she can to get more. I doubt she has much money left."

"I'm sorry she upset you. Listen, I just had a quick break. I'm at the airport waiting to pick up this guy who arrives in about two minutes. I just wanted to check in."

Tamiko again turned around. This time, she found herself standing five feet away from her new admirer. "Take care now, beautiful." He grinned and headed to the checkout line with a swagger.

Tamiko smoothed her hair behind her ear and spoke under her breath. "You, too."

"Who was that?" Jarod asked.

Tamiko turned and headed for the front door. "Just a guy in the store."

"Did he say beautiful?"

She reached in her purse and grabbed her car keys. "I think so. Anyway, are you coming by after you leave the club?"

"I am."

"I'll sleep lightly."

"You do that. Beautiful. I know what's up." His voice teased her.

"Bye, Jarod." She kinda smirked and hung up, keeping her focus while she stepped to her truck and got inside. She caught a glimpse of herself in the rearview while securing her sunglasses, and pulled off, listening to the radio.

"*The wife of rapper Big Mack, aka Mac McCoy, has filed a petition for divorce stating irreconcilable differences. Since the couple did not have a prenuptial agreement, she's asking for half of his assets from their eight-year marriage.*

"*McCoy was accused of assault in the case that involves the sex club called Erotic City. The club was charged with negligence. There has been a lot of controversy surrounding sex clubs, particularly in light of these charges. We have a show scheduled for April twenty-fifth to discuss sex clubs when our host Diva Sexton addresses the topic, and our spe-*

cial guest will be Milan Kennedy, who is the owner of Erotic City and the daughter of the deceased musician Charlie Kennedy. The defense attorney for the club has already appeared on behalf of the client, and both sides agreed with the judge's decision to set an evidentiary hearing date of May sixteenth while the charges are investigated further. The club's owner is expected to plead not guilty. No information yet as far as the date of the criminal charges against Mac McCoy. We'll have more information as it becomes available."

"Oh my goodness," Tamiko said out loud. "This mess is not blowing over easily."

19

"Cream"

⌘

Thursday, April 17, 2008
11:30 p.m.

The theme was Erotic City's second annual Red Hot Party. Red balloons kissed the ceilings while curly red ribbons streamed beneath each one. There were buffet tables draped in red with finger food galore. The bartenders served virgin punch with cherries. The sexy hostess girls strolled around passing out chocolate hearts wrapped in red foil paper. They greeted the members with red lipstick kisses. Folks were fired up and ready to get loose.

"I'll make ya weak at the knees. Make ya feel all right."

Under the shy lights and erotic ambience of the main purple room, the crowd stared with lusty eyes as though being hypnotized through some tantric ritual.

Some bobbed their heads to the old school beat by Steve Arrington. But all were deep into eyeing the two, dark-skinned young women who only wore generous swirls of whipped cream, freshly squeezed from the can by a tall mistress with short, spiked hair. She wore a red baby doll, thigh-high stockings, and five-inch heels. She'd drawn creamy, delectable body bikinis for all to devour.

One of the women lay upon the table on her back with whipped cream covering her breasts and encircling the shape of her Mohawk vaginal hair. A heart-shaped squirt surrounded her pierced belly button. The other woman lay on her tummy with drawings of cream along her firm cheeks. The tight skin of her muscular thigh had a red-and-black tattoo of Betty Boop.

"Come on and get a taste. You know you want to," said the mistress of seximonies, holding a microphone and strutting like she was the madam of all naughty delights. Brian, one of the guards, stood nearby and kept an eye on things.

A young black man with cornrows bent over to scoop up a mouthful of tittie, ending with a suckle of the young woman's hard nipple. He licked her brown areola and kissed her saluting tip.

She lowered her eyes and moaned while another man came to assist with the other coated nipple.

An older white man began pressing his lips to her goodie trail. She spread her legs open a bit to assist. He came around to the end of the table to get a head-on view, teasing her hairy lips until he hit her point of entry, and inserted his tongue. Her eyes were coated with lust. She swallowed hard and her moans grew louder. She found herself with three men while she lay back enjoying being the VIP, very important pussy dessert for the evening.

She flexed her toes and throbbed her own sex cream onto the white man's face. He stayed on it like he was savoring the experience of the nappy dugout. He backed away, licking his lips. The young woman placed her own middle finger into her vagina and pulled it out, while an older, slender, naked Hispanic woman gently took her hand and sucked all of her juices from her finger. She also licked the young woman's belly button clean. The Hispanic woman's tongue was long enough to touch her own chin. The receiving woman's eyes bugged. She gave a welcoming smile as she squirmed counterclockwise.

Her friend, who lay next to her, looked back toward her own booty as a woman flicked her tongue along the shape of her protruding buttocks. The giver managed to work her face in between the young woman's cheeks, sliding her elongated tongue down to the point of her meaty split. The receiver groaned just as another woman kissed the small of her toned back, tracing her tongue all the way upward to her neck. The receiving woman turned to the side to look at her and within two seconds their mouths meshed together and their tongues met. They kissed for moments on end, as though only the two of them existed. It was a soft, girly moment of estrogen only.

"That's what I'm talking about. Make it nasty. Make it nice. Make it wet. Make it erotic. This is Erotic City after all. If you can't get your freak on in here, where can you go?" the hostess asked with a healthy laugh.

Milan walked by wearing a long red sheer skirt that showed off her red boy shorts underneath. She had on a red silk bra and a leather collar around her neck. Her hair was wild and curly. She even had on red glittery eye shadow and fake eyelashes. She gave an approving nod to the mistress when she saw the crowd. Lavender was two steps behind her. Normally, Milan was a distraction when she'd mingle about, but at the moment very few heads even noticed her.

Milan said, "Those women have nice bodies. No wonder that crowd is staying put."

"Yes, they do." Lavender admired the young woman's breasts as he and Milan headed on to the next room. But not before he looked over at his coworker and buddy, Brian, and raised his impressed eyebrows. Brian raised his back.

"I'll be your freakazoid, c'mon and wind me up."

A few seconds later, halfway through the song "Freakazoid," Brian picked up one of the ladies and carried her to the nearby open shower, where she stood along the pale green slate tiles. He went back over and picked up the other woman, carrying her to the shower next to her friend. The females high-fived each other while the forceful sprays of water cleaned them up. The crowd now moved to where the ladies stood, getting a free, double shower view. The two women began hugging and grinding each other. It was an exhibitionist's feast.

Nearby, in the blue S&M room, the older Hispanic woman with the forever tongue now straddled a padded spanking bench, kind of like a riding post. It had a dark brown leather covering and wooden footrests. A blond man with a long beard walked up behind her and popped her ass with a black belt. The sound was deep and loud. She squeezed her eyes shut and jumped as though in pain, yet she poked her blushed ass back for more. And more he gave her indeed, this time with an extraexplosive dose of force. He whipped the hell out of her cherry-cola cheeks three more times.

"Oooh, ouch. Yes." Her face was as blushed as her

booty flesh. One side of her butt read "Woman" and the other read "Whore."

Just as the two young women from the shower walked by with white body towels wrapped around them, one grabbed the hand of the woman who was getting spanked. The woman opened her Maybelline eyes and moved her curly hair to the side as the young woman spoke close to her ear. All three of them headed to a private room and closed the door.

The master who had given the spanking now had another willing slave. A middle-aged woman stepped up to the bench and straddled it like she owned it. She had a chubby body and thick waist. She wore a silver clamp that bit into her left nipple. Her belly button was hidden by a few rolls of fat and her stretch marks were noticeable even in the modest light, but she sat up proudly wearing her very own birthday suit. Her face was pretty. Her short hair was laid. And she was ready.

She placed her hands along the front of his pants zipper and moved her head downward to kiss him in the exact spot as if she knew his dick personally. But they were strangers.

He backed her away, placing his hands on her shoulders, and tapped her ass. Her mulatto cheek gave a short bouncy-bounce in reply. "You touch me when I say you touch me," he yelled in domination.

"Yes, sir," she replied with apologetic eyes that dropped to her feet. "I've been bad."

He pulled his arm all the way back and met her nutmeg flesh with an abrupt, punishing pop.

She erupted in a loud scream and grabbed her wide,

sagging titties, biting her lip and yelling, "More, more. Give it to me just like that again. Give it to me the way a good master should." She played the submissive well.

This city of sin was alive and crackin.

Milan, now working the rooms all by herself, walked into the blue room and struck up a conversation with a middle-aged couple.

The man said, "I had no idea what to expect until we walked through the door."

"I see. So what do you think?"

"It's different."

"Yes it is. Just do your first time looking around and see if you like it. If you do, I hope to see you back again. It would be a shame to waste that membership fee."

The man looked unsure.

His conservatively dressed woman said, "Oh, I don't know who he thinks he's kidding. Trust me. We'll be back."

Just as the woman said that, and she and her husband shared a laugh with Milan, Milan glanced behind them, over at the spanking bench. To her surprise, the woman who was being dominated so completely looked very familiar.

Lavender walked up to Milan and stood next to her.

Milan told the couple as they started to walk away, "Thanks for coming."

The woman said, "Nice meeting you." They continued to take in their surroundings.

Milan's eyes remained on the naked woman who was getting her ass beat. "Lavender, do you know who that lady is over there?"

Lavender looked. His mouth dropped. He picked it up. "Oh no. Is that Beverly from church?"

"In the flesh."

Lavender inquired, "Damn, she didn't even ask for you?"

Milan grinned, scratching the back of her neck with her long, red fingernails. "From the looks of it, I don't think she cares about being friendly with either one of us tonight."

"Damn, who was it that said never trust a woman in a church dress?"

Milan looked away and took a step. "Backsliders need love, too. Besides, we all have freak potential. Let's go. I don't know about you, but I ain't seen nothing. Vegas rules."

Lavender looked away and said, "Seen what? I ain't seen nothin either. Beverly who?"

20

"Jack U Off"

❧

Friday, April 18, 2008
4:52 a.m.

Very early in the morning, a soft, golden, artificial light filled the room.

The sound of ice cubes cracking under the pressure of warm cognac soaked the air. Tamiko prepared a drink at the leather wet bar in her bedroom. She turned to view Jarod, who'd just arrived from work. He sat on the end of her bed taking off his shoes.

"Do you want anything?" she asked as the natural rose oil gave off its sweet scent.

"No. You go right ahead. It's too late for that."

Tamiko swirled the dark liquid in a circle and stepped toward him. She took a sip. "How'd it go?" Her aqua teddy was skintight.

"Uneventful. But the club's been packed every night recently."

"So no more drama?"

"No."

"Good." She sat next to him. "Do you always think of Erotic City as uneventful?"

"What do you mean?"

"I'm just not sure how a sex club is ever uneventful."

"It's just routine."

"So, you're like immune to it or something?"

"Pretty much."

"I can't even imagine that."

"I still can't believe you've never been curious about what happens there."

"Not in the least."

"That's somethin. How'd your mama and daddy raise such different daughters?" he asked.

"I can't tell you."

"Interesting." He rubbed his eyelids and leaned back against two quilted pillows.

She turned back toward him. "You look tired."

"Like I said, it was busy as hell." He looked over at her as she took another sip, eyeing her wardrobe choice. "You know I'm not too tired though."

"That's why I woke up. I know you."

He worked his way to a stance. "I'll be right back. I need to take a piss and take off these clothes that smell like smoke and sex."

"I'll be right here." Her third sip was the last of it. It was strong. But she put her glass down, lay back along the bed, and allowed its strength to take over her head.

It was the tail end of o-dark-thirty in the morning. Another ten minutes and the sun would begin to show. Jarod and Tamiko were deep into position number four.

Tamiko's grind downshifted into half the energy. She lay under him, being pumped by his lengthy dick like her pussy was created as a vessel for only his penetration. As he plunged into her, he grunted and groaned and began to sweat. She held her breath every time he went too deep. And suddenly, Jarod rolled off and stood next to the bed with his demanding dick pointing her way. He put his hands along his waist and stood with his feet far apart.

Tamiko stood in front of him, and knelt down at his feet. She took hold of his thickness while lowering her mouth over the head of his cock. She flattened her tongue and licked the top portion of his penis like it was a blow pop, and began her deep throat maneuvers, making sure to focus on his head. She gave double-handed strokes to his shaft while she sucked.

Jarod ground strongly, flexing his large, muscular ass. He moved one hand behind her head to make sure the precision of her movement was consistent and straight on, just for one good, long minute. She felt him swell and he grunted as loud as she'd ever heard him grunt before. His fluid spilled. First a quick creamy shot, and then two long squirts. Her mouth was full of his warm sperm. She pulled away to swallow. As the final remnants of his load seeped, he looked down at her and patted her on the head.

"Good girl."

Tamiko inched to a stance and wiped her mouth. Jarod held on to his dick while she headed to the kitchen. The new light of morning licked the other side of the maple kitchen blinds. She'd only had three hours' sleep after waking up to be with Jarod.

"Hey, baby, bring me some water, would you?" he asked from the bedroom.

Tamiko poured herself a cold glass of fruit punch and sipped it slowly while glancing into nowhere. Once she finished, she grabbed a bottle of water, closed the refrigerator door, and headed back to her man who had collapsed on his side of her bed.

There was the man who she'd claimed as her own for the past year. The man who she'd made such a point of pleasing. The man who she'd gotten used to. To her, this was the way sex with him needed to be. He was faithful, even though he was hard to please. But she continued to please him. Even at six o'clock in the morning. After all, he was her man. He belonged to her. And she wanted to keep him.

21
"Miss Thang"

❧

Friday, April 25, 2008
3:28 p.m.

Milan's mind was occupied. Her ears were buzzing with drama. Even the few cups of extraleaded black coffee didn't help. She stood in her kitchen while looking out of the window at the beautiful, cottonlike clouds. The afternoon sight didn't match the tone that buzzed in her ears. Later that afternoon, she and Lavender were scheduled to meet their lawyer for dinner regarding the case against the club. Her first stop, though, was the radio station for an interview with Diva Sexton. But as for right now, she had a crazy phone call to finish up with. Nothing else crept into her mind other than her conversation.

It was the nightmarish, annoying, foolish voice that belonged to Ramada Hart that was speaking as though she wrote the book on how to be a total, unadulterated bitch. "You know what? You're just gonna have to deal with me," Ramada warned as though she were a female dog, like she was yipping and yapping at a passing car.

Milan said with a tense jaw, "Believe me, I do not have to deal with anything. Especially you."

"First of all, I have been in Lavender's life for more than ten long years. And I'm not going anywhere."

"Whatever. You're the one who insists on calling my home even after we've told you not to. So if you're sure you're not going anywhere, then why are you making such a fool out of yourself? You can't stop me from being his woman."

"But I can stop you from playing mother to my son. And mark my word, just like I used to be his woman, one day you'll be is ex, too. Lavender can't be faithful to one woman longer than a couple of years before he starts getting ants in his pants. He did it with me and he'll start itching on you, too. Believe me, you'll get boring soon enough. And just like me, you'll find the only way to keep him is to fuck other women right along with him."

"That is some crazy shit. You did that because your bi-sexual ass wanted to. After all those years, I don't think you know Lavender at all."

"Call it what you want to. What I do know is, that man will never make an honest woman out of anyone."

"So if you know that, what are you so worried about? According to you, he'll be free soon. And besides, I'm satisfied just the way it is. And since he's been through so much after losing his parents and his grandfather and then his boxing career, if you were there the whole time, then you should know that he doesn't need the crap you put him through. And you're using his son against him all because you can't have him. That's just a damn shame."

"What's a damn shame is that you have to give a man a fucking job to be with you. And that the only way you can make a damn living is to run a whorehouse for people to fuck. But then again, that goes along well with the fact that you're a damn ho anyway."

"Oh, so I'm the ho, huh? You, Miss Swinger Atlanta herself, who was fucking anything that moved while you were with him, and then you plotted to come in the club exactly one year to the day after you lost him, the night all this shit hit the fan, sucking dick and eating pussy like you lost your damn mind, and I'm the ho?"

"I was a victim while in your place of business. Hell, you should be paying me for making your club more popular, so get it right. By the way, can you spell contributory negligence?"

"I can spell crazy-ass bitch. And the only victim was that poor man who came in the club with you who seemed like he really cared about you. You put him in the middle of all this shit, pretending like he was your boyfriend, all in the name of trying to make Lavender jealous. You are really sick."

"You know nothing about me or him. And you have lost your damn mind if you think I'm gonna sit back and let you end up being my son's stepmother, cookin him tired-ass spaghetti after you stole Lavender from me last year. That'll never happen. That much I'll make damn sure of. I promise."

"What will never happen is you calling here again. Get all your calls in today because as of tomorrow, this number will be changed. Good-bye."

Milan slammed down the phone and closed her eyes. Her heart sped up too fast for her breaths. She steadied her windedness and stood still. She looked out of the window again. "What in the hell am I doing?" Milan snatched her shiny leather handbag from the counter and headed out the door, slamming the door shut behind her.

She hopped in her ride, backed out of the driveway, and fought to get her head together. She popped in a tape of a sermon by Pastor Michael on Provoked into Good, and drove slowly, only taking in the words, and only focusing on reversing her foul mood.

The funky mood she'd allowed herself to be shoved into.

22

"Living in a Glass House"

&

Friday, April 25, 2008
5:01 p.m.

With a glass partition between them, Milan sat across from ashen-skinned and dark-haired, nationally syndicated radio host Diva Sexton, who made the introductions. Milan wore studio headphones and prepared to speak into the microphone just under her chin. One of the show's producers stood up against the wall, just in front of Milan so that he could direct her if necessary. It was a peak-hour show with thousands and thousands of drive-time listeners.

The Diva's voice was always high-pitched and hyper. "I've asked you to come on today mainly to address the controversial issues regarding your swingers club, called Erotic City, which has been in the news quite a bit lately. First of all, can you give us a brief rundown of what happened recently regarding the charges against the club?"

"Well, I think it's public knowledge that one of our members accused another member of allegedly assaulting them with a deadly weapon, though this has not been proven."

"And what was the club charged with."

"Negligence. But that's all I can say."

"Okay, well, I'll move aside from the legal aspects and ask you a question from a moral standpoint, just as far as swinging is concerned. I've looked over some of the e-mails we've received from our listeners in the past day or so, and the one question most have asked is, do you encourage safe sex at your club? Seems that's a big concern."

"Yes we do. The health department of Georgia has strict guidelines that we must adhere to. But honestly, I would make sure that we encouraged safe sex even if it wasn't required. There are condoms available at the front door and in every room of the club, including the restrooms. We keep them all around, in large bowls, and we encourage people to use them."

"Do you require it?"

"No. We could never fully enforce that."

"So how does it work—I mean people come into the club and pay the membership fee, show ID, and then what?"

"You can walk around and dance and drink, which is on a BYO basis. As soon as you walk in, you might see people having sex. And the great thing is that it's up to you as to whether or not you want to do anything."

"And how does one go about doing that?"

"There are certain ways to approach people. If you see someone you like, you should strike up a conversation first, though some simpy ask, Do you play?"

"Interesting. And what if they do?"

"You head off to a room and enjoy yourselves."

"And what if they say they don't want to play."

"Then you respect that and move on. No absolutely means no. And most people adhere to the rules."

"So you're likely to just see people naked and having sex right there."

"Yes. Some people leave their door open and some don't. Some will have sex right where they are. Most of our members are over thirty and pretty mature. I believe that a lot of them, the ones who are there with their mates, are in fairly secure relationships and they have a great deal of trust between them. But there are some exceptions."

"Are you an active swinger yourself?"

"I'm in the lifestyle, and I'm in a relationship with someone. We agreed that we have no desire to be with other people. I guess I get my fill just from being around it all."

"I'll bet. And we know, your significant other is former boxer Lavender Lewis, right?"

"Yes."

"I will say that you two make a great couple."

"Thank you, Diva."

"So let me ask you, do you encourage people to at least try it?"

"No, not everyone can separate love and sex. It's not for everybody."

"Okay, well let's take some calls. The phones are ringing off the hook. Line one, you're on 107.2 *Let's Talk*. What's your name and your question for Milan Kennedy?"

"Hello, Ms. Kennedy. My name is Willow. I wanted to ask, how did you get into this business?"

"Hi, Willow. I guess I got familiar with the world of group sex when I was younger. There was a house around the corner from where I grew up that had these orgy parties. I'd see cars wrapped around the corner for blocks. Some of my friends in the neighborhood found out what was going on and we'd gossip about it. I was maybe sixteen. Later, I did actually go into that house. And years later, after going through some very personal things, I thought about opening a business. I just wasn't the dress-shop-and-coffeehouse-type girl. I ran into a friend of mine while I was out partying in Smyrna one night who told me that the club next door was a sex club called Club Fellatio. I ended up talking to the owner for over an hour. One year later, Erotic City was opened."

Diva Sexton asked, "So, to you, the world of sex was like, nothing shameful or wrong?"

"I grew up believing that good girls can have sex without guilt. My mother taught me to be an out-of-the-box thinker. She was part of the sexual revolution in the sixties, so I've always been very open minded."

"We have another caller. Line three, go ahead. What's your name and your question please?"

"My name is Lori. Miss Kennedy, so you believe that it's okay for single women to explore their bodies?"

"Yes, I do. And married women, too."

"Of course you do know that some women have been abused at a young age. Some women have been raped and molested. Some women have a difficult time with the concept of pleasure."

"Yes. I understand that. And please keep in mind that I am not a therapist. But, for those who are already enjoying sex, but would just like a little bit more variety, or want to try to live out a fantasy, I think those people should give themselves permission to talk about and learn about their bodies, learn about how to feel good by pleasing themselves. Sex is meant to be pleasurable. I think sex between consenting, twenty-one-and-over adults should be fun."

"But isn't your profession about more than just sex? Don't you promote a sinful lifestyle? A lifestyle that promotes promiscuity?"

"I think there's a difference between sex and love. You don't have to love someone you have sex with. There are people who simply want a one-night stand, not a lifetime of love. They just want sex. That goes on every day, whether we admit it or not, and that's their right. I provide a place where mature people can come and explore. It's up to each individual as to whether or not they want to have sex."

"But sex with a stranger is, excuse me, that just seems straight up ho'ish."

"Don't knock it till you try it."

"Line four, go ahead. Please tell us your name and your question."

"Yes. My name is. Well, I'd rather not . . . let's say my name is Jane."

Diva Sexton shrugged her shoulders. "Okay, Jane."

"You know, I'm sitting here listening and the bottom line that no one has said yet is that what you're condoning is sex outside of marriage. And sex outside of marriage is a sin."

"Yes, sex outside of marriage is a sin, but the reality is that there are single people engaged in sex in bedrooms and kitchens and cars and backyards all over the world all the time."

"But that doesn't make it right. You're only making that problem worse. Are you a churchgoing woman?"

"I am."

"Then you understand some people think you're a sinner?"

"I do."

"I'd call you a female pimp. I mean, you take money so people can sin."

"Oh so I'm basically a pimptress, huh?" Milan grinned at the Diva. "Okay. The way I see it is, I provide a place. No money is exchanged between those who decide to have sex. It's kind of like a hotel. You could rent a hotel room and have sex. Would that make the hotel owner a pimp? What you do in your own mind or with your own body is your business."

"The way I see it, though, you're encouraging sex."

"I think people are already very encouraged to have sex. The adult porn industry generates fourteen billion dollars per year. And eighty-five percent of women either purchase or rent porn. We are not the prudes society has made us out to be. There are millions of lifestylers in the world. The popularity is growing for some reason."

"I have a problem with the misuse of porn, and the misuse of sex. Sex was meant for reproducing. Not all this casual mess that's going on these days. I just can't wrap my brain around it."

"Right off the bat we were taught that sex is dirty. That it's negative. Sometimes in life, we're told what to think instead of how to think. What if you had been the one to decide years ago whether or not it was wrong, instead of being told it was wrong and you'd better not or else? Some societies teach kids that they'll go blind and deaf if they masturbate. It's so natural to seek pleasure. And, yes, there are boundaries. I just stress safe sex between consenting adults."

"You will burn in hell." The caller hung up.

Diva Sexton responded quickly, "Sorry about that, Milan. Callers, please watch your comments. We don't have to bleep that word, but, Miss Kennedy is a guest on our show and we should show her some respect."

"It's okay. Our lifestyle is always going to be seen as sinful. It's here to stay though. Sorry."

The Diva said, "And I'm sure with you being a woman, and a young woman, you get a lot of that."

"The good thing is that more women are the ones running the clubs. That means women are becoming more liberated. We women are way too uptight about sex and there's nothing to be ashamed of. Years ago it was the man who wanted it all the time. When the movie *She's Gotta Have It* came out, it was groundbreaking because we didn't think of women in that way. We need to free ourselves from our guilty conscience. And the lifestyle is becoming more and more mainstream. It's not going anywhere."

"You know I agree that with marriage being such a sacred intuition, thinking in terms of an alternative lifestyle is like mixing oil and water. There will be a backlash from puritanical America. But I think the taboo is lifting."

"I hope so. This is all about how we view our own sexuality. Sex clubs are legal. They require a business license and a permit to operate. It is simply your choice with another's consent."

"Okay, we'll take a couple more calls. Your name and your question please."

"Hello. My name is Beverly and I'll be honest. I go to your church. I just wanted to tell you that no matter what they're saying, you know, among the people in church, I think it's just as wrong to sin Monday through Saturday and then on Sunday come in there judging people like you. Some people probably masturbated before they came to church on Sunday morning."

"Wow," the Diva said.

"I'm just saying, some probably cursed people out when they drove to church, and lie to people as they walk inside of the Lord's house. All of that is sin. All sins being equal, I'd never judge you."

"Well thanks, Beverly. I appreciate that."

"Don't let anybody make you feel ashamed. Just because there are some things we don't agree with or understand doesn't mean we have to try to shame people."

The Diva said, "You're right about that. Everyone's entitled to their own opinions."

"When you live in a glass house, don't throw stones. So you go ahead on, Miss Kennedy. I might come check out your club myself."

"Hey now."

"And come to church for you and no one else."

"Thanks."

"And I'll just say this before I go. All I know is if God turned away every sinner, the church would be empty. Thanks for your time."

"Thanks for calling," Diva Sexton said. "Line four, you're on."

A woman said, "That other caller was right. You're a female pimp."

"Excuse me, ma'am, but what is your name?"

Click.

"On that note, I think we've covered the pros and cons fairly well. It definitely seems people feel strongly about it either way. But we want to thank you for taking the time to come out and share your knowledge about the swingers lifestyle and about your club, and we thank you for taking the questions, Milan."

"I appreciate you for having me. Thank you." Milan had a tiny smile on her face, yet gave a light sigh.

As the Diva continued on with the show, Milan no sooner walked away from the microphone and said good-bye to the producer than Lavender called. She walked down the hall while reaching into her purse, answering her phone while also reaching for her keys.

She stepped out of the building and down the street. Lavender said, "I just know that wasn't spank-my-ass-and-call-me-slave Beverly." His energy was high.

"Okay?" Milan laughed as she stepped to her car and got inside. "You see I didn't bust her out."

"Yeah, but I know she's gonna hear about that in church on Sunday."

"I doubt it. It's not like anybody's gonna say it to her face anyway."

"True. She's brave."

"Listen, I'm on my way. I'll see you in about an hour at the restaurant to meet Hunter."

Lavender sounded like he was mobile, too. "Why don't you go back home and I'll pick you up. I'm headed that way now."

"Sounds good. I've gotta talk to you anyway."

"About what?"

"I'll tell you in a minute." She started the engine and pulled off.

"Okay. And you did a great job, by the way."

"Thanks," she said as they disconnected. She stared ahead and thought back to her interview. The last caller kind of sounded like Ramada, but Milan wasn't sure. Either way, she knew how people saw her. The business she was in was not easy to swallow. Just before she reached for a CD, the song on the radio was Mary J's, "Just Fine."

Milan bounded her head to the beat and tapped her thumbs along the steering wheel and sang along, "*I ain't gon let nothing get in my way / No matter what nobody has to say.*"

She added, "Exactly."

23
"U Got the Look"

❧

While Milan and Lavender wrapped up the evening meeting with Hunter Wyatt, Jarod checked things out downstairs at the club and Brian made his rounds upstairs.

Jarod stepped past the larger-than-life bouncer at the front door and went outside into the nighttime air, keeping an eye on the valet guy who hurriedly returned from parking a car.

A very tall, very curvy woman stood near the circular driveway, looking up at the well-lit sign as Jarod approached.

"How are you?" His glances were full. He focused on the ample, fleshy part of her body from behind.

"Good." A slight evening breeze whisked through her dirty-blonde hair.

"Can I help you?" he asked.

She took a step closer. "No, I'm just looking for the owner."

"She's not in. Can I help?"

She smiled. "No."

He nodded. "Are you coming in?"

Her hands gestured in agreement with her words. "Oh no." She held tight to the leather strap of her miniature N-initialed black purse.

He took a step closer. "Why not? No harm in looking." She was eye to eye and inch for inch to his six two frame. "You're a big girl, right?" He looked down at her two-inch heels.

"I guess you could say that." She hesitated. "You meant that in a nice way, right?"

"Most definitely." He offered his hand. "I'm Jarod."

She extended hers. "Nancy."

He held on for a brief moment, taking in her stare head-on, and released his grip. "Nice to meet you. How do you know the owner?"

"Oh, I just wanted to see her business. I've heard so much about it. Mainly on the radio this afternoon." She began to walk toward the door as he walked beside her. She read the notice near the door about being an Equal Opportunity Lifestyle Organization.

"Yes, I heard it when I was in my car earlier. Pretty interesting."

"It was. So, I'm just curious."

"Then I suppose it's good if all the curious folks come in."

"I guess so."

"Here's how it works. We charge a hundred-dollar membership fee for women. Is this your first time?"

"Yes."

"Once you pay the membership, the first-time door

charge is free. Normally it's fifty for single women. It's the single men who get charged a hundred each time they step in here. Couples are cheaper."

"Really?"

"Yes, really. You are single I assume?" He opened the door and stood aside for her to enter.

"Yes, I am." She paused for a few moments, stepped inside, and smiled, looking around at the deep-gold walls and the very contemporary setup. "I guess there'd be no harm in just checking it out for a minute."

Jarod stood at the entry booth. "I guess not."

The bouncer checked her with his metal detecting wand, also rummaging through her tiny purse.

Jarod spoke to the front desk girl. "Rita, can you help this young lady join the City please? She's a first-timer."

Nancy stepped up.

"Sure." The girl pointed to the side. "Would you mind stepping right over there to the computer and entering your information in the fields. It'll only take a minute."

"Okay." Nancy stood aside and entered her name, address, and date of birth and checked each box that applied to the membership agreement and clicked enter. She stepped back to the girl as Jarod kept close watch.

"May I see your ID, please?" Rita asked.

Nancy opened her purse and took out her driver's license. "Here you go."

"And if you would just sign here."

"Can I have a copy of this? I like to have a copy of whatever I sign."

"No problem. And that'll be a hundred dollars."

Nancy nodded as she signed. She looked back at Jarod at the same time she handed the woman her money.

"I'll see you inside," Jarod said, noting the fact that she caught him staring.

"Yes you will," she said, giving him a sticky smile.

Jarod stepped away with a look that said, *That's what I'm talking about*, and he went on inside.

Rita gave Nancy a copy of the agreement and a purple membership card. "Here you go. We have a coat-room here if you need it. Valet, in case you didn't use it this time, is free. They just work for tips. Once you go through those doors, there's a bar area. You should bring your own and give the bartender your five-digit membership number and they'll write it on the bottle." She pointed to the number on Nancy's card. "You'll see a big dance floor and a lot of rooms, with a bunch of naked people in them. The orgy room is nude only and requires that you leave your clothes in our lockers. And we have condoms here and in all the rooms." She pointed to a large glass bowl on the counter. "And we say safe sex or no sex. Condoms are a girl's best friend. Enjoy."

"Thanks, but I won't be needing to," Nancy said, stepping toward the tall doors to erotic land. "I'm only here to watch."

Rita buzzed her in while the bouncer checked her out.

Nancy saw seductive visions of people mingling in the purple room. The music was J. Holiday's smooth, slow groove, "Bed." She made a beeline to an area just to the side of the dance floor and sat down on a white-cushioned bar stool. She sat with her back straight as a board. Her hands rested on her lap, covering her purse. She took it all in.

A black woman walked up and said, "My man said you have a nice ass." She eyed Nancy below her waist.

"Please tell him thanks."

"If you want to tell him yourself, he's right over there." She pointed.

Nancy looked over and smiled. "Thanks."

The healthy-looking woman, who wore a brown bikini and heels, stepped back to the sofa next to her man. They both sat back and stared her way.

"So this is what all of the buzz is about?" asked a woman sitting next to Nancy. The woman held on to a cup containing clear liquid. It was filled with straight and smooth, p.i.n.k. vodka. It was eighty proof with caffeine. She nursed it slowly as traces of her Corvette red lipstick kissed the cup.

"I guess so."

"Would you like some of my drink? I brought vodka."

"Oh, no thanks."

They both faced the large dance floor. Both sat with their legs crossed.

"Your first time here?" the woman asked.

"Yes. How'd you know?"

"You have that first-time sticker on your forehead." She smirked.

Nancy grinned generously. "Oh really?"

"I wore the same one last week."

"I see."

Jarod spoke from behind Nancy's left shoulder. "I think they call it the virgin look. The nervous newbie look. Someone's gotta bust your first-time cherry."

Nancy turned toward him. "Jarod, right?"

"Yes."

She pointed from him to the woman next to her. "Jarod, this is . . ."

The woman said, "Heidi."

"Hello, Heidi." Jarod nodded her way.

Nancy put her hand out toward the woman, who looked even more delicious than the scent of her fragrance, called Be Delicious, smelled. "I'm Nancy, Heidi."

They exchanged handshakes.

"Nice to meet you both," Heidi said. "I was in here before with my new man but we just watched. He said he wanted me to keep myself on the sidelines. I decided then that I would come back alone."

"Oh really. So, is he history now?"

"No. I just snuck out. He thinks I'm at Wal-Mart."

"Wow. Sounds like this'll be a quickie then," Nancy said, looking half impressed.

Jarod leaned closer to both ladies and asked, "So, what are you into, Heidi?"

"What am I into?"

"That's a question you'll hear a lot. That, and do you want to play."

Heidi raised her perfectly waxed eyebrows. "Oh okay. Well, Nancy, whatta ya say? Do you want to play?"

Nancy's throat got stuck on a simple swallow of saliva and she shook her head. "Wow. No. I'm just observing."

Heidi said, "Okay. Well, I guess now you know you've got someone to play with when you're ready. For a little while anyway." Heidi brought her drink to her lips and sipped. Her long fingers choked the cup. Her nails were a plum color and she had a pink tourmaline ring on her middle finger.

Nancy noticed all of it. "Yes, I guess so. Thanks."

Jarod spoke close to Nancy's ear. "See how that works."

"I do."

He asked, "Would you like a tour?"

"Sure." Nancy looked to her right. "Heidi, would you like to come with us?"

"Sure."

The ladies stood, securing their small purses under their arms. Heidi kept her drink in one hand and grabbed Nancy's hand with the other.

Looking back to notice Heidi's cute face and small waist, Jarod walked one step ahead of them. "Follow me."

24

"If I Was Your Girlfriend"

ଙ୍କ

Friday, April 25, 2008
11:18 p.m.

Milan and Lavender rode in his platinum BMW 750 while heading south on 75 to the club. They'd had a two-hour dinner with Attorney Wyatt at Justin's in Buckhead, and then talked business over drinks.

Milan spoke while scrolling through her BlackBerry. "At least he's petitioning to have the negligence charges dismissed. But as usual your girl Ramada is trippin about it. Now that she has Judith Berg as her attorney, this is not gonna be easy."

"If it wasn't for Big Mack's name, Judith Berg never would have bothered with this case. No telling what she's got up her sleeve. She'll probably file civil charges to get some money from him."

"As long they're not filed against us. If so, we just might have to settle and get rid of it."

"For what? I say we wait and see if it goes to trial."

Milan deleted junk messages from her e-mail. "You have a lot of confidence in the system I see."

Lavender took the Tenth Street exit. "Not even. I just think it might bring out other fools who think they can do the same thing."

Milan read one of her messages. "Maybe. Here's a message from the guy who owns The Playpen. He suggests we check out the latest blog on the North American Swing Club Association site. I think folks are talking about our case. He's saying these charges are just another way to try to get sex clubs shut down."

"I believe it. It'll all work out." He leaned his right elbow along the middle console. "No worries."

Milan looked at him and then back at her phone. "You amaze me with your outlook. I don't know if it's optimism or naïveté. Ramada is the reason for the madness. She's a hot damn mess."

"That she is."

"Oh yeah, I forgot. What I was gonna tell you earlier was that she called the house again today while I was there."

"For what?"

"We didn't get around to why she was calling. We had it out."

Lavender made a lane change. "Damnit, I am so tired of this shit from her."

Milan put her cell on her lap. "Of all people, she had the nerve to call me a ho because I opened the club. Honestly, I don't know how much more of her games I can take."

"She called you a ho? Damnit. I've told her to stop calling your house." He gritted his teeth and frowned.

"And she said she'd be in your life for the rest of your life and she's not gonna let me raise Taj." She again resumed scrolling. "She also said you wouldn't be around long anyway. That you'll get bored and start cheating on me." Milan looked at Lavender.

He reached into the console and grabbed his phone.

Milan said, "Don't. That's just what she wants you to do is call her."

"I've had it." He stopped at a light before turning. "That's it." He put his phone in the cup holder slot. "We're gonna place a restraining order so she won't contact you. Why didn't you bring it up with Hunter tonight? He needs to know. Maybe he can do something about it."

She simply looked at him. "I already told Hunter when I was on my way to the station. He knows everything."

He looked over at her. "I'm sorry, Milan."

"Yeah, well, anyway. Right after that I had my number changed." She looked down and read a message while talking. "Effective tomorrow morning, she won't be able to reach me. But as far as her reaching you, now, that's a different subject."

"I know you've had that same number for a long time."

"To keep her from reaching me, it was worth it. As long as she doesn't try to call the club."

"Oh hell no. That would be stupid."

"Well. Stupid is as Ramada does. I'm not so sure she didn't call the radio station today. That last caller sounded a lot like her to me."

"I thought about that." Lavender pulled up into the reserved space near the front door. "I'll do whatever I have to do to make this go away, and to make this easier on you."

Milan grabbed her bag and shoved her phone inside. She sat and waited, looking around at all the cars in the parking lot.

Lavender's cell sounded and he pressed the screen. He put the car in park and turned off the ignition. "Hey, Great Mama. Yeah, Milan and I just came from a meeting. Yes, it went well. Taj is fine."

Milan sat still as she said, "Please tell her I said hello."

"Milan says hello." He looked Milan's way. "She says hi." He continued, "No, we're just pulling up to work. To Milan's work. Yes, the club. It's going well. And how are you doing? Good. Okay, well, you take care and I'll talk to you later. Love . . . She hung up before I could finish saying good-bye." He pressed the screen.

Milan asked, "She still thinks I run a regular night-club?"

"She's never asked. But she knows. I guarantee you, she knows." Lavender opened his door and came around to her side.

Milan sat still as he opened her door, looking up at him. "How would she know? Wouldn't she tell you if she did?"

"No. Not Great Mama. But I'll bet Ramada told her. I've known her long enough to know that much."

"That would be messed up. But, then again, it fits." Milan adjusted herself to exit the car when her phone signaled another text message. She reached inside and read it as she took Lavender's hand and stood. Her eyes grew large. "What? My manager said Maurice Black wants to schedule me for his radio show. Looks like it's to talk about black women who own sex-related businesses."

"You gonna do it?"

"I don't see why not. Radio's the best free advertising there is."

Milan replaced her phone into her bag and prepared to take a step.

Lavender pulled her close and looked into her eyes. "I'm proud of you. And like I said, I'm sorry."

"Just keep that, 'everything's gonna be fine' attitude. We're gonna need it," Milan said, giving him a half hug and walking away to head toward her sexual sanctuary.

Lavender closed her door and pressed the alarm, walking in behind her after greeting the parking attendant.

Milan stopped at the front counter. "Hey there," she said to the bouncer and then spoke to her front desk girl, "Hey, Rita. What's going on?"

"It's busy again."

"I can tell by all the cars." Milan gave a click of the computer and searched through the new member files. She kept clicking. "Wow. This is a lot. It's not even midnight. Wait. Who's this new member? The one named Clark?"

"Oh, she joined a little while ago. Really tall white lady."

"Did you write down all of her driver's license information?"

"It's on the back of the hard copy."

Lavender walked behind the desk and opened a black notebook that had sign-in sheets for all the employees.

Milan flipped through some papers and gave a quick read. She spoke at a faster pace. "Where is she now?"

"I have no idea."

"Lavender, let's go inside and look around, please."

"Why?"

"That birth date is August 18, 1965. I think Nancy's ass is here."

"Nancy, your stepmother, Nancy?" he asked, looking at Milan.

"Ex-stepmother."

"Why would she be in here?"

"Why wouldn't she be? She's a hot damn mess, too."

Lavender stepped from behind the desk after grabbing his usual pistol from the safe, and he took a two-way out of the drawer. He pressed the button and spoke. "Jarod? Jarod?"

"Where is he?"

"I don't know." He spoke into the radio again. "Jarod? Where are you?" He then called out on a different frequency. "Brian."

"Yeah, man. What's up?"

"Where's Jarod?"

"I haven't seen him in a while. I have no idea."

"Thanks." Lavender led the way and gave Milan a concerned eye. She returned the same.

They rushed down the hall, past the first-floor bathrooms, peeking in each room along the way. They went up three short stairs, past the lockers, to the pink room.

When they reached the closed door, Lavender turned the knob and pushed it open. The view that met their eyes made them both take a quick breath.

Nancy Clark Kennedy was bouncing upon the cigar-shaped, ebony strap-on that Heidi wore, riding shotgun, and her pussy was the holster. She was in the passenger seat, sitting on the woman's lap, facing away from her as Heidi sat on the floor. Heidi's butt was resting on the back of her heels. Nancy was squatted, with her knees up to her chest. Her horniness devoured the long, fake dick. And her face said she was in total ecstasy.

And in the corner, way behind the view of others, was Jarod, facing the female-fucking couple.

Milan's eyes dropped to where Jarod's hands were. He was straight in the middle of whacking himself off a mile a minute. His self-giving strokes were rhythmic. His brown dick was stretched far out into the air, and his hand was beating the skin of his shaft like he was in an X-rated panic. His pants were around his ankles, his two-way was on the floor behind him, and his eyes were glued to the hot, live, girl-on-girl action before him. It was like a close-up and personal Girls Gone Wild infomercial, only kinkier.

Milan yelled like she was about to explode. "O-fucking-K. Jarod, what the hell?"

"Milan?" Jarod's rounded eyes showed raw surprise. His mouth flew open. His hands froze in place. His dick began an instant collapse.

The cartoon caption above Nancy's head read, *Oh shit!*

Milan looked at her buck-naked stepmother with a deep down frown, flailing her hands about. "Nancy. Get the fuck up."

First Nancy stood, and then her strap-wearing accomplice, Heidi, stood as well. Heidi undid the buckles and held the long black dildo along the side of her thigh. She frantically began to look around for her discarded clothing. Nancy stood still, big tits, big hips, big legs, all six feet of her, towering over Heidi, paralyzed like her feet were stuck in place.

Lavender asked all three of them, "What's going on?"

"I was j-just . . ." Jarod began to say with a stutter. "See, w-what had h-happened was . . ."

Milan took over. "Jarod, this is my father's ex-wife. The one who's been trying to get half of his estate and you're up in my club yanking your dick at her?"

"She's who?" His forehead showed his shock.

"You have the nerve to fuck around on my sister with her own stepmother, and at work of all places? What the hell is wrong with you?"

Lavender spoke up with a stern voice. "Jarod, you're fired. Get the hell out of here."

Milan pointed to Nancy who stood there naked, only wearing black patent leather high heels while she scanned the floor for her skirt and blouse. "And take her with you."

Nancy looked bimbolike confused as she covered her double handfuls of breasts with her hands as best she could. "Milan, I'm not here to . . ."

Milan cut her off in an instant, boldly stepping up within an inch of her face. "I see why you're here. Leave now." Milan aimed her index finger toward the pink door.

Nancy blinked but did not say another a word. She bent down to scoop her clothes from the tiny pile and began to head for the door. Still naked.

Milan said, "Coming in here trying to live out your lesbian fantasies in my club. That is straight stupid."

Nancy awkwardly hurried along as she made her fumbling exit.

Jarod stuffed his major equipment into his boxers and pulled up his pants. He scrambled to reloop his belt.

Milan said, "I guess the thrill clouded your reasoning, huh? I told your ass, don't get your honey where you get your fucking money. Now your money from my water well has run dry. Get the fuck up out of here. Now." Milan pointed her hand toward the door for him, too.

Jarod simply exited quietly. His head was hung low.

Heidi hurriedly moved about, slipping back into her short cotton dress. She slid into her shoes. "Ma'am, I'm sorry." Her hyperactiveness was showing. The caffeine had taken over and she looked like she was about to straight lose it.

Milan's look was still one of raging anger, but she spoke to Heidi, who was now trying to tuck the retractable fuck strap into her tiny purse. "You can stay. But go find yourself some sane ass pussy."

Heidi flashed a smile two times fast and stepped away, still looking along the floor as she exited.

Milan headed for the door. "These folks are losing their damn minds up in here. Damnit," she said as she dashed out and down the long hall.

Lavender exited, too, shaking his head in wonder, with a bit of brotherly compassion.

25

"Un-Break My Heart"

∝

Saturday, April 26, 2008
6:57 p.m.

The full darkness of midevening approached after a long day of solace, a long day of thinking, and a long day of worry. Gray skies and a sudden mist of casual raindrops, mixed with a weak wind, matched well with the mood. Her mood from trying to debond from the hold that oxytocin had on her.

Exhaustion had seized Tamiko's very being. She had day-old mascara that still coated her lashes. Most of it had rubbed off and smudged, giving her raccoon eyes. Her nose was red. She cupped her left hand and blew into it, sniffing her own breath. She frowned in reply.

She smoothed her hairline, noticing she was in need of a meeting with a hairbrush and sank into her ivory leather love seat in the sitting area of her bedroom. The fireplace fought to light up her dim view. She leaned her head from front to back and then from left to right, trying to work out a nasty kink in her neck.

It was the day after her true nasty kink, the insatiable Jarod, was busted while giving himself the gift of a peeping-Tom hand job at the sight of her own step-mother getting fucked by a lady with a dildo.

Tamiko's mind battled between anger and sadness. Her Bluetooth hung from her ear as she spoke. She curled her legs to the side and placed her hand on her ankle. Her eyes were moist and her heart was heavy. "I can't believe those two fools really hooked up like that. And at your club of all places."

Milan spoke loudly as she drove to the nail salon a few blocks away from her home for a late appointment. "I never want to see that woman naked again in my entire life. That was absolutely traumatizing. Just the whole thought of Daddy doing her and there she was in front of me. My Lord. I can't believe Jarod didn't even know who she was. Didn't he ever see a picture of Nancy's trashy ass before?"

Tamiko leaned her elbow onto the soft armrest and propped her head up. "I doubt that I have many pictures of her other than in some old photo album somewhere. But this is just as much her fault as it is his. If she didn't know before, she knows now that Jarod is my man, or excuse me, was my man, and she hasn't even picked up the phone. She's been trying to be all brand-new ever since she turned forty I guess."

"I'm not surprised by her at all. What's worse is that he knows she was Daddy's ex. He hasn't called you?"

"No. I'll bet he's got his tail tucked between his legs, hiding like the mutt he is. I gave Jarod more credit than that. I would have never predicted this crap from him."

"That was just ignorant."

Tamiko gave a deep inhale and a slow exhale. "He's

got some nerve. They both do. And I was the one she called whenever she wanted to try to convince us that she was a cool person. Now I see Dad was right." Tamiko's cell beeped. Her heart gave a thump and she darted her eyes down toward the display. As much as she was disgusted, she hoped against hope that it would say Jarod. It read Gloria instead, the woman who was making a few samples for Tamiko's collection. It was a call she'd been expecting for days. She gave a long blink and let the call go. It no longer seemed important. The vertical line between her eyes was deep.

"Tamiko, didn't Daddy accuse her of being gay? Of foolin around with her trainer?"

Tamiko rubbed her temple. "He did."

"Now we know he was right about that. I thought her trainer's name was Sal, but maybe that was short for Sally." A honk could be heard. Milan said angrily, "Damn. Let me get over. These people out here are just rude."

Tamiko had a one-track mind. She somberly asked, "What was she doing in the club anyway? Trying to find herself a woman?"

"Who knows? Maybe just being nosy because of all the mess that's been in the news. But she had no business in there."

Tamiko's stomach growled. She leaned her head back and gave a long cleansing breath. She asked, "Milan, do you think they'll end up seeing each other?"

"That would be dumb, but when you're dealing with two dumb-ass people, who knows?"

Tamiko looked up at the empty ceiling.

Milan said, "Sis, I know you and Jarod seemed pretty

close. But I never felt he was as serious about you as he should've been, so please don't trip. He's just foul, just thinking with his dick. Please don't confuse sex with love. Don't lose any sleep over him."

Tamiko grabbed the chenille throw from the back of the sofa and smothered her legs with it. "What bothers me is thinking about the fact that he thought he could get away with it. Plus, he's always had a thing for white women. Every woman he's been with before me was white. It's just his preference."

"You see what that preference has gotten him now. He lost out on you. That's a hell of a price to pay to whack your shit over Nancy's big fat ass."

Tamiko allowed her tears to release. She wiped her face as they flowed and stared at the flickering flames of the fireplace. "Milan, why does any man do that shit? Why do men seem to need to cheat? I really thought Jarod and I were okay. I mean, I thought our issues were minor enough. And for him to not even pick up the phone and so much as apologize. I just don't get it." Tamiko's voice fell apart.

"Baby sis, don't cry. What he did was selfish. You know I don't too much believe a man can be faithful anyway. I think if Jarod had needs, he could have found a better place to do it than his own job, if he was gonna fuck up at all. Just because he was in a sex club doesn't excuse it. It was his place of employment, run by his woman's sister, and now he knows she was his woman's stepmother. All of that adds up to wrong."

Tamiko rubbed her nose. "Milan, why do I seem to meet guys like this? Jimmy just snuck off with someone and tried to lie his way out of it."

"Puh-lease. You're a good woman. And you need to be strong. Besides, an insecure woman is great for a man's ego, so don't even go there. Be strong and one day you won't be asking why anymore. It's not about you. It's about a man who got caught with his pants down, and a woman who doesn't care about anyone but herself."

Tamiko kept trying to imagine the visual. "I just can't get it out of my head. Jarod and my stepmother."

"She's not a damn thing to us, Tamiko. Now we know what Daddy knew. She's a slut. And now, it's on."

26

"Peaches and Cream"

⚯

Wednesday, April 30, 2008
10:34 p.m.

A full kiss on the lips.

An inserted tongue.

A squeeze of the buttocks.

A handful of stiff penis.

A finger fuck.

A nipple suck.

And then a dirty French kiss again.

Oui. Oui.

Their bodies were knotted up as though playing a game of Twister.

Left foot white.

Right hand black.

Her full white hips and rear.

His tight black glutes and six-pack.

Their foreplay was new and exciting. Nancy lay on her back with her legs spread like a wishbone. Jarod looked down and saw her pussy. Her light hair was long and plentiful. He wanted to be inside of her. He couldn't help himself. The sight of it had him at the point of no return.

He crawled up on her forty-two-year-old body and placed his hand on his twenty-eight-year-old dick and laid his chest upon her healthy breasts, placing his face near her neck. He prepared to enter.

"Eat me," she said as though he should have known better. She gave him a salacious look.

Jarod paused and leaned upward.

Nancy smiled an expectant smile. Her eyes were sweltering.

Jarod blinked a few times and lowered his body, heading straight downtown into muff-diving territory.

It was juicy.

It was a rosy shade of pink.

It was wide open.

It was heated.

It had a sweet scent. Like a feminine musk.

He kissed it and poked it with his tongue.

He looked up at her with eyes that said scrumptious.

He did a sloshing-tongue-tip insertion and screwed her creamy candy, like crème de la crème. He smacked his lips and smiled.

She smiled harder.

He was harder downstairs than before he'd sampled the delectable treat.

He adjusted the position of his face just below her pubic bone and maneuvered his lips to meet her clitoral pearl head-on. He saw her vulnerable fleshy nub exposed, without even having to pull back its rosy hood. Her pseudo-penis was enlarged.

He took the round, stiff muscle between his teeth and tongue and gave a sensual slurp. Her erect clitoris pulsated.

She jumped.

And he flicked.

She throbbed. The strength of it could be seen. It was undeniable. There was no lying about that.

And then he licked.

She flinched.

Her opening contracted multiple times. Her motion was strengthened by his obvious skill at pleasing. A skill much like riding a bike. Even though it had been a while, he managed to jump right back on and ride it just like before.

He allowed the fullness of her southern lips to surround the fullness of his northern lips, and inside his mouth, against his tongue, he met her tender point again, treating it to a suckling while slipping and sliding his lips along her tip like he was trying to get something out of it. He also probed the inside of her sugar walls with his thick index finger and his long fuck-you finger. He did the finger pliers, trying to stimulate the spongy tissue of her G-spot. The placement of his screw motion was at 11:00 a.m. and 1:00 p.m., strategically.

Her eyes popped open.

She gave a long purr.

He went faster, at two-point-five strokes per second.

Her white thighs squashed his ears.

He looked up and saw that her face was tense with ecstasy. Her eyes were now half shut, rolled back in a trancelike state of consciousness. Her mouth was pursed as if she was bracing herself for the strong emotion. Her teeth were clenched. And she pumped toward the feeling of her stiff little organ penetrating his mouth.

Her groans revved.

Her organ stiffened even more.

It jumped and she jumped.

She ground right into his mouth fuck.

She was being eaten.

Eaten alive.

And she cried out for dear life.

"Uhhhggh, uhhhggh. Yes. Yes. Yes. Umph." She pounded the toffee satin sheet with her tight fist. Over, and over, and over again.

She held his head in place as she ripped in his face.

Her secretions dripped and her thighs contracted and her hands flexed and her vagina squeezed tight around his deep fingers.

The thirst of her desire was quenched.

She got off in his mouth.

And one lone tear fell from her left eye.

He climbed up on top of her and rode her cum-filled pussy like the stand-up soldier he was.

He was the controlling drill sergeant.

And she was the obedient trainee.

It was his turn to have some fun.

Fun with a woman who took it deep, took it strong, and took it all night long.

Like the pussy champ she was.

He'd met his match.

And he came deep.

27

"Nasty Girl"

Thursday, May 1, 2008
10:34 p.m.

The next day, just before tall and thick Nancy turned around to take a seat next to Jarod, he reached up and grabbed a handful of plump ass. They were at her apartment in East Point, hanging out in her sunken living room. The circulating air smelled like butterscotch.

Nancy wore a mint-colored lace camisole and she was barefoot with clear toenail polish. The mango-colored candles flickered in the darkness.

He spoke like he was trash-talking to one of his boys. "I ain't never seen no ass like yours before."

"You say that to all the big booty girls."

"The hell I do. Damn, girl, what does your mama look like?"

She lowered her long body next to him, securing her womanly hips onto the blue gray woven sofa. "My mom? I guess you could say she's big. Or more like heavy."

"Well, God bless her." He talked like he was saluting.

He picked up his glass of Grey Goose and cranberry

on ice and swallowed while flipping through television channels.

Nancy asked, "Jarod, have you talked to Tamiko?"

"No. Why?" His eyes crept to her thirty-six-inch legs.

"You haven't even called her?"

"No."

"Are you going to?"

"I doubt it."

"You mean, you two don't need to talk? You didn't leave anything at her place, or maybe she left something at yours?"

"No." His eyes traveled up her six-foot body to her full breasts with nipples that showed themselves boldly.

"That quickly? That easily? Isn't there usually something that happens after you stop seeing someone? Something."

He blinked and returned his eyes to the TV. "Me and Tamiko are done. However quick or easy, I'm not sure."

"But why me, Jarod?"

"Why you what?"

"You could have gone back and asked her to understand. But, you didn't. And you're here with me. Even through my history with her dad?"

Jarod put his hand on her thigh. "I'm here right now because I want to be. I'm not sure what I'm feeling. But, after what happened in that club, in spite of her sister's feelings about me, or you, we just might be very well suited, you and me."

"You know that already?"

"I'm just enjoying this." He sat back and squeezed her leg.

She sat back. "You know I'm quite a bit older than you."

"And?"

"You've dated older women before?"

"Many times."

"But not for long, obviously. You're only twenty-eight."

"And?" he asked.

"And you know I'm fighting for a portion of Charlie's estate, right?"

"I do."

"That doesn't bother you?"

"That's on you."

"That's on me? We're not talking about some family out there who you've never met. We're talking about Tamiko and Milan Kennedy."

Jarod leaned his head back against the soft cushion. "Nancy, come on. Here I am, spending time with you after some great nights together." He looked down at her legs again. "You look good and you feel damn good. You're sitting next to me and my dick is hard. Again. I'm enjoying you. You turn me the fuck on." He looked at her softening face. "You have ever since the minute I saw you. I can't help who you are. There's no blood relation, even though I know both of them and what they must be saying about me. Or about us. The question is, can you handle this?"

Nancy looked him in the eyes and down at his jeans. She simply smiled and examined his broad shoulders and beautiful chest muscles. "If only I had met you in some other way, some other time, without all of this. But, who knows. Who's to say?"

"Yeah, but you didn't."

She leaned closer to him.

"Sit on my face," he demanded out of the blue with a stern look.

She giggled. "Jarod, you just ate me out last night."

"Come up here, woman."

Jarod moved over to the left side of the sofa and leaned back. Nancy stood up, unsnapped her camisole and lowered the shoulder straps, allowing her breasts to spring from its lacy cups. She brought her shapely right leg over his shoulder and then her left leg. She looked down and positioned her cookie to his awaiting face and pulled back her hairy lips, exposing her clit for him. He immediately took it into his mouth and began his butterfly-flick magic. Right away, his hands grabbed her plump ass, covering the womanly curve of her bottom. Her right leg shook. It was like he was pushing a magic coochie button. Her bushy pussy rested on his mouth. His fingers pressed her cheeks hard enough to leave reddish imprints. His dick stiffened behind her.

She squirmed toward him and fucked his face, riding his mouth. She ran her long fingers through her straight blonde hair and threw her head back. Nancy looked back and caught sight of his dark brown hands along her backside. Her pussy jerked.

She felt her rush arriving at ninety miles an hour and pulled away from his face and backed down to his penis, hurriedly making her way up against it.

It was as though her tight slit was begging to be fucked. He could hear it.

"You have such a pretty dick." She looked like she meant it.

"I've got enough to feed the needy, baby." He looked serious.

Nancy placed her ready-to-blow pussy opening to the point of easy access, inserting his dick inside. She braced herself with her legs, descending onto his girth, and moaned softly.

Jarod looked up at her as she lay upon him. His thick shaft was all up in her and she barely flinched. The feeling deep inside turned him on like a light switch.

She looked at his face and leaned down. She bounced upon him, bucking her pussy along his twelve inches. She kissed his lips, nose, cheeks, and chin, licking where she had been. She sucked his neck and pecked a kiss against his ear.

Jarod closed his eyes and looked as though his entire body had been swallowed inside of her. His legs flexed and his toes curled. He swelled north, south, east, and west, and she still stroked him inside of her walls.

Her wide breasts were squeezed flat against his chest. She sat up and they bounced up and down according to the rhythm of her grind.

She said loudly, "You'd better be glad my ass is six feet tall."

"You're damn right about that shit. You can take all this dick."

"I try."

She was stretched to the limit while he worked hard at poking himself all the way back. She did not shy away.

Her breathing spoke volumes to him. "Ohhh, baby. Jarod. That's it. That's it. Shit." She lost control and she moaned, "Fuck," making an *I'm about to cum* face. With a voice that sounded like it was inclined to break, Nancy grunted and let go of a hard, rolling, wet one with his name on it that oozed out alongside his coated dick.

They kissed again. With his tongue in her mouth, his balls tingled, his stomach flinched, his scrotum rumbled, and his juices began to travel the long journey from the base to the length of his penis, and out of his tip, right onto Nancy's ready, willing, and able pussy walls. His squirt caused him to pull his face away from her face and his whole body tensed up. His back arched and his breathing changed as he completely expelled his ejaculation. She was branded.

Their demanding libidos matched.

His spasms tapered off.

The height of her afterglow snatched her brain. She was sated. She spoke with a moan. "Ah-hah, I see. You're trying to get me sprung. You're a real bully in bed. A girl's gotta pack a lunch to get with you. This is dangerous."

"You're the one who's fucking Superwoman." He kept his eyes on her.

"Don't you forget it, Dolomite. Don't you ever fucking forget it."

She lay upon him.

He closed his eyes.

She closed her eyes

He hugged her tight.

The two fell asleep together, right there on the sofa, with his dick still inside of her.

All the while, even fast asleep, she bonded.

28
"Pop That Thang"

✑

Thursday, May 8, 2008
11:52 p.m.

Tamiko lay on her back along the dark blue, Egyptian cotton sheets in her bedroom. The nighttime skies had arrived. The light of the overhead fan was dim, and the fan was set on High. She was unusually hot.

Another day had come to an end and Jarod hadn't even so much as sent her a text message. But for some reason, today, it didn't even matter. Her anger over him not calling was overshadowed by the anger she felt over the fact the he was probably actually enjoying Nancy, or someone. She wondered if it was a broken heart that made her so miserable, or if it was a broken ego that was bringing her down. Again, she was unlucky at love. And she was growing pretty damn tired of it.

This time, it wasn't her river of tears that she was chasing away. It was a case of the hornies. And so, she pulled her lemon G-string to the side. Showing on her wide-screen television was a DVD . . . a dirty one . . . one that Jarod left behind.

She squeezed the green-apple lubricating oil and it dripped between the split of her cunt. Her legs were open and her fingers separated her labia. She rubbed her pussy lips with her index and middle fingers. Her right-hand fingers massaged the tip of her sex button, back and forth. She slipped her middle finger deep inside for a quick self fucking and back up to her turned-on clitoris. Indeed, she was wet and ready for her own busy fingers.

Her eyes took in a stimulating view of her ex's favorite big-ass porno star, Cherokee. The hardcore movie was *Phatty Girls 3*. The costar was Jada Fire. And Jada and Cherokee were alternatively getting their pussies invaded by the king of all monster cock, Dickzilla Johnson.

Tamiko propped two goose-down pillows behind her head and used the remote to turn up the volume of the barbaric sounds of Jada getting her asshole stuffed with a humongous penis while Cherokee straddled Dickzilla's face as he lay on his back with his head hanging off the bed. Cherokee was pumping her stuff toward his face like his mouth was an awaiting pussy and her clit was a full-length, probing dick.

Tamiko switched her stares between both women, and focused on Jada's sodomy scene. She moaned and asked out loud, "How's she taking all that?" She continued to watch while grinding toward the fingers that probed her tight insides. She turned to her right side and opened the nightstand drawer, locating the banana yellow, vibrating rubber clit massager, snatching it, and closing the drawer quickly. She flicked on the rounded power switch. The tiny toy hummed in her hot little hand. She took the short, hooked end and inserted it. And then she met the rounded edge of the vibrator to the flesh of her clit, moving the slick skin of her hood back to fully expose her most sensitive point. She allowed it to stimulate her directly and swirled it in a tiny circle, pushing herself against it and back.

She eyed the kinky threesome, now with Jada sucking Cherokee's brown, stiff nipples while Cherokee got her snatch rammed from behind. Her ass bounced and rolled about, and Dickzilla had a big, greedy, monstrous smile on his face. The close-up scene of his dick penetrating Cherokee's drenched opening made Tamiko breathe hard. She massaged her left breast and nipple while still feeling the powerful vibration against her tiny hardness. She closed her eyes for a moment and absorbed the overwhelming feeling, again looking at Cherokee's ass while Jada's long tongue flicked along her nipple. Jada had one hand inside of her own vagina and her cheeks were clapping as though begging to be backed up herself.

Tamiko began to think of what it would be like to have had Jarod in Dickzilla's position, wondering if Cherokee would have liked to fuck his Long Dong cock, and imagined Jarod watching another woman lick her nipple while he dug deep inside of her.

"Uuuhhhphm," she groaned and then said, "I'll bet that fool would get that nut over with then."

Dickzilla pulled out his glistening dick and Cherokee turned on her back while he brought his dick to her tits. Cherokee spat along her own chest and he pressed his dick between her breasts, up and down, while she squeezed her tits alongside his shaft. He banged her chin with his thick head and pulled back down and up. She continued to spit for him, and Jada now had her tongue deep into the crack of his ass.

Dickzilla looked back and gave one more hard press toward Cherokee's face and shot spurts of propelling cum onto her lips. Jada made a beeline to Cherokee's face and licked his sperm off her mouth and chin, kissing Cherokee on the lips and smoothing Cherokee's hairline back, kissing her forehead. She said in her ear, "You sexy bitch, you."

Just as Tamiko's cell phone vibrated once, twice, and then three times against the surface of the walnut dresser, Tamiko's massager continued to vibrate against her heated cherry. But the visual from the porno was too strong to turn away from. She shook her head and said with a throaty yell, "Yes." She screamed at full volume while the throb of her clit approached its height. Her vaginal muscles constricted until she wailed, "Ahhhhhh yes. Yes. Uuuuuuuuummmm. Yes." She licked her lips and pulled the massager away from her clit, turning to her side with her legs shut tight, holding her hand over her vagina. She gave a long, loud sigh of relief.

If she had been a smoker, she would have lit one up in celebration of her own technique and taken a long drag. She glanced back over to the movie to see that Cherokee was still at it. Tamiko said, "Now I need a penis."

As she slowly came to a stance, she looked to her dresser to check her cell phone. She saw that she had indeed one missed call. From Jarod.

"His dog ears must have been ringing," she said as she placed the phone back down, walked to the closet, and threw on a sweat suit. Within fifteen minutes she was at the local Love Shack, picking out and paying for the super-duper, replace-your-lover dildo. The sex toy, called a Jack Rabbit, rotated and had two ears that flank the clit and veins and ridges. It was made of jet-black flexible rubber.

Tamiko rushed back home and headed straight for her bedroom. She shed her clothes as soon as she closed the bedroom door. And in her mind, her fake penis had a name. It had a face. It had a physique. It had a voice. She imagined his lips and his eyes and his sexy young face. She pressed him in and out of her vagina just the way she wanted him to. And she kept it up, probing herself while her mind traveled. And before long, she busted another nut yelling, "Uuummmh, Kellen." Her nut rolled like a good vaginal orgasm should. Her cell phone chimed. And even if it had been Jarod again, at the moment, it didn't seem to matter.

As her chest rose and fell strongly, she stood up and tucked her new friend Kellen in the top drawer of her nightstand. And she pressed the button on her cell to see that the text read,

I'm sorry. I miss u. I love u.

She pressed delete and replaced her cell to the dresser. She turned off the television and hugged her pillow, pulling the covers closer, snuggling into the softness of her mattress.

The position she assumed jelled with the comfort level she was finally in. She told herself that the betrayer Jarod Hamilton would be nothing more than an unpleasant memory. And immediately, unlike the previous nights, Tamiko dozed right off to sleep.

Another message sounded.
But Tamiko simply slept.
Done with grieving over Jarod.
At least for one night.

29

"Cut the Cake"

❦

Wednesday, May 14, 2008
4:24 p.m.

It was an afternoon of clear skies, fresh from a day of Atlanta spring rain.

Lavender picked up Taj from school and was set to drop him back off at school the next day. They sat on the floor in Taj's room playing Madden. His room had a queen bed and everything was Atlanta Falcon red.

For the first time in three games, Taj had beaten Lavender fair and square.

"You the man. You beat me good on that one."

Taj pumped his fist and patted his chest. "See, Dad. I'm the king. Betcha didn't let me win that time."

"No way. That won't happen again. Listen, I'll be right back. I need to go listen to the radio for a minute."

Taj continued to press the buttons on his remote to set up another team. "Okay. And then can we finish?"

"We can."

"Can I listen, too?"

Lavender stood up. "Not this time. It's business. But I won't be long."

"Okay, cool. Then can I have some more pizza?"

"Sure. I knew you'd be headed back to do more damage. Got that appetite from your daddy."

Lavender exited the room and looked at his watch, making sure it was five-thirty. He headed to his bedroom, closed the door, and turned on his stereo. He adjusted the dial and heard Maurice Black's voice.

"Welcome back. It's a dirty eight-letter word called swinging. Our segment is called "Swinging Is on the Upswing," and you could call Milan Kennedy the queen of swing. She owns the popular adult playground in Atlanta called Erotic City. Atlanta's called the adult entertainment capital of the New South, ladies and gentlemen. Also known as the Black Hollywood. So, Milan Kennedy, Erotic City, huh?"

"Yes. Erotic City." Milan's voice was upbeat.

Lavender leaned back upon the bed and crossed one leg over the other.

"We had a woman who called in during the break saying she comes from a very strict Catholic background and got naked on a trip to Jamaica, I think she said on one of those hedonism trips, and didn't wanna come home."

Milan laughed. *"I hear that happens."*

"I ain't mad at her. So tell our listeners, exactly what is swinging?"

"Swinging, or the lifestyle, is consenting adults, usually couples but not all the time, who live a lifestyle that involves having sex with a couple, or a single person. It is sexual freedom between open-minded partners."

"Okay. And what kind of people are swingers? What's the average age?"

"I'd say early twenties to fifties. They're average people, like you and me, like folks you might work with or live next door to, who are taxpayers and churchgoers. Some are married, but not all of them. Different races. Most have very healthy relationships and high levels of trust. And most really don't believe we can be or should be monogamous, so why not explore."

"Oh really? I know a lot of men who think that way."

"See, I don't think either sex is monogamous by nature. I don't think a lot of people can handle it if their mate says they want to sleep with other people. The way I look at it, I'd rather be a swinger than a cheater."

"I agree. Well, that's why people lie. They don't want to lose their mates. I have no problem with guilt-free sex. Cut out all the sneakin. So, tell me, how did you get your club started?"

"I was looking for a business that would be a success. I met a man who owned a club and he showed me the ropes. And Erotic City has been a big hit. Far more so than I could have ever imagined."

"There's such a social stigma about swingers. I can only imagine the amount of flack your receive because of it."

"I have, but I understand it."

"Milan, tell me something. What is a fluffer? One of my producers said she heard that term. Can you explain that?"

"Fluffers are sometimes used in porn movies off camera to keep the guy hot, just in case he's not quite feeling the girl he's doin. I think some clubs have been accused of having fluffer women come in and flirt, strip, things like that. We don't hire fluffers. We have enough hot people who are real members."

"Now see, I would think maybe there are some husbands

out there who need a fluffer in the bedroom with their wives. No, I'm just kidding, really. Okay, let me ask another question before I get myself in trouble. Now, being that you are Charlie Kennedy's daughter, what do you think he'd say if he knew?"

"Actually, my dad came down to the club one night and he was proud of what I'd done. He wasn't one to judge since he'd been around the block more than a few times, if you know what I mean."

"He was very well known, so I'm sure he had a lot of opportunity to do a lot of things. Let me ask you this. Does size matter?"

"I think width matters more actually, just so it can be wall to wall. The top two-thirds of a vagina have no nerve endings anyway, and the G-spot is maybe three inches in. Most women reach orgasm with clitoral stimulation, which has twice as many nerve endings as a penis, so if a man knows how to satisfy in that way, most of us women are cool."

"I see. Not that I needed to know. I don't have that problem." Maurice chuckled and cleared his throat.

"Yeah okay." Milan laughed.

"Lastly, is it true that fathers bring their sons into the sex clubs to turn them into men, so to speak, and do women take their husbands there as a birthday present?"

"That's very common, yes. Both of those scenarios."

"Well, this is a hot topic for sure. Hey, I hope you stick around because we're going to interview other female business owners whose lines of work have to do with sex. One owns a sex shop, one runs a brothel in Vegas, and the other woman owns a strip club in Los Angeles. The trip is that more money is spent on the sex industry than motion picture and sporting events combined. Are women just as freaky-

deaky as men? Stick around. We'll be right back with more of Black Adult Radio."

Thursday, May 15, 2008
3:48 p.m.

Lavender had taken Taj to school the next morning. And by the afternoon, Milan had already said all the things your mother would wash your mouth out with soap for. And she said those things in about twelve different ways.

They were in her kitchen, she and Lavender. And in celebration of her highly rated interview with Maurice Black, her man was playing with her.

The flesh of her soft ass rested upon the gray and white, slab granite countertop. She wore a psychedelic skirt. Her bare feet rested along the edge of the now-heated counter. Her legs were bent with her knees spread apart. It was time for a little afternoon delight.

A crystal cake plate rested a few inches from her hands. A few hearty slices of yellow, caramel cake were missing. And the icing from half of what was left looked like someone had been finger-painting in swirling motions.

Lavender's fingers were the erotic culprits. And the object of the scooped caramel was Milan's opening. Lavender's fingers and tongue were swooshing the sweet, light brown frosting inside and outside of her own girlie cake. And he was feasting upon her pussy-dessert like he had a serious sugar habit.

She looked down at his cunnilingus precision and said, "Damn, you've got that shit on a plate." It was like she was his naked dinner.

He smacked and licked his meal in reply. He swallowed and added more icing and repeated his insertion, first his finger and then his wide, stiff tongue, in and out of her sticky hole. He twisted and teased his tongue to her hood and swirled her clit, gently scraping the tender organ with his teeth. He was an oral chef on a mission. He pressed two fingers inside and she rocked back and forth in reply.

She could hear him lap her up like he was a parched dog drinking water for the first time in days. And he would not stop. It was so intense that she quickly felt like she was about to lose it. She felt herself expelling onto his waiting face, saturating his skin with her love juices. She gave a sigh of pleasure and a look of appreciation.

Within one second, with his hard love muscle at full attention, Lavender stood and pulled Milan off of the counter, bringing her post-orgasm body to a standing position. Just as her feet hit the floor, he turned her around and bent her over, with her chin to the exact level of the counter. His favorite position.

She stuck her ass out toward him and he stood firm, bending so he could get inside. He spread her fleshy lips apart and inserted his cock, incrementally, pushing gently at first and then more with each thrust. Her boobs bounced beneath her body. Her slick pussy eased his entry. Her movement spoke of begging for more. He filled her up and she thrust against him, sliding her hips back at him, squeezing her cunt around his relentless dick. His heavy balls pounded against her ass.

"What do you think? Do I have enough width?" he asked.

"Oh hell yeah."

"Am I hitting that spot?"

"Shit yeah." She took his full entry. The crescendo of their rhythms meshed well.

After a few minutes of slamming into her caramel vagina, his body spasmed and his orgasm blossomed, causing him to shoot hot sperm that filled the depths of her womb. She inhaled as she took every last drop.

He pulled out, exiting where he'd been, leaving her lips wide open from his departure. His fluid leaked from her split to the inside of her legs.

He walked to the bathroom with his hand on his dick, shaking his head. "Damn. That was a record-breaking quickie."

She pulled down her skirt, also adjusting her top. She glanced over at the golden molested cake with her man's fingerprints all through it, and picked up a knife to cut herself a big piece. "I'll never think of a caramel cake in the same way again." She asked loudly, "Do you want some?"

"I've had enough, thanks," he said from the hallway.

"I ain't mad at you." She took a bite.

"Tomorrow's our big day in court," he yelled.

"Oh Lord, don't remind me please," she said while chewing.

"No worries."

"Lavender, you sure know how to ruin a fuckin celebration," Milan said, tossing the remaining cake into the trash. "That's bound to be one hell of a trip."

30

"Déjà Vu"

❧

Friday, May 16, 2008
9:17 a.m.

The court date for the negligence charge against Erotic City had finally arrived. Milan had about five cups of coffee before they left her home. Lavender had major problems dozing off. He just couldn't seem to shut his brain down. It was another day of battling Ramada in court.

Milan and Lavender's attorney, Hunter Wyatt, was tall, mid-fifties, with slightly graying sideburns that added to his look of distinction. He spoke authoritatively. "Your Honor, the prosecution has repeatedly appealed for potential witnesses to this alleged sexual assault. Mr. Mac McCoy aka Big Mack has denied the allegations. Other than the plaintiff claiming that he brandished a knife, we have not identified anyone who actually saw a weapon. Not the security people. Not the bouncer. Not the front desk person. Not the other people in the VIP room. No one."

The large downtown courtroom was full. The room was cold and everything was beige, from the bench seats to the beige carpet, to the scuffed-up tile flooring and the dingy latex paint on the walls. Bland was the theme.

The only movement was that of the attorneys, judge, and a court reporter. A guard stood by the door. There were a couple of news reporters who stood against the back wall. One scribbled on a tiny notepad.

Both dressed in slate blue, Milan and Lavender sat together next to Attorney Wyatt.

Ramada Hart wore a gray skirt suit with red-bottom shoes and she sat next to her attorney. Big Mack was absent.

Ramada's attorney, Judith Berg, said, "Your Honor, in spite of the fact that Miss Hart has dropped her criminal case against Mr. McCoy, this is a valid criminal claim against Erotic City for negligence in connection with assault on a patron." Her off-white Ann Taylor suit was classic. It framed her slender silhouette.

The white-haired, heavyset judge lowered his reading glasses to the tip of his nose. "Ms. Berg, I suggest you listen up and listen up good. There was no evidence of threats, grabbing, destruction of property, or other indications that an assault would occur against the plaintiff until the moment it allegedly happened. The evidence is insufficient to create duty upon the part of the club to prevent an assault, or to protect Ms. Ramada Hart against it. You can't apply hindsight in determining what a reasonable person would do. I've looked at how quickly the alleged events occurred. And from what has been proven, the club owners not only could not have anticipated something of this nature, but once they were notified, they immediately

removed the accused and the accuser, secured the premises, and called the police themselves within two minutes
after the plaintiff dialed 911 from her cell phone."

Ms. Berg replied, "Your Honor, we believe the owners
should have had more control over the situation. Claims
involving forced sexual activity can occur, and they need
to be responsible when they do."

"Ms. Berg, this is a sex club."

Milan looked down at a ruled notebook and took
notes.

"But, Your Honor, club owners at sex clubs should
not be held to a different standard than any other club
owner," Ms. Berg insisted.

"Perhaps. But right away, those patrons, as soon as they
enter the premises, are subjected to violations simply due
to the intimate nature of the acts they embark upon. I
have read over the club's membership agreement, and
the rules for this 'Alternative Lifestyle Swingers Club
Agreement' clearly states that there may be nudity and
sexual activity on the premises and that if it offends or
makes one feel it constitutes lewd or lascivious acts, then
they should not complete or sign the application and go
home. But she has already admitted to having oral and
vaginal group sex minutes prior to having oral sex with
Mr. McCoy."

Ramada looked over at Lavender, who focused straight
ahead. She turned and glanced back at a blonde female
with big eyes who smiled.

The lady attorney said, "No still means no, Your
Honor. You can't force someone if they decline, even
half way through an act. Plus, there was no security
readily available."

"This agreement, which Ms. Hart signed, does state that no means no. The question is did the accused adhere to that statement? And, Ms. Hart's signature is right here, agreeing that she releases the club, its owners, managers, directors, employees, agents, and servants from any and all liability arising from her participation in activities or events. That means if assumed or implied incidents occur as a result of personal activities or consequences of lifestyle choices, would the club be to blame for the fact that Ms. Hart's decision to say no was not honored? I don't think so."

The female attorney said with certainty, "Yes, but it also says no weapons are allowed. The club failed to detect weapons."

"And you, Ms. Berg, have not proven that there were weapons on the premises. And in my opinion, if that were the case, it would have been Mr. McCoy who violated the harassment and weapons policy. So convince your client, Ms. Hart, to sue him."

"Your Honor—"

The judge cut her off. "I'm about to make my ruling. I also have a copy of the agreement that Mr. McCoy signed regarding what he agreed to do. Need I remind you of that as well?"

"No, Your Honor."

Attorney Wyatt bent down and whispered in Lavender's ear. Lavender then whispered in Milan's ear. She nodded.

"Ms. Berg, since Ms. Hart dropped charges against Mr. McCoy, who in my opinion is the one who the civil and criminal charges should be directed to, then I don't know what else to say. So, if Ms. Hart wants to file a civil claim to see if a jury will find the club civilly responsible, meaning they determine the club is the reason for the cause, then so be it. But as for now, I do not recommend this case for criminal trial. This case is dismissed. Next case."

The attorneys gathered their files and stepped past the swinging doors with their clients. Attorney Wyatt patted both Lavender and Milan on the back, and Milan kissed Lavender on the cheek. He returned her gesture of congratulations.

Ramada stepped along in her tight skirt and stared Milan down, cutting her with a prolonged slice of her eyes. Ramada's blonde female friend stood and took Ramada's hand as they proceeded toward the door, but not before the female made a point of giving Lavender a lingering smile.

Milan caught the smile and asked, "Who's that? She gave us the eye earlier."

"That's the same woman Ramada and I got with at your club last year."

"I thought she looked familiar. Why am I not surprised?" Milan rolled her eyes.

Lavender and Milan followed their attorney into the hallway.

With briefcase in hand, Attorney Berg approached Milan, Lavender, and Attorney Wyatt. "So, do you want to discuss a settlement?"

Attorney Wyatt spoke right up. "No civil charges have even been filed yet."

"I'm saying just so we can save everyone the time and expense," Attorney Berg said. She looked at Milan and then Lavender.

Attorney Wyatt replied, "We need some time to discuss this. I'm inclined to say no."

"I agree," Lavender said.

Milan crossed her arms. "We'll see. We'll get back to
you."

Attorney Wyatt added, "We'll be in touch."

Ramada and her friend walked on to the elevator with
Attorney Berg. Ramada turned back, giving an evil look
down toward Milan's feet and up at her face, shaking her
head.

"She needs to quit," Lavender said with a deep exhale, noticing her stare of dismissal.

"That'll be the day," said Milan, looking everywhere
but at Ramada. "And you need to get that restraining
order filed that we talked about before."

"It's been prepared, we just need you to sign one, too.
It'll be filed. Don't worry." Lavender took Milan's hand
and they took the stairs to the parking garage.

31

"Brick House"

⨭

The almost-full moon cast its glow high in the almost-black sky. It was barely eleven o'clock at Erotic City. And just as it had been since the fateful night that Ramada made her accusations, the club was full.

Dakota, a regular, was also known as Dee, though some called her Good 'n Plenty. She wore a generous princess-cut diamond that glistened as her hand moved. Her shoulder-length hair was dyed sandy brown for the month and was gelled back away from her face. She wore a peach-colored teddy and a matching pair of sheer bottoms that were slit all the way up her thighs. Her cheetah-print thong was buried deep into the crack of her behind. And her hips devoured the leather stool beneath her. Even though Dakota was extrathick, thicka-than-a-snicka thick, two biscuits short of two-hundred thick, she was well proportioned.

They called her Dee because of her triple D, boobalicious tits that she always showed off. Her cleavage spillage was off the charts. The girls were about the same size as her fifty-inch hips. Her wide breasts were pushed together compliments of an underwire bra. The pale, alabaster skin of her bosom bubbled outward like pop and fresh dough, high and overflowing, damn near touching her chin. She had an itty-bitty voice that forgot she was a big girl, and a baby face that forgot she was fifty-five.

Dakota and her husband, Jed, found a semiprivate, cozy little room of their own to play in. The red-light special ceiling lights cast a sensual glow. The walls were painted black.

Jed lay beside his hot-to-trot wife. He was fully dressed, except he had taken off his shoes and socks. However, she now lay naked as a jaybird.

Dakota's name was etched in ink around her left ankle, her tramp stamp read Nympho, and a playboy symbol lived on her right shoulder blade. She lay flat on her tummy, with her amazing cellulite-free ass lounging upright, just letting it all hang out for the voyeuristic world to see.

And see they did. Two men kept walking back and forth, peering past the open door to get a glimpse of her wonderment. They noticed her every amazing curve. Jed noticed their stares. Jed lay on his side with his head propped upon his hand, his elbow taking the weight of his head. And under his pants, his hard-on came and went, depending upon their glances.

Dakota faced forward. She could see her nasty admirers through the wall-to-wall mirror. Another man looked inside and nodded.

Jed said, "Hello. I see you looking. Come on in." He gestured with his hands.

"Oh no. I was just walking by."

Jed said, "Yeah, but your eyes came on in for a visit. It's okay. She is something else, isn't she?"

He answered with a nod, "Yes, she's very beautiful. Is this your wife?"

"Yes. This is Dakota. People here call her Dee."

"Hello, baby. What's your name?" Dakota asked, looking at the young black man from head to toe.

"Braylon."

"Hello Braylon. Nice to meet you. Have a seat." She nodded toward the bed but he sat on the chair.

He faced Dakota. He sat still and quiet, leaning forward with his elbows resting on his knees. He looked around from wall to wall. Anywhere but where he wanted to look.

Suddenly, Dakota asked, "Can I kiss you?"

He sat up straight. "Yes. You can."

Dakota shifted her big-boned self around and sat in a yoga position. She reached toward Braylon. He stood and stepped to her, bending down. He met his face to hers and sat down on the bed next to her.

Her hand was behind his neck. He brought his lips to touch her lips and she opened her mouth. He opened wide and swirled his tongue with hers. She straightened her tongue and stuck it deep into his mouth while he sucked on it. Their lips stayed pressed together. She removed her tongue and laid a loud smack on his full, brown mouth and backed away, making sure to keep her eyes on his. She moved her hand from behind his neck to his crotch. She felt his thrill and smiled as she sized up his package.

"You need to step out of those," Jed said from behind Dakota.

Braylon did not need to be told twice. He stood up and dropped his pants to the floor.

"Mind if I leave these on for traction?" he asked, pointing down at his black Chucks.

Dakota said immediately, "Please do." She got up on all fours and propped her Mac truck rear end up high.

Jed gave him a condom but Braylon took one from his pocket. He secured it and moved up behind Dakota, placing his hands on her hips, pulling her extrawet, bald pussy onto his dick.

He went deep like a quarterback throwing a bomb.

She was the wide receiver.

And Jed was ready to play referee.

Jed stood up, removed his pants, and faced her with his penis at full attention. She took a deep breath and sucked Jed's uncircumcised white cock, licking his fore-skin with every motion. For every cock that pulled out on one end, a deep-diving dick was on the other. Her juices seeped and she let out muffled screams.

The door was still open, and within only ten minutes, there was a group of people watching the threesome fuck show live. Jed, at the sight of the group watching his wife get fucked by a big black dick, felt his balls release the heat of his turn-on. His fuse burned from his explosion as he quickly blasted his ejaculation deep against the back of his wife's throat. Dakota gave a few gulping swallows and then hummed the words, "Uuhm, uuhm, good."

Braylon, who had positioned himself in a firm Chuck-wearing stance, explored Dakota wall to wall, with her ass slapping against his balls. Like her tattoo bragged about, her nympho hunger was evident. Her excessive juices could be heard. That along with the sound of her silver bracelets jingling softly.

After a flurry of hard thrusts, Dakota made sure to ride through her slow-rolling orgasm by controlling her breathing, trying her best to make it last. She looked back to see Braylon's dark skin pressing against her white ass cheeks and she wailed.

Dakota sounded as though she was crying. She always did.

There were no tears, but she had this way of whining and sniffling, giving off weepy moans.

Braylon was impressed by her loud passion. He gritted his teeth and pounded her pussy for all he was worth, continuing to give it to her like he assumed she deserved to be fucked.

Jed had stepped back and regained his hardness, thumbing his tip at the ebony and ivory sight before him.

Braylon thrusted and worked his length into every nook and cranny he could find until he felt his dick swell to its max.

Dakota looked back and saw his *I'm cumming* expression. She braced herself, giving him all the access he needed so that he could blow. She focused on wringing his climax from him and milking his semen. She again moaned like she was in the throws of bereavement, like something hurt, bad.

Braylon shot his load like lightning, skeeting as she wiggled just for his personal visual satisfaction.

He slapped her ass and shook his head, and said, "Now, that is some good, tight pussy, there."

"You know it," Jed said, now seated with his legs apart, his dick pointing up toward the ceiling.

Most of the crowd began to walk away while giving off murmurs of appreciation. Among the people who remained, eyeing the threesome, was Lavender. He kept his eyes on Dakota and readjusted where his fully awoken dick lived and walked away.

Braylon backed away and scratched the back of his head, still eyeing Dakota's ass while the baggy condom covered his now-flaccid penis.

Within a few minutes, Braylon and Jed were dressed, Dakota stayed naked. Jed and Dakota went in the direction of the hot tub. Braylon left. They had departed just as easily as they came together.

Three bodies fucking.

Just taking enough time to hit it and quit it.

No bonding.

No phone numbers.

Taking *love thy neighbor* to a whole new height.

32

"Let's Work"

⊗

Sunday, May 18, 2008
11:31 a.m.

On Sunday at the second service, Pastor Michael stood in his tailored, wheat-colored suit with a rust tie and shoes to match. He wound down his sermon just before the offering. He downshifted the pace of his words yet still spoke at full volume.

"And so, you must have a new consciousness. A consciousness of good, of thinking good and doing good. You need confidence in order to position yourself for success. In doing that, your life will gravitate to the level of those thoughts. How you think is who you are. Expect to be blessed."

"Amen," some of the churchgoers replied all at once.

Milan and Lavender sat in their regular seats and listened intently.

"Yes, Lord. Become more in God's consciousness than self-consciousness. And now it is our time of giving." He picked up a small envelope and held it high. "You'll see that on the envelope the ushers handed out, there are a few categories as far as your offerings go." He perused the front of the envelope with his index finger. "One is the general love offering for tithing and giving, the other is for the building fund which goes toward keeping our beautiful sanctuary up and running. The third is a donation for our Open Word Big Sister Program where we actually mentor our high school girls and prepare them for college. A portion of the funds goes toward their college tuition. We'll present the young ladies at our anniversary dinner coming up soon. Please take a moment to fill out your envelopes."

The band played music for a minute or two and then the pastor spoke again.

"Now at this time, please hold your offering over your heart and repeat after me.

"I thank you for the ability to give and share with others knowing that our giving is returned throug' the circle of this blessing. For this we do give than' Amen."

Milan secured her check into the white envelo' licked the seal. On the front of the envelope, sh her name and address, e-mail address, and th of ten thousand dollars. She placed the env' basket as the person next to her handed passed it on to Lavender, who had filled lope and placed a two-hundred-dollar the basket as well.

"I saw that," he told her.

"The least I can do. That's a grea school girls."

"You've got a big heart."

"I, for one, know that I have beer

said in her head, *In spite of myself*, as the service concluded.

Monday, May 19, 2008
1:01 p.m.

The next day, after an uneventful evening at the club, Milan sat at her L-shaped, handcrafted desk in her home office, flipping through e-mails on her laptop while doing her PC pushups. She wore only violet panties. The CNN newscast was broadcasting in the background.

She opened an e-mail from an address she was unfamiliar with. It read

> Ms. Kennedy, By way of introduction, my name is Rowena Weber and I am a programming executive here at the WET TV Network in Los Angeles. Would you be so kind as to give me a call at the number below when you get a minute? I have something I'd like to discuss with you. Thank you. Sincerely, Rowena.

Milan immediately dialed the number and turned own the volume on her flat screen. She stood from her sk chair and headed to the love seat near the window. e settled herself square into the softness of the suede k-red sofa, and crossed her legs.

Rowena Weber's office."

ello. This is Milan Kennedy calling. Is Ms. Weber ble please?"

assistant asked, "Milan Kennedy. And you're with?"

"She sent me an e-mail less than an hour ago asking me to call."

"Okay. Hold on just one minute."

"Thanks."

"Uh-huh."

Milan sat back and cleared her throat. She tapped her fingertips along the sofa and uncrossed her legs. She stood up, taking the few steps to the window, looking outside at the neighborhood view of landscaped yards and beautiful trees. She smiled at the quaint sight as she heard through her cell, "Milan! Hello. Thanks for calling me back."

"Hello, Ms. Weber. How are you?"

"Oh, I can't complain. And please call me Rowena." The voice was chipper and bold.

"Okay, Rowena. I just got your e-mail."

"Good. I'm glad you were able to talk so soon. I did a little research and found your e-mail address, thank goodness. Listen, I'll cut right to the chase. We listened to your interview on the Maurice Black show. We'd like to meet with you if possible."

"Regarding?" Milan started to pace the floor, taking barefoot steps along the beige Berber carpet.

"Well, my sister-in-law lives there and tells me you did a radio interview with Diva Sexton not long ago, so I've been keeping an eye on you. Last Friday, I attended a creative meeting with our senior executive and she agreed that we need to talk to you. We'd like to talk about you being involved in a new cable television show we're creating called *Erotic City*. Great title, don't you think?"

Milan stood still. She grinned as her heart beat faster. "It is, if I do say so myself."

"Well, I'll tell you, the name of your club is a great name for our series. It'll be a mix of *The L Word* meets the *Cat House* meets *Sex in the City*. But, it'll introduce the viewers to the fascinating world of swingers. I see it as a suburban phenomenon. I understand swinging is three million strong and counting. And I do think it's quite fascinating."

Milan still did not move from her spot. "Wow. I must say that I'm shocked. I just, well, maybe I never thought the world would be ready to be introduced to the swinger's lifestyle in a format that would spell viewership."

"Why do you say that?"

"I mean, as you can imagine, especially if you heard about the Diva Sexton interview, I've taken more than a little flack for my business, not to mention the push back I receive when I talk about my sexual beliefs. I just didn't think enough people would be supportive of alternative lifestyles."

"I don't think people would need to be supportive to watch. That's part of the mystique of the forbidden. People live through other people, especially when it's labeled as forbidden. And one thing is for sure, WET TV is far from your conservative, good old boy network. We're an alternative to the white-bread standard. We think this whole concept of women and sexuality needs to come out into the forefront. To me, it's kind of like the whole tabloid magazine thing. People are just curious by nature. Yet no one wants to admit that they peek. But they do. We all do."

Milan twirled the end of her hair around her finger, again and again, in deep thought. "Well, you know I agree with that."

"So, whatta ya say then? Perhaps we can make a date to discuss this in person."

Immediately, Milan responded. "I say I'd love to. I have a manager who I'd like to bring with me. I'm not sure how soon we can get to L.A. though."

"It turns out that I'll be in Atlanta on Wednesday. You know WET TV is owned by Wallace Entertainment there in Atlanta. I'm meeting with our attorneys and some marketing people there. You pick a time and we can meet at the Wallace offices downtown."

"Wednesday should be fine. I'll check with my manager, but I'm sure we can work out being there that morning."

"Wonderful. I'll e-mail you the exact location information, including where to park. I know that area can be a zoo. And once you talk to your manager you give me a time that works best for you both. How does that sound?"

"Sounds good, Rowena. And thanks so much."

"No, we thank you. I look forward to meeting you, Milan."

"I look forward to meeting you as well."

Milan finally pulled her feet away from the spot they'd been in, and she headed to the sofa and sat down. She grinned from ear to ear while she called Lavender as fast as she could.

33

"Hot Thing"

Wednesday, May 21, 2008
2:03 p.m.

Milan was in overly excited mode. She looked up the sky and thanked the Lord over and over, out loud. "Thank you, Dear Lord, for all things."

The ride home seemed to fly as she was on the phone the entire time. She hung up when she put her car in park and hopped from her Mercedes, entering the kitchen from the garage and tossing her purse and portfolio onto the table.

She kicked off her pumps and plopped down on the sofa in the den while dialing her sister.

"Tamiko, I just stepped in the house from my meeting with the folks at WET TV. I would have called you earlier but I was talking to Lavender the whole way home."

Tamiko's voice sounded animated. "I've been waiting to hear. How'd it go?"

"Rowena's really cool. And there were a couple of other execs there, too. And an attorney."

"Who went with you?"

"It was just me and my manager, who ran it down. I barely had to say a word."

"And so, what happened? Tell me."

"It's *Erotic City*, the series. And I'll have show creator and producer credits."

"Milan, you have got to be kidding me." Tamiko was keyed up.

"Not."

"On the WET TV Network?"

"Yes, ma'am."

"You guys already sealed the deal?"

"They made an offer and we took it, with just a couple of minor provisions. But it was a very good deal." Milan leaned back and crossed her legs.

"Oh my God. You're about to blow up, sis. That is crazy. Starting when?"

"We'll get the official green light next week and then sign contracts. But they said they'd start casting right away. She said they want to use all unknowns. They plan to have the show ready for the new fall season."

Tamiko asked, "Are you writing, too?"

"Only on the pilot episode. They have staff writers standing by."

"Oh my God. What did Lavender say?"

"He's in shock."

"Milan. Has it even hit you yet? And can you do all this? I mean come up with an episode idea for a show like that?"

"Just watch me. One thing I know about is swinging."

"Please tell me the owner of the club in your show will be a woman."

"Of course. They want her name to be Shelby Garnett. She'll be absolutely fabulous." Milan snapped her fingers and waved her hand in the air.

"That is hot. I'm so happy for you. My sister, the creator of a TV show. What about the club?"

"It won't take up that much time. Besides, Lavender's got that." Milan sprang to her feet and headed upstairs.

Tamiko caught her breath. "Dang. Everything you touch turns to gold."

"Not quite. But I do know one thing. You and me? We're going to celebrate. I need to go to the Dana Buchman sale at Nordstrom Rack at your favorite place, the Mall of Georgia. I need to change out of this monkey suit and I'll be there in twenty minutes. Be ready."

Milan and Tamiko stood in the Nordstrom store in the mall in Gwinnett County. Milan searched the rack, looking for dress pants, checking the bottom hem for the longest pair she could find. She asked as she flipped the tag over, "What size is this?"

Tamiko frowned. "That is so last year."

"Why?"

She pointed down. "Wide leg pants like that are out."

Milan took it from the rack and held it against her leg. "In is whatever fits. And this would fit me just perfectly. It's long enough."

Tamiko looked her sister up and down. "You can fit into anything."

"Not with all these," Milan said, squeezing her left breast.

"Better than having all this." Tamiko squeezed her left cheek. "This is why I don't buy off the rack. I can't wait to get my own line going."

"I've already told people about Cheekz. They think it's already in the stores." Milan replaced the pair and kept hunting.

"I wish. I talked to the sales rep at Macy's here in the mall and they just wanna see some samples, so I need to get with this seamstress next week. I finally talked to her."

"You've got the logo patented and the company all set up?"

"All done."

"And once you show them the samples and they place their huge order, then what?"

"Then I get them made in volume. I'll probably use this factory this guy I know hooked me up with whose bulk prices are pretty reasonable." Tamiko stepped to another rounder and Milan followed. "I'm keeping my product close by so I can have access to what's going on. Hey. Let's go to this sample store on the second level. I need to talk to the owner for a minute."

"Lead the way," said Milan. "I'm all for my baby sister doing her thing."

Always the fashion plate, Tamiko flung her suede purse over her shoulder. She was dressed in a white skirt and a brown-and-white-striped zip-up shirt. Her pointy heels were deep brown. Milan had on pumps with light blue jeans and a gold tank.

They walked stride for stride through the huge mall while Milan flipped through her BlackBerry and Tamiko kept one eye on the window view of every single store they passed.

"Well, hello."

Tamiko looked to her left and said, "Hi." She stopped.

Milan stopped.

"How are you?" a guy asked with a very deep voice.

Tamiko replied while taking a closer look at his face, "I'm good. And you?"

He took off his wide Oakley shades. "Good."

"You're . . ." Tamiko stared at the young man who stood before her.

Just as it hit her he said, "Kellen."

"Kellen, right?" She smiled upon remembering she'd named her dildo after him. "Hi. What are you doing here?"

"Very good. You remembered. I'm just looking around. Need to pick up a few things. And you? Looking at fabric again?"

"No, just headed to a sample store"

Milan cleared her throat.

"Oh, Kellen, this is my sister, Milan."

"Nice to meet you," Milan said, extending her hand.

"Kellen Battle. The pleasure is mine."

A moment passed and Tamiko said, "So, well, it was nice seeing you."

He asked, "Are you in a hurry?"

Milan spoke up. "No, she's not. I'm gonna pop in here for a second. I'll be right back." She stepped away into the Coach store.

Kellen tugged on the rim of his black Yankees cap. "I don't mean to hold you up. I just wanted to, well, ask you how's the land of the beautiful and taken?"

"Oh, I'm not on taken land anymore."

His expression brightened. "Oh really. I'm sorry to hear that."

"Oh no. It's fine, really. He just surprised me, that's

all. You never know what someone is capable of doing, I guess." Tamiko secured a few strands of stray hair behind her ear.

"That's true. How long were you together?"

"Over a year."

"Wow. I know he's thinking about what a mistake he made. At least I know I would be."

"Who knows? So what about you? What's up with your love life?"

"I was with someone for three years up until last summer. We were engaged and she decided she wanted to get some of her playing days out of her. She actually asked me to wait for her." He glanced down at his black-and-white Adidas.

"So you told her no, right?"

"I did." He looked up.

Tamiko gave a sweet glance. "No doubt she came back quick."

"She did. But, hey. If the play was still in her, I'm sure she didn't get rid of it in two weeks. I saw it as a sign. I date a little but not as much as most."

"Oh, so you just follow women into stores, huh?"

A couple of guys walked by and noticed the way Tamiko was drawn. Tamiko missed it, but Kellen caught it.

He grinned. "Actually, I wasn't following you into the store. I was going in there, too."

"Why?"

"I'm an assistant to Dirty South and a few other rappers when they tour. Basically, that means I run errands. And if that means picking up things for their wardrobe people, or whatever, that's what I do."

"Really? Sounds interesting."

"It can be. So, obviously you're into clothing and I wanna know more. I know your sister is about to come back out in a minute, but do you think we can continue this over the phone if you have time?"

"I'd like that."

"Can I have your phone? I'll put my number in."

"Sure." Tamiko handed it over.

He entered his digits and name. "Here you go. Give me a call and let's talk."

"I will. And by the way, I'm Tamiko."

"Tamiko." He kept focused on her face only. "Nice. But I was just gonna call you Beautiful."

"Thanks," Tamiko said as Milan approached.

"Fa sho. I'll talk to you later." He looked at Milan, who stood one foot back. "Nice to meet you, sister Milan," he said with a smile.

She nodded. "You, too."

He pointed to Tamiko's phone as he took a step. "Hey, now. Use that, okay?"

"I will." She slipped her phone into her purse and watched him walk away. He put his shades back on.

Milan said, "Wow. You didn't tell me about him."

"I know. I ran into him the other day. It was no big deal."

Milan asked as they walked on, "And? He tried to hit on you then?"

"He did. But Jarod hadn't tripped out yet."

Milan took another peek back at him. "Well, thank God he did. That boy is fine. A little slim thug." She turned back around. "Young but fine. Looks like a damn model."

"I think he said he's thirty-one."

"You'd better ask for his ID on the very first date."

"I'll have to do that. Long as he's not a player."

"Screw that. And ask him if he has a brother."

"Yeah right. You've got a man."

"I'm afraid it's a man with more drama that I can deal with."

Tamiko rolled her eyes. "Please. You're not going anywhere. And anyway, I'm not looking for a man. I'm just making a new friend."

"Yeah right, friend. You need to have him come on by and tighten you up right quick. Have him fry up your bacon." Milan looked at her sister from the waist down.

"Whatever."

"And I don't know how you handled Jarod anyway, unless you were just dick dumb. That boy was the size of a Pringles can."

"Milan." She blushed.

"Hell, I saw him. Or should I say I saw it. You know he could give that Mandingo porn star guy a run for his money. Damn, Tamiko. You were just whipped, that's all."

"I was not. Besides, Mandingo or not, sex isn't everything. Jarod was my friend."

"Friend, huh? They say never trust a big dick and a smile."

"Anyway. Next subject."

At that moment, Tamiko received a text message. She grabbed her phone.

I miss r movie dates.

She silently deleted the message and kept walking.

Milan said, "You know what they say? A man will change his woman before he changes his ways. Just don't teach him that he can pull that crap and come back. Then he'll never stop."

"I know that. I'm not that naive."

"You know what, innocent one? What you need to do is bring yourself on down to the club and see what it's like. You missed my opening two years ago and promised to come and never did. Don't think I'm gonna let that continue to slide. Why do you avoid it like the fuckin plague?"

Tamiko's eyes drifted to the window display of Talbots. "Cause it is. And watch your mouth."

"You need to stop acting like such a damn prude and let that freak side come on out, Miss Goody Two-shoes." Milan answered her phone. "Hey, Lavender. Thanks. Love you, too. Bye." She hung up.

"Yeah. You're not going anywhere," Tamiko commented.

"Where I'm going, there might not be room for Lavender Lewis *and* batty-ass Ramada Hart."

34

"Get Off"

❧

Friday, May 23, 2008
11:07 p.m.

A couple of days later, Milan and Lavender were at work.

Milan walked around for a minute, greeting people and making small talk, and then she headed back up to her office to check out information on business laws in Miami, also researching possible locations, like the old site of the Triad hotel. Now that she had the money from the cable television show, she wanted to expand Erotic City as soon as possible. She also looked for data on possible future locations in Las Vegas, searching for spots that were thirty-five-thousand square feet or more, less than a half mile from the Luxor.

She surfed the Internet and made notes for a while and then opened her script software program and started the intro to her *Erotic City* episode.

They say swinging is like watching a soap opera. So many people do it but few will admit to it. I say it's established couples consenting to their partner's having sexual

*encounters with others, ranging from flirting, kissing, full
sex, or orgies.*

And speaking of orgies, Lavender had already glanced
into Milan's office, seeing her hard at work, when he
headed to the VIP room, and then to the orgy room.

He spoke to the guy who handled the lockers and
opened the door to peek inside at the large volume of
willing people. A man stepped in behind Lavender and
just stood there, looking at the many occupants. He had
a major hard-on and stared like he had no idea where to
start. The man's shapely woman walked up behind him
and took him by the hand. They stepped toward a mattress within a few feet from the pile of bending bodies
twisted up like pretzels and were all eyes.

Headlocks and corkscrews and interlocked jigsaw
puzzles and banana splits and sidewinders, and folks
speaking in tongues. The group intercourse was a sight
for sore, horny eyes.

Lavender grinned, closed the door, and left. But the
erotic party still went on like clockwork.

The orgy room members were fucking without feelings.

Strange hands against unfamiliar bodies.

The sign on the door said No Jealousy Allowed.

The song "The Freaks Come Out at Night" was
playing over the speakers.

The sweet scent of group sex was thick.

It smelled like a threesome.

Or a foursome.

Or a moresome.

With some who were bi, tri, or quad.

Big, beautiful titties jiggling in circular motions to
the sound of wall-to-wall, sweaty, flopping flesh.

Big, beautiful dicks were slinging deep and then shallow and then deep again, being milked to the liquid sounds of creamy feminine secretions.

Some were your everyday, friendly, neighborhood Joe and Jane Average.

Your bankers.

Your bus drivers.

Your day care workers.

Your coworkers.

Half were single.

Half were married.

But all were down.

For whatever it took to get them off.

It was an appropriate mix of about six couples, as well as two single vanilla women and one single chocolate man, sprawled out on wall-to-wall mattresses. Against one wall there were purple velvet drapes and another wall was all mirrors . . . mirrors of darkened glass for the Peeping Toms. Clothes were left at the door in assigned lockers.

The fifteen swinging members were engaged in a game of passionate and playful fucking, all huddled together, screaming with excitement, humping vigorously, getting off wildly. All of the uninhibited clutching and digging was accompanied by roaring screams that signaled the height of their frenzied spasms.

Two women formed a pink taco stand, pressing their pussies together, grinding against each other's opening. They had the exact same equipment. One of them moved from the grind to offer a pound of tongue to her temporary, same-sex mate, even eating her out from be-hind.

One sandy-haired woman was a biggun everyone was sho-nuff diggin. Her ass was the color of hot buttered rum. She looked butch but one would suppose she was a dick hound, as she appeared to be about ready to collapse into unconsciousness with a long, stiff one up in her.

One of the accountant-looking husbands had her bent over the mattress to fuck her in the ass in front of his wife. Her right hip read Georgia Peach. And his gloved joystick was deep into her anal cavity.

She looked back at him with her smoky topaz eyes and said, "Yeah. Fuck that ass."

The tight grip upon his dick signaled that he had reached his entry limit. His cave dwelling fetish was on high.

He tried his best to break her back, pumping in and out in the exact measure of her hysterical wails. His blonde wife was wide-eyed while in the middle of a missionary fuck by a long and slender, blue black dick, as one of the single, macadamia-colored women sucked her right nipple like she was lactating. The wife looked over at her husband while he wore out the big girl's ass, much like he'd worn out his own wife's pussy. The wife spanked her own clit and closed her eyes at the onslaught of cumming, ripping a squeal. She hit a high note like Mariah that showed itself between her legs, coating her strong lover's cock as it oozed from her extrahairy vagina.

Her husband took in an eyeful of her never-before-seen excitement and held on to the got-much-back, wonder-woman ass that was bent over before him. He continued to pound and his excited dick trembled. He shot a nut that was more intense than any nut he'd felt in all of his forty-something years. He looked like someone squeezed the wetness from him like a dishrag. The condom was full.

There was an older black couple on a nearby mattress. She wore extralong French braids. He had a head full of hair, a little more salt than pepper. They laid a few white towels under the woman's healthy butt while her boyfriend inserted a lime green Popsicle inside of her. As he pulled it out, she sighed repeatedly. The frozen treat came out much smaller than it went in, and the green juices traced a path down the crack of her ass. He again inserted it in and out until finally, there was nothing left. Her heated cave had melted it down to liquid that coated her sweet lips, and onto the towel beneath her.

He sucked what was left on the wooden stick and then tossed it. His face found her split and he cleaned her up, licking her juices and placing pussy kisses against her skin. Within one minute, he sat up and inserted his dick inside of her to feel what was left of the cold juices that had permeated her insides.

He pressed her legs back. "Fuck. That's so nice."

She said as though drunk, "Oh, baby, you have no idea." She looked to her left side. "I want him to fuck me, too," she said as her long braids flung over her face. One of the brunet husbands stood over his wife who was sucking a long one while he masturbated. After hearing the black woman's request, he looked over at her and stepped toward the couple. Her boyfriend pulled out and his eyes said *go right ahead*. The husband slipped on a Trojan and stepped up to her, inserting himself while her boyfriend went around toward her face to masturbate.

The man's Indian-looking wife saw him getting a taste

of another woman's pussy, and she backed away from the dick she'd hardened on contact, turning around on all fours to watch her husband, while the man stuck himself in her hole. She received him deep. She was aroused. He was aroused.

She growled like she had a tiger in her tank. "Get that pussy, baby. Fuck her good." She flung her long, dark brown hair to and fro.

Her husband looked back and said, "You know I will. You know how I do it." His dick was white but he spoke with soul. It wouldn't be long before he shot his load.

The black woman began a rhythmic holler as she turned to watch her boyfriend yank himself. She gripped the sheets and took the long ride to fuck-dom cum. She fucked the man like he was a G-spot dildo. Arousal engulfed her. Her boyfriend continued self-pleasing as the white dick dove into the course-haired brown muff of his woman of ten years. She pressed her curved, Bordeaux nails into the stranger's defined back and licked her abundant lips that matched her nails as she rode through her loud, tornadic cum.

Her erotic sex sounds of cunt choking cock were animalistic. They were barbaric. They were cavernous. And they were turning everyone in the room the fuck on. It was orgyville. The residents were living the fuckin "life."

35

"Let's Go Crazy"

❧

Saturday, May 24, 2008
9:31 a.m.

The next morning, Lavender took a moment to return a few calls from home. As was usually the case, he rarely answered his cell when he was at the club.

He made a call that he dreaded. His words were bland. "What, Ramada? Why do I have seventeen calls from you in a row? Is something wrong with Taj?" He was willing to bet Taj was fine.

She spoke loud and fast. "Do I always have to continue to wait until the morning hours of the following day for you to call me back when I leave messages? My God. When I woke up this morning, I was about to call that house I know you're probably at right now. Seems that's the only way I get your damn attention."

He frowned. "Milan changed her number a while ago since you just couldn't seem to show some damn respect. What's the big emergency?"

She popped her tongue. "Yeah, well, whatever. I need you to watch Taj today."

"What's up?"

"I have an appointment. A job interview. Like I said in the message, it's really important."

"A job interview on a Saturday?"

"Yeah. And? You got a problem with that?"

Lavender wanted to tell her what he really had a problem with was the fact that he even met her in the first place, but that would have meant no Taj. Instead he asked, "What time and for how long?"

"I can drop him off at your house at noon. My meeting is at one-thirty."

"So you're saying watch him for a couple of hours?" he asked, thinking to himself that would not be enough time to spend with his son. He didn't want to feel like a babysitter.

"I guess so. Unless it takes longer. Dang, you're usually beggin for more time with him." She acted like she knew him well. But she was wrong. "Now it seems like I have to convince you to see your son. Feels like I'm sellin something to you, like I'm peddlin Avon products, damn."

"I'll come and get him at noon and drop him off at eight."

"Well, excuse me."

He hung up without replying to her usual sarcasm.

That afternoon at Lavender's house, Milan walked into Taj's room just two minutes after Lavender left to get them something to eat from Checkers. "Hey, Taj. What's been up with you?"

"Not much." He stood from sitting upon his bed and

walked quickly to hug Milan. He held a Nintendo DS in hand.

She bent down and hugged him tightly. "Boy, you're gonna be taller than your dad soon, that's for sure."

He spoke as he backed away and headed back to his bed. "I hope so. I eat a lot. I'm trying to play football. But, I can't play sports. My mom doesn't want me to get hurt."

Milan leaned against the doorway. "Do you think you'll get hurt?"

"No. I'll knock 'em down."

Milan laughed at the way he used his right hand to demonstrate his strength. "I'll bet you would."

"Is Dad bringing me a lemonade?"

"I don't know. I'll call him and see, okay? I'll be right back."

"Okay. Thanks, Milan." Taj sat on his bed and turned to insert his iPod earpiece, bouncing his head to the beat.

Milan stepped away from his room and into the kitchen. She took her phone from her purse on the counter and prepared to dial, when she heard a knock at the door. And then the doorbell sounded. Over and over. And the knocking got louder.

She headed through the family room and into the foyer to the front door.

"Who is it?" she asked. But her view through the peephole answered her question. She gave a sigh and twisted her lips.

"It's Ramada." Ramada's voice was strong.

Milan turned the doorknob and opened the Blackwood door halfway. She kept her hand on the knob. "What are you doing here?"

"Hey, Erotica. I saw your car, dumb ass. Your man doesn't make room for you in his garage? Bad sign. The real question is what are you doing here? This was supposed to be Taj and his dad spending time together. Where is DeMarcus anyway?" Ramada peeked behind Milan's back.

Milan stepped out onto the brick, portico porch and pulled the door to. She stood barefoot in a light blue JLo sweat suit with her blood boiling. "Lavender's not here right now." She talked herself into keeping her words civil. She noticed Ramada's black car parked in the circular driveway behind Milan's Benz.

Ramada took in the close-up look of every inch of Milan, from the top of her long hair, all the way down to the tips of her French-manicured toes. "So, are you telling me you're here alone with my son?"

Milan fought to keep her voice down. "I'll ask you again, what are you doing here?"

"I'm here to get my son. Just like I said. Damn, you're a dumb ass." Ramada shifted her weight while her hand joined her hip. Her dark blue jeans and short black leather jacket were both fitting tight.

Milan shook her head and crossed her arms. "No you're not."

"I am."

"Taj is here until eight o'clock."

"Taj leaves when I say he leaves."

"That's not what Lavender told me."

Ramada took one step toward her car. "Screw you." She waved her hand at Milan. "I'm gonna call De-Marcus. Leaving my son here alone with you. Where's my damn cell?"

"Why do you throw stones, Ramada?"

Ramada stopped in her tracks.

Milan continued, "Because those are the same stones that could be thrown at your crazy ass?"

Ramada stepped back. "You run the damn whore-house, not me."

Milan positioned her cell and began to dial. "Considering you were one of my members, what does that make you?" She held the phone to her ear. "You need to be locked up."

Ramada used her eyes to point to Milan. Her voice went up a notch. "You're the straight-up freak. Everybody knows that. He must have you dick-drugged. And I'll have you know that I keep my personal sex life separate from my son. You do not. You live off of the sleazy, dirty-ass money you make. I make an honest living. You are feeding my son food that you bought with fuck money." Ramada watched Milan's every movement.

"Oh really?" Milan spoke into the phone but kept sight of Ramada. "Lavender, your son's insane mother is here. We're standing on the porch."

Ramada said, "I'll call him myself." She looked back toward her car.

"No, here." Milan pressed a button. "He's on speaker. Talk to him."

Lavender's tense voice sounded into the air. "Ramada, what are you doing there?"

Ramada twitched her nose toward the phone. "The question is, what's your problem, leaving my son with her?"

"Taj is at my house until eight. What I do in my home is none of your business."

Ramada's hand again made its way to her waist. She leaned forward. "Who you have around my son is my business. I was his full-time parent while you ran around living your playboy lifestyle. All I'm asking you now is to watch what you do around him. Otherwise, both of you will pay."

Milan looked back toward the door and pulled on it, making sure it was closed.

Lavender said, "You need to leave. I'm not about to have Taj think I'm the reason he can't stay until eight like I promised. And you can call whomever you want and do whatever you want. But he is staying. Milan, go in the house."

"You're gonna be sorry for this, DeMarcus."

"Leave."

Ramada asked with a look of tattletale in her eyes, "Did you ever tell her about us fucking Dee?" She asked him but stared at Milan.

Milan jumped on her question. "Yeah, he did. Anything else?"

Lavender said, almost in slow motion. "Good-bye, Ramada."

"DeMarcus, a year ago it was only an argument. But you had to run off with her and cause all this interference." She gave Milan a sneer. "And as for you, I'm checking my son for bruises when he gets home. Witcha fake ass, weave-wearing self." Ramada sliced her eyes at Milan's head.

Milan was stone-faced, but fingered the sides of her hair. "This is not a weave, dummy. Besides, where'd you get your damn name? Were you conceived in a hotel room?"

"Better than the seedy motel your mama turned tricks in. Bitch."

"You need to get your delinquent self the hell out of my damn face. "

Ramada pumped her body toward Milan. "Make me. I will fuck you up. You don't know me."

Milan's jaw was tight. Extratight. Her neck rolled around in circles. "You need to go to hell, that's what you need to do. All you do is fuck with us. You lost Lavender by screwing around when you knew the rules. So live with it. Stop being so damn jealous."

Ramada yelled, waving her hands in front of her, poking her finger in the air like she would poke a chest. Her eyes scanned the length of Milan's body. "You skinny-ass ho. I'm far from jealous. I used to let that man fuck other women right in front of me. I just refuse to have you around my child. Let me tell you, you don't want to fuck with me. I ain't no punk bitch. You'll see. I promise you. You will see and you'll be eating your words." She flung her long hair that was as red as her face and stormed away.

Milan said extra low, "Oh hell no. That bitch is crazy." She took the phone off speaker and opened the door, heading back into the house. She pressed the door closed with force and locked it. All she heard was Ramada starting up her car, burning rubber as she backed out and pulled down the street. Then Ramada laid on her horn as she turned the corner.

Milan spoke to Lavender as she entered his den and sat on the leather couch. She made a point to lower her voice even more. "Lavender, I'm telling you. I've had about all I can take. One day, she is going to go too far."

"I'm sorry about that. I'm right around the corner. Milan, listen. What I didn't tell you in front of Ramada is that I got a call from my attorney today. The one who's preparing to represent me on the child support petition? He called me, as well as Attorney Hyatt, and we had a quick conference call."

"And?"

"He said that he got a call from a man named Ray. It turns out he's the one who was with Ramada the night she came into the club starting all this mess. Ray told him it looks like Ramada has a female friend she just can't seem to shake, who I think is the one we saw in court with her. Anyways Ray got tired of hanging around so he threatened to leave her and take the Maxima I guess he bought her. They had an argument and that's when Ramada threw some things up in his face. One of them was that he didn't support her when she tried to set up the club. So after she hung up on him, he e-mailed her, and in her reply, which the attorney forwarded to me, not only does she threaten to blow up his Porsche, and her Maxima, she also admits to planning the entire thing, that she used him, and that there was no knife, no force, and no sexual assault. Therefore, there can be no civil charges."

Milan's mouth stayed open in relief, though she also had a look of exhaustion as she rubbed the creases on her forehead. She closed her mouth and stood up, passed by Taj's room and peeked inside to see that he was still listening to his music. She headed back to sit on the sofa, all without saying a word.

"Hello. Are you there? Hello."

"What the hell does she mean, fucked Dee?"

36

"She's Strange"

❧

Tuesday, May 27, 2008
6:27 p.m.

Lavender headed to Milan's home after he'd picked up Chinese food from Panda Express. Mandarin chicken, beef and broccoli, and chow mein were her favorites.

He noticed Milan's reserve as she greeted him at the door from the garage to the kitchen. It had been that way for a few days.

Her hug was weak. Looking down, she stepped away and silently searched the cupboard. She grabbed two plates and sat at the dining room table. He sat beside her and began to remove the food from the plastic bag.

Milan wore a frown to match the tone. "I know we got some good news because of that e-mail from that guy Ray, and the case will be done soon, but Lavender, I'm sorry. I don't think you're doing enough to keep Ramada in line and it's affecting my life. I just can't have this anymore."

Lavender opened each of the containers by touch while he looked at her. "What? The restraining order I had you sign has been filed. She won't be able to call you or come near you, or come to my home for that matter. And the visitation agreement will be modified to only pick up Taj at school."

"It's not just that. I think you almost enable her."

"So, you're saying it's my fault she's like she is?"

"I'm saying I feel like I have no choice but to put my foot down. I have to get her out of my life."

"So, you're willing to just walk away from me instead of support me?"

Milan grabbed two of the boxes and scooped the chow mein and the chicken onto her plate. "Lavender, you're a man. I'd like you to be able to protect me from that woman. But obviously, you can't. Maybe I need to just protect myself. My business life has been rough and I need my private life to be a safe place. That woman brings you drama all the time. How've you been able to deal with her all these years?" Looking puzzled, she twirled her plastic fork through her food.

"It's been because of my son. I made the choice to break up with her. But she is the mother of my son."

"Just like you have a choice, I have one, too. I'm telling you I'm about ready to end this, Lavender, as much as I love you. I just can't take it anymore. I can't allow her into my world any longer."

Lavender kept his hand on one of the cartons. "You accept me and my son and all that goes along with me being his father, but you're letting his mother break us up?"

Milan stared through him. Her tone was extratense. "No, you're doing that. You won't protect me from what goes along with her being a psycho-ass baby mama. I need peace in my life. I have a whole lot going on. But I'll always wonder what in the hell Ramada will do next.

What stunt will she pull today? How far will she go? And what bomb will she drop next, like her question about telling me who you two fucked."

Lavender released his breath. "I know that was messed up. And I know I should have told you that by now. That was way before you. But, do you really think it's gonna change your life for the better when you're without the man you say you love? You'd sacrifice that all in the name of your career?"

"It's about my sanity." She took a small bite.

Lavender sat back in his chair. "If we were married, would you just toss me aside like this? My son is a part of me. You can't just accept my half and not his. That, to me, sounds like conditional love."

"I care about him a lot. But, you have to figure out a way to limit her drama in your life. For you, and for your son, and for whoever gets close to you."

His eyes showed confusion. "So you're just gonna give her what she wants?"

"I don't know." Milan put her fork down.

"What about what I want? I'm ready to go to the limit with you. I haven't been willing to go all the way with any woman ever in my life. I made a choice to shake the mentality I lived with when I was in the ring, and the things I had to do to numb my senses when I felt like killing myself after I was told I couldn't fight." He spoke with dipped brows. He pressed his fist to his thigh. "I fucked my way out of depression, screwing around on Ramada all the time, and then slept with her and other people together, just so I could get my fill of the rush it brought. With you, I'm satisfied. I'm willing to do better. But I can't just erase Ramada from our lives. I hoped I'd be worth the fight."

Milan looked down as though he wasn't playing fair. "Lavender."

He pounded his fist again. "So I guess I'm not. Look at me."

She stood up and pushed in the dining room chair. "I just need to be alone right now." She stepped away from him.

"Milan. What about us?" he asked, springing to a stance and waving his hands.

"We'll see. I love you, Lavender." She stood by the kitchen door and reached back to hold it open for his exit.

He stepped right up to her. "Well, if you get out of this relationship, you'll prove to me that you really don't love me. You'll prove that you only love yourself. You can't be truly happy alone, only being successful at business, with no one to share your life with."

"Sounds like the movie *Mahogany*." She had a smirk on her face.

He shot his eyes away. "I'll talk to you later. And I am the one who loves you."

Lavender stepped out of the door and she closed it behind him. She locked it and headed straight to the table. She sat back down and finished her meal. Alone.

Five minutes later, as Milan sat in deep thought after her last bite, a text message chimed in. She reached across the table and yanked her purse closer, pulling out her phone and pressing a button.

I'm a fighter. I'm not going anywhere. U need 2 listen 2 the words 2 the song "All This Love."

Milan placed her phone on the table, stood, picked up the plates, and headed to the kitchen sink, all the while bouncing the familiar words around in her head:

I had some problems | And no one could seem to solve them | But you found the answer | You told me to take this chance.

She also said to herself, *Who the hell does he think is gonna put up with his dangerous, sick-ass son's mom? As it is, he should be happy I didn't trip about Dee. Bringing her up in bed when he'd already fucked her.*

She headed straight to her office and let off some steam by getting in some much-needed writing.

37

"Delirious"

❧

Thursday, May 29, 2008
8:40 p.m.

The front door was unlocked just for him as it had been the previous times he'd arrived, though another five minutes and it would have been locked and bolted and chained.

Nancy heard Jarod make his way to the back of her small apartment. He stepped inside of her room, humming a mellow tune, before he asked, "What's your problem? Why'd you hang up on me?"

Nancy said nothing as she sat up in bed.

He'd just returned from Marietta after going to his regular spot to get his head shaved.

Her bedroom was dark and so were her eyes.

Jarod flicked on the light. "And what are you doing in bed so early?"

Her voice was unfriendly. "First of all, I don't have a problem. Why don't you ask yourself the same question?"

"You mean to tell me you're mad because I'm ten minutes late? I said eight-thirty."

She licked her lips and stayed fixed on the TV screen. "I told you nothing's wrong."

"It doesn't take a degree to see that you're pissed off, Nancy." He placed his keys on her wicker dresser. "I know you."

"You know me?" She moved her eyes his way. "Just how well do you know me, really?"

"Well enough."

"Yeah right." She jabbed her vision back toward the TV. "If you knew me, you'd have known to apologize by now for spending all that time on the phone with Tamiko while you were driving here, and then when I called, you casually told me you're still talking to her but you're on your way."

He frowned. "Damn, woman. Who came and stole your cool?"

"You did. Just don't take my kindness for weakness. Don't let the myth of the naive white woman fool you. I was married to the king liar of all black men. Remember?"

"Please. One thing I do know is that you ain't hardly weak."

"Oh, I don't think you really know."

He sat on the corner of the bed. "Wow. This is amazing."

She looked his way. "Wow what?" She frowned. "And why are you talking to Tamiko now anyway? You told me that shit was over. You told me you two hadn't even communicated. What could you guys possibly need to talk about now?"

"She's pregnant."

She angled her head. "What?"

"I'm just kidding." He gave one hard chuckle.

"That is not funny, Jarod. I'm serious."

"Damn. I can see that. We talked about me. I left her a message and she called me back. We just talked. Talked about a lot of things. We even talked about you."

"Oh Lord, please, don't talk to her about me. My business with you is none of Tamiko's business."

"But it is."

"Jarod, you made that none of her business when you came to me the day after you got fired, got in my bed, and asked me to be with you."

"Just because Tamiko and I aren't together doesn't mean I don't still care about her."

"Yeah right." She reached back and fidgeted with her hair. "She'd be a fool to believe you give a damn about her. Showing someone you give a damn is not about what you say, it's about what you do. You left her and ran to me and then you didn't call. She'd be hard up to even give you the time of day. I know her. She's a big girl. She doesn't need me or you worrying about her."

He faced her. "And since when did you stop giving a damn about her? You're her father's ex-wife. You're her stepmother. You lived with her for years, and from what I know, you and she were closer than you were with Milan. How easy has it been for you to just shut her out of your life now?"

Nancy poked her head toward him. "Ask yourself that. You shut her out, too. But hell, excuse me. I guess it wasn't too easy, you seem to be running back to her now. Milan and Tamiko shut me out of their lives, not the other way around. The last time I talked to Tamiko she was cruel.

What do you suggest I do, invite her over for dinner? I'd be a fool to let her into my life. She never liked me even when I was trying to get along with her. And especially now that you and I became . . . hell, what are we anyway? Fuck buddies. I guess that's obviously all it is."

"Bottom line is, Tamiko didn't do anything to either one of us. We hurt her." He focused down at his Jordans.

"Okay, so we hurt her. So please tell me why in the hell she even talks to you at all."

"We loved each other." He cut his eyes back to her. "Did you ever love her? Hell, did you ever really love anybody?"

Her voice grew. "Fuck you, Jarod. Of course I did. But it's obvious when you say you *were* in love with her, what you really mean is that you're still in love with her."

"Yeah. But see, I know I don't deserve her. Not only because I got with you. But I don't deserve her because I didn't even leave a message to say that I'm sorry. That's what bothers her."

She clicked her tongue. "Oh please. So now you feel sorry for her? Tamiko is not the saint you think she is. She's more like her sister than you know. I've known her a lot longer than you."

"Since you've known them so long, do me a favor and fuck their estate and the money."

She looked like a lightbulb had gone off. "Oh, now I see. Did she ask you to talk to me? She's going to use this to her advantage. That's some damn nerve." She managed a brief, sarcastic laugh.

"No she didn't. But my opinion is, they deserve what their father left them."

She put her hand over her heart. "Have you even stopped to think about what I might deserve, Jarod? Oh yeah, that's right. You don't know me well enough to give a damn. But see, you made a smart-ass comment about who I could have ever loved. I was with their father for sixteen years and loved him more than I loved myself. I put up with what he said was a failing marriage to his first wife, and I dealt with his daughters, who rejected me from day one. People called me a home wrecker and I was even blamed for him dying, like I gave him a heart attack. That man lived fast until the end. He had a chick on the side in every city and put me through hell because he thought I had one affair. And here I am left with nothing as if I never even existed. Mark my word, those girls are going to look for men who are just like their fathers. Come to think of it, Tamiko probably would take you back in a heartbeat. Men who fuck around is all she knows."

"And whose fault is that?"

"It's Charlie Kennedy's fault. It his fault they learned men are dogs and men cheat. And it's his fault he left me with nothing. I loved him. And contrary to popular belief, he loved me." Her eyes were clouded with tears.

"So why go after his daughters? You're punishing them. What'd they ever do to you? If it was your father, you'd do the same thing."

"They just happen to be in the middle."

"In the middle of you and a dead man."

"Jarod, stay out of this," she said with warning.

"Stay out of it? Okay. Since it's none of my business,

maybe this is. Are you with me to get back at them? Did you come into Erotic City looking to fuck right up in the very place that Milan owns just to screw with her? Or did you go up there snooping, trying to find a way to shut her club down?"

"Where the hell did that come from? Tamiko must have put that junk in your head. You're the one who got caught hiding in the corner choking your overgrown chicken. Maybe you're with me to get back at Milan for firing you. Is that why you ran to me?"

"I take full responsibility for my dumb-ass stunt. It was stupid. I got caught up."

"Yes you did."

He abruptly stood. "Nancy, you know, it's obvious this won't work after all."

"Why? Because I'm suing them? That was way before you. But all of a sudden you're being their little advocate to make sure I never file the claim. I want what's coming to me."

He grabbed his keys. "I think you'll get something coming to you but it won't be money. What would it take for you to feel like you have enough? You got your divorce settlement."

"Yes, I did and what do I have to show for it? I'm driving a ten-year-old, raggedy car and renting a tiny apartment that I'm almost three months behind on. What do I have to show for a life of loving that man, one of the most well-known musical legends in the world? It's like it was all a dream. I at least deserved a house to live in. But all I got was escorted out of my own home by Milan. I want half of his earnings from the time I met him till the day of our divorce. I wanted that before you and I still want it now."

"Let me tell you something." He stood near the bedroom door.

"Don't tell me. You're willing to end this all because I want my money."

"Good luck." He turned toward the door.

"You know what?" she shouted.

He turned back. "What, Nancy?"

Her eyes were tight. A tear traced a path from her eye, right into her mouth. "You're as big a dummy as your big-ass dick. That's all you've got going for you anyway."

"Oh Lord. Like I said, good luck." He headed out of the room and down the hall.

She jumped up and yelled at his back. "Fuck you, Jarod. You don't know a good thing when you see it. You had to ruin it and stick your nose in where it doesn't belong."

He said while walking, "You need to stop being so greedy and get happy. Maybe you can start by getting a job."

"I'm not the one who got fired, baby boy!"

"Good-bye." He opened the front door.

Her hands flailed about. "Go ahead and run back to Tamiko. She'll laugh in your damn face."

He laughed out loud as he walked out the door. "On second thought, go get you a full-time woman."

"Asshole," she said, grabbing hold of the closest thing she saw. She hurled her cordless phone toward his departure just as he slammed the door. It burst into pieces along the entryway linoleum.

She held her head down and cradled her face into her hands, crying like a baby and yelling at the top of her lungs. "Damnit, Charlie Kennedy. It's all your damn fault. Now what? Now what am I going to do? I need that money. The money you fucking promised me. You lying bastard. What the hell am I gonna do?"

38

"Can U Believe"

❧

Friday, May 30, 2008
6:00 p.m.

Man, you know I was in the fast lane from the time I was born." Lavender ran it down to his coworker, Brian, sitting at the oval bar area of the dark, upscale, Sambuca jazz cafe in Buckhead. The sexy sounds of a tenor sax swirled in the air. A live jazz band played along the small, raised stage, and a slew of singles mingled about. It was the height of the happy hour rush crowd.

Lavender continued, "I'm a lot like Milan. The world I was in caused me to travel more by the time I was five years old than most people do by the time they're thirty. And Dad raised me till around the time I was in high school and then he died from liver disease. So his mom and dad were all I had." He sat upon the cherry leather–padded barstool with his forearms resting on the bar with a glass of Crown Royal before him.

"I can't imagine what that was like. I know it's tough, man. So who showed you the ropes as far as boxing?" Brian nursed a cold bottle of Miller Genuine Draft.

"My dad was trained by his dad, who trained me, too. My grandfather became my role model and my trainer. My everything. As soon as I graduated from high school, I was in the ring being sought after like crazy. I was being wined and dined like I fucking mattered. It was like I was a rock star or something. Hell, they all went away when I got hurt."

"Sounds like you've always had all the women you've wanted, twenty-four-seven."

"Man, I had women thrown at me. I screwed anything in a skirt, whether they were virgins or going through menopause. Money was thrown at me. Drugs were thrown at me. I fooled around on every woman I promised to be faithful to, especially Ramada. I saw our mutual interest in swinging as my license to fool around. Fooling around kept me feeling something. Who knows what the hell I was looking for, but I felt lucky just to have found a woman who understood me wanting variety. We shared women and she let me fuck them right in her face. She loved that shit. And I loved it, too, hell, until I saw that guy last year. I know it was a double standard. But I just couldn't deal with it."

"And Milan's not having that, huh?"

"Hell no. Meeting Milan's been one of the best things that ever happened to me. I had so many fucked-up days before meeting her. The only thing that got me out of bed was going to work and the first thing I wanted to do when I got off work was sleep or fuck or drink. Milan was the only woman I've felt has really loved me as a man, not a boxer. She accepted the fact that I was running security at a damn retail store. And she accepted and trusted me enough to go into business together with the little bit I had to invest in the club. We like the same things. The sex is great. We seem to come from the same worlds. We both lost our parents and came from the fast lane. She's open-minded, but she's not sharing me any more than I could share her. But, man, what we have is unraveling right before my eyes." Lavender took a long sip of his drink.

"So what now? What do you want to do?"

Lavender set down the crystal glass. "I've wanted to settle down. I've wanted one woman who would trust me and who I could trust. I come from a long line of Lewis men who've had sons. I want to have children with a woman who I'm married to. I wanted to marry Milan."

Brian sat back a bit. "Wanted? Then do that. Man, you've gotta go for what matters to you. If Milan is enough for you, fuck what the world thinks."

"Funny. Milan has told me that so many times, fuck what the world thinks. She's got that shit down pat. But she can't deal with Ramada being Ramada."

"Dude, you need to go ahead and step up and settle down if that's what you want. Make it work." Brian sucked on his beer bottle again.

Lavender shook his head. "Not if she's gonna run out on me when times get tough like this. Besides, I'm just not sure that I can. Truth is, I just don't know if I have it in me to be a one-woman man." He glanced down at his half-empty glass. His eyes traveled across the bar to the angelic face of a woman who looked his way. Just before she could give a full smile, he looked back down at his drink. He brought the glass to his lips and swallowed what he always called liquid courage. He hoped it could bring him enough courage to keep his eyes off of the woman staring him down.

Brian looked around from left to right, noticing how crowded the place was. They sat silent. He asked, "Then what's holding you back?"

"Milan will not deal with Ramada's psycho bullshit anymore."

"Sounds like Ramada will never change." Brian leaned forward.

"Man, she wanted a baby so bad years ago that if I would've spit in her she would've gotten pregnant. She was a damn fertile Myrtle. You know, she was so pissed after we broke up that she had a yard sale and sold the shit I'd left at her house, including some of the crap that I bought her.

"That's a straight-up *Waiting to Exhale* move."

"She even checked my e-mail for a month after we broke up and kept e-mailing Milan, telling her shit. She was the password-cracking queen. One night, she cussed me out and tried to choke me and when I tried to leave her house, she lay in the driveway behind my car so I couldn't back out. Other than not seeing Taj at all, I'm gonna have to deal with her for the rest of my life. Lord knows if I had my way, Taj would be with me all the time."

"Is she the one who pulled the dine-and-dash over at Copeland's last year?"

"That's her."

"You need to try and get permanent custody."

"Don't think I haven't thought about it."

"If you don't mind me asking, how much are you paying her for child support? It's gotta be steep. You were getting paid well."

"Three grand a month."

Brian's eyebrows lifted. "Damn, that's like a full salary. For one child?"

"Shoot, that's nothing to her. I ain't saying she's a gold digger, but . . . hell, she is." Lavender gave a weak laugh. "Whoever gets with her better be big in the pockets, open-minded, and ready for some drama."

"Probably would've been cheaper and less drama just to keep her. You ever think about going back there?"

"I'd rather die. You don't sleep with the woman who set out to destroy you."

The bartender set down another bottle and took away the other one. "Thanks," Brian said.

Lavender raised his glass to Brian and guzzled the remaining amber liquid. He felt a tap on his right shoulder. He turned back and so did Brian.

"Excuse me, but I was just watching you from across the bar, and, well, I know this sounds corny but don't I know you?" a tall, smiling woman asked Lavender. Another woman stood behind her.

"Do you?"

"You look so familiar."

"Really?"

Her brown eyes said she was trying to think back. "Yes. Are you from Atlanta?"

"No. I'm from Miami."

"I see. No, I've never been to Miami. Anyway, hello, my name is Angel. And this is my friend Sharon." She pointed toward her back.

Her friend stepped forward a bit.

Right away, Lavender's eyes disobeyed him and looked at her chest, leaping from tittie to tittie. "Hello. I'm Lavender." He pointed to his buddy. "This is Brian."

Brian nodded to them both. "Hello."

"Hi," the ladies said together.

"Lavender?" Angel's friend Sharon said as though a lightbulb flashed. "Lavender Lewis, the boxer?"

Lavender said, "Yeah."

Angel asked, "Boxer?" at the same time she perused his bicep where his boxing glove tattoo resided.

Lavender made sure to say, "It was a while ago."

"Oh, Angel, it wasn't that long ago. He was a heavyweight champion. Remember?"

Angel seemed to be thinking hard. "No, I don't."

"Surely you do." Sharon's eyes were big.

Angel said fast, pointing to Lavender, "No. I know where I've seen you. You work at Erotic City, right?"

"Erotic City?" Sharon asked.

Angel looked at her friend. "You know, the club I told you I went to a couple of months ago."

"That sex club?" Sharon's nose was turned up.

Angel asked Lavender, "You work there, right?"

"I handle security there." Again his eyes went on a journey, roaming the length and thickness of Angel's body.

"Oh my goodness. That's right." Angel sounded a bit seductive. "I remember seeing you and wishing you were there for more than protection." She giggled. "Really, though, I came in as a freshman. I was just in awe of everything I saw. But I didn't get lucky."

Sharon's mind was stuck. "I still can't believe you went there."

"I went with John from work. We're just friends. But he got hooked up with this woman thanks to me. I just walked up to her, brought her over to him, and they didn't even say a word, they just started rubbing on each other and next thing I knew, they walked away and I never saw him again until we left."

Sharon frowned. "That's just nasty."

Angel said to Lavender and Brian, "Please, she's no prude. She'll come with me next time."

"I will?" Sharon asked, jerking her head back.

Angel stayed focused. "What nights are you open?"

Brian said, "Thursday though Sunday."

"So how about tomorrow night?" Angel suggested.

"Us, go to the club?" Sharon replied, looking hesitant.

"Yes." Angel only looked at Lavender. "Is that okay with you, Lavender? You'll be there, right?"

"I'm always there."

"Good."

Sharon asked, "What about you, Brian? You ever tried it?"

He said, "Ah no."

"I see." Sharon's voice dipped.

Lavender followed up with, "He'll be there. He works there, too."

Sharon gave a brisk smile. "Nice." She secured her purse over her shoulder and elbowed Angel.

Angel said, "We'll see you tomorrow night then."

Lavender replied, "Okay." He said to Sharon, "And you'll have fun. It's not as scary as you think."

She said, "You might see me. But it was nice meeting you both."

Brian gave a parting smile. "You, too."

Angel's eyes were focused. "Bye, Lavender."

"Bye."

She jokingly asked him, "Now, what's my name?"

"Angel."

"Say it again, this time slower." She purred as she moved in closer and swiped his ear with her index finger. She giggled again.

Lavender again said, "Good-bye."

"Bye, gentlemen," Angel said as they walked away switching.

Both Brian and Lavender kept their eyes on the ladies' backside departures.

Brian shook his head as he again faced the bar. He put his hand on his beer bottle. "Yeah, you still need the cookies. Damn, you're a fucking pussy magnet. A lifelong, professional bachelor. That shit is always gonna be thrown your way."

"It's not like that. I'm far from some sex-crazed hound." Lavender paused. "Not anymore, anyway."

"Yeah right. I'll believe that when I see it." Brian took a big swallow. "I'll believe all of your clean-up-your-act shit when I see it. Angel was fine as hell though. Sharon had a hellabody, man. It was bangin. But she was a butterface."

"Oh yeah? Everything looked good but her face?"

Brian aimed his beer bottle at Lavender. "That's it."

Lavender laughed. "Yeah, I guess I'm always gonna look."

"Me, too."

The bartender approached and Lavender said, "Hit me with another Crown please." He looked at Brian. "Yeah, that Angel is fine," he said as though he shouldn't.

39

"Daddy Pop"

✵

Saturday, May 31, 2008
3:30 p.m.

Tamiko said to her sister as they met at Starbucks near Perimeter Mall, "Oh so now you're the one with your chin hanging down past your breasts. "What's wrong with you?" Tamiko wore all tan with raisin-colored Ugg boots.

It was a still, cloudy day but it was slightly warm. They sat outside underneath a dark green umbrella, sipping on their favorite brews. On the sidelines, two men stole glances while playing chess and smoking cigarillos.

Milan wore a Falcons cap. She spoke unhurriedly. "I'm tired, Tamiko. I'm just tired."

"Tired? You're the creator of a cable television series. You should be on top of the world."

"You know all the mess I go through being with Lavender. I just don't know. We're about done." Milan had on brown Chloe sunglasses.

"What? Is Ramada's still trippin?"

"It's always about Ramada and her bitchassness."

"Milan, you really need to wash your mouth out sometimes."

"Oh please." Milan dismissed her sister's shock and shooed her away with her hand.

"My goodness." Tamiko gave almost a motherly look. "Anyway, you mean to tell me you'd let her get in the way of you and Lavender?"

"Please. You sound like Lavender."

"Milan, you'd hand him right to her?"

Milan held her cup under her mouth. "You don't know what it's like to be in love with a man who has a baby's mom like her. It's pure-dee hell." She took a slow, cautioned sip.

"It's gotta be more hell for him than you."

"All because he lets it be."

"And if you break it off that'll be hell, too." Tamiko shifted her hips back into the wrought iron seat. "Milan, you know these women out here can be a trip. But how can he control her? All he can do is go through the courts to get them to set the limits legally. He can't force her to be sane."

"Yeah, that's all they ever seem to do is go to court. She's sue happy. Who wants to have the courts make a decision like whether or not that poor child has surgery to correct a snoring problem? That shouldn't have a thing to do with the courts. That woman is gonna continually throw all kinds of crap at Lavender. But that's on him."

"Please, these women out here nowadays want a man like Lavender so bad they'll put up with it just to keep the other woman from getting him."

"Well, you know me. I do not fight over a man. And I am far from the jealous type. If they end up together, then more power to 'em. I'm not insecure about her. I'm just tired of her damn mess." A group of businessmen walked by and their stares lingered. Milan pulled her cap down farther.

Tamiko smiled their way. "Jealousy is a social condition that we all suffer from."

"Some of us."

Tamiko took her vanilla latte in hand. "Do you think Lavender really wants it this way? I'm sure he'd rather be able to reason with her than fight it out in court. Even though she is certifiably loony."

"Tamiko, what do you know about a loony baby's mama? The men you dated never even had kids."

"I do know that just because he's not doing things as fast as you want him to doesn't mean it's not going to happen. He's doing what he thinks is best and it's obviously different from what you'd do. But it's not you who's going through it. It's him." She sipped her drink.

"What he goes through, I go through."

Tamiko explained like she was the big sister, "Exactly. That's how it's supposed to be. Lord knows we're going through some drama with these men. Mom made hanging with Dad look a whole lot easier than this. And Papa was a rolling stone for real."

"Yeah well, even she ended up moving on."

"So, what's gonna happen with the club? I mean if you guys break up."

"I don't know."

"And think about it. How are you gonna run Erotic City and all the other things you want to do?'"

Milan pulled off her shades and looked at her sister. "Well, I'm glad you asked that."

Out of the blue, a voice behind them said, "Charlie the Scatman Kennedy's daughters, right?" An older man pointed their way.

They both turned back.

"Yes, sir," Tamiko replied.

"Go ahead on now. I love that song, what was it, 'Try a Little Tenderness'?" he asked, looking back as he walked.

Tamiko pointed in return.

"Me, too." A grin spread across Milan's face so strong that her dimple appeared. They both turned back around as memory lane popped into Milan's head. She continued, "Damn, he looked just like Dad." She refocused. "But what I was thinking was, maybe I could get someone to run it when I'm not able to get there, whether Lavender's there or not. Like, you maybe."

Tamiko jerked her head back. "Run Erotic City? Why in the world would I wanna do that?"

"Because I trust you. It'll only be a couple of nights a week. Just try it. For me. I'll give you whatever you want." Milan batted her eyes.

Tamiko sat back. "What I want is not to be a part of that club."

"What do you mean *that* club?" Milan asked, jerking her head back, too.

"I don't mean because of the sex part of it. No, I'm lying, I mean that exactly. It's just not something I wanna be around."

"Well, Lavender and I made plans to expand, so if that happens, I'm gonna need someone even more when we travel. Tamiko, I can trust you."

"I'm still nervous about starting my own clothing line,

so you know I'd be clueless when it comes to knowing how to run a club like that. Not to mention what goes along with swingers. I'd be totally lost."

"How about if you start out just giving it a try? I can teach you what you need to know." Milan reached over and patted Tamiko's hand. "Besides, I need to get busy and finish writing this pilot episode. We signed contracts and everything's done."

"Milan."

"Tamiko. Please. I've got way too much going on right now. I need some help."

"And I don't? I'm trying to get stuff in order, too."

"Please."

Tamiko rubbed her temples. "I'll check it out. But I can't promise anything."

"Okay, no promises. I promise." Milan flashed a smile.

"Very flippin funny."

"Flippin? Oh Lord." Milan reached down and grabbed her purse. "Any flippin way, for starters, how about if you come down tonight? Have you ever even set foot in a swingers club?"

"Never."

"Then tonight's the night."

They stood as Tamiko said, "Good Lord. What am I in for?"

Milan reached over and hooked her arm through her sister's arm. "Sis, it's time for you to live a little."

40

"Who Is She 2 U"

༜

Saturday, May 31, 2008
10:55 p.m.

That night, Tamiko actually set foot in Erotic City. She stood in Milan's office in awe. She was dressed in a heavy sweater and leggings, with low-heeled boots, almost as though trying to completely shield her body. She stared out at the view from Milan's office while Milan sat at her desk.

Tamiko said slowly, "Look at that guy just strutting around with his shang-a-lang hanging."

Milan did not look up. "It's a penis, Tamiko. Stop acting like a virgin when you're really and truly an undercover freak."

Tamiko sounded serious. "Oh, I know what a penis is, but just all exposed like that, like it's hanging from a tool belt. There's another guy. His is teeny-weeny. I didn't know everyone just walked around naked."

Milan said, "Not everyone does."

"And that woman with the stretch marks, and her man just walked up and took that lady's hand, and they kissed. They're going into that room. They closed the door." Tamiko narrated the play-by-play.

"That's how it's done."

"Wow, that guy has stab wounds or something."

Milan said, "And some probably have cigarette burns and beer bellies. That's how real-life bodies look, Tamiko. This is not a movie. Besides, most of the women in here could shop at Lane Bryant. You've been looking at too many *Cosmo* magazines."

"I watch dirty movies, too, now, don't get me wrong."

"But that's my point. These are your average people. Some women are going through the change and their confidence is low. They come here and people find their bodies attractive," Milan said as she stood. "Here, let's take a tour. Come on."

"Are you sure now's a good time?"

"The sooner the better," Milan insisted as though she really needed to. "I wanna show you around."

Tamiko joined Milan as they walked down the spiral staircase and through the VIP room, the silver room, and the dungeon, showing her the layout and making sure she met the bouncer and a few regulars, like Dakota and Jed, and one of the mistresses.

Milan greeted Jed with a hug and found herself eyeing Dakota more than usual. Dakota hugged her. Milan got over it and continued the tour.

She spoke as though reading a script. She had it all down pat. "I'll give you a copy of the membership agreement that people sign. We search bags here and use a metal detector at the door before we buzz them in. Cameras are at the main reception door and one of the fire exits. There are a lot of rules. No drugs. No smoking. No pressure. No pictures or cell phones. Most people adhere. We encourage safe sex, or as we say, fuck responsibly. I'm sorry about my language, but that's the term. Also, we have bowls of every size condom, just sitting around like peppermint hard candy, but most men bring their own depending on what they're packin. We can't actually serve liquor, so people bring their own and that's pretty standard at any sex club. The most important rules are that our members practice safe sex and be respectful to each other. You've got the freshmen and the big dawgs. We call the freshmen, newbies, and the big dawgs, old hands. Dakota and Jed are definitely old hands. There are those who flirt only, some just watch, the soft swingers pet and do oral, and then there's the full swap and group sex. Some start out shy but once they start to get intimate, all the shyness seems to go away.

"Most swingers are couples and single chicks, so you'll see a lot of girls in here who are bisexual. Some men like to watch their women with another woman so a lot is female-female-male, but it can be male-male-female, if the man can handle that. Jed seems to have no problem whatsoever.

"We encourage people who arrive as a couple to leave as a couple. They need to be sensitive to their partners since there are a lot of insecurities here. But most have no shame in their game. Oh yeah, and employees may not engage in acts of a sexual nature while at work."

"Oh, I know all about that one." Tamiko spotted a young man sitting back in a dark corner with his head leaned back and his eyes closed while an older woman sucked his dick. "This seems so sneaky to me."

"Tamiko, these people aren't sneaky. This isn't forbidden fruit. They bring sand to the beach. They're right up front with what they do. Most of the time, that is."

"Either way, it just seems wrong."

"I tell people all the time that sexual expression does not mean sexual deviance."

They passed the dance floor where a Hershey Adonis–looking man and a Halle Berry–looking woman were grooving to a marathon slow jam, doing the slow dance switch with other people, changing partners for a pelvic grind every thirty seconds. One woman, wearing a skimpy nightie, backed it up on a man who wore only a towel.

Tamiko looked like her eyes were being molested. "This is just so recreational, like nobody's taking it seriously, like people have a license to be a freak. I mean, how do couples even bring up that they're interested in coming here if they're in a relationship? How do these people come together and agree on screwing strangers together?"

"Some bring it up if and when a woman wants to experience another woman. They might fantasize in bed and he'll sneak in a question and then he might find the right time to bring it up outside of the bedroom. There are also online groups and blog pages where people meet. Not to mention sites like the Adult Hookup, and Booty Call Anonymous, where straight or gay, you can hook up within minutes, right through the Internet. It's the whole friends-with-benefits thing. Believe it or not, they even have a site where men can seek other men who will fuck their wives right in front of them, or each other. Tamiko, there's a whole world out there. Anything can be arranged. Trust me. Anything."

"I guess so. But while you're busy sharing your significant other, seems they could get stolen."

"Like I said, anything can happen. This club is not for those who fuck around on the side. It's for those who fuck right in front of you."

As they stepped away from a dark-skinned woman who lay flat on her back in an open room with her legs spread-eagled, Tamiko noticed that the woman wore a strap-on and the man was between her legs, sucking her bright pink dildo while stroking his woody. The woman was wearing black pumps and a black mask. Her hands were tied above her head with a silk scarf. She wiggled into his suckling. Her legs were shaking like she was getting off. She was silent.

Tamiko's eyes leaped and her mouth opened.

Milan said, "And if the door stays open, looking is definitely fair game."

Tamiko stopped at the door but Milan kept walking. Tamiko's mind went back to remembering the scene of the crime when Jarod came in and whacked himself in front of Nancy. She struggled to shake the thought of the naked couple in front of her doing things Jarod and Nancy may have already done together.

Milan suddenly saw Lavender standing over two women who were sitting on a lounge chair.

They were all smiles.

Lavender was all smiles.

He leaned over so that one could speak into his ear, and he stood straight up, laughing.

Milan stopped.

Tamiko almost bumped into her sister as she proceeded without looking, and then shifted her brain to

Milan's vision. Already feeling her own tinge of personal frustration, she frowned and pointed. "Who are they?"

"I don't know."

"You don't wanna know?"

"Lavender meets so many people in here. We both do."

"Well right about now, since whatever you might have left is hanging on a very thin string, you need to follow me." Tamiko made a beeline to the threesome. Milan was a few steps behind her. Tamiko said, "Lavender. Introduce us."

"Oh hey, Tamiko. Milan. This is Angel and Sharon."

Milan said, "Hello."

Angel was all smiles, in her short dress, fishnets, and high heels. "Oh hi. We met Brian and Lavender out at Sambuca the other night and they invited us over."

"They did?" Tamiko asked, looking at Lavender.

"Yes," Angel said.

Lavender spoke. "Milan is the owner."

Milan looked at him like she was waiting for Lavender to add another title to the introduction.

Angel said cheerily, "Oh. Nice place. This is my second time." She looked at her friend. "And I had to force her to come along. She's had her mouth wide open ever since we walked in."

Sharon's eyes were wide. "I must tell you. I'm speechless."

Milan said, "Tamiko's my sister. She's new, too."

"Oh so, you're a newbie, too?" Sharon asked, wearing a neck-to-ankle leopard bodysuit.

"Yes. You know Milan and Lavender have been together for what, over a year now, Lavender?" Tamiko cut her eyes to her sister's man.

"About that."

Angel said, "Oh really?" She looked at Milan. "And you and Lavender work together. That must get to be extremely challenging."

"Why would it be?" Milan fought off a frown.

"I mean, just with the sex all around. I know there are a lot of couples who do this and all, but I mean, working in these surroundings all night would definitely be enough to keep my libido fired up."

"We do just fine in that department. We've been around this flavor of life for a long time and we each turned in our personal swinger's cards a while ago." Milan shifted gears as she watched Lavender looking around the room in any direction but hers. "Listen, you guys enjoy. I'm headed over to show Tamiko the bar area."

Angel said, "Okay. It was a pleasure."

Tamiko gave Lavender a look like he should be moving along, too.

He told Tamiko, "See you later." Milan had already walked away. He stayed put.

Tamiko followed Milan but looked back as she said, "I'd keep an eye on them if I were you."

"Lavender and I already have the cheating thing handled. If he wants to, he can. And he can also deal with whatever I choose to do after that."

"But dang, are you two still officially together?"

"That's on him." Milan approached the bar and swung the bar top portion open as she and Tamiko stepped behind it. She looked up and saw Brian approaching. She said loudly, trying to talk over the sounds of "Rumpshaker" by Deelishis. "Oh, Brian, you know Tamiko."

"Yes, I do. Hello."

"Hi there."

Milan said, "I'm trying to get her to manage the club a few nights a week so I can get some things done."

"Uh-oh. The new boss, huh?" he joked.

"Hardly. I'm just taking it all in."

"There's a lot take in."

Milan asked him, "So, everything's cool?"

"Yeah. We've got it covered."

Milan pointed to Lavender. "Lavender's over there with the women you two met the other night."

"Yeah. I saw them."

"Brian, are you trying to get with one of them?"

"No. Not my type."

"Okay, well, you know I don't miss much." Milan took in the sight of Lavender still talking to his new friends. "No. I don't miss much at all." She flagged down the bartender to come to them.

Milan looked over and noticed a man, maybe about twenty-two, who approached Sharon and they walked away together. They entered a private room and he shut the door behind them. Lavender and Angel continued to talk until Jed stepped over and Lavender introduced him.

Milan said, "It didn't take her long. It's always the ones who are the most wide eyed who are the first to hook up."

"Not me," said Tamiko, looking around like her skin was crawling.

Milan watched as Lavender leaned down again to hear what Angel had to say. She brushed her hand over his bicep as he stood up straight, laughing.

Lavender began talking to Jed.

And then Angel saw Milan watching.

Angel's eyes welcomed her.

Angel actually blew Milan a kiss.

Milan looked away. And looked back. And looked away. And she looked back, returning the gesture.

Their eye contact lingered.

Milan blew a kiss back.

41

"Two-Fisted Love"

❧

Sunday, June 1, 2008
1:55 a.m.

Right around two in the morning, the legendary Big Booty Trudy hooked up with another regular named Dexter St. Cyr and they began undressing each other in the corner of the silver room.

Dexter removed his white Air Force Ones, army green hoodie, and Sean John jeans and then stripped Trudy down to her rhinestone goddess thong.

Sturdy Trudy grabbed the sheer fabric of her underwear and bent down slowly, shoving her smack-it-up ass into the air and slipping her panties down to her ankles like a stripper at The Pink Pony down the street. She stood up straight and stepped her metallic, open-toe shoes out of her undies, taking a second to kick her skimpy drawers onto a nearby love seat.

Trudy immediately turned her back to the voyeuristic crowd that had already started to gather. She made sure they had a full-on view of the big booty she was named for.

An ooooo and an ahhhhh could be heard.

Trudy grinned and began smacking her wad of bubblegum, giving it a pop.

And kneeling down on his knees with his dick at full attention was Dexter, 100 percent naked.

Trudy began the process of rough riding his face. While receiving his genuine mustache ride, she didn't just stand there, taking what she was given. She worked hard to make sure it looked like she was the one doing the fucking. Fucking his tongue, chin, nose, teeth, lips, whatever he was offering to get her off. She put her hands on each side of his Rastafarian head and straddled her legs at the most appropriate level of meeting his mouth. She bounced her soft ass like someone was behind her pushing her cheeks up with their hands. Her legs barely moved. It was all ass muscle and all sheer booty momentum. She was the freak of the week.

Dexter made sloppy saliva swooshing sounds, lapping her up as though his tongue was a ladle and she was the gravy. Her pussy smiled thigh to thigh. He varnished her cunt lips with a fury, sopping her up and down. He backed away and brought his fingers right up to her drenched opening. He put one hand on his mocha dick and began to stroke himself with long, steady movements.

He looked out and saw a man choking his dick in both hands. There were two women wearing little to nothing. One woman only wore lip gloss and gigantic chandelier earrings. The other woman made soft moaning sounds at the sight of the superhero lovers.

"Is he well endowed or what? And damn, she has a body that looks like she was drawn that way."

"Yeah, like an ebony Jessica Rabbit or some shit."

"Shoot, she must have been the first in line when they were passin out booty."

"I'll bet she can clap a beer bottle between those cheeks."

"I wish they'd let somebody else get soma that shit."

It turns out that Lavender and Angel were also standing at the door. He stood behind her and she moved up to get a closer view.

She said, "Look at that. I want soma that myself." She was all eyes.

Trudy lay back on a padded-leather block and spread her legs while Dexter positioned himself between her. He grabbed a tiny, clear bottle of Ultra Glide Lube and squirted it onto her lower lips, allowing it to drip along her slit. He rubbed it back and forth, and inserted his finger, and then another, and then another and another until he had four fingers inside of her.

Trudy shut her eyes with a look of complete ecstasy and sucked on her wad of gum, pressing it flat to her tongue.

Dexter inserted his thumb and pressed his hand deeper until her vagina swallowed his knuckles and clasped down on his wrist. He impaled her, pressing his hand deeper until it was no longer visible. His entire right hand occupied her pussy. Trudy began to grind and his fist rotated left to right, hitting her spot, filling her up completely.

"Hell yeah," she said, opening her eyes and moaning like she was in another world.

He placed his mouth on her clitoris, which sat straight up, looking at him. He sucked her clit like a nipple. Her legs began to buzz while he gave sweet strokes, fisting her with strength. His bicep muscles flexed. She was breathless through his probing. The pleasure crashed through her body like a twenty-five-car pileup.

Trudy remembered that just as she liked she was being watched. She looked to her left, seeing a sea of people. An Asian couple had walked up. The man was pinching his own nipple and his woman was finger fucking herself.

Trudy's eyes searched the group and she felt her heat intensify while Dexter stroked the walls of her sex. She began to close her eyes at the onslaught of her cumming and she saw Angel's sweet face. She quickly drew in her breath and shuddered, and felt a rush. She clamped tighter around Dexter's hand and he slobbered nastier on her clit. She could not control herself.

She flexed her muscles and propelled her hips forward just as Dexter yanked his fist out of her cavity. Trudy spurted a long hot stream of liquid orgasm straight up into the air. The sensation rolled harder and harder with every shot of warm fluid. Her explosion of tremors quaked. She shook violently while the cascading orgasm began to subside. She gave a long blink and tried to catch her breath. Her chest told on the pace of her beating heart. Her drenched pussy still squeezed in reply to the fainting waves of cumming. Her lower body was soaked.

She came out of her dizzying spiral and opened her eyes, looking back at the group who still stared, but some had dropped mouths. As mascara from Trudy's lashes ran and stung her eyes she searched for Angel in the crowd. Suddenly, a fully clothed Angel walked up to Trudy, unbuttoned her own blouse, removed her black satin bra, and began feeding Trudy her plentiful titties. Trudy removed her gum from her mouth and happily obliged.

Dexter gave a deep semilaugh and said with strong lingo flavor, "Wait, me think me left me watch in dat punash." He grinned and grabbed his monster dick, stroking himself while watching the ladies play.

Lavender stood spellbound while Angel asked Trudy as she looked down at her, "Can you teach me how to do that? Make it rain like that?"

"I can," Trudy replied in between sucking major nipples.

Angel's face showed that she enjoyed Trudy's suckling skills even though she now kept her sexy sights on Lavender.

She nearly slapped Trudy's face with her breasts as they flopped about. Lavender had to force himself to walk away.

But it was very, very hard.

Angel was no longer a newbie.

She was definitely ready to play.

She wanted Lavender to know it.

And he did.

Temptation had him by the balls.

42

"Dirty Mind"

❧

Sunday, June 1, 2008
3:02 a.m.

Tamiko placed her phone on the shelf of her headboard after sending Milan a text that she'd made it home. She'd left the club at two o'clock in the morning, unable to stay until closing. The four hours she'd spent there, in her mind, was way more than enough.

The quiet and stillness of Tamiko's bedroom cheered on the inspiration for her mind to race. She was actually amazed at the level of comfort that the members of Milan's club had. They were secure with their bodies and they knew what they were there for. It was a level of freedom she'd never experienced. Even though she played it off like it totally bothered her, it piqued her curiosity a little. She just couldn't get it out of her head.

The tingling between her legs got her attention. She thought back to a couple of the men in the club who had kept staring at her. Looking at her in a different way than they would at a regular nightclub. There was a bit of ease and relief being around people whom she knew were into a style of life that involved being open to sex and being liberated enough to explore having sex, right then and there.

Tamiko had received the *I want you* nods. The *come fuck me* winks. The *let me eat you* below the waist stares. She denied her attraction and her level of turn-on. But lust was kickin her ass.

She opened her paraphernalia drawer and pulled out her rabbit named Kellen, named after the young man from the store she'd been playing phone tag with. She lay on her back and slipped off her panties, opening her legs and rubbing herself, inserting only her middle finger. She was unusually wet. She flicked the tiny switch and two seconds later . . . she flicked it off. She reached over to her nightstand and pressed the button to call the very person she knew she shouldn't, but the bad girl was in her. That, mixed with the nagging of her hungry pussy, was way more than she could handle.

It was like sending a drunk text, but she was sober. It read,

Call me now.

Within thirty seconds her phone rang in reply.

She answered it with "Jarod. Hi. Can you come by please? Now. Hurry. I need to see you. Bye."

Totally surprised and overly excited, Jarod stepped out of his jeans as he stood over Tamiko's bed after she let him in and she ran back to lie down on top of the covers. She only had on her white lace bra. And she wore a look on her face that said she was high off lust.

He and his foot-long cock examined her brown legs and waxed V-shaped vagina, thick, pretty lips, and big eyes. "You look good."

He looked like such a stranger in her room. He looked almost forbidden in a way. And this particular night, she found that to be just the turn-on she needed. "Kiss me," she demanded like a newfound sexpot.

Jarod, now only wearing his unbuttoned shirt, crawled on the bed and shifted himself to lie beside her, kissing her cheek softly and leaning over to plant his mouth on hers, opening up and extending his tongue to trace hers, doing a slow tongue ballet. His hands touched her skin. She sighed. It felt like heaven.

Her mind wanted her to think clearly, but her pussy was still calling the shots. She felt her nipples harden. Without looking, she reached down and grabbed his hella-dick. It was ready for duty. Again her mind wanted to race into thinking straight. She shifted gears and prepared to straddle Jarod to ride him just like the porno movies he craved, but he stopped her by putting his hand on her shoulder. He pressed her onto her back and rolled on top of her.

Ring. Ring. Ring.

His cell went off. He barely missed a beat. He kissed Tamiko's neck and then her collarbone.

Ring. Ring. Ring.

Tamiko shook her head to chase away the voice that kept trying to get her attention.

He kissed her cleavage and reached under her to unsnap her bra and release her twins. He kissed one and then the other, sucking both, back and forth, giving equal time, tracing the circle of her areola with his tongue.

Ring. Ring. Ring.

He said nothing.

Tamiko couldn't help but wonder if his phone was in his pants pocket on the floor or what. She glanced in that direction, over toward the foot of the bed.

He continued to suck her breasts, palming each tittie and squeezing them together.

"You smell good," he said, inhaling the essence of her familiar God-given scent that he'd craved. With his right hand, he rubbed her between her lower lips and got a sample of her excessive soaking. "Damn, you are ready aren't you?"

"I am. And I need your dick inside of me."

Ring. Ring. Ring.

Tamiko exhaled. Her rumbling mind insisted that she ask, "Do you need to get that?"

"No."

"Do you want to turn it off?" Her voice showed stress.

A single tone sounded.

"It's a message. It's cool."

Jarod slowly lowered himself. His mouth traveled down from her tits, to her belly, to her baldness, and then to the point of her candied clitoris.

Tamiko's eyes were wide. She did not blink. She did not move. Her only inclination was to pinch herself, but she thought if she did, she might wake up.

She could feel Jarod open his mouth. He was breathing on her split. His breath was hot. He had his palms on her tits while he went . . . down there. He took a whiff.

He stuck the tip of his tongue inside of her tender opening and kissed her glossy vagina loudly.

She jumped and her eyes bugged. *Oh my goodness*, she said under her breath. *No he's not.*

Ring. Ring. Ring.

She yelled out, "Jarod."

He spoke from down below. "It's okay."

Tamiko closed her eyes only for a second. His new trick made her nervous. She could not believe that he was trying to go fishing. She looked down at him, seeing those lips that were once upon Nancy, now upon her. She exhaled and lifted herself up, moving back away from his face. She sat up and put her hands to her face.

"What's wrong?"

She avoided looking at him. "You need to go."

"Why?"

She waved her hand and stood. "I can't."

He rolled over and lay upon his back. "Tamiko. Let's talk. I understand we haven't talked in person."

Ring. Ring. Ring.

"The only person you need to be talking to is whoever that is blowing up your phone at four in the morning."

"Tamiko."

She grabbed her peach-colored robe from the door hook. "Good-bye Jarod."

He sat up. "I need you to listen. I've been trying to think of a way to make this better and get back what we had."

"Jarod, who is that trying to reach you?" Her tone was angry and bossy.

"I don't know."

Ring. Ring. Ring.

She pointed at the floor. "Well, check it. It's obviously important."

He bent down and reached into his pocket to grab his phone. He looked down at the display and then picked up his clothes. With a long face, he stepped into his jeans and buttoned his shirt.

"It's Nancy, isn't it?" She slid her arms through the sleeves and pulled her robe closed.

"Yes."

"Good-bye."

"Tamiko, we're not . . ."

She used her hand as a stop sign. "Don't say it. Obviously somebody is. And next time, put your phone on silent, like all good players do."

Jarod's face gave away the fact that he wanted to say more. He put on his shoes and followed her to her front door. She held it open. He shook his head and placed a soft kiss on her forehead. She turned the other way as he stepped out. She closed the door.

Tamiko's tears began to flow while she leaned her back against the door and melted down to the floor.

"I still love him. I miss him. I want to forgive him. He's such a jerk. He's a greedy, dirty dog. Would it be so bad to have him back?"

There was a knock at the door. "It's me. Please let me in. I left something."

"What?"

"Let me in," his voice begged up against the door.

She braced herself upon her knees and crawled to a stance, unlocking the door and pulling it open before her. "What?" Her sigh was impatient and she wiped her cheek.

"I left you before. This time, I'm not leaving."

She let his sentence saturate her brain over and over

and she looked at him sideways. Her words jumped. "Good-bye, Jarod. Go home to Nancy." Tamiko slammed the door in his face.

She stood with her face to the door when she heard Jarod's footsteps just after one-half ring of his cell. "Stop fucking calling me, damnit. Grow the fuck up. I don't have any money. No. I can't come by." Each word got more faint in equal measure to the disappearing sound of his departing footsteps.

43

"Seven Whole Days"

❧

Thursday, June 5, 2008
10:40 a.m.

Milan awoke alone on a Thursday morning, lying in bed nude, feeling Lavender's absence. It had only been their three off days, though it actually felt like seven days of missing Lavender. She reached over to her cordless and dialed.

He greeted her as though energized. "Good morning."

"Good morning. Lavender, are you coming to the club tonight?"

"Of course I am."

She replied fast, "Of course? I thought I might need to ask. What's going on with you anyway?"

"Nothing."

"Lavender, something's up. Are you trying to get ghost on me?"

"I thought you needed space."

"I did. But something's up with you. You said you weren't going anywhere."

"I haven't gone anywhere. Actually, the only thing I've been trying to do is line up a meeting with one of the investment guys Jed told me about. I want to talk to him about putting some money into me opening a regular nightclub."

"You opening a nightclub? Since when did you decide to do that?"

"Since I talked to Angel and Sharon, those women who were in the club when Tamiko was there the other night. One of them, Angel, is a Realtor and she told me about this spot in Stone Mountain on Hairston that would be perfect. It's been in my head for while. I think it's a good location for a nightclub."

"You never mentioned that to me."

"Milan, it's just a thought."

"So why'd you call the guy if it's just a thought?"

"I got his number from Jed and called. I left a message. I'm waiting for him to call me back."

She lay on her back as she spoke. "I don't know. It just seems funny that you ask me to include you in what goes on with the court case, and then you don't even bother keeping me in the loop before you start exploring opening a club of your own. Is that how things are between us now? Now I guess it's yours and mine, not ours. All because I told you I'm at my wit's end?"

"You didn't do that when you made that deal with the WET TV Network."

"Oh, so you see me making things happen with the show, being focused on business, and you suddenly decide to move ahead with new plans of your own?"

Lavender gave a nasally chuckle. "Are you trying to say I'm jealous?"

"I didn't, but are you?"

"See, I always support you and now, when the shoe's on the other foot, you blame me for wanting to line up my own projects. This is not about you. And be responsible for the fact that you all but pushed me away, and now you want me to act like you're my wife. So much for you being happy for me."

His sarcasm caused her to blink a mile a minute. "Lavender, do you want me to buy you out of the club?"

"No. Erotic City is an investment for me."

"We've both made good money with the club, so whenever you're ready to see the books, or have someone come in and look at them, you're more than welcome to." Her edge was razor sharp.

"I know that." He sounded exhausted with the topic.

"And if you do open your own club, wouldn't that affect Erotic City?"

"We'd work it out, just like we'd do if we expanded. We'd hire people."

"Okay. But you must admit that the only time we see each other lately is at work? That must make Ramada pretty happy."

"What?" Annoyance coated his one word.

She spoke louder. "Or whoever's pleasing you in the bed nowadays. Because it's surely not me." Milan turned to her side and readjusted her pillow.

"Like I said, you're the one who asked for space. It's only been a few days."

She was one inch from yelling. "For you to not get fucked every night isn't like you either. You were over here every day before I got serious about my concerns about her."

They both paused.

She took a deep breath and said, "Don't you see what's happening to us?"

"You just need to relax. I'm fine."

"You don't act fine."

She could hear him exhale.

"Lavender, we're not the same as before and you act like you can't even see it. Why is that?" She turned onto her back again, looking straight up.

He said, "Then maybe you were right. Maybe we both need space. Maybe we need to take a break."

She quickly switched the phone to her right ear and spoke fast. "One minute you say you're not going anywhere, and then you're the one suggesting a break. Seems to me you're ready to test the waters with your new Angel or Sharon or whoever."

His tone was calm. "You've got it all wrong."

"No, I think I've got it right."

"No, you don't."

"It seems to me this is exactly what you want. You ask me to listen to the song 'All This Love,' and then you run right back into player-hood like before."

"Milan, hold on." There was a rustling sound of him moving the phone. "Wait, let me call you right back."

"Why?"

"I've got a call."

She spoke louder. "From who. Who is so important at this moment?"

"It's from Ramada. Good-bye. I'll call you right back." Lavender clicked over in spite of Milan's tone.

Milan sat straight up yoga style. She stared at the display to see if indeed the call had ended. "What the?

Foolish chick must have gotten the news of that order
being filed. I can't believe he just clicked over like that."
Her anger and confusion were written all over her face.
A call came in. "Hello," she said with an edge.

"Milan. It's Jarod."

"What?" She accentuated the last letter, pulling the
covers over her legs. To herself she said, *Oh Lord*.

The sound of a Kenny G tune was behind his voice.
"I've been debating whether or not to call you."

"And I see that your better judgment lost out. What?"
she asked again, making it obvious she was in no mood.

"I'm headed home. I've been going through a lot.
And first of all I want to apologize. I lost the best woman
I've ever had in your sister, and that's one hell of a price
to pay."

"I agree."

"Nancy's been showing up unannounced. She's been
desperate and, the truth is, I'm a little worried about
her."

"That's between the two of you. You ran off with your
MILF preference. You made that bed. You fuck in it."

"Milan, I don't blame you."

"I wish I could say that to you. Jarod, I know you
didn't expect me to not be pissed off. Now other than
you being worried about Nancy, who you probably hurt
as well, what else do you want? Because I'm about to
hang up."

"I totally understand your anger. I deserve that."
He waited. "What I did cost me a job I wasn't ready to
leave."

"You must have been." She shook her hair and tossed
it back.

"I wasn't. I enjoyed working there. I appreciated you for hiring me."

"Yeah well. Your upper head won out. Are you done?" Milan's frown was deep set.

"What I wanted to tell you was, and it might be nothing at all. But, I was at the airport today, picking up a client, and I saw Ramada, Lavender's ex. The one who came in that night?"

She gave a long blink and sighed. "So?"

"Well, she was with Big Mack. And they were obviously together, if you know what I mean."

"Ramada and Big Mack?"

"Yeah."

"Maybe they just ended up on the same flight. But when was this? She just called Lavender."

"Then she must have just called him from the plane because they were just headed out of town not long ago. To Las Vegas. And believe me, Milan. They were very, very together."

Milan just sat, wondering what the hell Ramada was up to now. And how Ramada could actually be involved with the very man she accused of forcing himself on her at knifepoint. It was just another sign that Ramada Hart was off her rocker.

Milan hung up and then called Lavender, but it went straight to voice mail. She didn't leave a message.

44

"Try a Little Tenderness"

❧

Thursday, June 5, 2008
4:12 p.m.

Milan sat at the desk in her home office after opening the envelope that contained her second check from the WET TV Network. She opened the document on her computer and read over the completed copy of the premiere episode that she'd turned in. She reread a portion of her script called "Adrenaline Rush."

> We, he and I, needed it. It was an adrenaline rush for my boyfriend and me. Adrenaline is a funny thing. It's defined as a hormone released into the bloodstream that initiates bodily responses. It can affect the heart rate and blood pressure. Is that what that was when a strange man would stick his dick up my ass while my boyfriend fucked a girl in her ass at the same time? Was that what that thump, thump, thump was in my chest? A response to the fear factor? The fear of engaging in the forbidden? Fucking people we'd just met was

hot as hell. Little did I know that one day, he'd take the road of the straight and narrow, the road of the cloth, and leave me here, still swinging from limb to limb, dick to dick, all fucked up from an adrenaline rush bonding. All in the name of, as he now calls it, sinning. For now, though, I have a new fear factor. And that's my man's ex-girlfriend. She must have adrenaline rushes twenty-four-seven. Because she is one crazy broad.

Just as she took a deep breath and exhaled, preparing to take a break, her phone rang. A 404 number appeared.

"Hello."

A female voice said, "Milan Kennedy?"

"Yes."

"Ms. Kennedy, this is Grady Memorial Hospital. We're calling about Nancy Clark Kennedy. Your mother."

"Yes. I mean no. Well she's my stepmother. What's going on?"

"Nancy is here. You've been identified as next of kin. I'm sorry but you might want to come here right away. Nancy has been raped."

Milan stood from her chair. "Raped? What happened?"

"She was found screaming in the backseat of her car. She has injuries to her back, arms, legs, and neck."

Milan plopped back in her chair. "Oh my goodness. How is she?"

"She's in stable but serious condition."

"What happened? I mean where was she?"

"Someone passing by on the street near Cascade Road

saw her in the backseat yelling for help. She told them that when she was sleeping, some man attacked her. Ms. Kennedy, is she living in her car?"

"No. Not that I know of."

"And I need to tell you that, she lost her baby as well."

Milan leaned forward. "Her baby?"

"Yes. She was only about six or seven weeks along. She had a miscarriage. And it may have been due to trauma, or due to her age, we're not sure. I'm sorry. If you'd like to come and see her, she's here."

"I'll be right there."

"And a Jarod Hamilton is here as well. He's the one who gave us your information as next of kin."

"Jarod is there?"

"Yes. Apparently, he was the baby's father."

"I'm on my way."

Within ten minutes, Milan was in her car, headed downtown toward the hospital. She drove faster than she thought she would. She felt anxious. She felt worried. And she was surprised that she wasn't actually mad. It really wasn't anger that she felt. It was confusion from a ton of questions rattling about in her head.

Does this woman even deserve my time? Should I show up like this when she hurt my father and threatened to sue us? Especially after she got with Tamiko's man? Even when she got pregnant by him.

Again she felt anxious. The instinctual answer to her questions was no. She then wondered, *What was she doing sleeping in the backseat of her car anyway?*

She kept driving. Fast. She thought about her own

mother and how Nancy had stabbed her in the back by playing the other woman.

"I feel like a traitor," she said out loud. "Am I doing the right thing?"

She inserted the Jill Scott CD into the player but fumbled with it. She pushed one button and the radio played loudly. Just as she turned it down, a song began to play. It was the song that made her father famous. "Try a Little Tenderness."

Milan turned it back up, lowered her hand, and listened to the words. *You know she's waiting, anticipating, for the things she'll never possess.* She felt the heat rush over her body and she swallowed hard to make room for her breathing. She sang, *"Try a little tenderness."* She sang the line twice.

She slowed down a bit.

She calmed herself and answered her phone when she was less than a mile away from the off ramp on 85. "Hello, Lavender."

He said, "Hey. I have Taj with me. I just wanted you to know."

"This early on a weekday? What's going on?"

"You know when I got the call from Ramada?"

"Yeah." Milan held her breath, waiting for his reply.

"Well, it was Taj calling from home. Ramada left him there."

She swallowed hard. "Left him?" She breathed.

"He'd been home all night and the house alarm went off. She wasn't planning on coming home for three days. He was missing summer school."

"What? Oh God. Then I guess that's where she was going when Jarod saw her. That's why I called you back.

Jarod called and told me she went out of town. He saw her at the airport. I just assumed Taj was with a baby-sitter or something."

"He saw her?"

"Yeah. And she was with Big Mack."

"Hold up. She was with who?"

"Big Mack."

"She was with him after all that mess about him forcing her?"

"That's what Jarod said. That they were definitely to-gether."

"And she had the nerve to leave my son alone and run off?" Lavender sounded as angry as Milan had ever heard him.

"Did you call her?"

"Yeah. She didn't dare answer. Now I see. She's been busy with somebody who got her distracted by his money. Makes perfect sense. I wonder if she was with him that day she wanted me to watch Taj for a few hours when she came back early starting mess with you."

"Who knows anymore with her? What I don't under-stand is how she could think she'd get away with leaving an eight-and-a-half-year-old alone like that? Taj must've been scared to death. Was someone really trying to get in?"

"Everything was fine. All the doors and windows were secure. The police came out and put it on record that I have him."

Milan turned the corner and shook her head. "I must say I'm not surprised. Crazy leaves clues, you know? Ra-mada is a nightmare. She should have been born without eggs."

"Well, I'm filing a petition to get full custody in the

morning. No more of this pick him up from school and you get your days, I get my days. He won't be around her at all. She basically abandoned him. And, I already talked to Great Mama. I'm flying her out tomorrow so she can help take care of him for a while. You know she's been going crazy being in Florida by herself. It was driving her up a wall anyway. Eventually she wants to sell her house and move here. She wants to be near Taj. And I'd feel better having her here anyway."

Milan managed to smile. "Good. I'm happy about that."

"And for now, I want you to know I'm gonna put off my plans to open Lavender's."

Milan felt surprised and relieved. "Oh really? Was that gonna be the name of it?"

"Probably. Just a thought. Gotta get this Taj thing handled first. Where're you headed?"

Milan paused and then said, "Nancy is in the hospital. Believe it or not, she was raped."

"When did this happen?"

"I guess last night."

"And they called you?" Lavender sounded amazed.

"Jarod gave them my number."

"Jarod and Nancy are still talking? I thought Tamiko said they were done."

"He told me that, too. Seems she wasn't letting go too easily either. And, she had a miscarriage. She told the hospital it was his."

"What? I have to say that I'm shocked. But I'm more shocked that you're headed over there."

Milan pulled into the hospital parking lot. "Tell me about it. Please tell Taj I'm glad he's okay."

"I will. And maybe you can stop by when you're done. I was gonna play basketball with Brian but I'm here with Taj."

"I'll do that. I'll call you."

"And I won't be at work tonight. I'll be here with him."

"Okay. We'll make do." Milan turned off the ignition and opened the door.

"And I really do hope Nancy's okay."

"I didn't think I'd feel this way, but I hope she's okay, too. This just might all work out. I had a thought. I'll tell you about it later. Bye."

"Okay. Bye."

Milan disconnected the phone and looked up at the sky and said, "I'm still saying it. Thank you, Dear Lord, for all things."

45

"Soon as I Get Home"

❧

Thursday, June 5, 2008
10:01 p.m.

I just don't picture you being a Hennessy-type-a girl."

The fireplace was lit and the smell of burning wood was in the air.

Tamiko sat in the living room of her new friend Kellen's home. They'd connected over the phone the day after Jarod left and agreed to have dinner. They'd planned on meeting at Johnny Carino's Italian Grill in the Camp Creek Marketplace because Tamiko had scheduled a meeting nearby to look over some samples that her seamstress had made, but the meeting was re-scheduled for the following week. Tamiko called Kellen to talk about meeting somewhere else since he lived in Fayetteville near her home, and he offered to cook Italian once he got home from work. She found that to be an offer she could not refuse.

Tamiko spoke with the strong drink in her hand. "Neither did I. I was always into wine but a friend of mine left a bottle over at my house after a party and that was all she wrote. It does the trick."

They sat next to each other on his brown microsuede-upholstered couch. He held on to a cold bottle of beer. Kellen's newer, three-bedroom home had bay windows, high vaulted ceilings, and beautiful hardwood floors. His color of choice for everything was chocolate. And his taste was very contemporary.

After sitting at the dark walnut table in the formal dining room where they'd devoured his Ragù version of lasagna and a Caesar salad, they were in his large living room listening to Keyshia Cole's "Love" and talking.

Kellen said, "I was glad you called after we met. Sorry we had trouble connecting. I've been looking forward to this."

She sat barefoot, wiggling her toes while she talked. "Hey, I needed to get out. Though I really must say I wasn't expecting a home-cooked meal."

"I'll bet you deserve it. Sounds like you stay locked in a lot?"

"You could say that. But I needed to get my mind off of stuff." She took a sip and then licked her lips.

"I see. Moms taught me how to make the quick version of lasagna. Gotta be self-sufficient, you know."

"I see that."

"Yeah, so I'm glad you could come by since we're not too far from each other." His voice was hip and young and sexy.

She found herself feeling the sexy part more than anything else. "You know they say it's a real no-no to go over to a man's house on a first date."

"Really? Are you cool though? I don't want you to feel uncomfortable or anything."

"Oh no, I'm fine."

"Good. Good." He looked down at her naked feet and said, "Listen, I wanted to ask you, do you date a lot? Or should I say, did you date a lot before your last relationship?"

"Not really. I've had four long relationships. Not a lot of casual dating really. Honestly, I don't really enjoy dating. People try and put their best foot forward, and it just seems like an audition sometimes."

"I agree. I don't like it either. But, hey, whatcha gonna do? Gotta get out there and meet people."

"True." Tamiko looked around toward the den area. "This is a nice house. How long have you been here?"

"Just a few years. I had an apartment for a while and I took the money I'd been saving and put it down on this place. Got tired of paying someone else's rent, ya know? Had to get me my own home."

"You got a nice one."

"Thanks." Kellen took a swallow of his Corona. "I'll be honest with you. Until you called on my home number and the caller ID came up, showing your last name, I didn't know who you were."

"Who I was?"

"I mean when it said last name Kennedy I remembered your sister's name and it was like a bell went off. So I checked the Internet and not only did I see all the reports about the accusations against your sister's club, but I even saw some pictures of you two on Google Images from when you guys were somewhere with your father. Your dad was big time I see. That must have been a trip. I mean, what was that like, being the daughter of someone that famous?"

"I was so young when he was at the peak of his fame. You know, to us he was just dad. He was gone a lot. We didn't really get close to him until he slowed down after he got sick when he was older."

"I can tell that you and Milan are very close."

"Oh yeah, we're best friends. We've been though a lot." She sipped a bit more.

He nodded. "Let me ask you, if you don't mind. I mean, with your sister having a club like that and everything, is that something you ever thought about? Swinging?"

Tamiko wore a small frown. "Oh no. I went there once the other day since I was thinking about helping her run it for a minute while she's out of town, but I'm leaning toward not doing it. It was more than I could have ever imagined."

"Not your style, huh?"

"Not even. How about you? Have you ever tried it?"

"No. Not that I haven't thought about it, you know. I mean, a lot of people that I know have tried it."

"I guess you just have to be curious enough to want to try. And I definitely am not." She crossed her legs.

"It does sound like she's doing okay for herself over there."

"She is. They're making money off of it. Their bad press proved to be good for business."

Tamiko took another swallow of her potent drink and it burned as it traveled to her belly.

Kellen aimed the CD remote to play Lauryn Hill's "I Used to Love Him." "Tell me about you and what you do as far as business. How'd you get into designing clothes?"

"Oh, way back when, my mother had a sewing machine that she never used. I took a sewing class in school and started making my own clothes. I even made my own prom dress. I got pretty good. Guess I just have had a knack for it. My dream is to have my own line called Cheekz."

He eyed her legs and said, "Nice name. You know, you could be a model yourself. You're very beautiful. You know that's your name, right? Beautiful." He did a stretch and yawn move, reaching around to hug her.

She moved an inch closer and nodded. "Thank you."

He grinned. "It's true. So what's stopping you from getting your line off the ground? That name is hot."

"I'm working on it. I'm getting some samples made and then I'll get out there to the buyers. I have a meeting next week to go over some skirts and pants I designed."

"You know, I can help you if you want me to." He eyed every inch of her face.

Her eyes lit up. "How?"

"I know a lot of buyers. We sometimes book blocks of time for celebrities to shop alone and they close down the designer stores. So the managers tend to pick up the phone when I call. What you need to do is showcase your designs and invite these guys."

"I'm working on it. So, you've got some serious hook-up power, huh?"

"I do know a little bit about the business. I had a line of caps called Positivity. I sold that a while back."

"Positivity was your design? With the positive slogans and stuff?"

"Yep. That idea is why I have this house."

"Impressive. You'll have to tell me all about how you got that started."

He watched the movement of her mouth. "I will. Hey, ah, Beautiful?"

She noticed him noticing. "Yes." Her voice became shy.

"You've got the sexiest lips I've ever seen. I'm telling you." And with that Kellen brought his face to hers and began kissing Tamiko. She closed her eyes and followed his lead once their tongues met. He slowly pulled away, but not before his tongue lingered to trace the design of her lips. The parting made a smacking sound. And then it was Tamiko who moved in to his mouth, kissing him, placing her hand on his shoulder. She backed away and waved her hand to her face, looking flushed.

The white pepper and mandarin scent of his Burberry Touch cologne tickled her brain. "I shouldn't have kissed you back like that."

"Why not?" He saw the shape of her hard nipples showing under her tight T-shirt.

She set her glass on the coffee table and uncrossed her legs. "As nice as that was, I just need to get to know you first." She looked at her wristwatch. "Plus, it's very late. I'm usually in bed by now. I don't think I should even be here. I should've left earlier." She began to stand.

He took her hand and guided her back down to the couch. "Who says? Just try to relax." He pulled her close.

"I'll be honest with you. I just don't want to get intimate so soon."

"I understand. Please don't think you need to go slow because I might think badly of you. I just enjoy having you here. No pressure."

Tamiko rubbed her forehead as she spoke. "It's just that, I haven't been with anyone but my ex in more than a year. And now that it's over, I really don't want to have that rebound sex. You know? I just need some more time." She turned to him and realized that she was a little buzzed.

He looked her in the eyes. "Okay. But I still don't think you need to be driving. I know you don't live too far but, you can sleep in my room. I won't touch you. I promise."

"Your room?"

"My room. And tomorrow, I'll take you to breakfast and we can talk some more. How's that?"

Tamiko gave a long blink, exhaled and said, "That'd be nice."

"Good." Kellen stood up after finishing his last sip of beer. He walked back through the den and down the hallway. His voice traveled. "I'll find something for you to sleep in. And I'll get the bed ready. I'll sleep in the guest room next door."

Tamiko spoke loudly. "Okay." She also said under her breath, "What am I doing?" As she heard a beep sound, she looked down at her purse, which was on the floor, and reached inside to get her cell, noticing that her battery was low. Just as she started to press the power button, her phone died anyway.

She replaced her phone and sat back, securing her back onto the cushion, and sipping the last of her amber liquid. She stayed.

By three-thirty in the morning, Tamiko awoke. Her eyes widened little by little and she gave a jerking motion, as though she forgot where she was. The room was pitch-black as she looked at the large red numbers of the digital clock over the television. She pulled back the soft sienna blanket from the panel bed and got up, walked to the bedroom door, and went to the next door. Her head spun slightly as she stepped. She knocked. "Kellen."

"Yeah," he said, sounding groggy.

"Can I come in?"

"Yeah."

Quietly, she turned the knob and stepped inside of the handsomely furnished guest room, walking along the plush carpet on her tiptoes. The flat-screen television was muted.

He asked, "Are you okay?"

"I am. I just have a tiny headache." She stood over his side of the four-poster king bed. "Do you mind if I get in with you? I don't want to be alone. I mean, I'm just wondering if I should. It's just that being alone in your bed made me think it would be better, I mean since I'm here and you're here, if we just, well you know, slept in the same bed." Her face showed the same uncertainty as her words.

He gave her a major grin. "Yeah. Come on." He patted the empty side of the bed and she crawled over him. She wore a big white T-shirt and white panties. "Do you want some Tylenol or something?" he asked.

"No thanks. I just need to sleep it off." She snuggled under the mocha-embroidered covers and backed up to him, hugging two foam pillows with her left arm.

"Do you mind if I go with you to that meeting next week?" he asked in her ear.

"That would be fine."

He rested his arm along her waist and found her hand. As they interlocked fingers he said, "Good-night, Beautiful."

She could feel his nature rising behind her butt. "Good night," she replied while grinning just as major as he was.

46

"Give It Up, Turn It Loose"

⌘

Friday, June 6, 2008
9:50 a.m.

Where've you been all night?" Milan asked after answering her kitchen phone, sounding tense. "Your phone went straight to voice mail."

Tamiko was driving from the Waffle House toward her home. "My phone died. I have it plugged in the car charger now. I was at Kellen's."

"On a first date you went over to his place?"

"I did. We just had breakfast."

"Dang, Tamiko."

"Dang what? Wasn't it you who told me to live a little?"

"And? What happened?" Milan's voice was expectant.

"Nothing."

"Yeah right." Milan sat at her kitchen bar area, sipping on cinnamon coffee.

"Milan, I'm telling you the truth. He was a perfect gentleman. What's up with you?"

Milan spit it out. "Nancy's in the hospital. I went by there last evening. I was gonna wait until today to call you but when the club closed, I decided to try you on my way home. She was raped."

Tamiko's voice got higher. "Raped?"

"Yes."

"And you went by to see her?"

"Of course."

"Of course?"

"The hospital called me. What was I supposed to do?"

Tamiko gave an exasperated breath. "Okay, with you being the one to tell me it was on as far as Nancy goes, what do you expect me to think? I know she didn't give them your number?"

"Jarod gave it to them."

"Jarod was there?" Tamiko's voice cracked. Her sigh was audible.

"Yeah. And I think they're, well, he was still there when I left." Milan slipped her index finger over the rim of her coffee cup and traced the edge.

"Oh my goodness. I guess he rode in on his black horse to save the day for real."

"Can you come by for a minute? I have an idea."

"What is it?"

"Just stop by. Please. I'll tell you what happened and then you can tell me about your night."

Tamiko sucked her teeth. "I'll be there in a minute." She hung up.

One hour later, after Milan and Tamiko talked while they sat at the bar area in Milan's kitchen, Milan picked up the phone and dialed while speaking in a low tone to her sister. "Tamiko, we've gotta do this. I'm telling you. She has to get on her feet and she has to decide to give up her claim to Dad's money. Nancy's no fool." Milan heard someone answer and then she said, "Nancy Kennedy's room please. Thanks." She sat on the teakwood stool next to Tamiko, who was quiet as a mouse. A frowning mouse.

"Hello."

"Nancy?" Milan asked.

"Yes." Nancy's voice was low-key.

"This is Milan."

"Hello."

"How are you? Any better?" Milan asked as Tamiko cut her eyes away toward the floor.

Nancy's voice dragged. "I'm adjusting. My back still feels like it's broken. I think I'm immune to naproxen. I'm just trying to do whatever I can to keep my mind off of the pain. The police came by again this morning. They don't have any leads and no one saw a thing."

"I'm sure the police will find the guy."

"I hope so."

Milan said, "I talked to Jarod while I was there. He shared some things with me."

Tamiko bounced her legs.

"He did?"

"He told me how you really felt about what happened after my dad died. My feeling is that we might not agree on a lot of things, but bottom line is, you were my dad's wife. And I, for one, tend to agree with you. I know that he loved you."

"I believe he did."

"When you really stop and think about it, to be with someone for sixteen years, that's gotta be love."

Nancy spoke faster. "I want you to know that I came to the club to talk to you. And I wanted a copy of the agreement to look it over. I did have a little bit of law school you know. But, things just happened."

"You could have called if you wanted to help me."

"I didn't think you would've taken my call. I barely got Tamiko to talk to me."

Milan watched her sister sitting with her legs and her arms crossed. Staring. "Nancy, in spite of what we've thought about you, you were my dad's wife. And for whatever reason the marriage didn't work, I know my dad wouldn't want us to be the way we are with each other."

"I agree. And truly, I know you girls are being protective of him. You always have been."

"Nancy, the reason I called this morning is because Tamiko and I have talked, and when you get on your feet, we want you to live in the house in Miami."

Tamiko mouthed, "We?" and twisted her lips, cutting her eyes.

Nancy was silent for a second. She then spoke louder than before. "You cannot be serious."

"I am."

"Milan, I don't know what to say. I'm shocked."

"It's the right thing to do. But I have to ask you, were you, are you living in your car?"

"I was but—"

Milan talked over her. "Now see, we can't have that. Our attorney can draw up the lease. Just find a way to pay four hundred a month to take care of utilities. That's not a lot but you'll need to find a way to make some money once you get out there."

"Milan, your dad obviously wanted you girls to live in his two homes. Especially his house in Miami."

"You were not in the situation then that you are now. I don't believe he wanted you living in your car. The house is unoccupied. I just ask that you take care of it."

Tamiko was now eyeing her sister down like she was imagining sticking needles in her eyes.

"Milan. I don't know what to say."

"What you must do is agree to waive any rights you might have to claim anything against our dad's property ever again. And this document will be much more specific than the divorce settlement agreement."

"Okay, but I want you to know that I never filed a thing."

Milan sat up straight. "I understand. First things first though. You need to get well."

"Milan. Thank you so much. You have no idea what this means to me. This morning I was wondering maybe, you know, that maybe I deserve what happened to me. It's probably karma for all that I've done in my life."

"You're human. Anything can happen. I'm just trying something different."

"And I apologize for all that I've done to both you and to Tamiko."

Milan watched Tamiko's blank face again. "I forgive you. And you can tell Tamiko that yourself. She's right here." Tamiko widened her eyes at Milan.

"Okay."

"Hold on."

Tamiko's forehead buckled. She balled up her fist toward her sister with one hand, taking the phone with the other. "Hello, Nancy." She sounded like she was truly forcing it.

"Hi, Tamiko. How are you?"

Milan stood up and walked out of the kitchen.

Tamiko said, "Okay. I hear you're doing better."

"I am. You don't have to do this."

"I know."

"I don't know what to say."

Tamiko leaned toward the bar and spoke up. "Maybe you can say one thing. Like tell me why. Why you still messed with Jarod once you found out he was mine?"

"Tamiko?"

Tamiko was firm. "No, really. Why?"

"I guess I, I must have been mad. Mad about being discarded like I didn't exist."

"So you took it out on me. By hurting me. Just like you hurt my mother then, right."

"Tamiko. I can tell this isn't the right thing for me to do, by staying in the house. And it doesn't seem to be the right thing for you either."

Tamiko stood and began pacing the kitchen floor. "The right thing would be for you to tell me more than you were mad. That's not good enough."

"Well, first of all, I know that I've always had issues. Being with your father made me, I don't know, feel like I was somebody. Plus he was older and I never knew my father." Nancy swallowed and became silent.

So did Tamiko.

Nancy continued, "You know, I had six abortions by the time I was eighteen. I never even thought I could have children or that I could even get pregnant again at forty-two years old, and here I find out that I was and that I lost it."

Tamiko held her breath. She didn't know that little detail that her sister had spared her. She felt her heart race.

Nancy continued, "What your dad gave me was the self-esteem I needed. His popularity gave me that." She sniffled.

Tamiko waited and breathed heavily. She then asked, "Oh so, it doesn't matter whether or not you loved him, right? You just used him?" She continued to pace.

"I loved him like no one I've ever loved. He put up with me and gave me the life I'd never had. My child-hood was the complete opposite. It was hell."

"So at forty-two years old, you tried to make my life hell, too."

Nancy continued explaining. "I was mad, like I said. I guess I felt Milan discarded me and the last time I talked to you, I could tell you were upset because of my e-mail about the claim for money. I was wrong for still seeing Jarod after I knew who he was. And I'm sorry."

Tamiko again walked the length of the kitchen and back. "Well, it would've been nice if you'd picked up the phone and told me that yourself. What you did told me a lot more about you than I thought to be true. And I wanna know. How did you go from needing a father figure to needing a man who's almost young enough to be your son? I'm still just trying to figure out what you two were thinking."

"I can imagine you are." Nancy's voice retreated.

"You need to know that Milan wants this. I don't

know what tree fell on her head but you will live in that house. I'll fly you out there one-way, first class, whatever. Milan thinks it's the right thing to do. I'm going to go with her on this. But honestly, I don't ever want to hear from you again. And I can't say that I give a darn about you losing a baby or getting raped. You can marry Jarod for all I care." Tamiko threw up her hand.

"Tamiko, please—"

"Don't." Tamiko walked back toward the bar just as Milan walked back in. Tamiko and Nancy and Milan were quiet. "And by the way, what in the heck did you do with all the money my dad gave you?"

Nancy's breathing was loud. She again sniffled. "I won't lie. I was with someone when I moved out of your dad's house. It was my trainer. And he asked me to help him open a gym. I did. Next thing I knew, we'd gone through the money and when it was all gone, he left."

Tamiko's face said she was through. "Hold on." She shoved the phone toward Milan and stormed out of the kitchen. She could be heard saying, "With her jungle fever, dyke self."

Milan sat down, looking at the wind from the trail that Tamiko blazed out of the kitchen. "Nancy, we're gonna go. Do you have someone to take you home when they release you? Where are you going?"

"Yes. To Jarod's." Nancy sounded as though she knew the truth did not sound good.

"I need to talk to him so ask him to call me. And I left my new home number by your bed. Let me know when you get on your feet and we'll set a time for you to meet with my attorney to handle everything. Take care of yourself."

"Okay. Thank you again. Thanks to you and to Tamiko. And again, please tell her I'm sorry."

"Good-bye." Milan hung up the phone and rushed out of the kitchen to find her livid sister. But she had left.

47

"I've Got to See You Again"

☙

Friday, June 6, 2008
11:20 p.m.

Tamiko was right back at Kellen's house for the second night in a row.

The long blades of the ceiling fan above them sliced the air, cooling their bodies from the heat of June, and from the heat of their combined passion.

The accumulation of her bouts with anger helped her to swallow her apprehension. There was no more doubt. Right off the bat she was getting a serious, longtime-coming tongue-lashing. Kellen was taking care of business like a real man should.

Her breaths signaled arousal. She was propped up on her knees. Kellen's tongue slid across her clitoris from behind and she was seeing stars. She squirmed and tried her damndest not to lose it. He feasted on her pussy like she was an all-night buffet.

Their empty wineglasses rested upon the dresser. Soft light from the Sea Breeze aromatherapy candles flickered against the skin of their naked bodies. Soft, panty-dropping music serenaded their ecstasy. But the panties had long been dropped already. The song was "There'll Never Be" by DeBarge.

"Ah, Kellen. That feels so good." She nearly meowed.

He said yes with a moan that vibrated between her legs.

"Since, we are lyin here ah / For the first time, you and I."

The lyrics made her mind swoon and she hung her head low with her hair draped over the pillow. But two minutes later her head shot straight up and she screamed, "Oh. Oh wait. I can't take it."

He did not stop.

Her lips separated as he inserted his tongue like it was a dick fuck. His tongue went in waves. One minute his tongue was pointed and then it was flat, and he never neglected her clit, running it back and forth. He pulled on it lightly and gave a tug with more pressure. His nose rubbed against her opening while he treated her to a suckling.

Tamiko arched her back even more and stuck out her ass. His face was lost. He never seemed to come up for air. He put his finger around the outside of her asshole, slowly inserting it.

"Oh, Kellen. Oh. Oh. Oh. Shit!" The bad word sprinted from her mouth and she broke out in an all-over, 100-yard-dash orgasm that caused her to shake against his face. She could feel her cum oozing and her clitoris throbbing like it never had before. She panted, "Kellen. Kellen." It was like her voice was begging him to stop.

He backed away and said, "Yeah," looking extra-innocent.

Tamiko collapsed onto her stomach. Her head swam. "That was amazing." The attention to detail had her wide eyed and impressed.

He smiled and lay on his side. "That was one good, hard cum. That's what that was."

She looked at his average but thick penis and licked her lips. "Can I do you now?"

His eyes were on her cheeks. "I just wanna be inside of you."

"Okay." Without hesitation she turned onto her back.

"No. Can we face each other? Sitting up?"

She seemed curious. "Show me."

Kellen sat on the bed with his legs in front of him. He directed her to sit on his lap, facing him with her legs spread open. He pulled her closer and she widened her legs even more. He began kissing her on her face and all over her erogenous neck.

She moaned.

He looked her in the eyes and touched her face and hair, tracing her hairline and her profile with his fingers. He nibbled on her ear and explored her from the neck up.

Tamiko's desire intensified. She began kissing him from tongue to tonsil. Their mouths danced until he backed away.

He reached over and took a condom package from the checkered bedspread, ripped it open, and rolled it over his erection. He took his dick in hand. She prepared to take him in. Her eyes were expectant.

He pushed toward her and he was inside.

His girth took over her.

He moved slowly and Tamiko wrapped her arms around him. She held on tight. He hugged her back and thrust deeper.

She could feel his dick touch a place and said, "Oh yeah." It curved to a soft spot that was sending signals to her clit.

He felt her squeeze. "Uh-huh."

They worked together until the stroke of midnight while she lifted and lowered her hips on his dick, working her wet pussy muscles to hold his penis tight.

Their hips stayed locked together and again they kissed. Her chest was pressed to his.

It was syncopated rhythm for another fifteen minutes.

That was until he froze and began to grunt. And groan. And yell. "Uhh, yeah. Oh yeah. Fuck. Damnit." He released his streaming, urgent orgasm and she still moved her hips.

The heat of his body and the pressure of his pelvic area against her clit made her lean her head back in amazement. She felt dizzy just as she came again. She saw a white light. Her body shuddered.

Twice in one night.

Twice in one hour.

She said while trying to come down from her satisfied high, "That's the shit I'm talking about right there." She high-fived him with her pleasured, dirty voice.

He said, "Beautiful."

And again he kissed her softly.

48

"Diamonds and Pearls"

∝ℛ

Friday, July 18, 2008
11:05 p.m.

It was four weeks before the big premiere of Milan's cable television show. She sat in her office e-mailing invites to members, friends, and business associates. She had planned for it to be huge, lavish, and well attended.

She received an e-mail from the church, inviting her to the upcoming Big Sister dinner and thanking her for her financial contribution. Her heart smiled.

She also received an e-mail from Tamiko that read,

> Sis—I know we've been at odds about Nancy. You are not one to fight fire with fire and I know that. I understand your reasoning behind letting Nancy stay in the Miami house so she'd leave Dad's estate alone. I know you felt sorry for her. I feel like something's wrong with me though, because though I'm glad they caught that guy who raped her, I still don't feel a bit sorry for her. Not even deep down.

But my biggest thing was trying to understand why you're so generous to Jarod again after what he did. And I'm going to move on from that. As you know I'm happy with my life and things are going well. I'm also happy that Lavender's grandma is here. At least now you guys can go back and forth to Miami and not have to worry, and work later nights. And if you ever need me to babysit I'll be there for you. Oh, just so you know, I really did have fun when I went to the club that night. Honestly, I was a little turned on. Okay, a lot turned on. But I'm not looking to start swinging anytime soon. N-E-WAY–I can't wait for your big night. I love you, big sis. T.

Milan immediately clicked reply and began typing.

Sis—Thanks for letting me know that you understand. I debated about whether or not I was doing the right thing and I just think it's best to forgive and give. Jarod made a big mistake and so did Nancy. They've also paid greatly. They lost a baby.

Thanks for being happy for me but I'm even more happy for you. Happy that you and Kellen are getting to know each other and that he helped you put everything in place for your big night. Your first fashion show. You guys seem good for each other. I love you back, baby sis. Talk to you tomorrow. M.

She hit send and a smile spread across her face. She stood, taking a moment to look out of the mirror to check out the scene of her thriving sex palace.

In the red room on the dance floor, there were about two dozen lively people doing the shuffle to "Cupid Shuffle." An older couple did a switch move with a younger couple and they began kissing each other's mates.

Milan's desk phone rang and she rushed to catch it. She jerked the receiver from the base and said, "This is Milan."

Click.

The caller ID read *private number*.

She hung up and immediately turned back, looking at the goings-on in the silver room. There were about four people standing at the entrance, eyeing down a woman who was getting fucked by a man who used a doggy-style enhancement strap on her ass. And he was deep-sea fishing. Well.

The main purple room had people mingling about with breasts and asses everywhere. The fuck flick for the evening was *Desperate Blackwives 3*. Milan saw Brian walking by, making sure everyone behaved.

And the black VIP room had groups of people sitting upon the leather sofas, mingling and laughing. One woman with a definite bubble butt looked like she was giving a focused lap dance to two guys at once. The looks on their faces said it would be an on and crackin, male-male-female all-nighter.

Milan saw Jed walking from the bar to where Lavender stood, in front of the VIP room. Milan took hold of the radio.

"Hey, Lavender. Can I talk to Jed for a minute please, honey?"

He joked, "It's gonna cost you."

"Oh no problem. You know I'm willing to pay whatever the cost."

He looked up at her and grinned. "I'll remember that. Hold on, baby."

Jed also looked up toward her office window, taking the radio. "Hey."

"Hey there. Listen, I need to know if you and Dakota wouldn't mind running Erotic City until we get the Miami location off the ground. Only for a few months on and off. We'll be back and forth."

"Starting when?"

"Next month."

"Sure, I can definitely help you out. I need to have something to do. This retirement thing is driving me crazy."

"Good. Can we meet later on? Just go over what you'd charge, and some other things?"

"Sure. And what about Lavender here? What happens to security when you guys are gone?"

"Jarod's coming back to do that."

"The one who got fired?" Jed asked, sounding skeptical.

"That's the one. I've decided to give him another shot."

"Okay. You know best."

"Let's hope so."

"Well, I'll be up there later."

"Good."

Milan hung up as she saw Jed give the two-way back to Lavender and they walked off. She then spotted the same woman who was doing the lap dance before, now straddling a lounger, getting double penetration, filled by two erections, while the bystanders watched in ecstasy.

She spoke out loud. "Yeah. This is the place to cum alive all right. I've gotta remember that one just in case I write another episode. Or maybe I'll write a book called *Hollywood Swingers*. The city of the stars, movies, women, and cars."

Milan's creative mind was on fire just as her phone rang again. She stepped back to her desk to catch it. "Hello."

Click.

This time the display read *Ramada Hart*.

49
"Soft and Wet"

❦

Sunday, August 3, 2008
5:12 a.m.

Saturday night had slipped into early Sunday morning.

Great Mama and Taj were at Lavender's sleeping while he followed Milan to her house. Earlier, she'd sent him a sex text while they worked that read,

My erotica bed is lonely.

Though they had not engaged in 5:00 a.m. sex in a long time, it was time. The room was filled with the sultry red light from a stained-glass Tiffany lamp.

Milan blindfolded Lavender while he lay upon her black lacquer bed, erect. He waited patiently as he heard her fumbling around.

She made final adjustments to transform the bondage bed into a fetish play space.

She then lay down, grasped the shaft of his dick, and stroked it, stimulating the head with her giving mouth.

Without the visual, it drove him crazy and he surrendered to her every move. She ran her tongue around his base, around the shaft, and to the rim.

She moved her mouth down to his balls and licked him up and down like he had a vagina, still stroking.

He breathed extra heavily like he was desperate and began to give a loud rumble.

Milan stopped just in time so he could save it.

He was just about to cum.

His rumble stopped.

He lay back wondering.

She stood up upon the pillow-top mattress and adjusted her right leg through the hanging strap of the canopy and secured the Velcro cuff around her ankle.

He was quiet.

He and his dick were still waiting.

She grabbed the hoops to lie back upon the black leather fantasy swing, raising her left leg into the other strap.

"Fuck me like I really am your ho," she demanded while restrained for his pleasure. "Take that damn blindfold off."

He removed the black silk scarf and sat up, coming to a stance on the bed. He saw her suspended with her legs spread from wall to wall. His eyes grew. He knew just what to do.

As she lay back, hanging there, faceup, he grabbed onto the overhead suspension bars. The level of access was supreme. He positioned himself between her legs and right away inserted his teased dick into her vagina.

She jumped from the pressure of his entry. Her pussy had been waiting longer than usual.

He jerked upon the sensation of her heated wetness.

Fucking her was like melted butter. The angle of her vagina was perfect.

He held on and gained leverage, thrusting his third leg deeper and deeper.

She was supine.

And he was taking full advantage, swinging her just so, giving new meaning the word *swingers*.

When he was in the middle of an upstroke, Milan asked, "Did you fuck Angel?"

"Yeah." He'd answered immediately.

"Tell me about it."

"She got on her knees and sucked my dick. She sucked it like she enjoyed sucking dick. She told me she gets her excitement from feeling a dick in her mouth."

"And then what?"

"She sat on me. She has strong legs like a gymnast and she bent down on my dick. She told me to jack my dick off with her pussy."

"And did you?"

"Yeah. But only after she asked me if you like your clit sucked."

"And?"

"I told her yes." Lavender's penis stabbed Milan harder and harder.

"You did?"

"Yeah."

Milan got wetter and wetter. "And then?"

"She asked me if your cum tasted sweet. I said yes."

Milan revved up. "Uh-huh."

"Then she asked if you'd like to suck my dick after she came all over it."

"And you said?"

"I told her you'd like that. And that you'd like to kiss me after she came on my face. She raised up from my dick and brought herself to my mouth, smothering me with her pussy. Next thing I knew, she came in my mouth. I stuck my tongue inside and tasted her. From behind her, my cum shot up on its own and then dripped back down onto my dick. She moved down to lick my sperm off my skin."

"Uh-uh, yes. Ummuh. Yes." Milan seemed lost. Her eyes were closed.

"And before Angel came she yelled your name."

"She did?"

"Yeah." His eyes squinted like he was in pain and their rocking motion ceased.

"Uh, ahhh, da, damn, damnit, Lavender," Milan screamed slowly as her orgasm unraveled.

But Lavender was fighting to hold back the volume from the intensity of his own first squirt of cum that shot one second before hers did. He had that pained look on his face and the veins in his neck and forehead protruded and his nostrils flared. He gritted his teeth and gave a quick, angry grunt.

Her eyes reopened while her intensity slowly subsided. "Don't you play with me. Your bedroom talk is getting nastier and nastier." She panted and laughed. "Get me down from here."

Lavender gave a slow swallow and a long breath. He carefully pulled out and picked her up along her back and legs, pulling the ankle strap apart as she wiggled her feet free. He laid her down gently.

She watched him as he positioned himself to lie next to her while his hard-on gradually subsided. She said,

"You know your ass is wrong. I know you really fucked that girl."

He leaned over and kissed her on the forehead. "Just bringing a fantasy to bed with us. As usual."

"Yeah right." She cut her eyes and then closed them. "Good night."

Milan was still asleep at 11:00 a.m. Lavender had been up to call and check on Taj. Lavender stepped back in the room and said softly, "I can't believe Great Mama says that boy hasn't snored one night since she's been with him."

Milan did not move a muscle. She was knocked the fuck out.

He crept back into bed and pulled the top sheet from her nudeness with an idea to serve her the sandman surprise like he used to.

And she now awoke to discover that the heat between her legs was being devoured by her man's face, treating her to a morning tongue ride. "Good morning," he said from down below.

At that moment, Milan's home phone rang and went to voice mail after three rings. Both she and Lavender acted as though they were deaf.

She stirred and her eyes quickly took in the view of the top of his head, right at the level of her pleasantly awakened vagina. She whimpered. Needless to say the eroticism carried her away. It didn't take long for her to show a creamy stream of appreciation. Her mind drifted. The forbidden fuck visual in her head was nasty and lustful. She thought back to the not-so-pretend fantasy that Lavender shared with her while his dick was probing her insides. Her breathing grew deeper. "Awww, baby. You've got my mind racing like crazy. This one is slow rolling and hard . . . fuck, oh damn, this is a good-ass nut here. Yes. Ahhhhhh." Milan trembled and tightened her body and ripped a long one. Her hands choked the cotton sheet. She bit down on her bottom lip and then said softly, "Uhhmm, hook that shit up."

"What?" he asked with a mixture of pride for his super pussy-eating skills and an air of trying to play things off.

Her lustful mind returned. "That shit with Angel. Hook it the hell up."

He nodded with his nose an inch from her drenched pussy lips. "Okay." He gave a final lick of her nectar before adjusting his body upward to lie next to his woman and secured the covers back over their bodies. They were both silent, enjoying their intense connection and the thought of what could be. Lavender halfway slipped back into reality and asked from behind her, "By the way, who was that calling anyway?"

Milan leaned forward to the nightstand and grabbed her cordless, eyeing the display. "It was a blocked number." She began to think about it, replacing the phone and then lying back down next to Lavender. "I meant to tell you, Ramada called my office number the other day."

He spoke up. "Why? For what? I mean what did she want?"

"She just hung up on me. Still playing tired-ass games. Even with a restraining order on her."

He sighed intensely. "God only knows what that was about, or where she was calling from. I'll call Attorney Wyatt in the morning."

"She's one person with whom trying a little tenderness does not work." Her voice grew softer. "For now, let's enjoy the rest of this. And by the way. Good morning to you as well, sandman," she mumbled and moaned. She cuddled back to him.

It was like it had been before. Simply-a-fucking-mazing. And now, it could only get hotter.

50

"Purple Rain"

❧

Saturday, August 16, 2008
9:40 p.m.

It was the long-awaited night at Erotic City. Flood-lights glared from the street outside of the midtown club, shooting up into the warm summer sky, signaling the exact location of the big celebration in honor of the very first *Erotic City: The Show* episode.

There was a full buffet of everything from seafood to soul food. The club was decorated in purple from ceiling to floor, and folks strolled in wearing some shade of purple. Milan and Lavender wore formal evening wear. Hers was a sequined, low-cut, purple gown with slits up the left leg, and Lavender wore a black tux with a purple cummerbund and bow tie. They were out as a couple on Milan's big night. Great Mama was at Lavender's home watching Taj.

In the main room, seated at one table were Jed and Dakota, looking around the room, all smiles. Sitting next to them was Jarod, who was unescorted. He scrolled through his Smartphone after receiving a text from Nancy who now lived in Miami. Milan's blonde-haired and blue-eyed, very female manager sat next to Jarod, also unescorted. Jarod turned off his phone and they shared a couple of Amaretto Sours on ice.

At Milan and Lavender's table were Tamiko with her new man, Kellen. Jarod fought not to look at her, so he continued to chat with Milan's manager. But Kellen, who kept his arm around Tamiko, kept an eye on Jarod. Tamiko only focused straight ahead at her happy sister.

Milan stood from her seat and approached the small stage of the main room, looking up at the three levels of wall-to-wall people who had just ceased their generous applause upon her arrival to the microphone. Brian stood behind her a distance back, keeping an eye on the crowd.

She spoke as though she was accepting an award. "Thank you. Thank you very much." Milan pointed upstairs toward the orgy room. "All of you getting your groove on anywhere in here, take a fuck break please, just for a minute." People looked around and gave off some giggles. Milan saw her lingerie-wearing, church-going buddy Beverly in the front of the crowd and brightened her eyes toward her. She also saw the woman who showed up in court with Ramada the day of the hearing, the one who Lavender and Ramada had slept with the night they broke up. The woman gave Milan a wink and then an instant evil stare. Milan looked away at friendlier faces and continued.

"First of all, before I get started, I'd like to introduce the interim manager of Erotic City Atlanta, Mr. Jed Grant, and also Mr. Jarod Hamilton, who will temporarily run security for the club while Lavender and I work to expand Erotic City. Please give them a hand."

Milan glanced at both Jed and Jarod. She smiled while onlookers put their hands together in acknowledgment. Jed and Jarod looked around at everyone, nodding and raising their hands.

"What we plan to do is open a club in Miami, where Lavender and I were born, and then one in Las Vegas. Who knows, maybe even in Los Angeles one day."

The crowd began clapping in reply.

Milan held her head up high.

"I want to thank all of you for coming out tonight to support me as the creator of the series, and writer of the pilot episode of *Erotic City*. Also, I want to thank our regulars, Jed and Dakota, Dexter and Trudy, for supporting the club since the very beginning, as well as all of the other members and valued employees. And of course I want to thank the WET TV Network folks for seeing the vision behind exploring our misunderstood world of swinging.

"You know, the lifestyle isn't for everybody. I understand that. But in my eyes, it's good to know that we as women, in particular, seem to agree that we need a sexual alignment. Good girls are told to keep our legs together, and so we're even afraid to look at our own vaginas. How can you spread your legs for someone else if you can't spread them for yourself? For a black woman like me to open a successful sex club when sex is one of the most taboo subjects in society today, and have that club not only make money, but expand like we're doing with Erotic City, is unheard of. The truth is that

whether the subject is unspoken or not, swinging is happening, and it's not going anywhere.

"During my initial conversations with WET TV, we
talked about whether or not people would be curious
enough to tune in and check out the show. The mystery
of how and why swinging evolved from wife swapping
to what it is today is a story in itself. The word *swinging*
was actually created to elicit light and happy thoughts as
opposed to the word *swapping*. Swinging is indeed more
mainstream than ever before. And it's my hope that the
stigma of judging those who choose to have sex with
other consenting, like-minded adults will ease.

"I am very aware of how sex with strangers is seen. I
know how negatively lust is viewed in our society. But so
are greed and wrath and envy. Yet for some reason, sex
is so frowned upon, when it is really one of the greatest
pleasures of life. Contrary to what some people think,
this club is not a brothel, and swinging is not symptom-
atic of deviance. And while some encounters end badly,
a large number of them work out well. Purely and simply,
swinging can be fun if done responsibly. I wrote this first
episode with that in mind. It's not meant to convert
you or turn you on. It's only a glimpse into the lives of
swingers.

"So get ready America. A third person is coming into
your bedroom. You'll meet her in a minute. So sit back
and loosen your jockstraps and your G-strings, because
tonight I present to you the groundbreaking WET TV
cable television series called *Erotic City*."

The crowd erupted in applause as she stepped aside
and headed to the table to have a seat in between Lavender and Tamiko. Tamiko offered a lingering hug.

"I love you, sis."

"I love you."

The projection screen dropped from the rafters and the lights were dimmed.

As the opening credits rolled across the screen, the song "Erotic City" by Prince began to play and everyone in the club started singing the well-known lyrics.

On the screen, a sexy woman pulled into a reserved parking space in the sparkling evening air of midtown Atlanta. She stepped out of her ebony Maybach, wearing thigh-high stockings and spiked Manolos, a red satin bustier, and a matching miniskirt. She grabbed her designer bag, exited the car, and pressed the alarm with her long red fingernail. She strutted toward the tall double doors like a supermodel and stepped inside like she had the world at her feet, pleasantly nodding at the doorman and the bouncer along the way. And as she stepped past the double doors and headed up the many stairs toward her third-floor office, she spoke toward the camera.

"They say swinging is like watching a soap opera. So many people do it but so few will ever admit to it. I say it's consenting adults having sexual encounters with others, ranging from flirting, kissing, full sex, or orgies, or all of the above. Aside from the occasional documentary or exposé on a small group of swingers, the lifestyle, as it's called, had been conveniently ignored. The topic is rarely tackled, even on talk shows, in favor of spousal abuse or transsexualism. It seems as though those topics are easier to digest. Swinging is very hush-hush. You do it by night and lie about it by day. But not anymore. My name is Shelby Garnett and I am a swinger. I am also the proud owner of Erotic City, a sex club in Atlanta, Georgia. And I'm about to take you on what I

hope to be an ongoing ride into the weekly lives of those who swing. Please join me as I take you to my sex-in-the-city club called Erotic City."

The long-haired woman flicked on the light and stepped inside her grand office, set her oversize purse on the desk, and immediately looked through the tinted one-way glass, out among the many members who patronized her sexual mecca.

She crossed her arms and began to narrate, as the camera zeroed in on the kinky happenings.

"The first time I ever swung, it was me who got turned out, not my Creole boyfriend, as we'd originally planned. See, I always have preferred that a man express details of his mental fantasy out loud just before he ejaculates while saying my name, as opposed to closing his eyes and secretly fucking someone else while his dick is beating up my pussy. Most people do it, you know—fantasize about someone else. They do whatever it takes mentally to get them off physically. It was like that when my boyfriend, who lived around the corner when I was in high school, said her name when we were fucking . . . the name of his best friend's mother. I'd seen him flash a lingering look at her one day when she drove by in her Volvo and he waved like he was trying to hail a cab.

"The next time he and I had sex, he brought up her name again, saying he wanted her to suck his dick. And the time after that, he asked if I'd like to eat her pussy. The next night, as young as we were, we were down the street at this sex house we'd heard about called the Castle, watching people walk in who thought like we did. Who were open-minded like we were. Who were swingers like we were. It was a safe place to be. It was a family of people who lived out their fantasies without judgment.

"Here's what happened." The scene flashed back to 1995. *"It was thirteen years ago. I was very nervous, but instead of having a woman for him to fuck first, I got my ass fucked doggy style by a very hung stranger in front of a crowd of naked people for about a half hour. We were on the middle of a pool table and he just took me right there. Viagra hadn't quite made its premiere yet but if it had, I would have bet money that he'd overdosed on it because he worked me like a stallion. And little did we know that our neighborhood friend's mother was there . . . watching us. Right when I was done getting drilled to kingdom-cum, she took my boyfriend by the hand and took me by the eyes. I followed them into a private room. And the rest, as they say, is swinger history. Here, allow me to show you . . ."*

The crowd was all ears and all eyes as the next scene reenacted an up-close and personal flashback of that swinger-virginity-busting threesome.

Milan and Lavender held hands.

She looked extraproud of her show.

He looked extraproud of her.

He brought his mouth close to her ear. Her scent was her trademark tea rose. He squeezed her hand tightly. "Congratulations, baby. You did it."

She looked ahead at the show and her dimple flashed. She glanced down after feeling Lavender fidget with her finger. She looked closer and saw a pear-shaped, four-carat, brilliant lavender diamond on the ring finger of her left hand. She held her breath and readjusted her vision just in case her eyes were playing nasty tricks on her. She extended her shaky hand, exhaled, and turned her body toward Lavender. This time it was she who squeezed his hand tightly.

He said with a playful smile, "And by the way. I'm not hooking up a damn thing. I want papers on you."

She sounded little girlish. "Thank you, Lavender. It's beautiful." Her eyes fought back the tears and she struggled to speak low. "Thank you for, well, thank you for loving the 'Jezebel' in me." She put her hand on his back and traced his spine with her fingertips. "And thank you for wanting to be my man only. I love you," she said as she wiped her soggy eyes with her index finger.

"And I love you back." Lavender kissed her on the cheek. They sat shoulder to shoulder and resumed watching the erotic episode with the rest of the crowd.

In an instant, the glaring sound of a high-pitched alarm sounded as everyone's sights darted away from the screen and up at the ceiling, and then in a panic, people looked toward each other and all around, covering their ears.

Lavender grabbed his two-way. "What the hell is that?"

The bouncer replied, talking fast, "It's the upstairs hallway access door. Someone's opened it." The deafening sound suddenly stopped just as the lights were turned back up.

Crackkkkkk! The blasting resonance of glass breaking ripped through the club. Milan's body flinched and Lavender jumped to his feet, realizing he wasn't wearing his holster. Voices shrieked and people began to yell at the top of their lungs as another intense sound belted. *Crashhhhhh!* Milan looked up at the second floor near her office and saw that the one-way glass that overlooked the club was broken into a million pieces. Milan sprang to her feet and pointed upward, just as Lavender looked up in the same direction.

There stood Ramada, with a Louisville Slugger baseball bat in her hand, swinging at anything and everything around her, including banging up Milan's computer, her desk, and anything else she could reach.

Ramada's loud voice was filled with the same rage that took over her angry face as she turned around. Her livid eyes we fixated on Milan. "Fucking bitch. I told your ass you'd never raise my fucking son. Over there playing house like I fucking died. Bitch, bring your ass up here now." She then gave Lavender a spiteful glare. "And if anyone else comes up here, I will burn this motha-fucka down. I'm telling you now." She dropped the bat and held up a glass bottle of clear liquid. She also held up a 22-caliber pistol. "Or do you prefer that I just start shooting people one by one? Get your ass up here now, bitch. I said nowwwwww!" She shouted so loud her head shook and face turned red.

Lavender's radio went off and he heard the bouncer say, "We've got the police on the way."

"Well fuckin hurry. She has a gun."

"Got it."

"And find out how the hell she got in."

Milan looked over and caught a quick glimpse of Ramada's female friend, who had just returned to stand among the crowd. She again gave Milan a daring look.

"I'm waiting," Ramada roared viciously.

Lavender spoke toward Milan while keeping his eyes on Ramada. "You're not going up there."

Milan's eyes were now back on Ramada, too. "Yes, I am."

"No. You're not."

"I'm going. She's not gonna start shooting people. No way." Milan took a slow step.

So did Lavender. "I'm right behind you."

Ramada yelled at the very top of her lungs. "Back the fuck away from her." She pointed to Milan. "I will count to ten and I want you halfway up those stairs before I get to five." She held the pistol up high and shouted. "Try me. One. Two."

Milan began to make her way through the stunned crowd. All eyes were on her. Mouths were gaped open. Milan turned back and saw her sister being comforted by Kellen. Tears streamed down Tamiko's face. She had one hand over her mouth and the other hand over her heart. Milan fought to focus and immediately ran to the stairway in her evening gown, pulling up the beaded fabric along the way.

Looking at Brian, Lavender spoke into his radio in a low tone but stood still. "Brian, get in position to take this bitch down."

"I'm there."

Ramada continued to count. "Three."

Milan kicked off her high heels and took two stairs at once.

Ramada screeched, "I will kill every fuckin body in here. You get your ass up here and talk to me." There was a depth to her voluminous tone that was absolute no nonsense.

"I'm coming," Milan shouted, striding until she reached her office door and quickly approached Ramada. "Here I am." She held up both hands in surrender.

"Milan." Tamiko could be heard crying her sister's name from downstairs. "No. Oh my God."

Milan took a deep breath and exhaled a long breath. Her chest housed her thumping heart. Her hands shook. Her nerves were a wreck.

Ramada, wearing flats, tight jeans, and a black, wrinkled peasant top that barely contained her heavy, free-hanging boobs, looked Milan up and down with a turned-up nose. Steady words spewed with dark malice. "Skinny-ass bitch. You took my baby and now I'm gonna take yours."

"Ramada, don't do this. Please."

"Oh, so now you wanna beg me to not do something, huh? I've never seen that look in your eyes before, Milan. Where'd that look of wanting come from? Where'd that shit-talking face go that you always wore before?"

"This is not gonna help anything."

"It'll help if it teaches your ass a lesson. You need to believe people when they tell you something. And how dumb were you to think I couldn't get your sorry-ass home number? All I had to do was tell my son to call me from your nasty-ass house. I know he was back there. Now, why the hell are you playing mother to my son?"

"I'm not. Ever since you went out of town he's been with Lavender and with Great Mama. Sometimes I just happen to be there, that's all." Milan's left hand shook more intensely.

Ramada kept her eyes on Milan's ring finger. Her jaw got tighter. She spoke through clenched teeth. Her hair was messy and wild. "Oh, that's all, huh? So you don't tuck him into bed after he takes a shower, or drive him places, or nurse him when he's sick, or make his little lunch for school? See, you're trying to give me that innocent-act shit. You know you've been happy ever since I ran off to Vegas. You know you hoped I found a new man and never came back. Well, guess what? That man was an asshole, too. So, I'm back."

"I knew you'd be back. Taj is your son."

"Bitch, please. Don't act like you know me. What the fuck do you know about me really? And what do you know about what children mean to a mother? Where's your slanted-eyed mother?"

While Ramada was talking, she began pouring the liquid from the bottle onto the carpet and furniture, taking careful steps while making sure her back was to the wall. She stayed away from the broken mirror. The office reeked of acetone.

"My mother is dead. But she was a good mother. She loved my sister and me. And I know how much you love your son."

Ramada stepped up toward Milan. "Do you? Then why the hell did you do all that homework shit and cooking for his ass? You had your plans set to be his mother from the first time you met him."

Milan shook her head. "No, I didn't."

"Oh yes you did. Look at you, all dressed up and on top of the world. See, I knew tonight would be the perfect night to fuck with something that means a lot to you. This big premiere at your club, your so-called baby, was the perfect time. Thought you were on top of the world, didn't you?"

"I'm sure that killing people just to get back at me won't be worth the price you'll pay in the end." Milan looked at the silver gun. "If you want to see Taj again, please put that bottle down, and that gun down, and let's just make this all go away. Please."

Ramada gave a spiteful look. "You sure are pleading like the weak ho you are. It's too late for this shit to just fucking go away. I'm already accused of abandoning my son, so now your no-good man is trying to take him from me for good anyway. So as it stands now, I really don't have much to lose."

"You still have your freedom."

"Losing my freedom knowing I fucked with your shit will feel a whole lot better. I vowed I would never have another woman trying to parent my son while she lives the very life with my child's father that I can't live. When I was Taj's very age, I was left by my sorry-ass mother. My father married some damn piece of shit woman whose teenaged son fucked me for breakfast, lunch, and dinner. I need to be with my son. Not you."

Lavender's deep voice vibrated in the room. "Ramada, put that down." He stood at the door, and then walked in careful strides with his hands in the air. He stepped up beside Milan. The permeating vapor of the liquid was even stronger.

Ramada cut him with her eyes and shook her head, raising the gun his way. "No, you step the fuck off." She looked at Milan with hate and extended what was left in the bottle. "Or better yet, how about if I pour this nail polish remover on top of your little bitch-ass woman here. Burn all that long, pretty hair I bet you pull on when you're fucking her flat ass from the back." Her demonic eyes shifted to Lavender. "Would you like that, my dear baby daddy?"

He replied with intense frustration, "Ramada?" He ended the slow roll of her name with a tinge of pity and frustration, and a long question mark.

Her words were fast and furious. "Fuck you. I see that

little ring on this freak's narrow-ass finger. Did you think you could just run off with this whore and live life like it's some happily ever after shit?"

Milan looked back and forth between the two of them and then into the steel barrel of the gun. Her face owned a frightened frown and her eyes were glassy.

"Don't do this." Lavender slightly lowered his hands and took a step.

Ramada screamed, "Back off DeMarcus," and abruptly turned the bottle toward Milan and began to shake all of its contents onto her face.

Milan turned her head and automatically squeezed her eyes shut, bracing herself. She gasped and held her breath.

Lavender leaped toward Ramada's hand just as her finger squeezed the trigger of the pistol. A vibrant red, butane flame ignited and extended from the gun's tip directly toward Milan. The immediate journey of what was a torch lighter could be heard as a quick, swooshlike wind.

Milan screamed with a sharp, plaintive wail.

Lavender, with unbridled fury coating his face, reached for Ramada's slender throat with his irate, powerful weapon of a hand and punched her dead in her jaw with his right fist.

She dropped the bottle and slammed against the floor upon her back with a thud. The glass broke into pieces beside her. She collapsed and was still.

Lavender hurriedly turned around as Milan fell to her knees, shielding her face and head. He raced to lay her on her back, covering the flames with his entire body.

The loud, trampling shuffle of hurried footsteps

that belonged to Jarod, Brian, and a slew of policemen sounded outside of the door as they had their guns drawn in the hallway toward the door. "Is everybody okay?" was the question as the stench of something burning pervaded where the threesome resided. The answer to the question was no.

EPILOGUE

❧

Saturday, November 8, 2008
9:03 a.m.

Great Mama and Taj had been awake since eight. Turkey bacon and hash browns with onions took over the air, along with a trace of freshly brewed vanilla bean coffee. The happy sound of Taj's laughter could be heard down the hall.

Suddenly, the bedroom door burst open just as Taj's voice became full. "Dad. Wake up. It's morning." Taj plopped down on the black leather settee. He was hyper.

Lavender's eyes jetted open. The sun battled with his craving for the pillow as he turned to face his energetic son. "Good morning, Taj. Just a couple more hours, okay?" His voice was lazy.

Great Mama stepped into the room wearing a white housecoat and fluffy slippers. Her gray hair was in a short ponytail. "Taj. Come on now. Didn't I tell you about that?" She tightened the polyester belt around her thick waist.

Groggy and exhausted, Milan sat up after gradually opening her eyes. "Good morning."

Great Mama kept her sights on Taj but spoke to Milan. "Good morning, sweetheart. Sorry about that."

Milan yawned and then said, "No, it's fine. I'm getting up anyway."

Lavender pulled the covers over his head. "For what?"

Great Mama grinned at her grandson.

"Dad. Come on." Taj's tone was insistent.

Lavender spoke from under the covers with a tone of loving firmness. "Just a little longer."

"I wanna play Madden. Please." Taj's face wore a boyish pout, as if he knew it would soften his dad's resistance.

Milan brought the tan Frette cotton sheet to her chin. "How about if I play Madden with you?"

Taj asked, looking shocked while pointing at Milan, "You know how to play?"

"I can try."

He said, "Okay. Let's go." His energy remained on high.

"You're a brave one," Great Mama said to Milan as Taj stood. She took his hand and looked at Milan. "Brave in many ways."

Milan smiled. Her nose, right cheek, and top lip barely told on her trauma. Her scars were minimal, considering the second-degree thermal burns to her face only three months earlier.

Taj broke free from his great-grandmother's hand and stepped to Milan's side of the bed. "Come on. I'm ready. Plus we saved you some breakfast." He touched her arm.

Milan gave him a warm smile and he leaned in to hug her, resting his frame along her side.

Their embrace was strong.

"Hey, be careful. Not so rough, Taj. Don't lean on her leg. You know she was still having pain from the skin they grafted." Great Mama tapped Taj on his back. "Besides, let them get up when they're ready. They got in late. You know that."

Taj backed away from hugging Milan but his eyes stayed fixed on her. He asked, "What does grafted mean?"

Milan explained while lightly touching his cheek. "It means they borrowed a little bit of skin from my leg to use on my face."

"Skin from your leg? Where'd they put it?" he asked, coming in close to inspect her.

"Boy, come on now. Leave them be." Great Mama tugged at him and closed the door after she and Taj walked out.

Lavender said, "Get some more sleep, baby." He pulled the covers to his chest and turned onto his back.

"I'm okay."

He looked over at her. "Are you sure?"

"You know I am. Don't start your doting. I went back to work last week, didn't I?" She removed the sheet from her body and sat on the side of the bed.

"You did. And you look good as new. That plastic surgeon did one hell of a nip-tuck."

She turned back toward him with a look of doubt. She touched the side of her lip where a tiny bit of the pigmentation still varied. "Oh, you're just being nice. I can still see where the stitches were."

"Well, I can't."

She immediately said, "You're lying."

"I'm serious." He turned onto his side to face her. His eyes were weighted.

She stood up. She actually had on champagne-colored, silk pajamas.

He asked, "Why are you getting up so soon, anyway? We just got home not long ago."

"I want to play with Taj." Her energy was upbeat.

"He can wait. Come on back to bed."

Milan headed to the closet door to grab the matching silk robe from the hook. "He's excited. Plus he's been good about all that's gone on. I want him to know he can count on me."

"You're his stepmother now. You've shown him what he means to you in many ways."

"Lavender, his mother is serving decades for trying to murder me. He needs all the attention he can get." She draped the robe over her back. "Besides, the smell of that coffee is driving me nuts."

"Look, stubborn. In another hour, he'll be just as excited and he'll still get your attention. Only you'll get another hour's worth of sleep. And then you'll get in that office and continue writing that premiere episode for the second season of *Erotic City* they paid you for."

Milian paused, removed the robe, and placed it back on the hook. She headed back to the bed. "Okay," she said in surrender. She lay down and snuggled up to him, face-to-face with her husband.

He told her, "I just want to say again. And I know I've said it many times before. I'm sorry. Sorry you were nearly disfigured by the very woman you knew was off enough to do something stupid from the very beginning. I still can't get it out of my mind. If I'd protected you by grabbing you first . . . if I'd not let you go up those stairs . . ."

"Lavender, don't. I told you, everything happened just the way it was supposed to happen. It could have been worse."

"It's just always in the back of my mind." His face showed regret.

Her eyes agreed with her heart. "We're past that. We're husband and wife now. We've been blessed enough to buy the house next door for your grandmother. And thanks to you working so hard while I was laid up, our club here is fine, and we have another club about to open in Miami next summer. We're blessed."

He nodded. "Yes, we are."

"I know one thing. You marrying me in that hospital room was cool and all, but you owe me a wedding." She gave him a quick peck on the tip of his nose.

"I got you. That's gonna happen."

"Good. Because this is for life." She adjusted the covers over her shoulder and his. While he closed his eyes, she told him, "You know, I looked up the meaning of *swinging* yesterday when I was doing research for the script, and it said swinging means to cause to move to and fro. Like to move in an alternate direction."

"Yeah."

"Well. Is that gonna be something we do after we get tired of each other? Do you really believe in monogamy?"

His eyes reopened and he spoke sounding groggy again. "Like I told you when I put that ring on your finger that night, I want you all to myself. None of that to-and-fro madness. There is no other direction. Not after all we've been through. After all, our destiny is better than our history, right?"

"Definitely right." Her eyes showed surrender.

His eyes showed more alertness. "Milan, no matter what we do in life, no matter how hard we play or what risks we take or what type of lifestyle we surround ourselves with, life is all about love. It's all about family. And I have all that I need right here in this house." He kissed her on the nose.

"Okay, Mr. Lewis. I believe you."

"Life has a way of showing what really matters," he said as they snuggled even closer.

"It does."

His eyes closed again.

And hers did as well.

Taj's voice could be heard from down the hall. "Mom, come on. Let's play. Your son is ready."

Milan took in his words and grinned. "That's the only alternate direction I'm going in." She opened her eyes and slipped out from under the covers, coming to a stance. She grabbed the robe again and exited the room in a dash with a smile upon her newly repaired face, feeling as though through it all, her life really and truly had . . . come alive. She said as she stepped away, "Thank you, Dear Lord, for all things."

Lavender smiled and fell back asleep. Satisfied.

MILAN KENNEDY'S
WOMEN HAVE WET DREAMS, TOO

☙

Twenty-one and over, please

I've wanted to get the word out about how we as women have been taught to think of sex in terms of being wrong and dirty. But the truth is that we women have wet dreams, too. By the way, you might wanna take notes.

As you know by now, I'm very in touch with my sexuality and I'm very in tune with my body, so I might say some things that some of you find offensive. I'm just warning you now to consider that. If you think you'll be offended, move on.

I want to talk to you about pleasuring. Sex is pleasurable and it is not bad to feel good. So when it comes to you and your mate, I say be as bad as you both wanna be. I want you to think about whether or not you even know what your pussy looks like, inside and out. More about that later but think in terms of presenting it proudly. We need to be bolder.

Get in touch with your womanhood. I am a sexual being and I believe we can be sexual creatures and still be 100 percent woman. Don't be afraid to speak up. Show him what you're working with. Who said men are the only ones who can be sexual aggressors? Ladies, it really is okay to have sex on the brain. You don't need permission. Sex is a beautiful thing. It's okay to be bad. I'll tell you right now, my man thinks I should be given a Porno Award for fucking and I am damn proud of it.

First of all, we need to exercise. And I don't mean with a barbell. I'm talking about strengthening your PC muscles. They form the floor of your pelvic area and are the muscles you use when you pee. They're the same muscles men use, located between their ballsac and rectum, to clench to keep from cumming. If they're premature ejaculators, they can exercise it, too. We women need to do what I call PC pushups, or Kegel exercises. Dr. Arnold Kegel was a gynecologist in Los Angeles by the way. I want to thank Dr. Kegel.

I have discovered that the stronger your PC muscles, the easier and more frequent and more intense the orgasm. Every time you stop the flow of urine, those are the muscles you want to exercise. Maybe once you wake up in the morning you could just lie still before you get up and just squeeze, release, and repeat. Even while you're driving to work you can squeeze, release, and repeat. I get turned on just thinking about it. You can do it while no one even knows, just you and your very own pussy. That's the beauty of it. Squeeze, release, and repeat. I know more than half of you are squeezing your pussies right now. I can see you. Yeah, you're bad girls, all right.

Also, we must dress sexier. I'm telling you, if you do, you'll feel sexier. Don't dress like your aunt, even if you're an aunt yourself. And please start with your underwear. Toss out your old undies or granny panties. Wear underwear you'd wear if you knew you were going on a romantic rendezvous with Brad Pitt or Denzel. You may believe no one knows you're wearing them, but the most important person who knows is you. As far as what you wear to bed, toss that flannel nightgown, please. And I don't just mean do it because a man is crawling into bed with you. Do it even if you're single and home alone. And include tossing those ugly skirts, blouses, and casual wear. Do they de-sex you? Not good. This is all a part of, as I say, a sexual alignment. Have a fashion show for yourself. Hell, buy something leather. Be brave.

Next, buy some ho shoes. You know the shoes that look so sexy you could see yourself wearing them while your knees are bent back to the headboard? The fuck me pumps. Those shoes. Something with a very high heel, maybe bright red, or a pair that'll show off a good pedicure. And get your hair *done*. Get rid of that ten-year-old bun and try a new look, a wig or weave or haircut, just try something different. Natural or fake, just go for it. Stop trippin about the men who make jokes about fake hair, shoot, it's your head. Try what you want. Even a new hair color can work wonders. Go blonde and pretend you're Beyoncé. Fantasize.

Go to a spa and get a sweet honey facial or hot rocks massage. Think of it as a makeover without surgery. You'll have a brighter outlook and it'll build your self-esteem. The better you feel, the "badder" you get.

Practice a sexy walk, buy a new fragrance, do some floor exercises that involve rolling your pelvis, lifting your lower back off the floor. That's very sexy. I heard even yoga can help your sex life. It all allows you to move your hips. Heck, take a stripper class.

Then, how about talking sexy? Get over the fact that saying the words *penis* or *pussy* makes you blush. Blush on. Then think about where that came from. And why can't we talk dirty in bed? Who said we can't? Good girls don't what? Well, who wants to be a good girl in bed, or on top of the kitchen counter? Silence is not golden. And please don't be shy about telling him to move a quarter of an inch to the left. We can tell him everything else, like how to drive, and then we shut our mouths in bed. No more silent sex.

Get yourself a sex symbol voice. You don't have to be a bimbo to sound sexy. You must have bad girl vocabulary skills. Don't panic, I'm not saying talk like that in the office or within earshot of your kids. I'm talking about with your lover. Be able to say the right words at the right time. Tell him to take all the pussy he needs or ask him to fuck you like he's mad at somebody. And if you don't curse, tell him to stick his tongue so far up you that he can taste your cervix. *Cervix* is not a bad word, is it? It is? Oh, you're gonna take some work. And why not use foreign accents in bed? Try a Hispanic voice. If you can't speak it, speak fake Spanish. He won't know the difference. Be different people. Fantasize, ladies, and have fun. You can even learn to breathe sexy. That can help to intensify your orgasm.

And then there's masturbating. Did you know that most adult films are made mainly for purposes of masturbation? People please themselves through visual stimulation all the time. So, yes, rent a movie for you and your mate. Triple X-rated movies facilitate our need for fantasy, that's why we show them on the wide screen at Erotic City. It's healthy when used in the right way. They're meant to be instructional. Some men watch porn flicks so they can learn from them. And some men need to learn, so please do let him watch. And I'm not talking about the movies that end just because the man shot cum. What about us? We want our pussies eaten just as much as they want their dicks sucked. Don't we?

Now, as far as knowing what your pussy looks like, have you ever taken a hand mirror to your vagina? You have these beautiful outer lips called labia majora, and inner lips called labia minora, that protect the vaginal opening. The vagina looks like a flower, like an orchid, it's really very pretty. Go to the hood and pull back that retractable skin that protects your own beautiful clitoris. It's pretty in pink and the focal point of pleasure. Actually, its function is solely to induce sexual pleasure. It is your most sensitive spot. We all know we have a G-spot but I call the clit the X-spot. I love my happy clit. When it's aroused, the clit engorges with blood and extends beyond the hood, some way beyond, like a little penis. How about the urethra? It's below the clit and it's the opening that we pee from. And of course we know our vaginal hole, right? It has glands called Bartholin's that produce lubrication. And we have a portion of skin that's between the bottom of the vulva and the anus called the perineum. It's a smooth stretch of skin and for some it's very sensitive. Take a minute and look at it and visualize what it looks like. Touch it and see what that feels like. Not to mention the anus. Call it an asshole, but it's an erogenous zone. Take a minute to look at it, too. Slip an ice cube in there. Whether you want it to be an exit only is up to you. But, it's yours.

Touch yourself, ladies. Become a sexpert in the bed, but an expert on you. You should be the biggest fan of your vagina. We've been taught to be ashamed of our vaginas and I, for one, love my pussy. Learn to love your body, including your pussy.

The vagina secretes a scent near the outer lips that is a sexual stimulant. It's a true aphrodisiac. Be happy about the fact that you have your own scent. Don't be ashamed of it. Now I'm not saying don't keep it clean. Don't have him come running to me if you don't wash it. But washing it together can be a great part of foreplay. Maybe you can even let him shave *her* for you. And that's another thing. Name her. Call her Juicy Janet or Hello Kitty. Own it like that because she belongs to you and the good thing about it is, you don't need to have a man to enjoy her.

And let's not forget when we plan to have sex that we can make a home-cooked meal, and light a candle, and put on sexy cucumber melon body butter, buy lavender incense, play romantic music, or put on a hot movie. Get him, or her for that matter, whatever floats your boat, and you in the mood. Watch a football game with him while wearing his favorite team jersey and no panties, with the rule that he can't touch you until the game's over. And pick a team. He'll get turned on if you determine a reward for the winner. That'll do it. Basically, don't be afraid of your erotic fantasies. Shatter the myth. Are we ready to be more erotic? Women have wet dreams, too, you know. I'll be back for more next time. Until then remember, condoms are a girl's best friend. Now get going and name that sweet pussy. Ciao.

P.S. And as far as Big Booty Trudy's intense waterworks skills go, or shall I say, Trudy's art of female ejaculation, only 10 to 20 percent of women actually have a squirting pussy, having actually experienced the erupting expulsion that, some say, can cause you to cry, just from the sheer, intense, erotic pleasure it brings. It really does feel like you're going to pee on yourself, but making yourself comfortable, free from stress, and having a listening and patient partner, all help in learning to get past the urge to hold back, so you can let it flow. And it's not urine. Most times it's clear and odorless. It is a female ejaculate. If you'd like to read up on it, you can check out http://www.the-clitoris.com/f_html/ejacula.htm. There you can learn how to first masturbate while in the bathtub. Let me know how it goes, or cums.

LIVE YOUR
SEXY DREAMS!

❦

PYNK

PREVIEW CHAPTER

SEXAHOLICS

by Pynk

October 2009

1

This Is My Confession

❧

"My name is Miki Summers and I'm a sexaholic."

"Hi, Miki," the warm, smiling support group members sang in unison. The walls of the east hall meeting room of the outpatient treatment facility in Santa Monica, California, were lined with framed twelve-step traditions and Sexaholics Anonymous posters.

Cocoa brown Miki looked down at the chair as she took her seat at the same time that her best friend, Valencia, stood.

"My name is Valencia Hooks and I'm a sexaholic."

"Hi, Valencia."

Valencia nodded and sat, crossing her legs and clasping her sweaty hands.

A woman from the other side of the circle stood and spoke. "My name is Teela Raye and I'm a sexaholic."

The group again gave their standard cheery reply. "Hi, Teela."

She took her seat.

A petite, dark-skinned woman sprang to her feet. Her voice was melodic. "Hello there, everyone. I'm happy to be here." She flashed her capped teeth. "My name is Brandi Williams and I'm a sexaholic and an alcoholic."

"Hi, Brandi."

Brandi bowed and then scooted her backside back into the chair, nodding her head and eyeing each member. She rocked back and forth and crossed her arms, embracing herself tightly.

The tall, redheaded support group leader spoke from her seat. "Thank you very much, newcomers. Anyone else?" She looked around along with others who scanned the room, giving time for anyone who was left out. "No? Okay." She hugged a clipboard and a small dark blue notebook to her chest. "Welcome to Sexaholics Anonymous, or better known as SA. We at SA welcome you and appreciate the fact that you have shared a little bit of yourselves with the group. We want you to consider this group your extended family." Dr. Rachel Cummings, the Sexaholics Anonymous counselor, crossed her thirty-four-inch legs and flashed a Colgate smile, securing a retractable pencil over her ear.

"The focus of tonight's meeting is to familiarize you with the promise of recovery. So, first of all, right off the bat, I think it would be healthy and necessary for the new members to go ahead and get your biggest sexual act out of the way now. There has to be an admission in order to have victory over any addiction, and I know it's scary. But, if you wouldn't mind, please tell us the wildest thing you've ever done sexually. Preferably, the wildest act would not only be the one that possibly shamed you the most, but also one that you may have enjoyed the most. So, let's think back and speak in truth without fear of judgment, shame, embarrassment, or shock. It's time to confess. And remember, we are your new recovery family."

The older members of the group of ten looked around at the newer ones, flashing encouraging, nudging smiles. The newer members checked each other out as if hoping someone else would step up as the first guinea pig of the night but no one budged.

Dr. Cummings spoke encouragingly, giving eyes just as friendly as her voice. "Does anyone care to go first? How about you, Miki, since you gave the first introduction? Would you please?" Dr. Cummings motioned her hands upward, encouraging a standing position.

Curly-headed Miki began to speak at the same time she stood. She hung her hands at her sides and shifted her weight to her right leg. She placed her hand on her shapely hip as her mind traveled.

"It was all about me. I didn't care about anything else. I remember the creaking sound of footsteps in the hallway but our animalistic moans seemed to drown them out. He was tall and big and heavy, and his bulging belly needed to be lifted up to find his penis. I'd already sucked his huge dick for about thirty minutes but he didn't ejaculate. The taste and smell of his precum stuck to my tongue while he literally pounded my flesh. I remember wishing I had a stick of gum." A woman sitting on one side of Miki put her hand on Miki's slender arm for comfort as Miki gave a nervous giggle along with the group. Miki paused and swallowed audibly and closed her eyes. She continued.

"As much as his body repulsed me and the smell of his sweat that dripped onto my titties was musty smelling, my vagina throbbed rapidly and took him in like I was getting away with a crime. My pussy was wetter than it had been since I was in my teens. I was dripping slippery fluid and he was turned on to the point of having a heart attack. He breathed unsteadily. He kept grunting louder and louder, and he went deeper and deeper. I kept groaning and grinding faster and faster with an urgency I'd never known. I mean, my clit felt like it was about to burst. I felt the pressure of his powerful shooting cum deep inside of me just as the bedroom door flew open. I noticed someone standing there in broad daylight, but I didn't care. Not even about the fact that it was Adore, my younger sister, who had just absorbed an eyeful of our carnal fucking. Not even the fact that the man who had just shot his sperm deep inside of me was paralyzed with fear. He froze. I didn't care.

"I didn't care enough to cease my panicky grind or downshift my pleasure-filled grunts. As I said, it was all about me . . . getting off. I spewed my cum while my clitoris clenched repeatedly until I slowed down to the stillness of busted reality.

"My baby sister said, 'Not with my husband, Miki. Not with my Tommy.' She yelled with watery eyes and shaky hands. I lay there almost giving her a look like she had the nerve to dare interrupt. I pulled the covers over my body and scooted back. She called me a bitch and a whore and ran out. He ran out after her, just as naked as he was when we lay down. I sat back and lay still. Maybe it was out of shame, but I ended up taking a one-hour nap and then went to work like nothing had ever happened." Miki simply opened her eyes and stopped talking. Her brown skin was flushed. The members were silent as if maybe she wasn't quite finished. It was like the video player in her mind simply stopped. She sat down. She flashed a glimmer of her right dimple and her chest rose and fell.

"Very good, Miki," Dr. Cummings said. "That must weigh heavily on you for perhaps feeling as though you betrayed your sister. We'll speak on that as we go along, and we'll help you work through the feelings involved. Very good. Next."

Tall and brown Valencia came to a stance, looking down at her friend Miki who'd managed a mini-smile, and then Valencia spoke while taking a mannequin-like pose. Only her pouty lips moved. She didn't even blink.

"I push the limits. I have always pushed limits. I pushed them in middle school doing something as minor as ditching class, or as major as giving my math teacher a blow job for an A. I was only thirteen.

"I have always been bored with twosomes. I had my first threesome when I was fourteen. It was with my cousin and her boyfriend. In college I met a man who matched my freak level to a tee. We'd go online and look for adults who wanted to experience group sex with strangers, we'd fuck with another man, we'd fuck with another woman, we'd go to private house parties and end up on huge beds with ten people, just swapping and swallowing cum and eating pussy and taking it up the ass. Both of us. And I watched him suck dick. I got off on it. I'll masturbate to an exercise video if necessary and he'll masturbate right along with me. I love to fuck. I can't think of the wildest time because it's all been wild." Valencia now flailed her hands about with urgency.

"I've fucked while smoking weed, I've tried ecstasy while giving head, and I've drunk seven shots of straight one-fifty-one rum and then had sex outside in a park in broad daylight. I love riming, I'll screw a man in drag, I'll lick pussy until it's raw. All I know is that I can't stop thinking of new ways to push my freak button. My man has threatened to leave me if I don't stop. His curiosity has been more than satisfied. My mind is constantly racing to find new ways to get my rocks off. I have no limits. Piss on me, tie me up, choke me, make me bark, or slap me. Doing whatever it takes to get a rile out of me only makes me hotter. Today, I hate living like this. But when I'm in the middle of it, I love it." She slowed her speech and her voice cracked with exhaustion and shame. She spoke at a low tone. "I'm here to break my addiction to sex. I'm a freak. I've had enough, but I can't do it alone. And I don't want to lose my man. Thank you." She sat back down and Miki reached over to hug her. Valencia placed her head on her friend's shoulder and wiped her left eye. A sniffle followed.

A bald-headed black man sitting across from Valencia gave her a wink of approval, and then glanced over at Miki's legs where his eyes lived for more than a few moments. The woman next to him had a tear running down her cheek. She played with a balled-up tissue and looked at her lap.

"Valencia, we thank you as well. I see that your addiction has caused you much frustration. I understand and we are here for you. The good thing is that you are at your wit's end. That's the point where most need to be before they seek help. Your glass if full and that is a major turning point. We'll get through this together, Valencia. Thanks again."

Valencia nodded and smiled. Teela stood, smoothing her hand over her pixie-cut hair.

"My name is Teela, as I said. I am a voyeur. I love to watch and I get turned on by being watched. Valencia, I can relate to the park thing. I do that on the regular, maybe once a week. My lowest moment was when I peeked in the room to watch my mother and father having sex when I was a teenager. I felt shame, but still, I took that curiosity into my adult life. I will peek at neighbors or simply watch my man sex up other women without even getting involved. I've never been with a woman but I have no problem approaching them at clubs and persuading them to fuck my man, only I sit back and fuck myself with a dildo or a cucumber or a hot link or with my fingers or whatever until I'm satisfied. I'm not the least bit jealous.

"I'm here because two weeks ago, I went into a sex shop and sat in a booth watching an old Vanessa del Rio movie. It was one of those seedy rooms where other people can peek in and watch you like perverts. I guess that includes me, huh?" she asked the group, looking around as others shook their heads in disagreement. She blinked rapidly. "I was leaning back with my panties to my ankles and I knew that two sets of eyes were watching me rub my clit and stick my fingers in my ass. But I still jerked myself off over and over, and then I came so hard that I squirted pee on myself. One of the men stuck his dick through the glory hole and I sucked it until he came in my mouth. And when he left, I put on another movie and lay back. I looked up to see that I was being watched again, and I saw a set of eyes, only one pair of eyes. They were dark brown and the lids were iced with deep-set wrinkles. The whites of the eyes were cloudy. I jumped back and pulled up my underwear, closing my blouse, putting on my pants. Turns out the eyes belonged to my uncle. Uncle Chester was always trying to hug me a little too tight when I was younger, slyly pressing against my breasts. I always had a bad feeling about him. I hadn't seen him in five years, but there he was jacking off at the sight of his niece masturbating. This world is getting way too small for the type of sick problem I have. I want to be rid of this obsession. That's why I'm here."

Dr. Cummings showed no shock. She only beamed with approval. "That's very good, Teela. It sounds like your admittance is going to get you through this. Your honesty and shame can work together toward your healing. We thank you."

"Yes," a couple of members said aloud, in particular, the long-legged black man next to Teela as she shifted her thick body back into her chair.

Brandi said, "Yes," too, as she sprang to her feet. "I suppose my name suits me well as I've been an alcoholic for the past ten years. I'm thirty years old and started drinking in college. I never believed in AA meetings or even admitted that I had a problem. But the combination of this sexual addiction and the alcohol addiction will surely kill me if I don't surrender. I cannot bond to anyone.

I guess you can say I'm a love cripple. I have never had sex with the same person more than once in my entire life. I get off on the thrill of a stranger. I have a problem.

"And I recently posed as a hooker just to surround myself with men who were expecting a one time wham-bam, without all the intros. We went to the seedy motels or hopped in the backs of cars, and when it was all over, I ended up feeling as though I had gotten more out of it than they did. I wouldn't even take their money. But the last straw was when I got arrested for solicitation of sex. The embarrassing charges were eventually dropped but this addiction is interfering with my job as a fourth grade teacher. I'm afraid I'll run into one of the student's parents one day, or worse, get fired. I am a sexaholic and I'm ready. Ready to get well. I'm ill. And I admit it."

Dr. Cummings handed over a wide smile as chocolate Brandi took her seat.

Brandi looked down after smiling back.

"Wow, I must say those are some very good examples of the extreme side of lusting and being lusted over. Brandi, you have a two-headed demon to tackle, with sex and alcohol, but it's not unusual. Some people have addictive-type personalities and you'll probably find that you are addicted to many other things as well. It will not be easy, but the fact that you're here means that you are sick and tired of being sick and tired. Your tomorrows will not be like your past, not if you don't want them to be. Thank you, Brandi. Thanks for sharing. Now, unless anyone else who hasn't shared before wants to share, we'll continue on. No one?" She eyed the group. "No problem. Since we have so many new members involved tonight, the first thing I will tell you all now is that it is time to stop lusting and become sober. Please repeat after me. Stop lusting and become sober."

"Stop lusting and become sober," the group said as one.

"Very good. The one thing you all have in common is that you have all been driven to the point of despair. That's why you're here. I want all of you to see that each of us, each and every one of us, as sexual addicts, takes from others in a sexual way what is somehow lacking in ourselves. But what we end up doing is giving away our power through the forbidden. At some point in our young lives, because of some event or experience, we tuned things out with fantasy and masturbation, probably because someone took away our power, too. This is a physical, emotional, and spiritual problem, and therefore, healing and sobriety must come in those three ways as well. When you lose control you no longer have the power of choice. I want to give you back your power of choice. I want you to give yourself back your power of choice. Your stories tell me you want to gain control, and you want to live a life of making positive, healthy choices that do not spell addiction.

"This is a twelve-step recovery program. This will follow you every day for the rest of your lives. The only thing that differentiates you from the next new person who comes through that door is your sobriety. How long can you abstain from the act itself, not engaging in unhealthy sex? That number of days will add up to mean your anniversary. It will be part of your identity. You will be one day, or three months, or one year, or ten years sober, and you will celebrate like it is the first day of your life. And each day that you fall off the wagon and engage in intercourse and sexual acts, you start that number all over again. It's all up to you. It can be done. I won't give up on you. Will you?"

The group replied no all together.

The doctor continued, "And by the way, I am fifteen years, two months, and six days sober. I could tell you the number of hours if necessary. I had daily sex with my married neighbor while his wife was at work. Next thing I knew, his teenage son joined in to make it a threesome so I began sleeping with both of them, the father and the son, sometimes together, sometimes not. The parents didn't know why but the son got so sprung that he tried to kill himself. The father's wife confided in me that she knew her husband was fooling around on her. The final straw was when I ended up fucking the wife, too. He had no idea where she was all night long when she was lying in my bed right next door. She left her husband for me and is still with me today. He moved away in shame. Nothing you can say to me would shock me. My name is Rachel Cummings, and I'm a sexaholic also."

The members of the group, two men and eight women, eyed each other and raised eyebrows and nodded and smiled at Dr. Cummings. Some had heard it before but still wore their thoughts on their faces. Some scooted back and some uncrossed their legs, some sipped bottled water and some looked around the room. But a cleansing feeling of shaking off all of the admissions permeated the air and an anxiousness of knowing that it was time to learn and heal and deal, as equals, as addicts, took over.

After thirty more minutes of going over the first step

in the twelve-step program, admitting to being powerless over sex and that their lives were now manageable, the doctor ended the session and promised to see everyone back next week, same time, same place.

Valencia and Miki left hand in hand, with more pep in their steps than they had going in. Teela and Brandi exited in a different direction.

Valencia dropped her hand to reach in her purse for her cell phone. She said to Miki, "I'm proud of you, girl."

"You, too, Valencia. To sum all of that up was harder than I thought." Miki's short jean skirt was fitting like it was painted on.

"You didn't make it look hard." A slight breeze blew Valencia's flat-ironed hair away from her oval face.

"Thanks, girl. Where are you headed?" Miki asked with keys in hand as they stepped out of the clinic front door.

Valencia spoke, looking down at her dark red phone. "I'm headed to Adonis's place. I see a few missed calls from him. He's so excited about the fact that I agreed to get help. I'm getting excited now, too."

Miki stopped suddenly as the young bald-headed man who was in the group walked up and stood in between her and Valencia.

"Hello. How are you doing? My name is Dwayne." The man towered over Miki's average frame. He had on a white T-shirt and jeans.

Valencia continued to walk, car alarm remote in hand and cell to ear. "I'll see you later," she said to Miki.

Miki nodded and spoke to Valencia while looking toward Dwayne's massive frame. "Okay. I'm headed home. Drive safely."

"Sorry to interrupt," he said.

Miki put her hand out. "No problem. My name is—"

"I know. Miki, right?" He shook her hand and kept it.

"Nice to meet you, Dwayne."

He still held her hand while they began to walk toward the parking lot together. "I heard your story."

Miki beamed with a marriage of embarrassment and attraction. "I feel as though you know me. But what's your story?"

"I'd actually love to share it with you."

Miki stopped. "Your place or mine?"

Dwayne answered without missing a beat. "Yours." He released his grip and reached into his pants pocket, keeping his eyes on her, handing over his business card. "My cell number is at the bottom."

She read each and every letter and number. "Oh, okay. I'm in Inglewood. I'll call you. See you in an hour."

"I'll be there."

Miki began to walk away and looked back. "And bring a condom."

"I'll bring a few." He promised with a naughty grin.

Miki spoke in a private tone to his wide, V-shaped back as he hurried toward his silver Corvette, walking like a stud. "Damn, I'm gonna fuck the shit outta his fine ass."

PYNK'S SEX DICTIONARY FAVORITES A–Z

Acorn The head of the penis.

Bagpipe Slang term for the performance of fellatio.

Chocolate Starfish Slang term for the anus.

Daisy Chain Sexual position involving multiple partners.

Etch a Sketch To draw a smile on a woman's face by twiddling both of her nipples simultaneously.

Facial A slang term for ejaculating on someone's face.

Gang Bang The term for many men having sex with one woman simultaneously, or in rapid succession.

Hard Swap Allowing your partner to have sex with someone else while not in your presence.

Icing A slang term for semen or female cum.

Jack Rabbit 1. Common name for an electronic device used primarily by women for sexual stimulation. It is a one-piece device that includes a vibrating and rotating dildo head that is inserted into the vagina and a smaller vibrating stimulator that has two flaps (the ears) that flank the clitoris. 2. A term used to describe a man whose lovemaking style is characterized by rapid thrusting.

Kinesophilia A term for deriving sexual pleasure from exercise.

Labia Majora The labia majora are the outer lips of the vulva, pads of fatty tissue that wrap around the vulva from the mons pubis to the perineum. These labia are usually covered with pubic hair and contain numerous sweat and oil glands.

Macrophallia The medical condition of having a large penis. Interesting!

Nooner A sexual encounter during the lunch hour.

One-Eyed Trouser Snake A slang term for the penis.

Pansexual A person who is attracted to all genders and all forms of sex.

Queef The discharge of air from the vagina, sounding like flatulence (a fart)—it's talking to ya, daddy! I call it an airgasm!

Rotisserie The term for when a woman is bent over, performing oral on one man, while being penetrated from be-hind by another man.

Shrimping The act of sucking or licking a partner's feet or toes for either partner's sexual gratification.

Tit Tunnel Virtually self-explanatory. Where a woman's breasts are pushed together with the penis between them and slid back and forth. Lubrication is frequently provided from the woman's lips if the penis is of sufficient length and she is able to drop her head sufficiently.

Up on Blocks A slang term for the time when a woman is menstruating (i.e., out of action, like a car in a garage).

Vulva The name that collectively refers to the external female genitals.

Whisker Biscuit Another name for the vagina.

XXX or Triple X A term for highly pornographic materials.

Y Trail Tracing a line with your tongue from the vagina down to the anus (okay, I made that up!).

Zelophile A person who is sexually excited by their partner's jealousy. Damn! Is that what that was?

READING GROUP GUIDE

1. Have you ever experienced a ménage à trois? If you did have a threesome, would you prefer male-male-female or female-female-male?

2. Have you ever patronized a swingers club or attended a swingers event? If not, would you?

3. Is it unrealistic to think that spouses can have sex only with each other throughout their entire marriage? Could you watch your spouse/mate have sex with someone else?

4. What was the most erotic scene in *Erotic City* and why? Have you ever masturbated after reading a hot and sexy scene in any book?

5. Which character in *Erotic City* would you prefer to have sex with?

6. Was Milan's unconventional openness about sex, mixed with her desire to know the word of God, an understandable mix? Did you see her as a Jezebel?

7. Would you be okay with your lover verbalizing who they're fantasizing about while having sex with you?

8. Have you ever experienced a negative baby-mama situation? Would you have stayed with Lavender or left because of crazy Ramada?

9. Did you understand Tamiko's fervent desire to satisfy Mr. Big Stuff Jarod sexually? Do you always have to get your orgasm, or are you fine only giving your lover one?

10. In your opinion, was Nancy entitled to a portion of her deceased ex-husband's estate?

11. What message did you get from reading *Erotic City* relating to alternative lifestyles? Is swinging a sin?

12. Have you ever experienced squirting?